Gretchen Berg was ~~born in the East~~ ... in the Mid... ...
spent a number of ye... ...
English in Sou~~th~~ ... ...in Iraq and ...wed
the other co~~ntinents~~. ...graduate of Iowa State University...
Chicago, Illinois. *The Operator* is her first novel.

Praise for *The Operator*

'What if you could listen in on any phone conversation in town?
Irresistible!' Kathryn Stockett, bestselling author of *The Help*

'Glorious, gossipy, delicious and perfect'
Jill Mansell, bestselling author of *It Started with a Secret*

'Funny, sweet, secretive, and full of fascinating 1930s, '40's, and
'50s period details . . . A poignant look at life in a small town with
its nosy neighbours, thorny families, imperfect romances,
scandalous pasts, and gratifyingly just desserts'
Laurie Frankel, bestselling author of *This Is How It Always Is*

'Funny and fast-paced' *Heat*

The
OPERATOR

GRETCHEN BERG

REVIEW

First published in Great Britain in 2020
by HEADLINE REVIEW
an imprint of HEADLINE PUBLISHING GROUP

First published in paperback in Great Britain in 2021
by HEADLINE REVIEW
an imprint of HEADLINE PUBLISHING GROUP

1

Cataloguing in Publication Data is available from the British Library

ISBN 978 1 4722 6413 8

Off   14 44/17 700   W ll   MT   I   /MW 6 M   Keynes

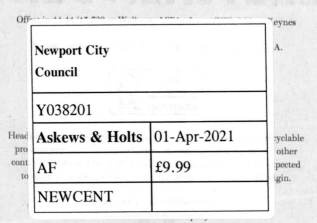

Head   cyclable
pro   other
cont   pected
to   igin.

Carmelite House
50 Victoria Embankment
London EC4 0DZ

www.headline.co.uk
www.hachette.co.uk

For Elaine Gladys McAnaney Stoddard,
Grandma

The
OPERATOR

Chapter 1

Vivian Dalton's worn old ankle boots crunched over the packed snow in front of Freedlander's, the bright lights of the department store spilling right out onto the sidewalk and mixing with the glow of the streetlamps. Vivian gave a quick, polite wave of a gloved hand to Betty Miller, who'd caught her eye through the flocked glass of the main display window. Freedlander's fancied itself right up for the holidays with the lights and the bells and whatever it was they put on the window to make it look like it snowed inside.

Vivian had heard it called flocked glass but couldn't tell you what flocked was. She might've guessed something to do with geese. Flock, flocked. Who knew? Vivian just knew she would've liked to be inside the bright store, on the other side of that flocked glass, herself, all nice and toasty, instead of out freezing her toes off walking to work in the boots that might as well've been made of Saran Wrap, for all the good they were doing.

Betty Miller didn't have to work, did she? No, *she* was nice and toasty inside the department store with her two youngest, Little Bitty and Charles Junior, waiting in the long line to see Santa Claus, and that didn't surprise Vivian one bit. This year's Santa was a pretty good one, Vivian had to admit. Fat, jolly, and sober, at least, so the Millers were there, and the lines were much longer than they had been last year. Last year, Jimmy Hixson had said Santa's breath smelled like the Sunoco filling station. Jimmy's older brother Albert worked at the filling station, so he would know.

When she'd heard what Jimmy Hixson said, Betty Miller had been the first mother to boycott the Santa line and the other mothers quickly followed her lead, like they always did. She hadn't bothered with a courtesy phone call, politely explaining to Freedlander's with all her over-enunciated consonants, "Your *San*-ta Claus seems to be *fright*-fully *ahem* em-*balmed*." That would've taken up too much of her time. Vivian didn't know exactly what it was Betty did with her time, but she knew Betty thought her time was more precious than anyone else's. Betty Miller knew the boycott would work, and the other mothers knew it, and soon Freedlander's knew they'd better get themselves a new Santa Claus. No matter what Little Bitty and Charles Junior said to Sober Santa, up there on his shiny red North Pole throne, Vivian Dalton knew the Millers were going to have a marvelous Christmas this year. The Millers had a marvelous Christmas every year.

That was the thing about small towns. Everyone knew everyone else's business. Vivian certainly knew everyone else's business, but more important, she knew people. Vivian Dalton knew people, that was for certain, and she'd be the first to tell you that. She'd say it was more from intuition than from eavesdropping on people's telephone calls, but her daughter, Charlotte, would say, "No, it's from the eavesdropping."

Charlotte joked with her friends, putting on airs for amusement, saying her mother was *privy* to *myriad* conversations among the good people of Wooster. Now, "privy" and "myriad" were two words Vivian would've used if she'd known what they meant. She wasn't stupid, but her schooling hadn't gone any further than grade eight at Bowman Street School. Vivian never would've seen "privy" and "myriad" printed next to the splashy photos in her fashion and movie magazines. Charlotte had to roll her eyes and sigh as she explained to her friends, "My mother doesn't trust people who read books."

It was a shame Vivian didn't know words like "privy" and "myriad," because she would've loved them. They sounded fancy and expensive. They sounded like words the four-flushers on the north side of Wooster probably used all the time, even at Buehler's when they were buying whatever it was they bought there. Their prime rib and lobster claws and bushels of caviar or whatnot. Vivian eavesdropped, and also did her share of peering into people's shopping carts at the grocery store. Yes, people like the Millers probably used words like "privy" and "myriad" at Buehler's. All four of their rich kids probably privyed and myriaded all over the place. Little Bitty and Charles Junior probably used those words when they were talking to Sober Santa at Freedlander's.

Vivian wasn't thinking about the words she didn't know as she crunched along on her way to work, blowing out little frozen clouds as she exhaled. She was thinking about how glad she was that Betty Miller had seen her wearing her new hat. There'd only been one left at Beulah Bechtel's that afternoon, and Vivian had set it on the counter next to the cash register with shaky guilty fingers that really should've been pushing the hat money across the counter to the bank teller to put into her savings account instead. She'd seen Betty hovering near the fur coats, eyeing the hat hungrily. Looking at it like she'd almost eat it for lunch if she could, with her pointy little white teeth. Betty Miller's teeth weren't really pointy, that's just how Vivian imagined them. Pointy teeth in a vicious mouth that seemed just as likely to tear the very flesh from your bones as it was to smile and comment on the weather.

Vivian had saved for months to buy that hat. Just that one hat. The beautiful hat that she knew hadn't really been made for someone like her, but maybe, if she bought that hat for herself, she'd feel a little bit of what the four-flushers felt. Worthy of something nice. Boy, if she'd told Edward how much it cost, he would have put her in the lunatic asylum. Betty Miller probably could've bought four or five of those hats that day, right there. If they'd had any more, that is. "You're lucky," the salesgirl (Doris, maybe?) had said to Vivian as she wrapped the hat in lavender tissue paper. "This is our last one."

Vivian, in her worn-out ankle boots but fancy new hat, stepped out of the frigid night air and into the brick building, pulling the door closed behind her with a "Brrrr!" before making her way to the cloakroom. She shrugged out of her coat and then carefully removed the beautiful new hat. Doris at Beulah Bechtel's had said it was "Prussian-blue," but Vivian didn't know what that was. She thought it looked more like a dark navy. Beulah hired girls from the college and Doris probably went there to study Prussian or something. Either way, the blue complemented Vivian's eyes, and she especially liked how the hat dipped low over her right eyebrow on the one side. *Chic*, she'd read in her fashion magazines, pronouncing it "chick" in her head. She carefully balanced the hat on top of her old winter coat on one of the hooks in the cloakroom, and then trod over the worn wooden floors into the switchboard room, pulled out her rolling chair, and rolled herself back up to the counter to put on her headset.

"Who takes a wife?" she asked Dorothy Hoffman, who was already seated, and probably had been for fifteen minutes.

"What?" Dorothy pushed the earpiece into her hair behind her ear, turning to face Vivian.

"Who takes a wife, in 'Farmer in the Dell,' who takes a wife? Is it the sheep?"

"The sheep?" Dorothy's penciled eyebrows furrowed into a jagged *M* on her pale forehead.

"No?" Vivian asked, studying Dorothy's eyebrows. She should've been using brown eyebrow pencil instead of black. Black made her look angry, and Dorothy was probably just a little annoyed, like she always was when Vivian was a little late and then talked about nursery rhymes.

"Why would the sheep take a wife?"

"I don't know. For some reason that's what stuck in my head. Something about the *eee* sound." She turned back to the blank board in front of her and studied it, head tilted to the side. "*The eeee takes a wife . . .*"

"It's the farmer who takes a wife," Dorothy said, because even though she was annoyed she couldn't let Vivian think the sheep took a wife.

"The farmer? Are you sure?" Vivian turned back to Dorothy, the doubt plain on her face. It was a nursery rhyme, for chrissakes. Why couldn't the sheep take a wife?

"I don't even think there is a sheep in the rhyme. You're probably thinking of 'the cheese.'"

"The cheese?"

"Yes, honey, the cheese."

Vivian turned her attention back to the board, giving a vigorous shake to the dark barrel curls she'd carefully arranged to look like Bette Davis's in *All About Eve*.

"Well, the goddamned cheese wouldn't take a wife," she muttered, then started to giggle at the image of two wedges of cheese in front of a pastor. One wearing a veil.

"It doesn't." Dorothy looked skyward for help, like she did sometimes. "The cheese stands alone. *The cheese stands alone, the cheese stands alone.*" Dorothy sang the words as she held her hand over the mouthpiece.

Every once in a while there'd be a short in the wiring circuits and even if the operator remembered to flip the muting switch, you could still hear her voice over the active line. Dorothy had learned her lesson about the wire glitches the hard way and was now extra-careful to flip the muting switch and cover her mouthpiece when talking to the other girls in the switchboard room. Wooster's very own mayor had overheard her say the *f*-word, and that'd gotten her suspended for two weeks without pay. Vivian never said the *f*-word, but she said all the other ones, and was careful to keep her hand over the mouthpiece when she talked to the other girls in the room.

Vivian frowned at the board for a moment, back to thinking of that cheese standing alone. She could see it. A wedge of holey Swiss cheese lit up by a stage spotlight, all by itself in the middle of her dining room table. Alone cheese. Spinster cheese. Suddenly one of the board's lights blinked before her. She quickly plugged the rear key cord into the jack, flipped the switch, and adjusted her own mouthpiece.

"Number, please."

Vivian was a little bothered by the cheese standing alone in its spotlight, so she connected the call and flipped the mute switch. If she hadn't been distracted, she'd have listened in.

"You can learn a lot that way," she'd told Edward on one of their first dates.

Even though they weren't supposed to, Vivian and the other girls who sat at the switchboards of Ohio Bell on East Liberty Street listened in on the telephone calls. Each and every day they plugged their cords into the jacks, flipped their switches, and leaned into their headsets to find out what was going on around Wooster. You might say they were the ears of the town. If it were up to Vivian they'd be a lot more than just that.

She'd tell you she had a real sharp understanding of people and their personalities, and listening in at Bell only helped that along. She could tell you plenty about situations based on just a few details. For example, when Ray Barnes telephoned his mother from New York City to say he had a big surprise in store for her, Vivian knew that big surprise was a new fiancée, and she also knew that Mrs. Barnes wasn't going to like that one bit. Probably with good reason, if she were honest with you; that fiancée was likely a no-good slut. The good girls went *to* New York City from the small towns, not the other way around.

Ruth Craven had listened in the day Ray Barnes's mother called her sister in Mansfield to complain about the "fast New York City girl Raymond brought home," and how she was corrupting her "poor, innocent boy." "The Negro music he listens to now!" Ruth was good enough to tell the other switchboard girls all about it, and remind them about what Vivian had said. Some of them liked to tease her when she talked about knowing people, but they all looked at her with just a little more respect after that call.

"You don't need some fancy college degree, or even a regular old high school diploma, to know people," she'd say.

Lately, there'd been almost nothing to know about anyone, and Vivian had just about fallen asleep at the console a few times. The townspeople of Wooster were talking about the dullest things you could imagine. Take this week. On Monday, Mrs. Butler complained to Mrs. Young that her daughter, Maxine, never called anymore, and even after she'd sent Maxine that beautiful windmill star quilt she'd worked so hard on. On Tuesday, Earl Archer called his wife, Dora, from the ticket office at the railroad depot because he'd left his wallet on their kitchen counter again, and wanted her to please get on the bus and bring it to him. On Wednesday, Clyde Walsh called Ginny Frazier to ask if she'd go to the A&W with him that afternoon after he finished shoveling the sidewalk in front of his mother's house, and Ginny Frazier (for the umpteenth time) said no.

Vivian had connected all these calls, and, although they were dull, she'd listened in and made up her mind about them. She thought Mrs. Butler should drive herself down to Columbus, break into Maxine's house, and take that quilt back. She thought Earl should hustle his wrinkled old ass back to the house, rather than making Dora take the bus in this cold weather just because he was a careless, absentminded idiot. And she thought Ginny Frazier might want to think long and hard about her chances of doing better than Clyde Walsh. If he could overlook that frying pan face of hers, he was worth a hamburger and root beer float at the A&W. How many boys his age still shoveled the walk for their mothers? And she'd overheard enough of Clyde's calls to Ginny to know he meant business. Vivian felt that sort of romantic devotion should be rewarded. But Mrs. Butler, Earl, and Ginny would never hear Vivian's advice, and they'd be all the poorer for it.

Vivian didn't always recognize the voices of the callers, or the telephone numbers they gave her. Wooster was small, but it wasn't that small. If the voice or number was unfamiliar, it was impossible to know who was there on the other end of the line, but Vivian could still come up with solutions for their problems. There were days when she thought maybe the callers should know she could hear them, and maybe instead of just listening she could chime in and give them that good advice she knew they needed. They'd be all the better for it, that was for certain. But she couldn't do that. The telephone operators weren't supposed to listen in on the calls. Vivian couldn't tell you if that was a specific rule or just something that was frowned upon; it'd been so long since she'd read the rules. If confronted, she would've scoffed and said there wasn't anything worth listening to anyhow. Quilts and forgotten wallets and the A&W. Christ.

The calls that got the girls' hearts pounding and pulses racing were the ones for the hospital or the police station or fire department. Vivian had the good sense to put those calls through immediately. Although, yes, she'd sometimes listen in, if only to make sure the call wasn't coming from her own house. For, as clever as she was, Charlotte could be careless with the stove, and she'd gotten into the habit of making popcorn after school, and Lord knew Edward was bound to cut off one of his arms with one of those sharp tools in the shed, or hammer his hand to the workbench in the basement one of these days.

What she'd really like to hear was something scandalous. Something out-of-the-ordinary. Something like the Julius and Ethel Rosenberg business that Edward had told her about. Soviet spies! The intrigue was international news, but Vivian was mainly interested in the story because the spies had been a married couple. Now, *that* was intrigue. And if she'd eavesdropped on a call between Julius and Ethel, you can bet your bottom dollar she'd have had some advice to give them.

Based on what Vivian overheard when she was at the switchboard, there was no spying going on in Wooster. No, what was happening in Wooster was that Mrs. Butler had wasted her time making a quilt for an ungrateful daughter, Earl Archer was an absentminded idiot who took his wife for granted, and Ginny Frazier thought she could snag somebody better than Clyde Walsh. Also, it was cold outside, Christmas was a few weeks away, and Freedlander's had a nice, sober Santa Claus to remind everyone of that fact.

Vivian still had hopes for something more exciting on that cold December night as she sat at the switchboard. Restless, bored, humming nursery rhymes in her head, and halfway hoping to discover spies, or at least a scandal about a married couple, in their little Ohio town. If she'd been able to push aside the farmer, his dell, the lonely spinster cheese, and Julius and Ethel Rosenberg, she might've heard the voice of her dead granny saying what she used to say when you were asking for something that might get you into trouble. *Be careful what you wish for.*

Chapter 2

The switchboard stayed dark for a few minutes, and Vivian pushed up her mouthpiece and rested her chin in her hand as she thought about spies in Wooster. Not too likely, if you asked her, but Wooster'd had its share of excitement. There had been happenings. The kinds of happenings that stuck in the minds of the townspeople, and made them wonder to themselves in their spare, lonely moments. Got them talking to each other, you know, from time to time, long after the happenings had happened.

Like the excitement from five years ago with the attempted robbery and shoot-out at the William Annat Company department store at Christmastime. A shoot-out! In Wooster! Who would've believed it, but three armed men from Akron tried to rob the store. Akron, didn't that just figure. You'd never hear of a Wooster resident shooting guns off at a department store at Christmas, for chrissakes. If it hadn't been for a brave store manager and a quick-thinking salesgirl, who telephoned the operator to connect her to the police, who knows what might've happened? The quick-thinking salesgirl had been Vivian's younger sister Violet, and Vivian would've been positively out of her mind if she'd been on the phones that night. Ellen Leonard had answered that call.

"Mercy!" Vivian had exclaimed, when Ellen had described the commotion in Bell's switchboard room that night. "Jesus Christ almighty!" was what she'd said to Violet. Because she knew what to say in polite company, but didn't want to have to mind her mouth around family.

Violet had quit William Annat shortly after, because she had a husband, two kids, and two cats and didn't need those kinds of headaches in her life, and Ellen Leonard had taken her one night of switchboard crisis experience and moved to Cleveland to work at Bell there. She thought she was ready for a bigger city and its bigger calls. Vivian thought she'd better be, because if men from Akron were shooting up department stores at Christmas, could you imagine what the men in Cleveland were up to?

The robbery attempt had been the talk of the town for the next few years. At least until last June when that sneaky Gilbert Ogden embezzled $250,000 from the Wayne Building & Loan on North Market Street, where he worked as a teller. He took the money and absconded with the bank director's secretary, according to the front page of *The Daily Record*. Although Vivian could've guessed at its meaning, she'd decided to look up "absconded" in the dictionary she'd had to buy Charlotte for school.

Abscond:

: to depart secretly and hide oneself <He absconded with the stolen money.>

Charlotte was a sophomore at Wooster High School. She'd skipped the first grade after correcting the teacher on her usage of "break" versus "brake," and knew words like "abscond" and "privy" and "myriad." She also liked to read books, and was known to roll her eyes every time her mother boasted about how she "knew people."

Vivian had spent days wracking her brain to try to remember if she'd ever overheard any telephone conversations between Gilbert Ogden and the secretary, before they *absconded*. She said she "had a feeling" about that Gilbert Ogden, with his shifty eyes looking every which way behind the round, steel-rimmed spectacles, and the nervous way he used to fiddle with his bow tie with stubby fingernails that he chewed down past the quick. "That's the sign of a Nervous Purvis, right there," she always said about nail-biters, and you didn't want to get her started on the ones who wore glasses.

So, no, Vivian wasn't all that surprised when she read about the embezzlement. But embezzlement, while sort of exciting to a town like Wooster, wasn't the real news to Vivian. The real news had been Gilbert's illicit romance with the secretary Flora Parker. "Illicit" was a word she knew, because it was all over her movie magazines.

"Flora Parker, my stars! Who would've thought?" she'd said to Ruth Craven, during one of the early afternoon lulls at the switchboard. "Although . . ." She'd then paused with a finger to her lips. "Wasn't she from New York?"

Ruth had nodded. "From New York. And a little older. Pretty, though."

"They have any kids, her and her husband?" Because that would've made it worse, and the worse a scandal was, the better it was to talk about.

"Don't think so."

Vivian had shrugged and thought, *So, the trash ran away with the spoon.* That had been something unexpected. It was Wooster's own version of Bonnie and Clyde, and don't think Vivian didn't find it suspicious that Bonnie's last name had also been Parker. There was a lot more significance to names than most people bothered to notice.

Vivian had thought Flora and Bill Parker were one of those annoying happy couples, what with all the arm-in-arm walking around town and staring into each other's eyes she saw them doing. They were as swoony as a couple of lovebirds. But who knew what was really going on behind their closed doors? Vivian took her "knowing people" seriously, and especially since there was such a scandal around Gilbert and Flora, she was hard on herself for not having spotted the signs sooner (or at all).

She consoled herself with the thought that, although she saw Flora Parker every once in a while, she'd only actually spoken to her once, a few years before the robbery. It'd been in line at Buehler's, and it'd just been small talk.

"The cashiers are sure chatty today, aren't they?"

"Yes. It is slowing the line a bit."

Flora Parker had then found something interesting inside her handbag, and Vivian guessed she wasn't in the mood for conversation, although she could've gone on for a while about those cashiers. The few words between them really hadn't been enough for Vivian to figure Flora properly.

She had noticed the can of vegetable shortening in Flora's shopping cart, and that was something. If Flora'd been a good housewife, she'd have been cooking with lard or butter, but Vivian wasn't going to pass judgment on her over something like that. She'd also been preoccupied with her own thoughts that afternoon. It was her and Edward's ten-year anniversary, and Vivian was buying his favorite Amish Baby Swiss cheese, trying to plan the rest of their dinner in her head, and wondering what awful tin thing he was going to give her for a gift. Ten years was tin. Whatever it was, he was probably making it on his workbench in the basement. *It better not be another goddamned watering can.* She'd gotten one of those for a birthday gift one year.

Dorothy cleared her throat, bringing Vivian back to the present moment, where several lights were blinking in front of her on the switchboard. When she let herself drift off like that it took a nudge to get her back. With a snort of air through her nostrils, she plugged in the cord.

"Number, please," she said, and quickly connected the call before answering the next one. Maybe that one would be the call with the Communist spies.

"Number, please."

"Viv, is that you?"

"Yes, dear."

Edward never surprised Vivian anymore, after fifteen and a half years of marriage, but she was almost surprised her husband recognized her voice on the other end of the line. He had some hearing loss, or at least claimed he did. It seemed to come and go. It was at its most powerful, the loss was, when she was reminding him to trim his nose hairs or put his dirty socks in the warsh basket. But the moment she and Charlotte were talking about shopping for a new dress, or something else not exactly practical, boy, did his hearing improve. She was sure he'd be able to hear a dog whistle if the whistle was talking about spending any of his money.

"They canceled the meeting tonight, so I'm home." He sounded tired, as usual.

"Okay." Vivian had no idea what they talked about at those stupid meetings anyway. Freemasons. Huh. Grown men having secret meetings about God knows what. It all just sounded like a way for them to have an adult version of their tree house with the "No Girls Allowed" sign out front, and call it a "society." Edward was busy enough, working two jobs. If she hadn't liked having the house to herself sometimes, she'd be annoyed that he chose to spend most of his free time with a bunch of other men instead of staying home with his family.

"I'll leave the porch light on."

"Thank you."

She disconnected Edward, and reached to connect the next call.

"Number, please."

The caller, whose voice she didn't recognize, gave Betty Miller's home number, which she did. Vivian looked at the clock on the wall, which read ten minutes till eleven. That seemed awfully late to be calling someone who had a family with small children, didn't it? She assumed Betty Miller had made it home from Freedlander's, probably enjoyed a fancy dinner of roasted peacock or some such bird, on the rarest china plates and using real honest-to-goodness silverware, and then put her perfect, small, rich children to bed, probably in pajamas made of the finest spun gold. That made her think of Old King Cole. *He called for his pipe, and he called for his bowl, and he called for his fiddlers three . . .*

She was getting tired, though. Edward's call and his mention of the porch light had made her think of just how much she wanted to be home switching off the porch light, slumping up the stairs, and crawling into bed. Plus, she had no interest in hearing Betty Miller talk about how swell her life was, how her Christmas party was going to be the event of the season, how God himself would have cleared his schedule for a chance to sit in the Millers' living room and sip champagne with the crème de la crème of Wooster society. But something made her pause as the caller said, "Hiya, it's me."

The unknown woman's voice was low and secretive, almost seductive enough to make Vivian uncomfortable. Like the time when she was thirteen and had happened upon her brother and Edith Cramer in the backseat of the family's Model T. She shuddered a little and stifled a gag, then squinted at the board in front of her, as if the squinting would help her figure out who "me" was.

"You'll never believe this," the voice said.

And, although Vivian was sure the disbelief would just have something to do with a surprising new way to put lobster or crab or some other expensive seafood into a casserole recipe, she stayed on the line, held her breath, and listened. After just one minute her body had gone rigid, with her fingers pressing themselves white into the countertop. Her heart thumped in her chest and her mouth went dry. Vivian listened in a state of stunned paralysis, gaping at the switchboard and feeling like the rug of her life had just been yanked out from under her.

Chapter 3

It was a warm spring evening, the kind of evening where you wanted all the windows and doors open so you could smell the flowers, feel the warm breezes, and hear the crickets chirping. Ten-year-old Vivian McGinty was doing all three of those things while setting the table in the dining room. She was also lifting up each of the empty diamond-patterned water glasses, peering into them, shaking them lightly in the air next to her ear, and then setting them back down on the table. Uncle Frank and Aunt Emma and the Cutter cousins were driving up in the Sheridan from Apple Creek for Friday Night Fish Fry and, as usual, Vivian was full of excitement and dread. Excitement to see the relatives, and dread about eating the fish. The Fish Fry was a tradition Vivian's Pawpy had brought back to Ohio after visiting the Michigan and Wisconsin McGintys.

The McGinty ancestors had sailed to the United States all the way from County Tyrone, Ireland, sometime in the early nineteenth century. They'd arrived in port at Philadelphia and then scattered like blown dandelion seeds all over the mid-Atlantic and Midwest regions. Uncle Frank and Aunt Emma weren't McGintys, but they were kin, they lived within driving distance, and they enjoyed the Fish Fry.

Aunt Emma was Vivian's aunt on her mother's side. The Lancaster County German Mennonite side. The Kurtzes. "Happy as a pot of mice, are we?" was just one of the weird things Aunt Emma would say to Vivian's mother, speaking in Low German while poking her in the side, trying to coax a smile out of her sister. Myrtle Kurtz McGinty never seemed as happy as a pot of mice. She always seemed about as happy as the mice that Zipper the neighbor's cat dropped in a mangled heap on their doorstep. Myrtle needed to be coaxed into a smile. The McGinty side never needed coaxing.

"Paddy, how are you? How's the railroad business?" Uncle Frank asked, as he clapped Vivian's father on the shoulder.

The way Uncle Frank said it you'd think Patrick McGinty owned the railroad, but he just punched tickets. Vivian had once heard Uncle Frank call her father a "wickedly charming Irish robe," and she'd wondered if the robe was anything like Joseph's coat of many colors from the Bible. She'd asked Vera about it later, and Vera had laughed long and hard.

"Rogue, dummy, not robe. God, you're stupid."

As usual, Vera hadn't been helpful. Whatever it meant, robe or rogue, Vivian was proud that people talked about her Pawpy. He was popular around Wooster, and people liked him. She'd once heard a neighbor say, "Oh, that Paddy. He's got a ready wink in one eye, and the reflection of a passing woman's backside in the other." Vivian had squinted at his laughing blue eyes the next time she looked him in the face. She didn't see either of those things.

What she did see was her Pawpy trying to talk her mother into converting to Catholicism, and her mother refusing. She'd just shake her head slowly back and forth, grumbling under her breath. To Myrtle, church was church, and having to do a lot of standing up and kneeling during services didn't change that. And going to confession? She waved a rough, dismissive hand at the thought. She didn't have anything to confess anyway. Forest

Chapel Methodist was just fine for their purposes. Pawpy didn't go with them on Sundays. He claimed he went to Mass at St. Mary's, but Myrtle and the McGinty children thought it more likely that he prayed to the Patron Saint of My Wife and Kids Are Finally Out of the House from the comfort of his living room armchair.

The Friday Night Fish Fry became Paddy's version of Mass, and Vivian enjoyed it about as much as she enjoyed sitting in church. She had no problem eating the applesauce and fried potatoes, but when they were gone she was left with the fish. She'd look around at everyone else's plates to see if they'd eaten theirs yet. That fish was all that was standing between Vivian and the apple crisp for dessert, but she just couldn't bring herself to eat it. She couldn't eat it and she couldn't think of a way to get rid of it. It would sit on her plate until she remembered to push it around and around with her fork.

"Vivian, eat the fish," her mother ordered.

"Oh, now, Myrtie, Vivy doesn't have to eat the fish if she doesn't want to."

Vivian tried to hide her smile behind her napkin. She loved when her father was "half seas over," as he liked to say, because it meant he either wouldn't notice the kids' behavior or wouldn't care. On the days when Pawpy knocked off work early, he'd take the front porch steps two at a time up to their white two-story clapboard on Buckeye Street, fling open the front door, and go straight to the liquor cabinet. He'd open the whiskey while their mother was still stirring the boiling pot on the stove, which always smelled like it was dirty socks and bloomers rather than food.

"Doin' the warshing on the stove tonight, eh, Myrtie?"

After a few slugs from the bottle there was a good chance Pawpy wouldn't really be able to taste the meal anyway. By the time they sat down at the table and bent their heads in prayer, Mr. McGinty could've been convinced they'd already eaten dinner.

Vivian looked back at the fish on her plate. She tried to remember, at least at mealtimes and on her knees before bedtime, to be grateful she had food to eat. She tried to remember to be grateful about a lot of things, but it was harder when you were the middle kid. Henry and Will claimed they were middle kids, too, but Vera liked to remind everyone, "Vivian's the *real* middle child," with her voice full of oldest-child authority, "commonly overlooked and perpetually craving attention." *Perpetually*, Vivian repeated the word to herself. *Perpetually.* She wondered what that meant.

While the grown-ups and older kids talked to each other across their plates of awful fish at the long table, Will and Violet kicked each other under it. Forks and knives scraped against plates while Vivian, not quite old enough to talk to the grown-ups and a little too old to kick Will and Violet under the table like she used to, let her mind wander to what she had planned for after dinner. She glanced at the water glasses and began to fidget. Tonight it didn't matter that Ruby, Opal, and Vera wouldn't let her play with them afterward.

"We don't 'play,' Vivy," Vera would scoff, and then shut her bedroom door, leaving Vivian on the outside, every single time.

The last streusel crumb had been scraped from the plate and everyone had pushed their chairs back and made their way out of the dining room. Vivian stayed behind to help her mother clear the table and then brushed the dish towel dramatically back and forth across the rough grain, making a great show of cleaning up, getting a rare smile from her mother and a pat on the head from her Uncle Frank.

"Attagirl!"

Pawpy gave her a wink and then grabbed her mother by the hand, dragging her out to the living room while she protested. He'd never let her mother do the dishes right after a Fish Fry meal and she'd complain that the crud was going to set on the plates and pans if she didn't get to them right away. Vivian held on to the back of a dining room chair and rocked back and forth, toes to heels, toes to heels, as the grown-ups settled themselves in the living room. She waited until she heard the swinging rhythms and blaring horns of the Paul Whiteman Orchestra coming from the radio, and then she sneaked back into the kitchen. She reached for one of the empty water glasses next to the sink, wiped the rim on the hem of her dress, and tiptoed quietly up the stairs to the bedroom she shared with Violet. When the weather was nice, like it was tonight, Violet liked to play with her dolls in the backyard after dinner, so Vivian had their room all to herself.

Pawpy and Henry'd put the screens in the bedroom windows a couple of weeks ago, and Vivian could smell the neighbor's freshly cut grass and hear the crickets chirping. She could also hear the faint, faraway sound of Violet's little voice as she sat under the clothesline and talked to her dolls.

Vivian carefully laid the empty water glass in the middle of Violet's pillow before easing herself onto the narrow bed. It had to be Violet's bed because that was the one pushed against the wall between their room and Vera's. Vivian held her breath and moved slowly enough so the bedsprings wouldn't creak. Vera had ears like a bat. When she'd crawled herself into a comfortable crouch on her knees, she lifted the glass from the pillow and put the mouth of it against the wall, lining it up with the old faded plum-and-evergreen stripes of the wallpaper, and when she was pretty sure the glass wouldn't move, she squished her ear right up against the bottom.

It wasn't like being in the room with them, but the glass-against-wall worked just fine to help her eavesdrop on her older sister and cousins. They spent hours gossiping in Vera's room about the girls and boys in their classes at school. Ruby and Opal went to high school in Apple Creek and Vivian didn't know any of the girls or boys they talked about, but she still gasped quietly at the stories, which she could hear just a little bit better with the glass.

"...thinks he's the elephant's eyebrows, all right," Vera sneered. "And he used to go with Mabel Fiske. Mabel Fiske!"

Mabel Fiske, Vivian thought to herself.

"I can't believe you bobbed your hair," Ruby said, unconcerned with Mabel Fiske and who she used to go with.

Vivian rolled her eyes as she heard Vera say, "Well, believe it." Vera hadn't been able to shut up about her hair since she'd done it. She thought she was sooooo mature now. Vivian could picture Vera on the other side of the wall, smiling coyly and fingering the edges of her fashionable hair.

"Sylvia Emerich bobbed hers," Opal piped in. "And then she had to quit school to get married."

Sylvia Emerich, Vivian thought to herself, and then wondered if Vera would have to quit school because of her hair. But she wasn't getting married.

"Well," Ruby added, "that wasn't the only reason Sylvia had to quit school."

"No." Vera's response was low and disbelieving.

"Positutely," Ruby said.

"No!" Vera exclaimed again, this time so loudly that the word came through the wall as an almost forceful blow.

It was so loud that Vivian fell away from the wall and the glass bounced softly onto the quilt. She'd almost tumbled right off the side of the bed. *Boy, is Vera ever loud. What was the other reason Sylvia Emerich had to leave school?* Vivian steadied herself, then carefully crept back to her spot, picked up the glass, leaned back against the wall, and pressed her ear harder against the base of the glass. Ruby'd lowered her voice by this time, though, and Vivian couldn't make out what she was saying. She narrowed her eyes into a squint.

"What are you doing?"

Vivian gasped and whipped around, causing the bedsprings to bounce and squeak crazily, as the glass again dropped onto the quilt behind her. Her older brother Henry was standing in the bedroom doorway with his thumbs hooked in his suspenders and a sly smile dancing around his lips. Vivian hadn't even heard the door open.

"What are *you* doing?" she shot back.

"I asked you first."

"None of your beeswax!" She crossed her arms over her chest and shifted around on her knees to make sure he couldn't see the glass.

"Well, when you're finished with 'none of my beeswax,' Mom needs to wash that glass." He jabbed a finger in the direction of her right hip, before making an about-face to go back downstairs.

Vivian huffed and considered picking up the glass and throwing it at her brother, but knew she'd get the wooden spoon for that. Their mother knew exactly how many glasses, and plates, and bowls were supposed to be in the kitchen at any given time. She didn't like it when they went missing, but she really hated it when they broke. "These things all cost money!" Vivian wondered how much it would cost to buy herself her own glass. *I'll have my own telephone before Vera does.*

She listened and waited until she heard Henry's shoes hit the tiled floor of the kitchen below before she put the glass back up to the wall. The girls had finished the conversation about Sylvia Emerich and now Vera was talking about the ring. But Vivian wanted to know the *other* reason Sylvia Emerich had to leave school.

"It's Irish," Vera explained to the cousins, who weren't. "They call it a claddagh ring. It's gold and—"

"Our mama has a gold ring, too," Opal interrupted.

"Yes," Vera said patiently, in the way she always did when she spoke to Opal, who wasn't the brightest of the Cutter sisters. "But it's probably her wedding ring, isn't it? This is different. It's gold—"

"She has other gold rings, too, you know," Ruby said, quick to defend her sister and the contents of their mother's jewelry box. Vivian could almost hear her crossing her arms over her chest.

"Fine, but I'm telling you about *this* ring. We can talk about yours after."

Vivian recognized Vera's irritated tone. It was two steps from her shouting tone.

"Anyway, there's a heart in the center, with a crown on top of it, and then two hands that look like they're holding the heart."

There was a pause, to let the cousins picture the claddagh ring in their heads, or maybe Vera was miming with her own hands what the ring looked like, then she continued.

"If you're still a spinster, you wear it right-side up, and then if you're married you wear it upside down."

No, Vivian thought. That was what was annoying about a know-it-all. They sometimes got things wrong, but didn't know it. They never really knew it all.

"And my Aunt Catharine has one that's been in our family for about a hundred years, and she's going to give it to the first one of us girls who gets married."

"Ah," both Opal and Ruby said together.

"Since I'm oldest, it's going to be me."

"Positutely," Ruby agreed.

Vivian thought that if Vera was going to get Aunt Catharine's claddagh ring, she should at least know how to wear it properly. You wore it with the point of the heart facing up if you were still a spinster, but you wanted the point facing down, pointing at your wrist, if you were married. Vera was always so busy talking and telling everyone what they didn't know, she never listened to anything. Vivian listened.

She took the glass from the wall and collapsed back onto the bed, the springs creaking again.

"Vivian!" Vera shouted through the wall. "Is that you? What are you doing in there?"

None of your beeswax.

"I'm resting!" Vivian shouted back.

She thought about what her wedding would be like, and pictured herself in a beautiful white dress with a lace veil that went all the way to the floor. Her husband was going to be so rich, he'd buy her all the gold claddagh rings she wanted. Maybe she'd get one for each finger, although you were really only supposed to wear them on your fourth finger, but Vera didn't know the rules. She'd just see all those rings. How would Vera like that?

Uncle Frank, Aunt Emma, and the cousins never stayed past nine o'clock on Fish Fry nights, and at around quarter till, Aunt Emma called up the stairs.

"Girls! Time to go!"

The door to Vera's room opened and Vera, Ruby, and Opal emerged, still chatting away, and walked in single file past Vivian and Violet's room down the narrow hallway, making their way downstairs. Vivian climbed down from her bed holding the glass behind her back and followed them quietly.

At the front door everyone hugged and kissed their goodbyes, the grown-ups making plans for the next Fish Fry. Vivian's mother pushed the screen door open and hustled the Cutters out, waving her arms after them so the mosquitoes and moths wouldn't get in. The McGintys stood just inside the screen door and waved to the Cutters until the headlights of the Sheridan disappeared down the road. They all then retreated to the kitchen to sit around the table, and Pawpy would have just one more wee glass of whiskey while Mom scraped the dried crud from the dishes and complained, "I told you it would all dry up like this."

"What did you and the girls talk about up there, Vera?" Pawpy asked with a wink as he swirled the amber liquid around his glass.

"Oh, never you mind," Vera answered, tucking her bobbed hair behind her ear and looking at her fingernails in a way Vivian thought made her look like the secretary from the office at school. "That's girl stuff, Pawpy. You don't need to know about that."

Vivian hated to be left out of conversations, so she added, "Yeah, Pawpy, you don't need to know anything about Mabel Fiske or what that Sylvia Emerich is up to," and then crossed her arms over her chest and sat back in her chair with a satisfied smile.

"Vivian!"

Vera's shout brought all eyes to her, then to Vivian, who frowned and pulled her arms tighter against her chest. She liked attention, but not the bad attention.

"Mom!" Vera shouted again. "Vivian was eavesdropping on us!" and she lunged across the table and grabbed the collar of Vivian's best weekday dress with her office-secretary fingernails.

"Vera Eileen!" Pawpy's rebuke with middle name included was sharp, and he slammed his empty glass on the table, causing Vera to release her grip on the collar. "You do not attack your sister."

Vivian was still frozen in place, her eyes like saucers. She very badly wanted to straighten her dress.

"But—" Vera protested.

"You let me talk to her." Pawpy scooted his chair back, picked up his glass, and motioned with it for Vivian to follow him into the living room.

Vivian smoothed the wrinkled collar of her dress as she walked behind Pawpy, straightening the sailor tie and pulling down on the skirt that'd hiked up in the back. Pawpy seated her on the end of the sofa, in the farthest spot from the kitchen, before going to the liquor cabinet to refill his glass. He then returned to the sofa and crouched on the floor in front of her, taking a sip of whiskey.

"Vivy, love." He looked into the blue eyes that matched his own. "You shouldn't be listening in on your sister and your cousins, you hear me?"

Vivian's lip quivered as she nodded at the index finger pointing at her.

"You just need to make sure to keep those secrets to yourself. And next time you won't get caught."

He finished his lecture with a scrunch of his red nose, reached out and gave hers a quick tug with his fingers, and then lost his balance, tipping over sideways onto the braided rug and spilling the rest of his drink.

Her mother heard the glass drop and came stomping into the living room, hands on her hips.

"Christ, Patrick," she hiss-whispered at him. "Vivy, you go on upstairs now. Shame on you."

Vivian wasn't sure if the "shame on you" was for her or Pawpy, but she did what she was told and slid down from the sofa, pulling again at her skirt as she stepped over the spilled glass and across the braided rug. She then climbed the stairs to her room.

Later, Pawpy came to tuck her and Violet in. He steadied himself on the iron bed frame and leaned over and gave her a whiskey-smelling kiss on the forehead.

"You remember what I told you, love," he said in a low voice, tapping her on the end of her nose with his forefinger. "Just don't get caught."

With that tipsy endorsement Vivian's eavesdropping career had officially begun. She smiled and pulled the covers up under her chin, wriggling her toes under the blankets and hoping her dreams would be filled with secret conversations about high school girls getting married and scads of Irish claddagh rings. Instead, she dreamed that a fried fish with great big waggly eyebrows was chasing her around a huge water glass, and she'd forgotten how to swim.

Chapter 4

Betty Miller placed the telephone receiver back in its cradle and eased slowly back in the gold velvet chair, settling into the cushion like a satisfied cat. Her arms crossed over her bosom, her fingers with the shiny, scarlet lacquered nails tapping thoughtfully over her other arm. This was something new, now, wasn't it? It wasn't the everyday gossip they were used to in Wooster. No, this was better. More scandalous.

Betty didn't spend a great deal of time being introspective, as she disliked the feeling it gave her deep in her stomach, and she didn't know why she was so fascinated with the personal business of other people in town, but she also didn't question it. Wooster was a small town. It was natural. Some of her detractors, and even some of her friends, might have said it was the opportunity for comparison. Comparison always reassured her that she was setting the grandest example for the people of Wooster, with her sophistication and carefully cultivated way of life. She supposed she just preferred that things operate the way she wanted them to, without disruption. You wanted Betty Miller to approve of you, and you wouldn't want to get on her bad side, that was simply how it was.

Last December it had been Freedlander's, with their foul, grossly inebriated Santa Claus, endangering the innocence and wonder of Wooster's children, and polluting the very idea and spirit of Christmas. Jesus Christ was not born in a straw-filled manger in Bethlehem so that some filthy, drunken hobo could wreak havoc in the toy department of Freedlander's and desecrate the holiness of Our Lord and Savior's special day. That was what Betty had said to all her friends, who had then faithfully followed her boycott of the department store until Drunk Santa had been fired.

The year before that, Betty's ire had been unleashed upon Wooster's superintendent of schools for having the gall to consider integrating Quinby Elementary. The Negroes lived south of Bowman Street, and that was where they would be most comfortable attending school. It was positively ludicrous to make them travel outside their own neighborhoods, which had perfectly fine schools. It simply did not make sense. Betty and her husband, Charles, had also had to discourage the Hammonds down the road from selling their house to a black family in 1949. They just wouldn't have fit in with the rest of the neighborhood, and Betty wanted to ensure that everyone in Wooster fit in where they belonged. That was just common sense when organizing a community. "Everyone has their place, dear," she had said; surprised she had to belabor the point to Marilyn Dean during an afternoon tea party at Clara Weaver's. And you wouldn't want to get her started on the embezzlement scandal at her father's bank this past summer. You simply would not.

And now she had just been presented with some extremely intriguing information about Vivian Dalton's family. She had almost recoiled at Vivian's waving to her through Freedlander's window earlier. And in that Bechtel's hat. Who did she think she was, waving to Betty so casually like that? Accidental eye contact did not always warrant a familiar greeting. But Vivian did sometimes have difficulty remembering her place. She often led her family to sit in one of the first five on Sundays. Betty had seen that happen at least twice in the past year. She didn't think she should have to remind anyone that the first five pews should be reserved for the worshippers who donated at least a thousand dollars to Forest Chapel Methodist each year. Betty knew for a fact that the Daltons contributed far less than that.

Her *family*, Betty thought smugly, and then croaked out a hoarse laugh before slapping a soft, pale hand over her mouth. She didn't want to wake the children. They were so hard to put to bed these days. They'd get all wound up after *Howdy Doody*, with the hooting and hollering and that demonic clown honking his horn every two seconds. "Clarabell, Mom, it's Clarabell!" Now there was the added excitement about the upcoming school holidays and Christmas. She groaned, thinking of the increased noise level in the house, and the long days of sloppy wet snow, the children's clothing and boots tracking dirt and slush onto her pristine carpet.

She glanced at the perfectly decorated Christmas tree that stood in the corner of the expansive living room. Little Bitty had told her how excited she was to make ornaments at school next week, so Betty needed to remind Charles to set up the children's tree in the den. They could hang the clothespin Rudolph-the-Red-Nosed-Reindeers, and crooked paper snowflakes, and all the other charming, but unsightly, decorations they brought home on that tree. It was nice, and made it special for them, and Betty got to display her beautifully symmetrical, glass-ball-bedecked noble fir for the annual Miller Christmas party. No one's Christmas tree was more highly praised than Betty Miller's tree.

"She just has such an eye for décor!"

"Absolutely perfect!"

"Not a branch out of place!"

Because, as everyone knew, everything in Betty's life was always perfectly in place.

Her absent musings about people forgetting their place and the proper décor of Christmas trees soon shifted entirely to the Christmas party itself, and Betty spent fifteen minutes frowning over ideas for the hors d'oeuvres. As she imagined the silver trays floating about the living room and dining room, she tried to picture what the perfect tiny foods could be, with various free hands reaching for the offerings, while other hands were curled around festive holiday cocktails in the Waterford tumblers. She would have to remind Dolly to fetch the tumblers from the chest in the basement and give them a thorough washing. Although they had been wrapped in tissue paper and sealed in the chest, she wanted to make certain they were clear and sparkling for the event. The holiday tumblers were an entirely different set from the glassware the Millers used for day-to-day.

"Mommy?"

Betty turned her head to see Little Bitty standing on the lowest step of the staircase, hanging on to the post with one hand and rubbing her eye with the other. Her footie pajamas had started to pill and were looking worn. It was a good thing Santa was coming with a new set.

"Baby!" Betty cried in a hushed whisper as she rose from her chair. "What are you doing up?"

Little Bitty slipped down the last step with a thump and whimpered.

"Did you have a bad dream again?" Betty asked as she swooped Little Bitty up in her arms and hugged her close. Little Bitty was nodding and sniffing. She smelled slightly of the hamburger they'd had for dinner that night, and Betty groaned that she had forgotten to bathe her and Charles Junior. They always, always received a bath after any dinner that lingered in their hair.

"There, there." Betty stroked Little Bitty's hamburger hair and kissed her forehead. "Why don't we go back upstairs, and I'll read *Ginger Pye* to you until you fall asleep?"

Little Bitty didn't answer, but Betty could feel her head nodding. She shifted the little girl's weight to her left hip and mounted the stairs up to the pink frilled bedroom, tucked Little Bitty snugly under the covers, and settled onto the bedspread beside her. She only needed to get through two pages before Little Bitty finally fell asleep again.

Betty placed a hand on her sleeping daughter's torso, and then resumed her imaginings of the delighted smiles and gentle praise for her perfect Christmas party cuisine. Soon she began to worry her way through ideas for the perfect holiday music. Twenty minutes after that, she was pacing in her closet, her thoughts turned to the perfect holiday wardrobe.

Betty had quickly forgotten all about Ginger Pye finding the school where her owner Jerry went, Little Bitty's bad dream and hamburger hair, and Vivian Dalton and the phone call. The Christmas party had consumed her thoughts again. She was particularly concerned with finding just the right dress. It really was the most important aspect of the event. The dress had to be just right. She had been thinking about it the day before, but had been distracted by Charles Junior's frightening episode on the swing set in the backyard. It was, of course, too cold and snowy for swinging, but leave it to Charles Junior to discover the second most dangerous activity for a seven-year-old. It had been quickly remedied with a glass of warm water poured over his tongue to disengage it from the metal bar, but Charles Junior's awkward screams had disturbed her train of thought.

But, the dress. The dress was what she needed to focus on. Something tasteful, but still a bit tantalizing. Charles sometimes needed reminders of how good he had it, and it wouldn't hurt to show some of the other husbands how good Charles had it, either. She had been scouring Beulah Bechtel's for the past two weeks, but hadn't seen anything remotely close to what she wanted. She might have to make a trip up to Akron.

Shrimp turnovers! Betty thought as she sat in her peach satin nightgown, brushing out her hair in front of her vanity mirror while Charles snored in bed. Shrimp turnovers were just the thing.

Chapter 5

"Daddy, I have *just* the *thing* for you," had been the forceful, over-enunciated, and breathless greeting from his doorstep back in June, just after his personal disaster. J. Ellis had had to take a moment to process that, instead of the hordes of photographers with their infernal flashbulbs popping like cap guns, his daughter Betty was standing unaccompanied on the expansive fan of bricks. Purposeful, businesslike, and holding an ivory enameled cake carrier.

Now he rubbed both eyes with the heels of his hands, as if trying to rub out the memory of June altogether. The den was dark and quiet as he preferred it, with only the glow of the desk lamp illuminating the items resting in front of him on the smooth leather ink blotter. He reached for his fountain pen, scrawled his signature on the check for Phil Stanley and then did the same on the Christmas card for Betty, Charles, and the children. The one Florence had picked out for them.

J. Ellis Reed was one of the most respected men in Wooster. Depending on whom you talked to. He was definitely one of the wealthiest, if you could ignore the fact that his bank had been robbed of $250,000 six months ago. It had been all over the newspapers that week, and the town had refused to talk of anything else. "*Quite a withdrawal Gilbert Ogden made there, eh, Ellis?*" He had been furious and shaken, Wooster had been in a grand uproar, and then Betty had shown up to make everything all right with some sort of cake.

J. Ellis's children were a source of unending pride for him. Never a misstep with either of them. Johnston Reed, Junior, and Elizabeth Reed Miller were both college graduates who had married well, procreated well, and were known as highly respected, upstanding citizens of Wooster. Important pillars of their community. J. Ellis would never have admitted favoritism, but it was Betty. Betty was her father's daughter.

"Daddy, I know I said it before, but I *simp-ly* can-*not* believe it." She'd bypassed his outstretched hands and marched the cake carrier straight to the maple credenza in the dining room, placing it firmly on the lace runner. "How *dare* someone *do* this to *you*!"

She had brushed her white gloves together before tugging them off, one finger at a time, and set them on the dining room table, then with hands on hips demanded to know where the plates and the cake knife were. Oh, and the forks. The dessert forks.

J. Ellis had feared he might not have the energy for that particular visit from his favorite child and had leaned slightly into the front door he'd still held open. It had been a relief to let the sunlight in, since the photographers weren't there anymore.

"You know, if you'd hire someone like Dolly," Betty had scolded, "you wouldn't have to do all this yourself."

He knew. It was a conversation they'd had before, and J. Ellis would not be entertaining it again, particularly not when he had the bank business to worry about. He was simply not comfortable with hiring a colored woman to clean and cook for him. He had argued that he wanted Betty's mother to feel useful. She had a tendency toward depression when she didn't have enough to do (that was true). And, she had been named after Florence Nightingale, for Christ's sake. It was her *job* to take care of him.

"Where's Mother?" she said, as if reading his mind. "MOTHER?"

Betty had marched over to the foot of the stairs and shouted in the direction of her parents' bedroom, where Florence had been resting her eyes and her mouth. They'd had an argument about how J. Ellis was considering handling the aftermath of the robbery. J. Ellis had shaken his head at his daughter and finally closed the front door.

"Well, Betts, what do you have for us, then?" he'd asked, heading for the credenza.

His head had been throbbing for at least two days as he'd tried to wrap his mind around the robbery and what to do about it. He'd hoped whatever she'd brought would go well with a stiff drink.

"I *won't* try to take *credit* for it," Betty had chirped from the landing in front of the stairs. "You *know* how I *hate* the kitchen. Dolly made it, but I read the recipe to her from the *Home Comfort Cookbook*. I knew it was *just* the thing!"

Of course, J. Ellis had thought to himself.

"It's a *pineapple* upside-*down* cake," she'd gone on. "Because *that* is what those *rot-ten thieves* have *done* to our town, turned it *right* upside-*down*. I can-*not* be-*lieve* the *gall*!"

J. Ellis had noticed that his daughter was wearing a smart short-sleeved yellow and white suit, and he suspected she'd deliberately coordinated her outfit to the cake she'd brought.

"MOTHER!" Betty had shouted again.

J. Ellis had taken several long strides over to the liquor cabinet and reached for the Myers's rum.

"Elizabeth, dear, do stop shouting," the voice had floated down the stairwell.

J. Ellis hadn't needed to look over his shoulder to see the fallen expression, the barely perceptible slump in her shoulders. He'd seen it often enough. The visible dampening of Betty's high spirits that always accompanied each and every correction from her mother. "Stop shouting," "Speak distinctly," "Stand up straight," "Stop flaunting your bosom." Florence had missed her calling as an elegant, contradictory drill sergeant.

Florence Reed had descended the stairs in much the same way she'd walked down the aisle on their wedding day. Slowly, gracefully, and with a gleaming, forced smile. It was also the way she had modeled enormous ribbon-and-feather-festooned hats in Ladies' Fashions at the department store in Syracuse, where J. Ellis had first seen her. He and his fraternity brothers used to drive up to Syracuse from Colgate, just over an hour's drive in the motorcar, to watch the football game and "sample the local culture." The local culture was sometimes found in Ladies' Fashions at Dey Brothers.

J. Ellis had settled on Colgate after being rejected by Cornell, which he'd planned to settle on after his rejections from the Big Three (Harvard, Yale, and Princeton), and he still almost couldn't utter their names without spitting in bitter disgust. After Cornell's rejection, he'd chosen the next-best option, in his opinion, and closest both alphabetically and geographically. And then he'd just hoped it wouldn't make too much of a difference to Wall Street. Florence hadn't minded that he wasn't a Harvard man. She'd been a fine arts major. *The fine art of husband-hunting*, the fellows would snort as they tooted on their flasks of Old Highland, smoked their cigars, and waved their triangle flags.

He'd sighed. Colgate, Syracuse, and Florence. The triumvirate of his misery. Those Wall Street bastards had rejected him, presumably due to his not-quite-up-to-snuff background. He had to admit he'd dodged a bullet with the '29 crash, there, but things had eventually shaped up afterward, hadn't they, yes they had. Ohio banking had made quite an impact, hadn't it, yes it had. Those fat cats could take their Big Three graduates and their money and shove it right up their asses.

"Did your father tell you what he's going to do with *our* money?"

J. Ellis had stared intently as the rum poured into the glass tumbler, but he had felt Betty's eyes on him.

"What do you mean?"

J. Ellis had taken a large swallow from the tumbler as his wife reached the bottom step of the staircase. She'd kept one hand on the newel post as she leaned toward Betty's cheek for a kiss.

"How are you, dear."

It had been a statement more than a question, and Florence hadn't paused for a response.

"His plan is to reimburse the good people of the Wayne Building & Loan. With our money."

His eyes had closed as he tried to enjoy the feeling of the dark liquid coating his throat and sliding a warm path down to his stomach.

"Daddy!"

J. Ellis had run a hand over his pomaded hair and walked back to the credenza to inspect the pineapple upside-down cake.

"This is a beauty. How long did it take Dolly to make this?"

"Daddy." Betty's voice had sounded a warning.

This was not going to become a family exercise, he'd decided. It had been a mistake to even mention it to Florence, but the atmosphere had been sheer insanity. With the telephone's relentless ringing and the throngs of photographers outside the house. He'd started a verbal downward spiral about the whole thing, and at the end of the rant it had come out. He was going to use his own money to reimburse the Wayne Building & Loan customers. Or at least most of them. Of course the fellows from the club, that was just common sense. His son, John, had made a particular plea that he reimburse the Dalton family, which was easy enough. They hadn't had much to reimburse. And then J. Ellis would, naturally, repay the people who could potentially make trouble for him. The loudest complainers. If somebody like Phil Stanley didn't get his money back, J. Ellis would never hear the end of it.

He'd built up a majestic mountain of a reputation for himself over the years and he wasn't going to allow the lingering bank robbery nonsense to topple it. When you were as big a man as J. Ellis Reed, you had a responsibility to maintain a certain standing in your community. And if that meant spending some of your own hard-earned money, then that was what it meant. (His father might have punctuated this with a "By gum!" but he had been more of an Eagle Scout than J. Ellis.) When you were J. Ellis Reed of Wooster, everyone knew who you were. Everyone cared what you did and how you did it.

Chapter 6

"Oh, as if anyone cares what you do," Vera'd mocked when Vivian had a near-fainting spell over Pawpy's McGinty boardinghouse suggestion.

By April of 1931 the Brinkerhoffs next door had started letting two of their rooms to renters, a couple of men who'd lost their factory jobs in Cleveland and had moved to Wooster to find cheaper rent and, hopefully, work. Sixteen-year-old Vivian would watch in a curious panic, her breath fogging the panes of her bedroom window, as the strange men came and went from the Brinkerhoffs', day in and day out over the next year. When Pawpy suggested the McGintys open their doors as well, to earn a little money ("We'll call it McGintys' Come-On Inn!"), she'd twisted her hands almost bloody around her handkerchief at the thought of strange men from Cleveland knowing any of the intimate details of her life.

"*Intimate details?*" Vera had scoffed. "Where'd you even hear that? Did you read it in one of your magazines?"

As a matter of fact, yes, she'd read it in her *Motion Picture* magazine in either the Bebe Daniels story or the Carole Lombard story. She knew Vera had read it, too, but pretended she hadn't. Vera thought she was the only one in the family doing anything worth talking about, which may or may not have had something to do with one of the Brinkerhoffs' lodgers. Vivian overheard Mrs. Brinkerhoff talking about it with Mrs. Kessler.

The glass-pressed-on-wall trick wasn't practical for eavesdropping in all situations, but when Mrs. Kessler and Mrs. Brinkerhoff sat out in the sturdy wooden rockers on the Brinkerhoffs' front porch in the mornings, she didn't need it. Their voices carried up to the open window of Vivian's bedroom. Sometimes it was dull, but Vivian would still pull a chair up and just sit and listen. Boy, did those old ladies like to talk about their neighbors. Vivian was real interested in hearing about Geraldine Sigler, who lived across the street, and apparently suffered from the same troubling condition as Apple Creek's own Sylvia Emerich.

That'd been it. The *other reason* Sylvia Emerich had to leave high school. Having to leave school because you were carrying some farm boy's bastard was sure different than having to leave school because the country's economy collapsed and you had to go to work to help keep food on the table. It was enough to drive a person to curse.

As time wore on, Vivian grew to hate that goddamned Sylvia Emerich for what she represented. Vivian's lost opportunities, that's what. If Sylvia hadn't gotten herself into trouble, she could've finished high school, couldn't she? And maybe even gone to Wooster College to get a degree in something?

It wasn't Vivian's fault the country had collapsed into some great big depression, and she resented having school yanked out from under her, like all the other common folk who had to give up their dreams to scrape around for crummy jobs just to get by. What really burned her up was that Vera and Cousin Ruby got to go through all four years of high school before ever having to worry that Pawpy or Uncle Frank might need some help feeding their families. And they didn't even seem to care.

Cousin Opal made it through her sophomore year before she had to quit to work on the farm in Apple Creek, but Opal'd never been too smart anyway. Vivian once caught her French-kissing a honey jar that had a bee caught in it. Opal would only say that she'd been "practicing." The bee, probably scared out of its wits, had stung Opal's tongue and Opal spent a week whining for everyone to "gob gaffing" at her because the sting "iggy urg." She was lucky Alonzo Halstead married her, so she didn't have to do too much of her own thinking anymore. Or any more practicing. She had a baby the next year.

Mouths to feed and bills to pay. It didn't matter that the McGintys hadn't had any money invested. The stock market crash just knocked the first domino right into the rest of them. The crash sent everyone across America scrambling for ways to do things cheaper. Everybody loved the novelty of the automobile, but it cut right into the business of the railroad lines. With the automobiles came the trucks, and with the trucks came cheaper shipping, and the railroads started cutting jobs. Paddy McGinty's job was cut, and that was where they were in 1931.

The McGinty Come-On Inn suggestion had been swiftly slapped down by Vivian's mother, who was more worried that those strange men who needed room and board were part of the criminal element that was seeping into central Ohio during that time. Like a mudslide flowing from New England and New York State, itinerant men of all ages oozed into Pennsylvania and Ohio, riding the rails and following the rumors of cheap rent and fair wages.

"It's becoming a safe haven for criminals," Mrs. McGinty grumbled, as she shooed her children out the door to look for work themselves, while at the same time grumbling that they'd probably all just end up starving anyway.

Instead of starving, Violet and Will ended up pulling wagons full of discarded ashes from the coal-burning stoves up and down the streets and alleys of Wooster. They'd show up at the dinner table still smudged all over with soot, and then there'd be Henry and Pawpy, covered in paint splatters from sprucing up the houses on the north side of town, and Vera'd be covered in whatever the Dean and Thompson kids had wiped or thrown up on her when she took care of them that day. Turned out four-flusher kids were just as messy as any other kids. Vivian and her mother were the only ones in the house who showed up to dinner about as clean as they had for breakfast. Just after her birthday in June of that year Vivian had gotten herself a job at the switchboards at Ohio Bell, and there was no comparing a glass pressed against a wall to a headset plugged into the switchboard.

Years of being told what to do and when to do it, by father, mother, aunts, uncles, sisters, brothers, and now, at just seventeen, she had a grown-up job with regular hours and steady wages and only had to answer to one person, and her supervisor, Leona, was more of a watcher than a lecturer. She watched the operators, and you'd only hear from her if you messed something up. Vivian's job at Bell puffed her right up with importance. She was part of something certain, in a world suddenly full of uncertainty. Flashing lights, plug-in cords, flip switches, and total strangers counting on her to connect them to one another. She had responsibilities outside the McGinty household, and those responsibilities allowed her to help provide for the household. She'd never felt prouder than the day she handed her Pawpy a small stack of bills with a beaming smile. She'd faltered when she'd seen the tears shining in his eyes, and her heartbeat caught a bit when he rasped, "Proud of you, Vivy." The emotion made her uncomfortable, but the warmth of it felt good.

The switchboard job also gave her a tingly feeling of independence and possibility, and her first taste of power. For someone like Vivian, that was exhilarating, although "exhilarating" was a word she never would have used. She just would've said it was "crazy."

Vivian could hardly believe that people were counting on her to get their calls through. Little ole her, Vivian McGinty. Middle child. She followed the rules to a T in her first few months. But, once she was trusted to perform on her own, she began to stretch her authority.

"Number, please," she'd say.

"Gimme MAson-8812, sister, and make it snappy."

If the caller was like that? All brash and rude, without a "please," and with a "make it snappy"? Not on your life. Vivian'd flip the switch and yank the cord to break the connection, leaving the caller listening to dead air as she moved on to the next blinking light.

"Number, please."

"Yes, could you please connect me with GArden-3662?"

Now, that was more like it. A pleasant tone and a "please" meant Vivian would nod, flip the switch back, plug in the cord connecting the call, and then move on to the next blinking light.

Once, when Leona was on her lunch break, Vivian had felt a sudden urge as she looked at the mangled octopus of cords plugged into the board. Ooh, that urge'd been strong. She'd flexed her hands and thought, *You really shouldn't, you know.* But then the urge had overtaken her. She'd stood up from her chair and raised her eyebrows at the other girls. She'd bent her left arm and swept it under all the cords in one swift movement, unplugging all those calls at the same time and disconnecting the people of Wooster. *Pluck, pluck, pluck, pluckity-pluck, pluck* went the cords.

"Hey!"

"Hey, what . . ."

"What's the idea?"

"Hey!"

The other operators had sounded just like the cords being plucked out of their sockets. Vivian had felt a rush of excitement as the cords popped out and dropped with a clatter over the countertop. The accusing faces had turned to her all sourpusses and surprised Os, and a few with genuine anger. One (Mary Fletcher, that rat fink) had gone straight to Leona and told her what Vivian had done.

She might've been fired if Leona hadn't liked her so much. If it'd been up to Mary Fletcher, Vivian would've been out on her can. But Leona'd just taken her off the schedule for the next week, and Vivian'd felt horrible and full of remorse, mostly because of the lost wages.

What that little experiment had proved, though (Tattletale Rat Fink Fletcher aside) was that Vivian finally had some control. Never before in her life had she had such a sense of control. She couldn't have predicted that, some twenty-odd years later, that sense of control would be suddenly doused, like a flaming match dropped into a glass of water, with one late-night phone call.

Chapter 7

Vivian's sense of control at the switchboard had disappeared in about forty-five seconds of eavesdropping on that one call to Betty Miller, and had been replaced by blinking disbelief at what she'd just heard. When both women had said their good-byes in her ear, Vivian realized she needed to disconnect the call. She flipped the switch, pulled the cord, and then stared, unseeing, at the darkened board as her disbelief bloated into anxiety and fear. The kind of anxiety and fear she used to feel when she'd worried about her Uncle Hugh being in an accident out on the road on his highway patrol motorcycle, but this was much, much worse.

Moving from habit, she unplugged her headset and wrapped it into a bundle. She pushed in her rolling chair, and mutely followed Dorothy and the others who finished at eleven as they slid into their coats and pulled their hats snugly over their ears. She did the same, without thinking, and without hearing any of the "good-night"s that sang out around her. It wasn't until the icy wind hit her full force in the face as she stepped out onto East Liberty Street that the anxiety and fear froze in place, and from under that bubbled something hot. A roiling boil of hot anger. The churning lava flow of dark, horrible emotions coursed through her body as her worn, old ankle boots crunched back over the snow, retracing the steps she'd taken to get to work.

The temperature had dropped, but with her blood boiling the way it was, she hardly noticed. Vivian knew what rage felt like on the inside, and she also knew what it looked like from the outside. It looked like lifelong Democrat Roy Patterson when Herbert Hoover was elected president, and Jacob Starlin, when somebody stole his wheelbarrow from out of his backyard, and rage looked like poor Bill Parker, the day he found out about his wife leaving town with Gilbert Ogden after robbing the Wayne Building & Loan. *Absconding*.

Bill's neighbors said they could swear he had smoke coming out of his nose and ears and the top of his head, and Vivian could practically feel the smoke charring the inside of her Beulah Bechtel hat.

"It was genuine smoke!" his neighbors had insisted.

Bill'd slammed open the screen door and flown out of the house, shotgun in one hand, hat in the other. The tires of his car had burned over the pavement so badly, you'd still be able to see the black marks from the rubber, if they weren't covered with snow right now. Bill Parker's rage. That was the kind of rage Vivian was feeling, with her fingernails cutting into the lining of her gloves as her fists clenched inside her coat pockets.

The anger propelled her breath out into the freezing night air in short bursts. She stopped in front of Freedlander's window, now darkened and still, with no sign of all the festive holiday cheer she'd seen just a few short hours earlier, and no sign of that rich bitch Betty Miller, who was now sitting somewhere in her expensive house on Wooster's north side, with some dangerous new knowledge she shouldn't have. The woman in the reflection who looked back at Vivian was wearing her lovely blue hat, but was old and wretched, decades beyond her thirty-eight years. If everything under her feet hadn't been covered in a hard pack of icy snow, she would've reached down for a loose brick in the sidewalk and then launched it through that window, splintering the stupid flocked glass and shattering the image of the old wretched woman she didn't recognize.

The porch light was on outside, just like Edward said it would be; the rest of the house was dark. But not quite as dark as Vivian's mood. Her mind was a frenzy of confusion. Barely contained rage bumped up against a wall of disbelief and somewhere between standing in front of the window at Freedlander's and arriving at her own front porch a dull thudding headache had erupted in Vivian's head. Her body was tired and chilled to the bones. She trudged up the porch steps, which were mostly cleared of the snow, and grasped the doorknob, turning it and listening as the latch clicked and released from the jamb. Her limbs felt heavy, like they were made of wood and she was trying to pull them through water.

Once inside, she gave a sharp yank on the floor lamp's chain and watched the room brighten. She looked around at the furniture that had been familiar when she left the house earlier, but now seemed very strange, almost like it, too, was underwater. The wing chairs, the television set, the sofa; they all looked like they were floating. The side table, on which the telephone sat, also appeared to be bobbing on unseen waves. Vivian leaned back against the door and took a deep breath, willing the dizziness to pass.

They'd gotten it, their first telephone, just last year. A heavy black base with the handset resting in the cradle on top, and the thin cord winding its way down and along the floor to the outlet. There was no dial with numbers, like some of the phones she'd seen in movies. You picked up the handset and an operator would say, "Number, please," just like Vivian did, over and over, day in and day out.

Funny how she'd worked at Bell all these years, but the Daltons had only recently had a telephone installed in their own house. Edward's parents had had a telephone for years now. One of the old ones that hung on the wall; a great wooden box with one cone you spoke into, and the other you lifted to your ear. Vivian wondered what kinds of things Edward's mother heard through her telephone.

She reached down and slipped off the old worn ankle boots, losing two inches in height as her stockinged feet met the thin carpet. The big toe of her left foot had poked its way through the nylon fabric. She unbuttoned her coat and shrugged out of it, still standing at the front door, and still staring at the telephone.

Vivian climbed the stairs, counting them as she had when they first moved into the house. Thirteen steps. Thirteen was an unlucky number any way you looked at it, not to mention quite a fall if someone were to lose his balance.

The door to Charlotte's room was closed, as it always was by that time of night. No light shone in the crack at the bottom. Sometimes, but not always, Charlotte liked to stay up late reading. Books, not magazines, which, for the life of her, Vivian couldn't understand.

Edward was already sound asleep and snoring when Vivian entered their bedroom, the light from the hallway behind her outlining her silhouette in the doorframe. The room was filled with his deep, even, vibrating nasal growl. She flipped off the hall light, then waited for her eyes to adjust to the dark before stepping delicately over the rug. She stood on his side of the bed, watching his torso rise and fall in time with the snores.

She used to watch him sleep like this when they were first married. When she couldn't believe her luck in finding a guy like him. He, naturally, fell asleep immediately after their love-making, and Vivian would prop herself up on her elbow and gaze at the details of his face. His dark, wild eyebrows, the straight, proud nose that ended in just the cutest point. She'd sometimes take the tip of her index finger and lightly tap the point of his nose, making him snort and snuffle before settling back into his rhythmic snore.

She now studied the eyebrows that had grown wilder and started to sprout grays here and there, and the lines that had deepened in his cheeks and around the corners of his mouth, and the lips, which were looking thinner beneath the coarse mustache. Her eyes roamed around the hairline, which had stretched itself from a sexy widow's peak into a sharp V over the last decade, and then to his bulging Adam's apple, vibrating on and off with the snoring.

The alarm clock fit neatly in her hand as she slid it from the bedside table. The smooth face rounded against her palm, the glass sticking to her skin as her fingers curled around the metal edges. The light ticking of the clock matched the pounding in her head. *Tick, tick, tick, tick, pound, pound, pound, pound.* She watched the vulnerable Adam's apple and weighed the clock, the way a professional baseball pitcher might weigh the baseball in his hand before winding up, lightly raising and dropping it in a slow, measured bounce.

Chapter 8

Vivian couldn't keep all her parts from jiggling and bouncing as the Model A jiggled and bounced its way down Henrietta Street that mild winter afternoon. "It's the Roadster," Edward boasted loudly above the engine. "Got it for a song." That was no surprise, really, since newer models had come out from Ford and most people were more interested in having the latest thing. Edward's car was only five years old, but he drove it a lot and it tended to rattle. "Was that song 'Pennies from Heaven'?" she asked with an eyebrow arched, thinking that paying more than a few cents for this jalopy was nuts. A quick scramble to cover up the criticism, she tilted her head toward him with a winning grin. Edward smirked at the slight, unfazed. "It's got a rumble seat," he said, waggling his eyebrows up and down.

Vivian was grateful for Vera's hand-me-down wool coat (not the latest thing, either) that kept some, if not all, of her jiggling and bouncing at least a little under control. "Vivian, don't wiggle around like a whore," her mother had snapped once, surprising Vivian with the harsh words. She usually just huffed and grumbled her discontent. Either way, Vivian tried to ignore her. Every one of those little criticisms left chips in Vivian's self-esteem. By the time she was old enough to be considered a grown-up, her self-esteem, if she could've seen it, might've looked a little like a wedge of Swiss cheese.

The car was really jiggling around, though, and Vivian folded her arms across her breasts, afraid they'd jump right out of her dress *and* the coat, and she wanted to keep a little mystery where Edward was concerned. Mystery was an important part of romance, if you believed everything you read in *McClure's*. Still, she hadn't thought the car would be so small. She could smell his hair pomade, they were sitting so close. Something sweet, but she couldn't place the smell. A deep flush bloomed up and over her neck and face, and goose bumps popped up everywhere else. She cast a few shy glances from his hands on the steering wheel up to his profile, and the straight nose that tapered off to an adorable point, as he faced forward, keeping his eyes trained on the road in front of them.

A slight smile had crept into the corners of Edward's mouth as he steered the car with casual confidence over the uneven bricks of Henrietta Street. At one point he began to whistle, and Vivian stifled a giggle as she turned her head away from him and looked out the window, the brim of her hat shielding her face. She tried to focus her attention on the houses they passed, the Gerbers' and the Sawyers' and a few she didn't know, and then later the clusters of bare trees and bushes now dripping with melting snow. It was just perfect, the things that created the scenery of their own little private world inside the traveling tin can, sitting pretty on that tufted bench seat and breathing the shared air together as Vivian grew more and more aware of the tingling in her skin. She hummed "Pennies from Heaven" lightly under her breath.

By the time Edward pulled the car up to the curb in front of the McGintys' house the temperature had dropped back down into the numbers more usual for the month of December.

"They don't make heaters for cars," he said with an apologetic shrug. "But they should, shouldn't they?"

Although her parts had stopped jiggling and bouncing, she was starting to shiver and her teeth had begun to chatter. Edward cranked the gears into the park position.

"Go on, get in there," he urged, still with that big grin on his face. "I don't want you to freeze to death out here. They'd try me for murdering the prettiest girl in Ohio."

Vivian might've rolled her eyes if it'd just been cheap flattering, but her eyes were dancing as she looked down at her gloved hands in her lap and then out the fogging windshield in front of her. Cold as she was, she'd rather stay there in the car with Edward than go back into the McGinty house with all the noise and all the people. She wondered what it would be like to freeze to death right there next to him. The chill had crept in through the secondhand coat, and was working toward the top layer of skin, but her heart and the rest of her insides stayed glowing warm.

It might've been because she just kept sitting there, not moving, just looking at the dashboard because the windshield had now been completely fogged over by their breath. But, whatever it was, Edward finally remembered his manners and jumped out of the car and ran around to her side to escort her out and up the steps to her front door. *Finally*, she thought.

Vivian was ready to be worshipped. Like Douglas Fairbanks did Mary Pickford, or King Edward did Wallis Simpson. She'd seen the two of them in one of the magazines she liked to buy after she collected her wages from Bell. It was probably *Life*, because that was the one that mentioned international things, and if she were being honest she'd tell you she wouldn't have been too interested except the tabloid photographs of one Mrs. Wallis Simpson with King Edward VIII of England on a yacht were scandalous and Vivian couldn't resist a good scandal. The word "illicit" was dropped a number of times throughout the article, and Vivian declared to her younger sister, Violet, that Mrs. Simpson was nothing better than a home-wrecking whore.

"*Mrs.* Simpson," she hissed, pointing at the words on the page. "She's already married! She's wrecking her own home, for chrissakes."

"Vivy!" Violet was shocked by Vivian's language, but also secretly impressed. "Do all the switchboard girls talk like that?"

Vivian had shrugged. She and Violet followed the story of Edward and Wallis and when the King of England stepped away from his title and his crown in order to marry Mrs. Simpson, boy, oh, boy, did Vivian change her tune. All that illicit whorish home wrecking was forgotten the moment Mrs. Simpson divorced her husband and accepted Edward's marriage proposal.

Vivian found herself in a deep swoon over the romance of it all. A king who'd give up his kingdom for the woman he loved! It made Vivian dizzy, flushed and tingly in the places a decent girl didn't talk about. Oh, sure, there were a couple of boys in Wooster who came close to that kind of adoring devotion, because Vivian McGinty was a lively girl, and kept her lipstick fresh and her seams straight. She was "hotsy-totsy," as they said, and had more than her fair share of attention from the opposite sex, which went a little ways toward filling some of those Swiss cheese holes. But it was Edward Dalton's invitation to go out driving that came on the same day as the tabloid reports of the Wallis and Edward engagement. In her dreamy, dizzy frame of mind, Vivian had quickly accepted. It was as if the stars had aligned to create that perfect romantic afternoon drive down bumpy Henrietta Street in Edward's crummy Model A Deluxe Roadster. The Model A was a jalopy all right, but it might've been the closest thing Wooster had to a yacht, as far as Vivian was concerned.

She'd paid attention to the cautionary tales of Apple Creek's Sylvia Emerich, having to leave school and whatnot, and her neighbor Geraldine Sigler, as well as the other stories passed in whispers around town. Stories of girls who'd been baking their illegitimate buns in their ovens months, even weeks, before they married their husbands (or didn't!). It was all hushed up, though, and never, ever admitted publicly, but the whispers and rumors floated around town, sometimes through the telephone lines and switchboards at Bell, and wore away at the respectability of the brides-to-be. Vivian had even heard something about four-flusher Betty Reed, who'd seemed in an awful hurry to marry Charlie Miller. That rumor had never really gone anywhere, though, and since Betty and Charlie were both four-flushers no one batted an eye at their wedding. The Betty Reed rumor made Vivian feel almost smug about her romance with Edward. Even with the rumble seat in the Roadster, Vivian was better than that, and she knew Edward was better than that. She couldn't take full credit, it was really Pawpy's words ringing in her ears every time she greeted her dates at the front door: "If you get knocked up, you're out of here." He never said it mean, just matter-of-fact. So, *No, sir,* Vivian had thought, before she'd even gone on that first car ride, *that won't be me, if I can help it.* The people of Wooster would have to find someone else to gossip about.

Other than Vera and Mrs. McGinty, who was surprised when anything good happened, no one in the McGinty family had been surprised when Vivian got herself the job at Bell. They weren't surprised when Edward Dalton proposed, and they weren't surprised Vivian married before Vera did; a whole three years before Vera did. On a pleasant afternoon in June of 1937, Vivian Margaret McGinty married Edward George Dalton.

Money was still tight, and the beautiful long white dress and lace veil her ten-year-old self had daydreamed about would've been impractical. Vivian was a woman now. A grown-up. With a proper job, and a handsome bridegroom. Her "something old" was the gold Irish claddagh ring from Aunt Catharine, and she wore it proudly on her right hand as she stood in her smartest skirt suit and matching hat (her "something new" from Beulah Bechtel's). The fragrance of the Firmament lilacs pinned to her lapel (her "something blue" that matched her eyes) wafted around her head as Edward held her hand and leaned in close while they repeated their vows to each other. They might as well have been in the room alone, because everything around Vivian was a blur, and she couldn't see anyone other than Edward.

"I do."

DALTON-MCGINTY NUPTIALS
SOLEMNIZED THIS MORNING

Miss Vivian McGinty, daughter of Mr. and Mrs. P. W. McGinty, of South Buckeye Street, and Edward G. Dalton of Syracuse, N.Y., were united in marriage this morning at 10 o'clock at the Church of Christ parsonage, with Rev. T. R. Freytag officiating. The double ring ceremony was used.

The couple was attended by Miss Vera McGinty, sister of the bride.

The bride was attractively dressed in a three-piece tailored brown and grey suit, with matching brown accessories. She wore a shoulder corsage of Firmament lilacs.

Miss McGinty wore a grey suit with grey accessories. Her shoulder corsage of roses and sweet peas.

Mrs. Dalton has been employed by the Ohio Bell Telephone Corp. for the past few years.

It was official, and now everyone in Wooster would know. There hadn't been quite as many details about Edward, but Wooster wasn't *his* town. Forest Chapel Methodist was being renovated, and neither Vivian nor Edward wanted to wait for it to be finished, so they'd made do with the parsonage at the Church of Christ. As far as the wedding attire, Wallis Simpson hadn't worn a white gown with a lace veil, either, so Vivian wasn't too bent out of shape about it. Mrs. Simpson wore a designer silk crepe gown in "periwinkle blue," the magazines said. Periwinkle was just a shade off the Firmament lilacs the colorist matched to Vivian's eyes when he touched up the wedding photograph.

Vivian had thought it was both *important* and *significant* that her wedding to Edward was just two days after Wallis Simpson married her Edward. Vivian had made note to use the word "significant" more often, after church one Sunday, months earlier. "The J. Ellis Reed family has made a *significant* donation," the reverend had said. She also thought it was important and significant that the fancy and glamorous Mrs. Wallis Simpson was marrying an Edward, and she, the not-quite-as-fancy-or-glamorous Vivian McGinty, was also marrying an Edward. Names had importance and significance. More than most people bothered to notice.

"Listen to this," she'd said to Violet while she read aloud from her magazine. "*Edward Albert Christian George Andrew Patrick David, Duke of Windsor.* Garsh, that's a lot of names!"

Vivian didn't need a lot of names. She just needed her own. Her new one. She was Mrs. Vivian Dalton (pleased to meet you). She loved how fancy that sounded and couldn't wait to introduce herself to new people.

Although she'd later try to get him to admit that he'd picked that bumpy Henrietta Street for their first car ride on purpose, her husband, Mr. Edward Dalton, tried to deny any indecent motivation. But he denied it with a smirk. And anyone with an automobile, carriage, bicycle, or wagon back then knew what to expect on Henrietta Street, with its jumbled, uneven bricks. "And, boy, did I get what I was expecting!" Edward would hoot, then waggle his eyebrows, and give Vivian a pinch on the rear that would send her scuttling into the next room, flushing in embarrassment, her scowl threatened by hints of a smile.

The Daltons would eventually make it part of their anniversary celebration. A ceremonial drive down Henrietta Street. Sometimes Vivian would wear a flimsy blouse without her brassiere, singing "Pennies from Heaven" out loud, and wiggling around like a whore, because she was married then and it didn't matter. (So *there*, Mama!) And sometimes Edward would sing nursery rhymes like he liked to do to make Vivian laugh. She loved to laugh. His voice would joggle and wobble as the Model A bumped over the stones.

"Ma-a-a-ry ha-a-ad a li-i-i-tle l-a-a-amb . . ."

He was no Rudy Vallee, but he could carry a bumpy tune.

But those anniversary drives down Henrietta Street came later. After they'd moved back to Wooster.

Vivian was only superstitious when she wasn't giddy and thrilled about getting married. So, Forest Chapel Methodist wasn't available, and they had to have the ceremony somewhere else. So what? And she hadn't given it another thought when she'd dropped her handkerchief getting out of the car on her wedding day. If she'd been watching it happen to another bride, she'd have muttered, "Oh, Jesus, that's bad luck," under her breath. And maybe it was nothing. Maybe dropping her handkerchief wasn't the bad luck it was said to be, but having to move away from Wooster wasn't her idea of a great start to the marriage. It'd seemed to come out of nowhere.

"It means you'll have to quit the phone company," Edward had said when he told her about his new job.

Vivian's face had pulled into a deep frown, until she remembered that deep frowning caused wrinkles. She'd looked down at her wedding ring, which was already starting to feel a little heavier than she'd expected. She'd let out a small sigh. She was a dutiful wife now ("Mrs. Vivian Dalton, pleased to meet you"), wasn't she? Her salary was milk money compared to Edward's, wasn't it? And it would have been foolish to try to argue about it, wouldn't it? The answer to all those questions was, "Well, yes."

So, shortly after the day of her wedding to Edward George Dalton, Vivian moved away from Wooster, away from her family, and away from the job where she'd felt a little control and a lot of pride. Far, far away from the McGinty house on South Buckeye, and far, far away from Ohio Bell on East Liberty Street. The Edward Daltons began their life of marital bliss in a run-down yellow clapboard bungalow that was five hundred miles away from Vivian's hometown, and less than two miles from the Institution for Male Defective Delinquents.

The Eastern New York Reformatory in upstate New York was opened in 1900 mainly as a facility to handle the overflow of other prison facilities. Overflowing with thieves, murderers, rapists. If anyone had bothered to ask Vivian where she'd like to live as a newlywed, she'd have said, "Oh, near the park," or "It'd be nice to be close to the beauty parlor." Not, "How about a short drive from the Institute for Male Defective Delinquents at Napanoch?," which was the official name of the reformatory by the time Edward Dalton was hired there in May of 1937. Just a few weeks before their wedding. The reformatory was overseen by the Department of Corrections, and the inmates were men over the age of sixteen with IQs of under seventy, and their sentences were indefinite.

Other than the steady pay and the security that went along with it, the only thing Vivian liked about Edward's job as a prison guard was the uniform. Boy, did Edward look good in that uniform. Her favorite photograph was him standing with hands on hips, smiling, in his starched khaki shirt, black tie, and jodhpurs, with his thumbs hitched into his metal-buckled belt. That, by the way, was how he'd told her he had his position at the prison, the sneak. She'd been so busy at Bell, and with making plans for their wedding day, she hadn't thought to ask him anything about his new job. She'd assumed it was something nearby. And Edward didn't say anything about it until after she saw the photograph. He'd handed it to her, and waited for her reaction. He'd stood there, with that wicked little grin on his face, and she'd fallen for it. She'd blushed and gushed over how dashing he looked in the uniform. And he'd said, "Glad you like it," and then he told her they had to move to New York State. "Honey, I know it's not what you wanted, but I have to be close to my job."

"Not too close, I hope," she'd said on the drive in the Model A from Wooster to Wawarsing, some little nowhere town between New York City and Albany. After they'd crossed the Ohio/Pennsylvania border she'd finally stopped looking for her Uncle Hugh on his Ohio State Patrol motorcycle. That, at least, had given her a little comfort, knowing he was out there somewhere on the road. A thread of connection to the family she was leaving behind. It would've been nice to see another McGinty out there. She would've even been happy to see Vera, for crying out loud, flying down the opposite side of the road on her broomstick. Vivian snickered to herself and set her chin on her elbow leaning out the window, the wind whipping her face.

The stretch of highway had been endless, and the day cloudless and hot, with nowhere proper to stop when she'd had to go to the bathroom. She'd had to go wandering out into the woods to get away from the road, not that there were any other cars on it, mind you, because no one in their right mind wanted to go to Wawarsing, New York, in July, but that would've been just her luck, to get into a sweaty squat near the road and have someone suddenly drive by and honk at her. She knew Edward would've just laughed. He said he didn't have the same problems with modesty that she had. He called them problems, she called them manners. One thing she learned on that drive to Wawarsing was that being married was going to take some getting used to.

"How often do they escape?" she'd asked, wiping perspiration from her brow and looking uneasily out the open car window as they drove past the squat fortress set back from the road. She wondered how a place could look so gloomy and dangerous even in late afternoon July sun.

"Escape?" Edward laughed. "Who, the inmates?" and he reached out his right hand to ruffle her hair. "With me in charge?"

She hadn't been satisfied with that answer, but Edward had then pulled the Model A into the two dried-mud grooves off Lundy Road that led up to the west side of the house, put the gears in park, and before Vivian knew it she was distracted. The little yellow bungalow on Lundy Road had peeling white shutters with Christmas tree cutouts, a sagging roof, and a rickety front porch, and it was all theirs.

The Daltons' first house. Mr. and Mrs. Edward Dalton! Pleased to meet you, and welcome to our home! Vivian pushed open doors, and poked the broom into cobwebby corners, and put the wilting groceries away in the icebox. And then she'd stood at the back door staring across the overgrown yard at the little yellow outhouse.

"Jesus Christ."

Vivian spent her days tidying the house, washing their clothes and hanging them on the clothesline in the backyard, and preparing dinner for the two of them. Canned soups and vegetables that she'd heat up on the stove, and the occasional chicken or ham that she'd burn in the oven. Sometimes she'd eye the empty cans and think of the old telephone game she used to play with Henry when they were kids. Cans with the string pulled taut between them. And then she'd think of the glass pressed up against the wall, which then made her think of her old job at Bell. Octopus cords everywhere and a live person chattering in her ear every few minutes. She held the can of peas to her ear. "Number, please." She held it there for a moment as she swayed back and forth looking out the kitchen window. When she set the can back on the counter she let out a wistful "Whuff," bringing a corner of her apron up to blot her eyes.

Edward would come home from his shift at the prison looking exhausted and asking her not to ask him about his day, so they'd eat in silence. The same silence she'd had to listen to all day.

"What the hell's that smell?" Edward said one night when Vivian'd burned the soup again.

Except that he wasn't talking about the soup. He was in the bedroom.

"Well," Vivian shouted in irritation through the smoky kitchen, "that's our baby, roughing up my insides, is what it is."

She'd been using the sick bowl for the past few weeks. Goddamned outhouse was too far away. Today was the first day she'd forgotten to empty it.

So, that'd come out a whole lot more awkward than she'd planned, her special announcement. She wanted to do something a little fancier, maybe with candles and dinner that wasn't burned, with a bouquet of late autumn wildflowers in the crystal vase they'd received as a wedding gift from Edward's cousin Evelyn. The kitchen table wouldn't have held all of that at the same time anyway, but still. This wasn't the way she'd wanted to do it.

Goddammit.

She'd lain next to Edward in bed that night, wide awake while he snored soundly. The warm glow of Edward's excitement about the baby had worn off as soon as he'd fallen asleep and Vivian was already back to stewing about his complaint. Her moods had been getting sourer and sourer with every week. It was easier to be ornery than to be sad and sorry for herself. She couldn't let this hopeless helplessness swallow her whole, and who was he, anyway, to be complaining about smells? The sick bowl, the burned dinners. *He comes home smelling like a goddamned latrine on fire and I don't say a thing.* Boys, men. They never did learn to keep after themselves. Snips and snails and puppy-dog tails. She hoped her baby would be a girl.

Vivian got her wish, and little Charlotte Catharine Dalton (a lovely, significant, and important name) was born on February twenty-second, nine months and seventeen days after Vivian and Edward's wedding day. The pregnancy had been nine months of sick and grumbling and aches, and then the labor, whoo-boy, she wouldn't be going through that again. Vivian told Edward that would be it for her.

"You'd better like this one," she'd breathed, while propped up in the hospital bed, wan, sweating, and drained of energy. "She's going to be the only one." It would be too bad for Edward, she'd thought. He'd probably wanted a boy. He hadn't said as much, but she knew people.

Charlotte's birth made Vivian twice as anxious as she'd been when they first moved to the little yellow house the year before. She'd spent so much time worrying about the prison, the criminal inmates, and the proximity of their house to all of it, she hadn't had time or brain space to consider any other types of threats. Little Charlotte was just seven months old at the time of the attack.

Chapter 9

Charlotte's mother had struck her just four days after Thanksgiving. It was the first time she'd hit her in Charlotte's fifteen years and she was still a little rattled. Holy smoke, had that been a shocker. Right in the back of the head as she'd been storming out of the kitchen; away from the argument. *SMACK!* Open-handed and sharp. The cartoon stars spinning before Charlotte's eyes.

If Charlotte had had to pinpoint when her relationship with her mother started to show strain she'd have guessed it was a few years earlier; around middle school. When she really started to get excited about what she was learning. Although she didn't *really* figure it out until high school. That was when it dawned on Charlotte that there seemed to be a direct correlation between her bubbling enthusiasm over Robert Louis Stevenson's *Treasure Island*, or anything by the Brontë sisters, and her mother's scowling. Fifteen issues of *Movie Stars Parade*, stacked one on top of the other, measured up to the height of *Mansfield Park* as it sat on the side table next to the sofa, but there was no convincing Charlotte that anything in those magazines could measure up to what was inside the Austen book. She'd bet her mother hadn't even bothered with a glance at the book's title, and there was a small part of her that worried her mother might think Jane Austen was the president of Wooster's Trowel & Trellis Garden Club. *Oh, yes,*

Jane Austen. I think I've seen her at Beulah Bechtel's. The one with the chin mole and the blue rinse.

Smart, Aunt Vera had said. Charlotte had overheard Aunt Vera discussing her with Aunt Violet. Aunt Vera never had any of her own kids, but doted on Charlotte like she was her own. Doted on, but didn't coddle. The rest of that comment to Aunt Violet had been, *A little naïve, though.* Charlotte had gasped in indignation at that, and then folded her arms with a frowning pout, wondering what Aunt Vera meant.

She'd admit, she'd felt naïve about certain things, like when she hadn't understood why Rosie Gianetti's family hadn't been reimbursed by Wayne Building & Loan following the embezzlement scandal. Charlotte's parents had been reimbursed. Rosie's parents had not. "Why do you *think* they're not getting their money back, Charlotte?" Rosie had shouted, her fists clenched and face red, because the word around Rosie's neighborhood was that none of the Italian families were going to be reimbursed.

Charlotte had stood, dumbfounded, unable to answer what was really a rhetorical question. She remembered that Mrs. Betty Miller had organized an event in Wooster's Public Square to honor her father, who'd said he'd reimburse people who'd lost their money. The day had been a sweltering summer one and there'd been loudspeakers and Mrs. Miller was calling out to the crowd about this "celebration of simple human decency," saying that her father's generosity was the kind of thing all local communities should celebrate. Charlotte had even heard Margie Miller saying her mom thought there ought to be a statue of him in the square, and a special "J. Ellis Reed" holiday, which was a big eye-roller.

Charlotte had believed Mayor Reed about the reimbursements back then, but now Christmas was a few weeks away and Rosie's family still hadn't gotten their money back. But maybe it was just taking longer than they thought. "You just don't get it," Rosie had said, and Charlotte had stormed home and collapsed in a crying heap on her bed. At her age, Charlotte's most important needs were having friends and fitting in, and if you weren't a four-flusher, you had to work a little harder to get there.

Charlotte had recently been granted the honor of joining the Girls Athletic Association, which was a big deal for a sophomore; only four had achieved it this year. To qualify for the GAA you had to earn an established number of points by participating in extracurricular activities, and Charlotte had gone over-and-above to do it. Field hockey, swimming, softball, basketball, bowling. She was exhausted and extremely proud of herself. The successful members were announced over the school's PA system by Miss Vickers, the gym teacher, and the smile that had cracked wide open across Charlotte's face had remained plastered there until she'd walked through the front door of her house.

"So, you're a joiner now, are you?" her mother had asked in the same tone of voice usually reserved for mocking the four-flushers, her hand fluttering to her heart.

Her dad had squeezed her shoulder affectionately, then ruffled her hair with a "Good for you, Lottie. Good for you."

The GAA membership involved an initiation. One week where the girls had to do embarrassing things: approach boys in the hallway and sing songs to them, perform an Irish jig in front of a class, that sort of thing. During initiation week they couldn't wear makeup to school. They had to wear crazy outfits: mis-matched socks, plaids with stripes and florals, with crazy hairdos to match.

Charlotte's mother had dropped her spatula on the kitchen floor at the sight of her daughter, crinolines worn over a plaid pencil skirt sticking out from her winter coat, pigtails sprouting all over one side of her head while the other side lay limp and un-hair-sprayed, and a face with no makeup, about to leave the house.

"Charlotte, get back in here right now."

Charlotte rolled her eyes, but obediently stepped back inside the house and went to the kitchen.

"Where do you think you're going, dressed like that?" Her mother was aghast as her gaze roved over the hairdo and the clothing.

"It's part of the initiation."

"You're not leaving the house dressed like that."

Normally Charlotte would have agreed with her. She looked like she was dressed up for Halloween, and a small part of her wanted to skip the whole thing and stay home. But there was a stronger feeling, one of pride pushing her in the other direction.

"I have to," she countered. "It's not optional."

"Ohhh." Her mother's tone turned mocking. "It's not *optional*. Optional? What it is, Charlotte, is ridiculous, and you're not going anywhere in public looking like that!"

Charlotte looked desperately over her shoulder, hoping her dad hadn't left for work yet. But he had. He was always, always working. As she turned back to face her mother she felt the frustration bubble to the surface. She already felt absurd in the clothing, with her pigtails swinging crazily every time she moved her head, and one foot in a penny loafer, the other in an oxford. But this *was not optional for Charlotte.* This was part of belonging to something important, and she was not going to miss out on any part of it just because her mother didn't understand it. She might have meant to keep those thoughts private, but she heard herself speaking aloud.

"You don't understand any of this because you've never been a part of anything like this!" she barked, startled by the sound of her voice, and before she could stop it, "You never even went to high school!"

The words hung in the air like smoke as Charlotte whipped around to walk back to the front door.

SMACK! Right in the back of the head.

The smack caused her to stumble, and when she righted herself she paused for the briefest of seconds out of sheer shock. But then she kept going, striding purposefully through the living room in her mismatched shoes, and out the front door. Tears burning in her eyes. It would be years before she'd recognize the fear behind her mother's slap. The helpless panic Vivian felt as her young daughter pulled away and ahead of her, exceeding her in life. Tears would burn Charlotte's eyes then, too.

Chapter 10

1938

The smoke from the neighbors' burning leaf pile stung Vivian's eyes just a little, as it hung in the air over the Daltons' back-yard on that cold evening just before Halloween. *The upside*, she thought to herself as the outhouse door banged shut behind her, *is that it does cover up the smell.* She glanced at the few trees that bordered the yard as she wrapped Edward's overcoat back around her and shuffled quickly back to the house. They were still hang-ing on to their leaves, but, *Yep*, she thought, *winter's on its way.* Winter with that outhouse was something Edward had heard earfuls about last year, that was certain. Vivian knew she was just a crisis or two away from getting him to move them back to Wooster.

Little Charlotte was sleeping in her crib in the bedroom while Edward and Vivian listened to *The Chase and Sanborn Hour* on the radio. They always listened to the program to hear Edgar Bergen and his dummy, Charlie McCarthy, crack jokes. At ex-actly 8:12 p.m. there was a musical break in the program, and like he always did, Edward switched the radio dial from NBC to CBS to see what else was on.

"I don't know why you can't just enjoy the music until they come back on," Vivian groused, knitting needles clicking as she made some red booties for Charlotte. She didn't say it every time, but often enough that it got on Edward's nerves.

He ignored her and turned up the volume:

Ladies and gentlemen, I have just been handed a message that came in from Grover's Mill by telephone. Just one moment, please. At least forty people, including six state troopers, lie dead in a field east of the village of Grover's Mill, their bodies burned and distorted beyond all possible recognition.

"Jesus Christ," Vivian said, pausing her clicking. "Six state troopers? Where is Grover's Mill?"

Edward shushed her, waving his hand in a downward motion.

The announcement continued and Vivian and Edward stayed glued to the broadcast as several radio announcers described the horrifying attack unfolding at Grover's Mill, which Edward finally whispered was "in New Jersey."

Ladies and gentlemen, I have a grave announcement to make. Incredible as it may seem, both the observations of science and the evidence of our eyes lead to the inescapable assumption that those strange beings who landed in the Jersey farmlands tonight are the vanguard of an invading army from the planet Mars. The battle which took place tonight at Grover's Mill has ended in one of the most startling defeats ever suffered by any army in modern times; seven thousand men armed with rifles and machine guns pitted against a single fighting machine of the invaders from Mars. One hundred and twenty known survivors. The rest strewn over the battle area from Grover's Mill to Plainsboro, crushed and trampled to death under the metal feet of the monster, or burned to cinders by its heat ray. The monster is now in control of the middle section of New Jersey and has effectively cut the state through its center. Communication lines are down from Pennsylvania to the Atlantic Ocean.

Edward and Vivian looked at each other. Edward hadn't wanted to install a telephone in the house because of the expense, and the fact that he didn't see the need.

"Well," Vivian began slowly, trying to keep the panic from rising in her throat as she laid the knitting needles, yarn, and booties aside, "we can't check the telephone to see if that is true because we don't *have* a telephone. We won't know if the lines are down."

The threat suddenly seemed very real. They were just a couple of hours from New Jersey. Edward pushed up from his chair and swiftly made his way around the small house, locking the windows, yanking down the window shades, and then double-checking the locks on the front and back doors. Vivian had gone to the bedroom and gathered Charlotte up in her blanket, peeking at the tiny face to make sure nothing was wrong with her.

"Get to the cellar," Edward ordered, before switching off the light in the living room, and following her down the steps. He went to the wall shelf of the chilly cellar where he kept some of his tools and the small portable radio. He switched the volume on and tuned the dial until the alert came in.

They spent the next twenty minutes silent and shivering in the dank cellar of the little house, listening to the developments of the Martian attack. Vivian sat rigidly on Edward's wooden workbench, rocking Charlotte against her and anxiously bouncing a crossed leg while shooting hostile glares at Edward about the telephone.

As the broadcast blared on, the frantic tone of the announcer lessened and then there was a swell of music. Orson Welles introduced himself over the radio waves, his deep voice filling the damp cellar. The high-strung description of the attack had ended and now Orson Welles was talking about Halloween. Edward and Vivian stared at the little portable radio, confused, until they heard:

You are listening to a CBS presentation of Orson Welles and the Mercury Theatre on the Air in an original dramatization of *The War of the Worlds* by H. G. Wells. The performance will continue after a brief intermission. This is the Columbia Broadcasting System.

"Oh!" Vivian and Edward exclaimed at the same time as they looked from the radio to each other, startled. Edward was the first to laugh. He was the only one to laugh. Vivian said, "Oh!" a few more times, and then, "Well . . ." Then Charlotte began to cry, and Vivian snapped. She marched straight over to the radio and switched it off in a violent motion.

"Well, of all the . . ." Vivian clutched the crying Charlotte to her as she stomped up the steps into the kitchen, with Edward trailing behind.

She marched to the middle of the living room and stood there not knowing what to do next, and bouncing Charlotte in an attempt to stop her crying. She could not believe they'd just spent all that time in the cellar fearing a Martian attack, when it was just a stupid story. It had sounded so real.

"Here." Edward reached out his arms for the baby.

"I hate to be made a fool of!" Vivian spat while stubbornly clinging to the wailing bundle.

"Honey, come on, give her here."

She huffed, pushed the baby into his arms, and stomped to the back door, unlocking it and flinging the door open for some fresh air. The smell of burning leaves still hung there as she looked up into the moonless sky, tapping her toe in irritation, almost daring a Martian spaceship to appear. She heard the snapping of twigs and froze in place, her eyes following the sound to the shrubbery that bordered the far corner of the yard.

"Edward." It came out in a whisper. Her voice felt pushed down inside her chest, like something was pressing on it to keep it from escaping. Her fingers squeezed the doorknob and she took a deep breath.

"EDWARD!"

The shriek brought Edward running from the living room, clutching the still-crying Charlotte to his chest.

"There's something out there in the bushes!" she hiss-whispered to him as he pulled her back into the house with his free arm. He handed Charlotte back to her, and then stepped over the threshold onto the back porch, and then a few more steps out into the yard, squinting at the area she had pointed to. He stood stock-still for a full minute, staring at the shrubbery. The bushes remained still, and the only sound to be heard was the chirping of a few late-season crickets.

"Viv." He turned to face her. "It might be the Martians, so we'll just keep the door closed and locked."

Edward had rebounded from the earlier scare a lot quicker than Vivian had and she didn't appreciate it one bit. She scowled at him as he walked back into the house, closed the door behind him, and shifted the lock into place.

"I know I saw something."

He pulled her close to him and planted a kiss on her cheek.

"Who's afraid of the Big Bad Wolf," he sang.

"Yeah, you weren't so brave when you thought the Martians were coming," she muttered under her breath as she walked back to their bedroom to put Charlotte in her crib, where she instantly stopped crying. Vivian was secretly glad they'd both been fooled by the broadcast, because that was just the kind of thing he liked to tease her about. But, there you had it. Her husband was just as gullible as she was. As she sat on that thought, she considered it might not be such a good thing.

One hour later Vivian lay in bed, drifting off to sleep but then clutching the covers and jerking awake at every creak, groan, and pop she heard. Edward was sound asleep next to her, snoring away as usual. Gullible or not, he sure didn't have a problem with worry keeping him awake. She snuggled her back up against his and thought about the Martians. After a few minutes she was snickering into her pillow.

When his alarm clock rang at four a.m., Vivian was already sitting in the rocking chair, holding the bottle steady in Charlotte's little mouth. Edward rolled over to Vivian's side of the bed and switched on the lamp, then rolled back, swung his legs out, and rose to his feet. He pulled on his socks and jodhpurs, then buttoned up his shirt and fastened his tie before shuffling into the living room in his slippers to turn on the radio. He'd gone four steps toward the kitchen to make his coffee when the emergency alert crackled from the radio's speaker.

This time it wasn't Orson Welles, and there was no mention of Martians. The Institution for Male Defective Delinquents had had a prison break. Three prisoners had unknowingly chosen the night of the Martian invasion to make their escape.

Inmates are at large. Local law enforcement urges residents to lock their homes and remain indoors until further notice.

Vivian heard every word of the alert, and now hissed in the direction of the kitchen over Charlotte's now-sleeping head.

"Eddie! I told you something was out there!"

Edward frowned and went to the back door of the house, pulling the ruched gingham curtain aside to look out onto the yard. The sky was still dark and all he could see was that everything was still and covered in a light frost. He walked around the corner and into their bedroom.

Vivian jerked her head in the direction of the window overlooking the backyard. Edward looked out at the yard again. Just frost-covered lawn and the little yellow outhouse.

"You're gonna have to use the pot again today."

Vivian scowled and rocked in the chair. Civilized people shouldn't be doing their business in a salad bowl. They'd both had to use the chamber pot last night before bedtime. Vivian, because she had no intention of leaving the security of the house, and Edward, because he claimed he didn't want to leave her and the baby unattended. Vivian suspected that, in spite of his jolly singing and casual attitude, he'd been just as uneasy as she was. At least until he fell asleep.

"We," she said in a low voice. "*We* are gonna have to use the chamber pot. *You* are not going to work today."

"Honey, I have to go in."

"And leave me and the baby here, when those criminals are loose?" Her low voice rose into a squeak.

"The windows are locked, the back door's locked, and I'll lock the front door on my way out. You're safe as long as you stay inside."

"What if they break a window?"

Edward sighed and wiped his palm across his forehead.

"Fine," he said. "I'll stay with you."

Vivian turned her head into her shoulder and tried to stifle a few sobs.

"Honey, I said I'll stay."

Tears spilled over Vivian's cheeks and she sniffed a few times.

"I'm so tired, Edward. I'm just so goddamned tired."

"I know, honey." He took Charlotte from her and laid her in her crib.

"Edward," she continued in a whisper, measuring her words evenly. "Our next house is going to have a bathroom."

"I promise," he said, and made a crisscross over his heart with his index finger.

"A bathroom *inside* the house."

"Of course, inside."

"And a telephone," she finished.

"And a telephone. You bet. Nothing is too good for my girls." He leaned over and kissed Charlotte's forehead. "You know, you'd feel safer if we could get that dog I was talking about." He stepped back toward the rocking chair, took Vivian's face in his hands, and planted a smack on her pursed lips.

"Edward, we're not talking about the dog again. You know I'm allergic."

"Whatever you say, dear," he said, his tone signaling doubt. "Why don't you get some rest?" He helped her out of the rocking chair and over to her side of the bed, pulling aside the rumpled covers.

He waited until she'd fallen asleep and then pulled on his leather boots. *Which three?* Edward's pulse began to race as he looked out the front window, up and down the street, before stepping outside. *Which three prisoners?* He made sure to lock the door and then clicked the flashlight on and walked to the Ford, his boots crunching over the frost-covered grass. He swung the flashlight up and down and around the automobile as he circled, looking inside, outside, and then underneath. The neighborhood was still dark. Most of the neighbors had listened to *The Chase and Sanborn Hour* all the way through, musical interlude and all. They hadn't bothered switching to check the other radio station, and so they missed the terrifying Martian invasion. They also spared themselves the near-heart-attacks and the tongue-lashings from their wives. They should put that damned Orson Welles in jail.

Edward climbed into the cold leather bench seat of the car and sucked air through his back teeth at the shock to his backside and thighs. *Which three prisoners had made the escape?* The radio announcement hadn't given names. There was just one he needed to be worried about. One inmate who'd cause problems for Edward in the world outside the prison walls. Vivian was going to be sore at him when she woke up and found he'd gone to work after all, but she'd get over it. Inmate eleven-three-oh-five was the one he was worried about.

His mouth was set in a grim line as he worried about that one inmate, and prepared for the chaos that would greet him when he walked through the gates. He was already a half hour late due to Vivian's paranoia. But, as the car rumbled down the road, Edward's mind went back to the conversation he'd had with his wife before he put her to bed. He chuckled to himself as he recalled her demands. *A telephone.* Only a woman would want a telephone in the house. *All the better to gossip with, my dear!*

Chapter 11

Betty Miller wasn't the biggest gossip in Wooster; Vivian would've given that trophy to Bell's own Ruth Craven. She considered Ruth a friend, just not a friend you tell your secrets to, if you wanted to keep them secret. Betty Miller was not only *not* a friend, but she had an uncomfortable grip of influence in town. And now, after that telephone call, she had a secret that threatened to destroy Vivian, and Vivian had already felt the destruction begin. She was all alone with the black dread that hung over her thoughts like a death shroud as she walked to work that morning, a faint pink rimming the horizon. It had snowed a little the night before, so her worn ankle boots were making fresh tracks up the sidewalks.

How stupid did you have to be to agree to work an evening shift one day, and then a morning shift the next? Pretty goddamned stupid. The recent turn of events had the black dread extending to Vivian's self-talk. She was being much harder on herself than was usual. The self-talk sounded like her mother. But, really, she had some seniority now, and needed to remember that when Leona was making the schedule. Leona was getting on in years and needed some reminding. Never mind. She'd still have time to make the spaghetti tonight. For Edward. *For Edward.* She stomped her boots with the words, and on the second "Edward" hit a patch of hidden ice with her right boot that threw her into a clumsy slide with pocketbook flailing around her head as she struggled to stay upright. Her insides shivered with the threat of the fall, and once she'd found her footing again she huffed and straightened her coat and her Beulah Bechtel hat. Now she felt angry *and* foolish. At any other time she would've laughed at herself. Laughed and said, "Whooopsies!" and been thankful she hadn't landed on her backside. But today hot tears began to threaten. She shouldn't have bought the hat. She was being punished for her pride in buying the hat.

There was no one she could talk to. Not about this. She'd have liked to confide in one of her coworkers, but her friendships with the women at Bell were kind of, what was the word . . . superficial. Oh, sure, she'd told Pearl about having all of her teeth yanked by the dentist just so she could have a full set of dentures that were straight and even and looked nice, like Joan Crawford's, even though she felt a little silly about it. And, yes, she'd told Dorothy about her botched hysterectomy (after Charlotte there'd be no more Dalton babies), but that doctor with a butcher's license took everything out and then just tossed it back in willy-nilly. It'd been a disaster. She'd been left without a proper belly button, but what did she need a belly button for anyway? Dorothy'd been kind about that. "Who's going to know, Vivy? Don't give it another thought."

And Ruth. Good old Ruth. Always one for gossip, you couldn't tell her any secrets, but Ruth was great if you wanted a casual snipe and gripe about married life. Ruth's husband made Edward seem like a regular Rhett Butler. But only Clark Gable's Rhett Butler from the movie, not the one from the book. Charlotte had told her the movie was also a book. Sometimes Charlotte showed off like that, and it got on Vivian's last nerve.

Those social confessionals with Pearl, Dorothy, and Ruth were never more than surface skimming, through all the years she'd known them working at Bell. Nothing too deep and nothing too dramatic. Vivian couldn't have any of her friends or acquaintances thinking her life was anything other than just fine, because the people with problems were the ones who got talked about. *Don't wiggle around like a whore, don't embarrass yourself.* This was one storm she was going to have to weather on her own. And it was a downpour. A grab your slicker and galoshes, cats and dogs, gushing rainspouts and flooded cellars downpour.

It's raining, it's pouring, your husband is snoring . . .

But, had the storm already hit Ohio Bell on East Liberty Street? Had Betty Miller leaked the gossip from her no-good, mealy mouth? It'd only been about twelve hours. Nothing moved that quickly in Wooster.

Although it would've been plain impossible for the rumor to have made its way out of Mrs. Betty Miller's mouth yet (it was probably still just percolating in her brain), Vivian still felt like people might've heard. Her fear had eaten her common sense like it was a casserole. Her heart pounded in her throat and her skin prickled as she crossed the threshold of the switchboard room. It was a different kind of nervousness than she'd felt when she'd first returned to work at Bell, after Edward had finally quit that horrible job at the prison and they'd moved back to Wooster with little Charlotte. She'd only been away a couple of years, and Leona was still there, and most of the operators she'd started with were still there, Pearl, Dorothy, Ruth, and they were glad to see her. But she'd still felt a little like the new girl, and that made her a little anxious about her first day. That anxiety was nothing compared to the paralysis she was feeling now.

"And so I says to him, 'Sure ya do,' and then he says to me, 'You'd better believe it,' and so I says to him—Hiya, Viv!" Ruth interrupted her story to greet Vivian and offer her usual friendly wave.

Vivian paused and tensed, wondering if Ruth had interrupted her story because she'd been talking about her. Was there something exaggerated in Ruth's greeting? Did her fingers flutter just a bit too much in that wave?

"You'd better get a move-on, cutie-pie," Laura Eagan teased, with a quick swat at Vivian's backside as she passed her.

Vivian jumped, and then forced a twitchy smile, moving toward the cloakroom. Laura was about ten years younger than Vivian. She was still unmarried, and probably thought being cutesy and baby-talking was the way to get herself hitched. Vivian had made that mistake once. She'd tested out the baby talk with Edward on their second date. He'd cocked an eyebrow at her like she was sitting there on the park bench in diapers, sucking on a teething ring. From that point on, he sang nursery rhymes to her to remind her how ridiculous the baby talk was, and to make her laugh at herself. But Laura Eagan hadn't had the benefit of a second date with Edward Dalton. Lucky her.

Laura was newer to Bell, and Vivian wouldn't say she knew her all that well. She wondered if that'd been a sneaky, knowing look in Laura's eye, or if it was just the usual flash of bitterness that sometimes escaped when she was trying to be flirty and cute. *I'll give her a cutie-pie.*

"You just gave up your break," Dorothy said in a low tone, with her hand covering her mouthpiece. She nodded at her watch as Vivian pulled out the rolling chair beside her.

Vivian couldn't tell if Dorothy seemed angrier than usual about how late she was because she was wearing the brown eyebrow pencil today. Vivian was on time, most of the time, but when she wasn't, Dorothy was the first to let her know. But was her reaction more than just annoyance about the time? Or did she know something, and had she already passed judgment on Vivian? Her face felt flushed and her heartbeat was stuttering a rapid SOS.

She lowered herself into the chair and self-consciously pulled herself up to the counter. Her hands shook as she pulled the headset over her hair. The lights flickered in front of her, and the resentment rose in her like bile, overtaking the anxiety. Staring at those blinking betrayals, remembering each and every word of

the overheard conversation the night before, she felt the resentment boiling back into the fury.

"Vivian!" Dorothy hissed, and motioned to the blinking light
on the board.

Vivian picked up the rear jack and jammed it into the board
so hard that the whole thing shuddered. She ignored the stunned
faces of the other girls and answered the call as if it were just another day. Her diction was just a little sharper, and her tone just
a little more forceful than usual.

"Number, *please*."

She'd made it through an excruciating day at the switchboard.

Excruciating:
1: causing great pain or anguish: agonizing <the
nation's most excruciating dilemma—W. H. Ferry>
2: very intense : extreme <excruciating pain>

And now she stood at the kitchen counter in her white ruffle-
edged apron, holding the knife firmly in her right hand and,
with her left over the dull side of the blade, crunched evenly
through the carrot on the cutting board. With each crunch
Vivian remembered the surprised "Oh!"s and "No!"s of Betty
Miller's voice last night over the phone line, as she listened to
the story that would ruin her life. Edward had already left for
work by the time she got out of bed that morning, but now he
was sitting at the kitchen table reading the paper, calm as you
please, as the spaghetti sauce bubbled on the stove.

"Anything interesting?" Vivian said over her shoulder, the
bite in tone emphasized in the consonants.

"Hmm?" Edward didn't look up.

"I said, 'Anything interesting?' there in the paper tonight?"
Vivian enunciated each syllable through her teeth. "Any *interesting* stories?"

"Unh," was Edward's reply.

He finally looked up to see her standing there facing him and staring, supporting her right elbow with her left hand, the large knife waving back and forth like one of those Fourth of July flags they gave you at the parade.

"You going to cut me if I don't tell you something interesting?" He grinned as he looked at her, then looked back to the paper and took a sip of his beer. "Well, okay, then, they separated those Siamese twins in Chicago."

"Siamese twins," Vivian said flatly, then turned and took another carrot from the counter.

"Mmm-hm."

Crunch, crunch, crunch, crunch.

"Joined at the head, but didn't look anything alike, according to this. Imagine that."

Charlotte breezed into the kitchen, took one look at her mother's rigid posture, the knife crunching through the carrot, measured the tension in the air, and promptly breezed right out again, her scarf-tied ponytail disappearing in a wisp around the corner.

Later, there was silence at the dinner table as Edward, Vivian, and Charlotte swirled strands of sauce-soaked spaghetti in their spoons and deposited the neat coils into their mouths.

"This is really good, Mother." Charlotte, as usual, tried to ease the tension with a compliment about her mother's cooking, which was mediocre at best.

"Thank you, Charlotte." Her voice was terse. "It's the recipe Mrs. Tomasetti gave me."

"So, it's genuine Italian?" Charlotte had taken the first few bites and decided, with some surprise, that she would most definitely be having seconds.

"Mm-hmm."

"Tomasettis," Edward mused. "They live in Frogtown? With the rest of the Guineas?"

Vivian pursed her lips into a tight line. Maria Tomasetti worked with Vivian at Bell, and lived in the southeast part of Wooster, along with the rest of the Italian population. Vivian and Edward both called the area Frogtown, and couldn't have told you why. Just like they used the term "four-flushers" when complaining about the rich people in north Wooster. They said it, but couldn't have told you where it came from. Did "four-flusher" mean they were so wealthy they all had four toilets in their homes? Did it mean they were so wealthy and wasteful they flushed their toilets four times each time they used the bathroom? The Daltons really didn't know. What they knew was that the four-flushers were rich, awful, and probably up to no good with all that money they had.

The romantic fireworks that had brought Vivian and Edward together and sealed their union in the beginning had fallen and settled into a dampened pile of unsexy, but comfortable domestic ash, like it did with most married couples. Their partnership had grown into something mainly bonded by time, their daughter Charlotte, and their mutual dislike of anyone too different from them. On a normal night, Vivian wouldn't have even blinked at Edward's reference to Frogtown or the word "Guinea." Tonight, she resented the way it came out of his mouth. Instead of responding to his question, Vivian stabbed her fork violently around her plate until it finally pierced a limp piece of iceberg lettuce.

The next morning, the Second Morning, Vivian opened her eyes and remembered everything all over again and the flush of anger rose to the surface of her skin. The spot next to her in the bed was empty. Edward always got up early on Saturdays and went straight to his workshop, and was probably hammering or sawing something at that moment. Vivian considered how satisfying it would be right then, to be hammering or sawing, using heavy or sharp tools to pound or slice, and her fury gained momentum as she climbed from the bed and into her slippers and robe.

What she was also reminded of, as she moved about in a kind of heated daze, was that she didn't have anyone to share that fury with. It was fuzzy, her thoughts about her coworkers and the friends she didn't really have outside of work. Who had time for friends when you had a job and a family? Her hands shook as she took the dress down from the hanger. Who could she burden with this? Because she sure as hell didn't want to suffer this alone. Her sister Vera? Ha! That was a good one. Vera'd probably take an ad out in the paper to tell everyone else the news; host a goddamned party to celebrate Vivian's misfortune. Vivian's thoughts were pointed, sharp, but her legs had begun to wobble and her head to swim. She needed to stay angry to keep going.

If Vivian ever confided in any of her siblings, it was Henry, but Henry had gone and married Norma Barfield, whom Vivian couldn't stand, and had moved to Fredericksburg. They didn't really talk too much anymore, and she missed him. There was also Violet. Sweet, steady, warmhearted Violet. The only problem was, Violet was currently siding with Vera on everything. It hadn't mattered when they were kids. Violet was always too young. But now she was grown-up and had her own family, and she and Vera were thick as thieves. Although, let six months pass and Violet would probably be mad at Vera for something, and then she'd go running to Vivian and the two of them would put their heads together to complain about Vera. But that wasn't right now. Right now Vera and Violet were teamed up, and Vivian had no one to turn to. The discontentment, panic, and fear were like physical lumps she could almost see growing inside her head, her stomach, and her throat. No one to turn to. Nowhere to turn.

After Charlotte cleaned up the breakfast dishes, she scurried back upstairs to her room and Vivian was left alone at the kitchen table. Five minutes later Charlotte bounded back down the stairs, grabbed her coat and ice skates from the hall closet, and was out the door into the cold morning, headed to Christmas Run Park. Vivian watched her disappear, wishing she could follow. So young, so casual, so careless. Youth is wasted on the young. She'd never really understood that saying. Not now, and not when she'd heard it the first time, when she was in her youth.

She pushed her chair back, stood, and stalked into the living room, where she picked up one of the sofa cushions, held it to her face, and screamed. With her eyes scrunched shut and her mouth wide open, she screamed into that cotton-batting-stuffed beige cushion for a full ten seconds, and when she finally pulled the cushion away from her face she felt light-headed and had to sit down. She dropped onto the sofa, holding the cushion to her chest, the way she used to hold her dollies when she was little, and breathed slowly until the dizziness passed.

She stood up, replaced the cushion with a sound smack, returned to the kitchen, and tied on her apron. She banged around the cabinets and drawers, and took out the oversized mixing bowls, measuring cups, and the flour, baking soda, brown sugar, molasses, and all the other ingredients, and did what she always did at this time of year. She made her fruitcakes. And if there was any rat poison left in the box, maybe she'd make a special cake for Edward.

Christmas Fruitcake (double batch)

6 cups all-purpose flour
2 teaspoon baking powder
1 teaspoon salt
2 cups butter
2 ½ cups white sugar
8 eggs
3 cups raisins
2 cups red and green candied cherries
1 ½ cups dates, pitted and chopped
1 ½ cups candied pineapple, diced

1 ½ cups chopped walnuts
1 cup flaked coconut
4 teaspoons lemon juice

1.   Preheat oven to 300 degrees. Grease pan.
2. In a large bowl (but not the green one because the salad dressing smell wont come out) whisk together flour, baking powder, and salt. Mix in raisins, dates, cherries, pineapple, walnuts, and coconut. Stir until all fruit is coated.
3. In another large bowl, mix the butter and sugar. Add lemon juice, and eggs; mix well. Stir in fruit mixture. Spread batter into prepared pans.
4. Bake for 2 hours or until toothpick comes out clean. Cool completely on a wire rack.

Chapter 12

Vivian hadn't smashed the alarm clock into her husband's Adam's apple that first night, she hadn't stabbed him with the kitchen knife the night after that, and she hadn't poisoned him with a tainted fruitcake. Because, what if it wasn't true? *But it was.* What if that conversation she'd overheard had just been hateful, idle gossip; the kind Betty Miller was always involved in? *This wasn't idle.*

Vivian allowed her hostile fury to settle and fester just below the surface, while plastering on a tight, bright smile on the outside, lined in Revlon's Fire & Ice red lipstick.

"Fine, thank you!" was the automatic response to anyone asking how she was doing, or how her day was, or even just commenting on the weather.

"Sunny day today, isn't it?"

"Fine, thank you!"

That next week, she made breakfast like she always did, she dressed and went to work like she always did, and she listened to the phone calls like she always did. But she wasn't listening for everyday Wooster gossip anymore. The people could take their precious quilts, forgotten wallets, and trips to the A&W and just stuff them. Vivian was waiting for, and dreading, any calls that would expose her. How did she know it would happen through a telephone call? Who was to say people weren't getting together in person right now and talking about her? The truth was, she didn't really know. But it was December, it was cold, and it was right before Christmas and people were busy with their families. If only she didn't have to leave the house.

Every outing to a public place was now a test of nerves for Vivian. Who had Betty Miller told? Who knew? Who was talking about her behind her back? Every greeting was approached with cautious suspicion, every look was met with defensive, phony cheer.

"Fine! Thank you!"

A trip to Buehler's used to be a social opportunity wrapped in a grocery errand. She used to proudly parade down the aisles of the store, mentally ticking off everything she knew about everyone she saw. *There's Ann Metcalf; her father is in a nursing home and she doesn't want to visit because she can't stand the smell. There's Stewart Bowen's wife, whatshername. She'll have to go easy on the groceries because Stewart just lost his job.*

But now the trip to Buehler's was a tiptoe onto a minefield, because everyone at the grocery store might know about Vivian. She was terrified, and therefore overcompensating. She spent fifteen minutes more on her hair and twenty more on her makeup before walking out the front door of the Dalton house, as if extra layers of Spray Net and Max Factor Pan-Cake foundation could protect her from the judgment and scorn of Wooster. *Hair like Bette Davis, teeth like Joan Crawford.* She was doing the best she could. The dresses, sweaters, and shoes she usually reserved for special occasions, like weddings and holiday gatherings, were now in regular rotation for work, Christmas shopping at Freedlander's and Dari-Land, and grocery shopping at Buehler's.

"To market, to market, to buy a fat pig," a stony-faced Vivian chanted to herself, with her jaw set and her breath puffing out before her in the car as she drove. *"Home again, home again, jiggity-jig."* That was all it would be. A quick trip, there and back. For the market today, she'd chosen the cornflower-blue Dacron

poly-and-wool-blend dress, McCall's pattern #9150, which she'd sewn herself, with the faux-pearl earrings and rhinestone rooster brooch. Cock-a-doodle-doo! The blue of the dress matched the color of her eyes, just like Wallis Simpson's dress would have, back in the days of carefree romance and stupidity. If she didn't happen to run into her dinner guests at Buehler's, she'd wear the same dress that evening, with her black patent-leather pumps, instead of the worn-out ankle boots she had to wear to get through all the goddamned snow.

She sat holding the white steering wheel of the Buick Super with her gloved hands, gripping and releasing, gripping, releasing. She stared at the Schaeffers' car, parked across from her in the spot she had just pulled into, and groaned, wondering if she should duck down in the seat until she heard Madeline Schaeffer ease her bony backside into the car and then drive away. Vivian glanced around the parking lot to see if there were any other cars she recognized, but then realized she couldn't just sit there and wait them all out. If she weren't committed to hosting the intimate dinner party that evening, the trip to Buehler's could've been postponed. They had plenty of leftover ham noodle casserole, lentil soup, and cold cuts for sandwiches. But tonight was important, and she needed to pick up a few things for the special dishes she had planned.

As she began to walk down the parking row she saw Madeline Schaeffer exiting the store with one of the bag boys in tow. Roger or Michael, she couldn't see his face behind Madeline's giant fur hat. Christ, that woman was such a show-off. Vivian sidestepped between a green Ford and a white Chevy and bent into an awkward crouch, pretending to have dropped her keys. She stared at the dirty, packed snow around her boots, waiting until she heard the Schaeffers' trunk open and then slam shut. She watched her breath poof into tiny clouds and then disappear until she heard Madeline say, "Thank you, Roger," before probably giving him what Vivian guessed would be an embarrassingly small tip. And at Christmastime, too. Stingy when feeding herself, and stingy when tipping. *Eat something and give that boy a proper tip, for chrissakes.*

Vivian remained in her crouched position until she heard the engine start, and then waited fifteen more seconds until she was certain Madeline had pulled out of the parking spot and out of the lot altogether. She hooked her glove into the silver door handle of the Ford and pulled herself to a standing position, before brushing off her coat and narrowing her eyes at the store's entrance. She reached into her pocketbook as she walked past the other cars, and pulled out a handful of coins. She paused briefly next to the cheerful Salvation Army bell-ringer and dropped the coins loudly into the red bucket before stepping into the bustle of Buehler's.

With a death grip on the shopping cart, she kept her head high and pushed down each aisle with determined purpose, doing her best to keep her eyes on the shelf contents and not on the passing or approaching figures. She didn't know everyone in Wooster, but she knew enough that someone familiar was bound to pop up on this visit. She especially didn't want to run into her sister Violet or her mother today, because even if they didn't know what was wrong, they'd know something was wrong.

The cart's left rear wheel wobbled and rattled, setting her false-but-perfect teeth on edge. She paused in front of the Quaker Oats and thought she might want to exchange the cart for a different one before she rammed it into an unsuspecting shopper out of frustrated irritation. She glanced up to see Betty Miller's colored maid standing at the seafood counter at the end of the aisle. *I knew it. Expensive fish. Expensive, fancy fish for Betty's expensive, fancy Christmas party tonight.* Vivian started to swing the cart around to head back in the other direction.

"Vivian! Hellooo, Vivian!"

Vivian fastened her Revlon Fire & Ice smile in place, and

opened her eyes wide so as not to look like she was scowling, then turned to see Helen Harper waving at her.

Does she know?

"Why, Helen, hello yourself! You're looking well."

She really did like Helen. Charlotte's friend Barbara's mother. A dear, really, and on any other day she'd have enjoyed stopping to chat, but Vivian's current state of mind had made everyone a potential enemy.

"Who, me? Oh, *pshh*, you're sweet. I'm exhausted from the holidays already, and Christmas isn't until next week!"

Helen's rushed, cheery tone was the same as it always was, and Vivian saw nothing in her eyes other than overcaffeination and general holiday chaos. She relaxed her shoulders and stifled a sigh of relief.

"Now, Vivian." Helen's voice dropped to a lower octave. "I heard something . . ." She placed her hand on Vivian's arm and peeked over the top of the rhinestone-accented horn-rims she always wore.

Vivian's shoulders went rigid again and she struggled to keep her smile bright and eyes wide.

"Is it true that the cheerleading tryouts are held in front of the whole school? The girls are expected to perform in front of nine hundred people?"

Vivian sucked air in through her teeth, which Helen probably thought was a reaction to the number of students watching the tryouts rather than the conversational crisis she felt she had just avoided.

"Oh, garsh, I don't know," Vivian answered, not having considered it.

"That just sounds like an awful lot of people. I don't know how those girls do it. So brave!"

Barbara and Charlotte were both planning to try out for cheerleading in the spring, or something. If Charlotte made the team she'd need new saddle shoes. That was what Vivian had been thinking of when she thought about the tryouts. Having to ask Edward for money for new saddle shoes, although she hadn't thought of it since she overheard the Betty Miller phone call. Who gave a rat's ass about the size of the crowd watching them? Wasn't that all part of being a cheerleader? Shaking your taters in front of large crowds? How was she going to afford new saddle shoes on her salary if she had to leave Edward? Her inner voice had gone shrill.

"Oh, well," Helen sang. "That's quite a ways away. We don't need to worry about it now. If I don't see you again before Christmas, have a merry one!"

"FINE, THANK YOU!"

Helen was already thinking about spring, and Vivian's inner shriek had just considered leaving Edward. How do you like that? A chill shivered through her body. She gave a shake of her head, then looked down at the grocery list she was still pressing between her thumb and forefinger. Well, good for Helen for not having a horrible scandalous secret she was desperately trying to keep under wraps. The anxiety returned in a flash and Vivian pushed the cart quickly down the aisle.

She found the remaining items on her grocery list in record time, sailed through checkout with only a brief mention of the weather to Marjorie at the register (yes, Marjorie, it's still cold), and then stalked quickly through the snowy parking lot to her car, her boots keeping time with the rhyme in her head (*jiggity-jig, jiggity-jig*) as Roger struggled to keep up behind her with the grocery bags. *Home again, home again, jiggity-jig.*

The feather duster fluttered hastily over the tops of the curtains as Vivian stood on the sofa in her stockinged feet, stretching up to reach along the crease where the wall met the ceiling and into the corner above Edward's chair. The cobwebs hadn't quite had the chance to settle, although it'd been nearly a month since she had last dusted.

Vivian did clean the house every Saturday afternoon, but dusting seemed obsessive. Like something Betty Miller had her maid do every other day. She used a broom on the linoleum in the kitchen, and then spent about twenty minutes pushing the carpet sweeper around in the upstairs bedrooms and then the living and dining rooms. Other than that, it would take an explosive liquid disaster before she'd do any detailed scrubbing, like the time she'd been carrying the boiling pot of jam from the stove to the sink and one of the hot pads slipped and made a sticky strawberry spread of the kitchen floor, or the time when Charlotte had the flu and she hadn't made it to the bathroom in time. Christ, had that been a mess.

But tonight was important. She poked the broom's edge along the baseboards in the kitchen, and stabbed at a dust cluster in the corner, saying to herself, *Get into the corners, find every little bit.* She repeated this to herself as she pushed the carpet sweeper under side tables and pulled the chairs and sofas away from the wall. *Every little bit.* That was when it hit her. Do the same thing with the rumor. *Get into it, get under it, poke around in the corners. Find every little bit.*

She'd have to wait until tomorrow, but the idea gave her a new burst of energy for cleaning, and an agitated excitement for the dinner party. She smirked as she fluffed the pillows on the sofa and the wing chairs, and sneered as she polished the silver, an inherited wedding gift from Edward's mother, holding it up to the light and then checking her reflection in the shining surface.

"Charlotte, have you finished yet?" she called out to the kitchen, where Charlotte was ironing the tablecloth and napkins.

"Almost," came the reply. "Who is coming for dinner, Mother, and why are you making it such a secret?"

"Oh, don't you bother about it," Vivian said. "Just some very nice friends. Now, make sure you wear the coral dress, and pull your hair back from your face. I want everyone to look their best."

Edward wasn't yet home from work, but Vivian had carefully

laid out the outfit she expected him to wear across the foot of the bed. He was used to this, when they celebrated special occasions, or on Sundays, when they went to church. Vivian knew she wouldn't be feeling too much like going to church this Sunday, and maybe Edward could pick out his own stupid clothes. With their work schedules the way they were, she'd only been face-to-face with him twice since Monday night. Since the Betty Miller telephone conversation. She wondered if it even occurred to him that something was wrong; he barely looked up from his newspaper or his plate long enough to notice that there was someone else there with him.

Well, he'd notice it tonight. He'd sure be surprised, since he wasn't expecting any company, and most definitely not the company she had invited. And that was exactly how she wanted it.

Chapter 13

The doorbell rang and Vivian was right there to open the front door, with Edward's words from the other night ringing in her ears: *They don't bother me much. But I'd never have them in my house.* Out on the front porch, underneath the light, stood Maria and Dominic Tomasetti, looking shivery, polite, and a little nervous. *The Guineas from Frogtown.*

"Welcome!" Vivian cried, a little too loudly.

Maria handed a small white box to Vivian as Dominic removed his hat.

The familiarity Vivian felt with Maria at work did not extend beyond the confines of the Bell building. Without the switchboard and the cords and headsets and the hum of the connections, she suddenly felt self-conscious with Maria. Sitting next to her at the switchboard was one thing, or sharing a coffee in the kitchenette. But having the Tomasettis in the Dalton house was too far out of context. There was an awkward pause, and she wondered if she'd made a big mistake. It only took one look at Edward's unpleasantly shocked face to reassure her it was worth it.

"Thank you so much for this invitation, Vivian," Maria said, her movements halting with the same kind of uncertainty Vivian was showing, but Dominic guided her forward across the Daltons' threshold.

Edward had risen from his chair, but was unable to hide his

surprise. *That's right*, Vivian thought as she looked at him, *something a little unpleasant that you weren't expecting? Caught you off guard, did it? You sonofabitch.* Charlotte, in her coral dress with her hair pulled back away from her face, moved quickly to approach the Tomasettis with an outstretched hand.

"Hi, I'm Charlotte. It's very nice to meet you."

Every once in a while Vivian saw Charlotte wince when they said things like "Guinea" or "nigger." Vivian didn't know where Charlotte got her highfalutin attitude from, like she was above it all; probably from other kids at the high school, or from those books she always had her nose in.

"Mrs. Tomasetti, I just love your spaghetti sauce recipe! Mother made it this week."

Maria Tomasetti looked uncomfortable, and glanced down at her shoes. "Thank you."

Charlotte took Mr. and Mrs. Tomasetti's coats and hung them in the hall closet.

"Please," Vivian cooed, her voice decreased to an inside-appropriate level. "Sit!"

The Daltons and the Tomasettis carefully arranged themselves on the living room furniture, pulling their faces into polite smiles.

"That's a beautiful dress," Maria said to Vivian. "And I love your brooch. Is it a chicken?"

"Rooster," Vivian answered as she smoothed her palms over the skirt of the blue McCall's dress, feeling pleased by both the compliment and the fact that she'd been able to repeat her grocery store outfit for the dinner.

"Ah."

Vivian realized she should have switched on the radio just before they arrived. Background music would've made up for the lack of conversation. What would they possibly have to talk about with these complete strangers, and why hadn't she thought of that before? She stood up from the sofa, before the cushion had even had time to warm under her backside.

"Well, shall we eat?"

The Christmas color scheme was unintentional, but as everyone looked at the dinner table, it was impossible to miss. They started with a green spinach soup, with sour cream and boiled eggs. Maria tasted the soup, and then just stirred it around with her spoon until everyone else finished. The Jell-O with fruit was as green as the Wooster golf course in June, and chock-full of grapes, canned pineapple, and maraschino cherries. The Jell-O was Vivian's old reliable standard and she always brought it to events when asked to bring a salad. The beef Stroganoff had the slightest hint of red, as Vivian liked to add ketchup to things that didn't really need ketchup. She didn't find cooking quite as soothing as baking, and maybe put a little less effort into it. She gave herself a lot of credit for this evening's dinner, though, because she'd made it all from scratch. The green and red feast was capped off by the powdered-sugar-covered *pandoro* that Maria had brought in the small white box, and even though it sounded foreign, Vivian had to admit it was pretty good.

After dinner Vivian monopolized Maria's attention, praising her for her spaghetti sauce recipe and asking for cooking tips and the like. That was something to talk about. Food. Charlotte had excused herself to go upstairs to her room, which left Edward and Dominic sitting opposite each other in the wing chairs. Vivian ignored them, focusing all her attention on Maria. She had intended the evening to be tense and unpleasant, but Vivian found herself enjoying Maria's company. She'd been off the day Pearl Fry had sneezed into her mouthpiece while eavesdropping on Jean Cahill speaking to her mother long-distance, causing Jean's mother to exclaim, "Now, Jeannie, what did I tell you about catching your death, wearing those dresses cut so low in the front! What did I tell you!" The way Maria told the story, she just had all the mannerisms down pat. Vivian couldn't remember the last time she'd laughed so much. She couldn't remember the last time she'd laughed at all.

Vivian was confident Edward was not having as good a time entertaining Dominic Tomasetti. She'd been practically giddy when Dominic introduced himself. His accent was thick, and his English much less understandable than Maria's, and she knew Edward would be gritting his teeth throughout the evening about it. Maria had no accent, having come to the United States and learned English at the age of four, but if you'd told Vivian that, she wouldn't have believed you. The telephone company had a policy to only hire fluent English speakers, but Vivian still thought Maria had a pretty heavy Italian accent. Now that they'd spent a couple of hours talking, though, she hardly noticed it.

Maria told her how Dominic had come over to the United States just five years ago and worked at the Wooster Rubber Company, which had finally found its footing again after all the war rationing. His older brother Vincenzo (now Vincent) had settled in Wooster just before the stock market crash, and secured a job driving the delivery truck for City Dairy. Vincenzo Tomasetti had set his cap for Maria DiLucca, the prettiest, curviest girl on his milk route, and Maria admitted she'd gone on several dates with him.

"I gave him a little bit of encouragement," she admitted. "Just a little bit."

A little bit because she wanted to ride in the milk truck, and a little bit because she was flattered by all his attention. But then Dominic had shown up and, "That was it for me," she explained.

Vivian listened to the story. Boy, did she love a good love story. Her face was tilted toward Maria, one hand held her chin, and the other hand held a china cup with the last few drops of coffee. As Maria described how she and Dominic fell for each other, Vivian began to think about Edward. Without any awareness, she flashed an angry look in his direction. She slammed the coffee cup down on its saucer, and a tiny chip flew back toward the wall.

"Vivian." Maria's voice had risen a little, and Vivian snapped her attention back to her guest and forced a wide-eyed grin as

Maria said, "You've been at Bell so long, haven't you? How long has it been?"

"Oh"—Vivian let out a long breath and waved her free hand as she set the saucer and cup on the side table—"it feels like forever."

"I feel lucky to have been hired," Maria offered. "After the Building & Loan embezzlement"—she paused and looked at the floor—"we were in a bit of trouble."

"Oh, dear." Vivian's attention shifted completely away from Edward with this abrupt (and possibly intentional) change of subject. She felt a sudden and strange urge to put an arm around Maria Tomasetti's shoulder. Instead, she looked at her hands in her lap.

The whole town'd been singing J. Ellis Reed's praises when he'd told his bank customers he'd be reimbursing them. Everyone called him Wooster's very own George Bailey. His grandkids even made him a sash and a fancy pole to carry. (Charlotte had called it a "scepter" and said it was made of papier-mâché.) Vivian knew by now the bank hadn't reimbursed everyone who'd lost money, and she had little moments of guilt about it, especially about people she knew were worse off than her own family. That wasn't fair. But, as her mother was always saying, "Life isn't fair." She frowned for a brief second, then looked up and directly into Maria's eyes.

"Well"—her tone was matter-of-fact and she gave a nod of her head as she spoke—"whatever brought you to Bell, we're sure glad you're there."

Vivian was surprised to realize she really meant it.

Maria's expression went from pained to grateful and she reached forward, taking both of Vivian's hands in her own.

"Vivian," she said with some seriousness. "I should tell you something."

Vivian's breath caught in her chest and her fingers squeezed Maria's hands out of sheer anxiety. This was going to be it. Maria had heard about the rumor. She hadn't even thought of someone like Maria being the one to hear the gossip. She hadn't really thought of Maria as being part of Wooster. Her heart pounded in her chest and her smile froze in place, just as it had in the grocery store with Helen Harper.

"The sauce recipe I gave you." Maria's eyes darted over to her husband, who was staring at a spot on the wall behind Edward's head, as Edward silently sipped his coffee. "The recipe is not the recipe I use for my own family." Her expression was sheepish.

"Hmm?" Vivian wondered why Maria was talking about spaghetti sauce. These Italians sure did have a jumpy way about their conversations.

"I am so very sorry. We take our food very seriously, and so the recipe we give to other people is not the good recipe. Or, not as good as our own."

"Oh, well, garsh," Vivian said, still trying to figure out what Maria meant.

She hadn't heard the rumor, then. Vivian's palms had begun to sweat and she pulled her hands away and put them in her lap. She remembered asking Maria for a good spaghetti sauce recipe, during a lull at the switchboard one afternoon, thinking what good luck it was that she knew an authentic Italian.

"You have been so kind to us, and welcomed us into your home." Maria smiled, and crossed her own hands in her lap. She glanced up at the ceiling, as if unsure where to look at that moment. A small spider was ambling across the expanse of white, and seemed to be looking for something that wasn't there. Maria raised her eyebrows and tipped her head from side to side in a playful motion.

"You have earned the real Tomasetti recipe, if you would like it."

Vivian didn't know what to think. Her mouth had dropped open a bit as Maria stared at the ceiling, for some reason, and then gave a little shake of her head. Vivian had dropped the useless anxiety about the rumor and a weed of embarrassment had rooted itself in her belly. Maria's cute little head tilt sure wasn't going to change that. It was almost as bad as Laura Eagan's baby talk. Maria reached out and grasped one of Vivian's sweaty hands and gave it a squeeze. Vivian forced a laugh that, instead of being a charming hostess giggle, came out sounding like a donkey braying in the barnyard.

"Well, yes." She cleared her throat to get rid of the donkey braying. "I would."

She felt the color rising in her cheeks. She also felt foolish and offended, but was still a hostess, goddammit. This was why she had trouble with people. They always seemed to be keeping secrets from you. Just like her mother'd always said.

"Come to the kitchen. I keep my recipe cards in a box. I think I have a few blank ones. Maybe I could also get the recipe for the cake, what did you call it? Pandora?"

Edward watched from the window as the Tomasettis left the house and climbed into the rusted, early-model Ford pickup truck, Dominic helping his wife into the passenger seat before walking around to the driver's side. As soon as they'd driven away, he turned to Vivian and launched into one of his low-growl tirades. Vivian thought, *We don't need a dog, we've got Edward.* She responded by showing him her back and disappearing into the kitchen.

"How dare you," and "Guineas" and "my house" were barked out in repetition as Vivian circled the dishrag over the dishes in the sink. The volume of Edward's tirades never registered above a five on the dial, but that was almost worse than if they'd come at full blast. The anger and venom didn't have anywhere to go, just stopped themselves up inside Edward, or else trickled out of his mouth in little bits of invisible hateful slime.

Vivian scrubbed at the dried ketchup Stroganoff, the thickened glops just as stubborn as the smirk she refused to wipe from her lips. Edward stayed put in his chair in the living room, griping and swearing in her direction. Judging from the way Dominic Tomasetti helped Maria into the car, and how he helped her down the steps, Vivian guessed he probably never swore at her. She knew people. A couple of lovebirds, those two. She could just picture them, walking all lovey-dovey, arm in arm down the street, cooing sweet nothings. The Tomasettis respected each other.

"Ha," she scoffed, and slapped the dishrag over the faucet. Respect. She fished around the cooling dishwater for stray silverware and measuring spoons. Respect meant not lying to someone about something, now, didn't it? Vivian pulled the plug from the drain, leaned against the sink, and pursed her lips as she wiped her hands on the dry dish towel and thought about Maria's lie about the spaghetti sauce. Now, there were lies and there were LIES. Maria'd at least told her the truth tonight.

"Hmph." Vivian snapped the dish towel through the air in the direction of the living room.

The music from the record player grew louder above her and Vivian knew Charlotte was trying to drown out the sounds of her father's low snarling anger. Vivian hung the dish towel over its iron bar, whipped off her apron, and stormed out of the kitchen and up the stairs. Maybe tonight would be the night she would finally confront him. If he pushed her, she might. But as she removed her rooster brooch and placed it back into her jewelry box, she remembered her brilliant idea. The one about finding information. *Get into it, get under it, poke around in the corners. Find every little bit.*

Chapter 14

Not being found had become a way of life for Flora Parker and Gilbert Ogden, who were now considered "criminals" and "at large" following the embezzlement of the Wayne Building & Loan last June. And Flora would've agreed. Canada was indeed large. It was so odd to her that it was a completely separate country from the United States. She had been expecting something much different. But the people were the same, the language was the same, except for maybe a few extra vowels here and there, the cars and houses and buildings and streets were the same. The only thing really different was the money. The downside was that they'd lost about three thousand dollars with the exchange rate, but that was a small price to pay for a little more safety.

Flora remembered the day she and Gilbert fled the bank as the most exciting day of her entire life. She had hardly been able to button her blouse in front of the mirror that morning, with her fingers shaking the way they were. She had nearly stabbed herself in the head with her hatpin. It was then she'd had to give herself a little pep talk, because she would have to work the whole day knowing what she knew, and if she entered the bank that morning with her fingers shaking and her voice all jittery, she would have given the whole thing away.

Her handbag was heavier than usual, holding eight used

makeup compacts packed with vegetable shortening, which Gilbert had said they might need to grease any of the locks on the drawers, boxes, or vault. If anyone peeked inside the pocketbook they'd just assume she had a slight obsession with makeup, which she really did not. As her husband, Bill, drove her to work she took deep, slow breaths and told herself over and over in her head, *You can do this, Flora. You can do this.*

After saying goodbye to Bill, and closing the car door, every move she made was done slowly and deliberately. From the time she inserted the key into the lock of the bank's back door, to the phony, cheerful smile she gave Mr. Hunsicker when he arrived (forty-five minutes after everyone else who worked at the bank), to the friendly "Have a nice weekend!"s and "See you Monday!"s she said to everyone at the end of the day. She would never know if they had a nice weekend or not, and she wouldn't see them Monday, or any day after that, and the lie squished and sloshed in her stomach a little. For the most part Flora had kept to herself at work, but everyone who worked with her would have said they really liked her. But that had always been a large part of her daily existence, making sure she was likable.

The internal anxiety and thrilling terror she felt were coupled with the relief that she wouldn't have to keep up the charade of romancing her revolting boss. It was a role within a role and she had done such a convincing job of it, she just knew she could have made it big on the stage, or even in Hollywood. Mr. Hunsicker had to believe she fancied him, but wouldn't dare betray her husband. And no one else was supposed to know or even suspect any of it. Gilbert had made it clear that was terribly important. She had put on quite a production for that purpose, and could have given Barbara Stanwyck a run for her money. Barbara in *Double Indemnity*, though, not Barbara in *Christmas in Connecticut*. "Duplicitous" was the word she had been rolling over and over in her head while she worked. It helped put her in the proper frame of mind, and it helped her nail her performance.

Boyd Hunsicker was the kind of man Flora had spent much of her life trying to avoid. Overbearing, overweight, and overly confident, with a blustering manner of speaking, he punctuated his words with jabs to the air from an unlit cigar, because his doctor told him he shouldn't smoke. Flora winced as his inflated waistline brushed against the back of her chair, and wondered if there was anything else his doctor had told him he shouldn't do.

In the beginning, he simply used to watch her with an uncomfortable familiarity. His eyes traveled over the features of her face and the contours of her body, as if he were memorizing them. Flora broke a great many pencils out of burgeoning fear and anger, and tried to ward off the violated feeling that his prolonged and inappropriate stares provoked in her.

Over time Mr. Hunsicker grew bolder, feeling more secure in his position of power over her. "That husband of yours, Phil, what's he do?" he had said. "Bill," Flora would answer in a measured, patient tone, "his name is Bill." She was sure Mr. Hunsicker knew that her husband's name was Bill, and that what Bill "did" was split his time making deliveries for Barrett's Flower Shop and apprenticing as an electrician at Rambo & Long.

Mr. Hunsicker knew that her husband (Bill) didn't make enough money to support them, and knew that she needed to keep her job at the Building & Loan. Women with few options were always the best targets. In the privacy of his office, when she was taking dictation for him, he would recite a few lines regarding bank business, but then interject that her skirt that day "really got him going," and then almost in the same breath ask her, "How's Phil doing?" After a while she'd stopped correcting him, and let him call her husband by the wrong name. He seemed to enjoy it.

He took a grotesque interest in her marriage, which was almost as troubling as his interest in her body. It was all she could do to keep from gagging when he touched her. A fat swollen hand on her elbow, an intentional brush of his arm against her backside as she was leaving the office. He stank of whiskey and charbroiled steak, regardless of the time of day. But it was all for the greater good, and their future, and she stifled her revulsion and played her part admirably. She never rebuffed him directly, and twisted her suppressed gags into flirtatious giggles, making it seem like he was moving in the right direction, and that it would only be a matter of time. Stanwyck's Phyllis Dietrichson had nothing on Flora Parker.

Gilbert Ogden had a sixth sense for Flora's internal distress, and always made it a point to visit her desk after she had been in Hunsicker's office with the door closed. In the slightest of movements, unnoticed by anyone else, he would place a reassuring hand over hers as it rested on the desktop, and then smooth his suspenders, straighten his bow tie, and return to his seat behind the counter, where he'd chew on his fingernails, because he was nervous, too. Flora loved him for his efforts to comfort her, but she would still rush home and scrub her body raw in a hot shower to try to remove any and all lingering traces of Boyd Hunsicker.

Flora had never been prouder of Gilbert, who had planned the entire embezzlement and getaway almost single-handedly. She had seen how everyone at the bank had underestimated him, employees and customers alike, and how Mr. Hunsicker had bullied him. It was infuriating to watch someone as wealthy and powerful as Boyd Hunsicker berate and demean someone like Gilbert. He was much smarter and much stronger than everyone gave him credit for. His small stature belied a big brain and an even bigger heart. And Flora knew he would do anything for her.

The newspapers had gone crazy for the story of the Wayne Building & Loan robbery and the escape, with word reaching beyond the state of Ohio and up across the border into Canada. The outrage at the audacity of the crime, the mind-boggling amount of money that had been stolen, and some of the reactions of Wooster's citizens were detailed in dozens of publications in the region. The reactions of Wooster's citizens included a shudder-inducing snippet from Flora's next-door neighbors, who described the volcanic rage of her cuckolded husband as he had burst from their house, shotgun in hand, jumped into his car, and taken off in hot pursuit of his cheating, not to mention outlaw, wife. "There was smoke coming out Bill Parker's ears. Genuine smoke, honest to God."

No one could believe Gilbert had pulled it off. Even with the outright disbelief splashed across the front pages of the papers, and the calculated brilliance required to make such a clean get-away, Gilbert was adorably humble about the entire thing. He would wave a dismissive hand at any praise she gave him, and then somehow turn the focus around, laud her contributions to the operation, and ask her if she was coping all right.

There were moments when Flora grew wistful about leaving Wooster. She knew they could never go back, and she had grown fond of the tidy little town and its community. Gilbert had said they probably shouldn't even chance going back over the border into the U.S., much less all the way down to Ohio. Canada was their new home, Toronto more specifically, and with the money they had, it would at least be a comfortable life there, if just the ti-niest bit colder. He had smiled when he said that. "Just the tiniest bit colder, Flora."

He knew she hated the cold, and had bought her a full-length mink coat from Eaton's on Queen Street in October when the tem-peratures began to drop. It had been his first really expensive gift to her. They had been careful not to flash their cash around after exchanging modest amounts into Canadian currency. Just a little at a time, and never at the same bank twice. They rented a modest three-bedroom, red-brick bay-and-gable house in a quieter neigh-borhood of the city, and spent money only on necessities. Flora did hate the cold, but what bothered her more was the size of Toronto. "It's too big," she had told Gilbert, even though he had chosen a more intimate neighborhood, rather than renting something right in the city center. "It's truly unwieldy, Gil."

"We need it to be big," had been his response.

He'd laughed at her unexplainable affinity for Wooster, a place he'd never appreciated in the least. "Don't you find the people to be unsophisticated? After all, you lived in New York."

"A little." Flora would grin and her dimples would sink deep into her cheeks. "But I love it. I love the charm, the coziness, the predictability of it all. Mostly the people. They'll never really surprise you, small-town people, you know?"

Gilbert had raised one eyebrow and leaned back on the sofa with his hands behind his head as a slow smile spread across his face. Even when he felt he couldn't possibly know her any better, she'd surprise him. And she could always make him smile.

"But everyone knows everyone else's business." He liked to play devil's advocate with Flora.

"Not if you're careful," she had said as she raised both eyebrows back at him. "I like that you know what to expect," she'd gone on. "You know, when you step out your door, they'll watch you because they don't have anything else to do. When you're at the store, they'll peek at what you're buying, because they're bored and want to compare their lives to yours or his or hers. 'Ooooh, look who's getting the nice cuts of meat.' Or 'Did you see all the marshmallows in her cart? What on earth is she making with all those marshmallows?'"

Gilbert slapped a hand on his knee, laughing.

"They're always passing judgment on what you wear, what you eat, what you do, who you love." Flora shrugged. "And if you're smart enough to keep your distance, you can sit back and watch them the same way. Just enjoy it all, like you'd enjoy a stage play or a movie."

Flora had certainly seen a few people who swanned dramatically around their everyday lives as if Mr. Frank Capra had just called, "Action!" from behind his camera.

Chapter 15

The Christmas party had been the talk of the town; Betty's best yet. Yes, 1952's Savior's Celebratory Soirée (an unofficial title, but one Betty would evaluate for consideration) was going to be the one to beat. The decorations were outstanding, the food and drinks superb, and her dress had positively stolen the show. Not that the party had been a show, mind you. It wasn't as if it were a Christmas pageant, although if anyone wanted to refer to it as such Betty wouldn't have blamed them. But if it had been a pageant, which it really wasn't, Betty's dress would have won the competition. Not that it was a competition. Not a close one, at any rate.

She'd thought she'd have to go up to Akron or Cleveland, but Beulah Bechtel had come through for her in the end with a midweek delivery of a stunning deep crimson wool number, a heavy, substantial wool, with bracelet-length sleeves, and a perfectly cinched waist and flamboyant flared skirt, made even more dramatic by the petticoats underneath. She had added her own flair to the neckline of the dress by having Dolly stitch a border of fluffy white ermine, which both gave a nod to the timeless holiday apparel of Santa and Mrs. Claus, and also drew attention to Betty's décolletage. The décolletage was the only thing keeping Betty from wearing the dress to church services on Christmas Eve. As attractive as it was, especially for someone her age, it simply wouldn't be appropriate.

Vivian Dalton, apparently, didn't share Betty's feelings about what was or was not appropriate on the eve of Our Lord and Savior's birth, with her face painted up like a cheap B-movie starlet's. The moment the Daltons crossed the church threshold Betty was reminded of the telephone conversation. Her eyes widened as she watched them walk down the left side of the aisle. She could not be-*lieve* she had allowed herself to forget about something like that. Well, she could, what with the children's school Christmas pageants, and the Miller Christmas pageant (it really wasn't a pageant), and Charles's recent promotion and bonus news, she really wasn't surprised she had forgotten. Vivian Dalton hardly registered on her radar in the first place, although the story was shocking, and a true bit of scandal.

She watched as the Daltons took their seats in the pews, Eddie Dalton looking respectable enough in his wool Trilby and overcoat, and their daughter Charlotte, how old must Charlotte be now, high school, she knew that much, she was just a year or two older than Margie, my, she was a *gangly* thing, wasn't she, absolutely no bust whatsoever, and Vivian, wearing *that hat*, although who would notice the hat when she was wearing all that makeup. Betty gave herself a quick pinch on the soft skin under her wrist beneath her wristwatch where she'd attached the angel charm. It had been her analyst's idea, and was supposed to be a reminder to rein in her judgment. *Remember why we are here.* Vivian's fur-collared coat was quite lovely. Probably dyed squirrel, though. *It's Christmas*, Betty thought to herself, and then reflexively touched the sleeve of her mink.

She wondered if she should reconsider her original plan to disseminate the gossip she had heard. She cast a glance at the life-sized crucifix hanging on the far wall, and then lowered her eyes. She was bigger than that, really. She was a pillar of the community. It was up to people like Betty to set an example; to guide the rest of Wooster's denizens to be the very best they could be.

Just like she did every Christmas Eve, Betty had made sure the Millers arrived at the church early enough to greet Reverend Alsop before he adjourned to his study to do his last-minute preparations for the sermon. She made sure they were early enough to give the vestibule and worship hall a final once-over, and tidy up the holiday décor. Because, although Betty chaired the Worship Committee, Harriet Barnham was the one who oversaw the decorations, and everyone knew Harriet could get sloppy. After Betty had adjusted most of the pine garlands and holly branches linked together along the tops of the pews, and ordered Harriet to place a dish under every candle so she didn't burn the church down in a fiery inferno on Jesus's birthday, she then lined up her four children, Margie, Duncan, Little Bitty, and Charles Junior, next to their father, so that they could greet most of the congregation as they entered the church. Betty also made sure the Millers were all tucked into their pew exactly ten minutes before the service was to begin. Punctuality showed proper respect. Early arrival ensured that necessary adjustments could be made, and reminded everyone who was really in charge.

The interior of Forest Chapel Methodist Church was bathed in the warm glow of candles, humming with the melodic chorus of singing parishioners, and swelling with the magical aura of the Christmas spirit. Naturally, some of the younger children were restless and fussy, and some of the older children pretended they weren't enjoying themselves, but for the most part, the entire congregation became one swaying, praying, love-filled entity, which was precisely what Jesus deserved on the eve of his birth. *Praise the Lord.*

It was after the services ended that the warm and magical, love-filled, but also perfectly scheduled and structured evening began to unravel. For one thing, Vivian Dalton must have been launched from her seat in the pew by holy catapult before the hymn had even ended, as she was the first person up at the pulpit to wish Reverend Alsop a merry Christmas. Betty, who was always the first person to the pulpit, suddenly found herself second in line. Standing behind Vivian, fuming at that hideously tacky hat, and wondering if that was liquor she smelled coming from Vivian, as she had to wait her turn.

Betty shook Reverend Alsop's hand in both of hers and gave him the most fervent *"Mer*-ry *Christ*-mas" she could muster, in an effort to be the most memorable since she had not been the first. She then remained at the front of the church, and made polite small talk with Mary and Gerald Houder, as she tried to temper her fuming on the eve of Christ Our Savior's birth. Louder Houder, as some referred to Gerald in their less charitable moments, was testing her nerves. He refused to wear a hearing aid and always demanded that everyone repeat everything. "What's that? I can't hear you. Speak up. Louder!"

"I *SAID*"—she raised her voice to an almost-shout—"ARE YOU LOOKING *FORWARD* TO SPENDING *TIME* WITH YOUR *GRANDCHILDREN*?"

Vivian acted as if she hadn't even noticed Betty standing behind her, and had wished Reverend Alsop a theatrical "Merry Christmas," and then made her way back toward her family. From the corner of her eye, Betty could see Eddie Dalton was talking with John Randall, and the Dalton girl had plopped back into the pew next to Lacy Granger and they were probably talking about how they wished Margie would include them in her social group. Margie was extremely popular at school. Betty glanced between the Daltons and the faces of Mary and Louder Houder, and saw Vivian standing behind Eddie while he talked to John. The two men were likely discussing something related to snow shovels.

Betty knew Charles was probably thinking of the stiff martini he planned to pour as soon as the Millers returned home, and was shaking hands with their fellow worshippers, moving down the center aisle. When he reached Vivian Dalton, Betty's antennae shot up and her attention suddenly snapped completely away from Louder Houder. He had been able to hear her just fine this time, but only because he had moved to just two inches away from her, and had obviously forgotten his Clorets. She shot her glare in Charles's direction. Vivian was positively fawning over Charles, brushing imaginary threads from his suit, touching his arm repeatedly, and then fingering his pocket square; fluttering her eyelashes as she giggled in a manner better suited to someone much younger than she.

Betty squared her shoulders, flared her nostrils, excused herself from the Houders, and pushed her way past the Hoopers and the Chandlers, barely remembering to say, "Merry Christmas," through her tight smile. She quickly pinched her husband's elbow and pulled him away from Vivian, who then turned her attentions to Burt Chandler. Betty swore under her breath, casting an apologetic glance at Reverend Alsop, who had made his way from the pulpit and down the aisle, and was standing within hearing range, although she was certain he hadn't heard her.

"Merry Christmas, Reverend Alsop," she said again, this time through just slightly clenched teeth.

She waved in irritation to Margie and Duncan, who were holding Little Bitty's and Charles Junior's hands, but still standing in the pew up at the front. *We're leaving*, she mouthed, and continued to push Charles down the aisle toward the front entrance. At the vestibule she realized she had forgotten her mink back in the pew. She was rigid with irritation, and struggling to keep her eyes bright and her smile upturned as people passed them and sang, "Merry Christmas!"

"Darling," Charles said, with a hand on her shoulder, "where is your coat?"

"Here, Mom." Margie, in her red velvet dress with the white lace collar, was carrying the mink over her left shoulder and propelling Little Bitty, in her candy-cane-striped dress and bloomers, forward with her right hand. Duncan and Charles

Junior followed single file, in their matching charcoal-gray suits and evergreen silk ties, behind them.

Betty looked at her children and then at her husband.

"*Thank* you, sweetheart. You're a good girl." She gave Margie an affectionate pinch on the cheek, and then had three thoughts: how glad she was that Margie had her delicate features, how Christmas truly was the most wonderful time of year, and how Vivian Dalton would get what was coming to her.

Chapter 16

In the grand karmic scheme of things, Vivian wouldn't have thought she was due any sort of righteous retribution for any of her past actions or behavior.

> **Retribution:**
> ```
> 1: recompense, reward
> 2: the dispensing or receiving of reward or
> punishment especially in the hereafter
> 3: something given or exacted in recompense;
> especially: punishment
> ```

But she might've forgotten a few things over the years. Who remembered every little thing they said or did? Vivian was much better at remembering all the slights, taunts, and teasing she'd had to suffer than recalling anything she might've said or done to someone else. And, currently, she was suffering more than she thought she deserved to.

Since the Betty Miller telephone conversation, on the horrible, black day of December fifteenth, Vivian's emotions had run through shock, disbelief, rage, then anxiety, and were holding at a combination of the rage and anxiety. Christmas Eve had been the one night she'd tucked it all away in a lockbox in the very deepest part of her brain. It had been a mild distraction;

a dreamlike kind of event, where Vivian, who did not usually drink alcohol of any sort, had thrown caution to the wind and polished off a tall glass of cooking sherry before the Daltons left for church. She was a little tipsy when she retouched her makeup, but the dark circles under her eyes needed a lot of powder, and then the powder had made her look washed out so she'd added more pink rouge. And, what was a little more eye shadow? After all, Christmas comes but once a year!

The fuzzy warmth from the sherry had spread all around her insides and out into her limbs on the car ride to the church. The toilet paper roll in the cramped church bathroom made the funniest sound as she pulled hard and watched it flap-flap-flap-flap as it unrolled, giggling at the soft pile that fell to the floor when she finally ripped it free. By the time Reverend Alsop asked them to stand for "Angels We Have Heard on High," the candles were blazing in the stained-glass windows, the nave was filled with the scent of fresh pine needles, various perfumes, and colognes, and Vivian was bursting with the spirit of the Lord and celebrating the eve of His birth. Loudly.

By the final "Amen" of the service, Vivian's warmth and bursting spirit had tapered off a little, and she wanted to make sure she wished the reverend a "Merry Christmas" before all her holiday cheer turned into a mild headache and soft, sherry-scented belches. She wouldn't say she remembered too much of the evening, but, boy, if that sherry didn't make her like everyone at church just a little better! People weren't so bad!

When the Christmas decorations had been taken down, and all that holiday cheer swept off the floor of Forest Chapel Methodist Church, Vivian felt as if she, too, had been stripped of the holiday décor. What was left was her simmering hostility and extreme paranoia. During the next Sunday service she was too preoccupied with the congregation to pay attention to any of the divine guidance coming from Reverend Alsop at the pulpit. She barely noticed that Dora Archer was there by herself, and in the past that would've been the perfect occasion for a joke about Earl Archer's forgetfulness. The old fart forgot to bring himself to church! She also barely noticed that Stewart Bowen's wife had herself a new hat and coat, and maybe that meant Stewart had gotten a new job. And Maxine Butler was there with her mother, maybe up for the holidays and maybe she'd finally thanked her for the quilt. These things barely registered for Vivian. The focus for Vivian was herself. Herself and how everyone else was behaving toward her. Every one of her senses was attuned to the attention directed, or not directed, at her. The looks, whispers, and gestures coming from all around her. She was aware of Betty Miller, but careful not to meet her eye.

Vivian had made a trip to the stationery section of Woolworth's in between Christmas and New Year's, and had bought herself a small brown notebook and a small calendar booklet. She circled December 15 in the calendar booklet. The day that her life had changed. She made small checkmarks in the corners of each of the days that had followed that one. It was her own Advent calendar of anxiety.

The days leading up to Christmas showed a light penciled checkmark in the corner of each box. She'd been on her guard, listening in on each and every telephone conversation she connected at the switchboard, and keeping her other ear alert to the chatter and reactions of the other operators in the room, in case they happened to talk about something they'd overheard. December nineteenth showed a small x in the corner of the calendar booklet, instead of the usual checkmark. That was the night she'd succeeded in angering Edward with her dinner party for the Tomasettis. *How did that feel, Edward?*

More checkmarks followed that, but another small x had been placed in the corner of December twenty-fourth. Edward had sure been sore at her behavior at church, and had done more of his angry muttering during the drive home, and a little on Christmas Day. *Good.*

Checkmark, checkmark, checkmark, checkmark, checkmark.
Vivian's agitation settled into an uneasy quiet. The kind that
had a lid kept on it, just like the spring-loaded clown-in-a-box
before the final bar of "Pop! Goes the Weasel."

New Year's Eve was just another checkmark. Vivian claimed
an awful headache to avoid celebrating the evening with the Giffords next door. While Edward went off to drink a couple of beers
and smoke cigars with Quentin Gifford, and Charlotte went to
Sue Barker's for an overnight, Vivian sat up in bed in her flan-
nel nightgown and curlers. She took out her teeth, slathered on
her face cream, and played a few rounds of solitaire. *The cheese
stands alone, the cheese stands alone ...*

The raised voices and laughter from next door traveled up and
filtered through the walls of the Daltons' second-floor bedroom,
and Vivian turned toward the sound in irritation before reaching
for her drink. She tipped up the glass, draining the last few drops
of the cooking sherry. She'd wanted it to relax her, like it had
before church on Christmas Eve, but her mood had just turned
darker. She stared at the glass, squinting at the diamond pattern,
remembering the first time she'd placed a glass against a wall in
order to listen in on a conversation she wasn't supposed to hear.
She drew her arm back and hurled the glass as hard as she could.
It hit the tall dresser just beyond the bed and broke into pieces
that dropped to the carpet and settled into a small island of glass
shards.

Vivian had seen movies where a startling move like that had
triggered a breakthrough for the main character; awakened
them to the Truth of something. Shocked them into some kind of
realization, usually accompanied by the crash of cymbals or the
blaring of trumpets. But Vivian's broken glass hadn't done anything more than make a mess for her to clean up. She reached for
Edward's pillow, buried her face in it, and screamed.

There was no breakthrough, no shocking realization, and no
Truth until January third. January third was circled on the small

Woolworth's calendar with a dark ring of blue ink. A dark ring that had been circled with the pen pressing down so hard it made an indentation in all the other months of the calendar. The days that followed found Vivian sporting matching dark rings under her eyes, as if she'd circled them repeatedly, and violently, with the blue pen in her sleep.

Chapter 17

Vivian Dalton should have thanked her lucky stars Betty Miller had to go out of town during the week between Christmas and New Year's. Betty's goodwill toward men had dried right up with Vivian's little performance at church on Christmas Eve, but the following day was Christmas, and there was neither room nor time for anything other than presents and toys and family. So many toys! Santa had been good to them all. It was only after the children had gone to bed that night, full of chocolate, candy canes, and sugar cookies, that Betty had answered a telephone call from Marilyn Dean, and then promptly invited her over to the house for cocktails.

"Shhhhit," she whispered, with the *t* breaking off like one of the sharp icicles hanging from their house. She'd just inadvertently created an opportunity for Marilyn.

Once Betty's father had been elected mayor, everyone seemed to need a favor from her. It wasn't as if she didn't secretly enjoy the added influence she had over certain people, but when she wasn't in the mood for it, it was an annoyance. Marilyn Dean had been pestering and pressuring Betty to talk her father into appointing her husband, Farley, as Wooster's director of finance. Betty tapped a manicured index finger, Revlon's Fire & Ice red, on the side table and stared at the telephone. Should she call Marilyn back and cancel? No. No, of course she shouldn't cancel. What was she thinking? Goodness, that was selfish. It was Christmastime! And Marilyn had sounded more overwrought than usual. She most likely just needed to unwind after the Christmas Day chaos familiar to anyone with a houseful of overstimulated, sugar-soaked children. Little Bitty and Charles Junior had been so carried away with their new Mr. Potato Head kit, they'd poked holes in half the potatoes Dolly had meant for the au gratin dish. She'd had to run next door and borrow some from the Talbots. Betty had no doubt that Marilyn had had a similarly harried and chaotic day, but, just in case . . .

Betty had prepared herself to ambush Marilyn with the Vivian Dalton gossip as soon as she came through the door. But, to her surprise, Marilyn had burst through the door with her own crisis, desperate to talk, and it didn't have anything to do with the director of finance position. Betty hadn't been able to get a word in edgewise, as Marilyn went on and on about how Farley had spent the morning with her and the children, and then claimed to have something important to do at the office.

"And so he just left," she said. "Left the house on Christmas Day, to go into the office?"

Betty shook her head slowly and swirled her Manhattan around in the glass.

"He's an accountant. What accounting emergency could be happening on Christmas Day, that couldn't be handled on any other day? Hmm?"

Betty picked up the bottle of whiskey and topped off Marilyn's glass.

"Another cherry, dear?"

Marilyn nodded.

"It's not as if he's the sheriff, or even a local policeman. He's also not a doctor."

"No," Betty agreed with her.

She thought that if Marilyn was going to mention the director of finance position, that would have been her cue. *He's also not the mayor, and speaking of your father* . . . But Marilyn missed the obvious segue, and continued to propel the conversation forward, harping on her personal suspicions about Farley. Betty settled back into the floral-print davenport, and continued to half listen. The liquor cart was within arm's reach.

"But what really worries me"—Marilyn took a large slug of her drink—"is that I found his checkbook, sitting open on the desk in his study. Do you know how much he gave his secretary this year for a Christmas bonus?"

"How much?"

"Two hundred dollars. Do you know how much she got last year?"

"How much?"

"Fifty. Now, what sort of secretary goes from a fifty-dollar Christmas bonus to a two-hundred-dollar Christmas bonus? That's what I want to know."

The cocktails had kicked in, and Marilyn's face was flushed. She was beginning to slur her words a little.

"Oh, honey." Betty reached out to pat Marilyn's knee. "I'm sure it's nothing. Farley did really well last year, didn't he? That's what you told me." But she was thinking that a hundred-and-fifty-dollar increase in bonus sounded mighty suspicious to her. She tried to remember what Farley Dean's secretary looked like, and wondered if she should risk upsetting Marilyn further by asking her. She decided against it.

"Well." Marilyn held her highball glass next to her rouged cheek. "He did."

Betty pursed her lips, thinking what she'd do to Farley if she were Marilyn, but Marilyn wasn't quite that clever, nor did she demand the same level of rectitude as Betty.

"I wouldn't give it any more thought, if I were you," she lied, for Marilyn's benefit as much as her own. "You just go on home and get some sleep, and if you need to talk about it tomorrow, you just give me a call."

Betty was not eager to hear any more from Marilyn about her obviously cheating husband, and had extended her generous offer of a sympathetic ear the next day because she knew she wouldn't be home to answer the telephone.

"You know," Marilyn began, "I meant to talk to you about Farley and the director of finance position."

Betty took Marilyn's Manhattan glass from her and gently guided her to the front door. Unbelievable. He was cheating on her, yet she still wanted to help him advance his career.

"Of course." Betty smiled through her incredulity, certain that she wouldn't be helping Farley now. Marilyn was the one who'd be needing the help. "But let's talk about that tomorrow."

And before Marilyn Dean realized it, she was in her matching fox hat and coat, with her car keys in gloved hand, weaving her way toward the Coupe de Ville parked in the circular drive.

The next day, the Millers left town to spend the rest of the week with Charles's parents up in Cooperstown, New York. Betty wasn't home to receive Marilyn's telephone call, thank God, because that was going to be a long conversation and she had too many other things to worry about. Her mother-in-law, potential blizzard conditions on the road, her mother-in-law, keeping the children frostbite-free, and her mother-in-law.

It was only after New Year's Day, after Betty had returned to Wooster, that she was able to turn her full attention to the gossip about Edward and Vivian Dalton. *Well*, she said to herself as she opened the telephone book to the florists and pointed a sharp red talon at the top of the page, *since Marilyn was too preoccupied with her own personal scandal, I suppose I'll have to handle this one myself as well*. And she proceeded to go about planning an afternoon event where she could make that happen.

"Yes, I'd like to be connected with Barrett's Flower Shop." She reached for her notepad and pencil. "Hello?"

Silence at the other end of the line.

"Hello?"

Betty reached over and tapped aggressively on the telephone cradle.

"HELLO!"

Oh, honestly, these things are supposed to make life easier, she grumbled as she reached to dial the operator again.

Betty had Dolly hand-deliver the invitations to her afternoon tea, while she handled the flower, food, and drink arrangements, but she wondered if she shouldn't have done it the other way around. The arrangements took about three times as long as they should have, since the telephone line kept getting disconnected nearly every time she tried to make a call.

When Betty Miller extended a written invitation, women of Wooster clamored to respond in the affirmative. This had been a slightly unusual invitation, seemingly without occasion. It wasn't to honor someone's birthday, engagement, marriage, or baby, and it wasn't a fund-raiser. Betty Miller was big on fund-raisers. The month of January was supposed to be reserved for recovering from the chaos of the holidays. To catch the collective breath, the ladies would all agree. But there it was on the invitation: January 17, a Saturday afternoon tea, with watercress sandwiches and polite conversation. What on earth was that about?

Clara Weaver had been irritated with the invitation, not only because it interrupted what was supposed to be a relaxing January, but also because it meant donning an afternoon dress. She was still holding on to the extra seven (or ten) pounds of holiday weight she had accumulated (all Christmas cookies and fudge), and the most appropriate dress she could fit into was one left over from her last pregnancy. But she knew if you turned down a Betty Miller invitation, you would not receive another until she felt you had served your time in Wooster's social purgatory.

Clara had strapped a belt, loosely, over the dress and gone to the tea, as had everyone else on the invitation list. And they had talked about their respective Christmases, and they had eaten the tea sandwiches and cookies, and sipped the tea and fruit punch. And they had learned all about Vivian Dalton and her husband. There had been more breathless pearl-clutching and *tsk-tsk*ing that afternoon in Betty Miller's living room than last summer at the Wayne County Fair, when it was discovered that Lucy Kratz had stolen Ethel Armstrong's cherry pie recipe and passed it off as her own. Ann Metcalf had been so surprised by the Dalton news, she'd spilled Shrimp Louie down the front of the new orange silk shantung Beulah Bechtel dress she'd purchased just for the tea.

All the women at the afternoon tea were well versed in the art of displaying false concern. They continued to clutch their pearls and *tsk-tsk* as they wondered how on earth poor, poor Vivian was going to deal with this when it got out to the rest of Wooster. Edward Dalton had a second wife.

Chapter 18

"My mother has turned our tiny attic room into an office," Charlotte Dalton told Sue Barker over lunch in the Wooster High School cafeteria. Conversations were all held at a higher volume there than in the classrooms or hallways of the school, and the clank of silverware on trays was constant. The din surrounding them was a comfortable and distracting level of the muted chaos, which allowed Charlotte to share her increasing concerns about her mother's behavior.

"A few days after New Year's. She pushed all the boxes into the corners and set up a little table by the window for her typewriter and stack of paper and pencils."

"Why?" Sue asked, before taking a large bite of her liverwurst sandwich.

"Who knows?" Charlotte answered, with a shrug more casual than she felt. "She's been acting weird since before Christmas. Well, weirder. She seems really frosted at my dad, but he doesn't seem to have noticed yet."

"Ha, that's typical, isn't it? My dad's the same way. He has no clue."

"Yeah," Charlotte agreed, and took a bite of her apple. As she crunched, both girls scanned the rest of the cafeteria. "I mean"— she shifted the apple into her cheek so she could talk—"she seems *really*, really mad at him."

"So, really frosty frosted?" Sue scrunched up her nose the way she did when she made her little word jokes. "Like, her frosting is frosty frosted."

"We didn't even go to Akron this year to look at the Christmas windows." Charlotte ignored the frosty frosting comment because Sue, as usual, was making everything into a joke, and Charlotte felt like this was kind of serious. "We've gone every year, as a family. I was kind of looking forward to it. You know, shopping and having lunch at O'Neill's."

"Aw." Sue offered a supportive pout. "We went. It wasn't so great. Don't feel bad. Do you think I should get another piece of cake?" She craned her neck in the direction of the food line.

Charlotte knew Sue was just being nice about O'Neill's. O'Neill's at Christmas was always great. The weekend they were supposed to go, her mother had been sick. So sick, she couldn't get out of bed, and Charlotte had brought her orange juice and toast and chicken broth. Then, at around three p.m. on Sunday she just popped right up out of bed and insisted on cleaning the house, doing the laundry, and making dinner. Charlotte thought it had either been a really quick virus, or her mother had faked the whole thing just to avoid going up to Akron.

"She was actually being kind of scary." Charlotte stared trancelike at a spot just beyond Sue's shoulder, remembering her mother with the knife in the kitchen that one night, and all the plate-stabbing with the fork.

"And, did I tell you, she invited this Italian couple for dinner one night?"

Sue's eyes bugged out as she frowned over her mouthful.

"Yeah," Charlotte continued. "Some lady she works with. And after she made that big stink about how I can't bring Rosie Gianetti home anymore."

Charlotte stared back at the spot beyond Sue's shoulder, thinking about the weird, exaggerated, bright "hospitality" toward that nice Italian couple she had for dinner. And since when did her mother invite coworkers for dinner? She didn't even invite friends for dinner. Well, she didn't really have any friends, honestly. And then there was the erratic behavior at church on Christmas Eve.

"It's still really uncomfortable at home and, jeez Louise"—she broke the trancelike gaze to look back at her lunch tray—"I feel like, lately, she's been eavesdropping when we use the phone. She's asking all kinds of questions, asking my dad where he's going all the time."

"Ugh," Sue said. "Mothers."

"But, that one day, just after New Year's, jeez, was she ever mad. I don't think I'd ever seen her that mad."

"Really?" Sue asked, disbelieving. "Not even when you brought home the syphilis book?" As soon as she said "syphilis book" she burst out laughing.

Charlotte glared at her, not laughing.

"What's funny?" Barb Harper sat down next to Sue with her lunch tray, which held a carton of chocolate milk and a lump of canned green beans in a dish.

"Oh, nothing." Charlotte waved a hand in an attempt to appear nonchalant.

"Oh, *nothing*, nothing." Sue caught her breath, and glanced at Barb's tray, noting the absence of cake. "Remember when we had to read *The Myth of Sisyphus* for English?"

"Sue . . ." Charlotte warned.

"Yeah," Barb answered, peeling back the top of the milk carton.

"Well, Charlotte went home one afternoon after school, and she was carrying the book, and her mom saw the cover and went positively ape."

"Sue!" Charlotte slapped her hand on the table like she was trying to reprimand a misbehaving puppy.

But Sue kept going.

"What did she say, again?" Sue said, looking to Charlotte for assistance, but Charlotte had covered her face with her hands.

"Something like, 'YOU WILL NOT BRING PORNOGRAPHY INTO THIS HOUSE!'"

Everyone at the tables in front of and behind them turned and stared at Sue, openmouthed. Charlotte's forehead was now resting on the tabletop, her arms wrapped around her hair.

"She did not!" Barb sputtered, as shocked as the onlookers at the other tables.

Charlotte's head nodded from under her wrapped arms. "She did," her voice muffled by her arms. "She ripped the cover right off the book. Tried to rip the entire thing in half."

"Oh, boy."

Sue had doubled over laughing again, as Charlotte peeled herself up from the table and took a deep breath, straightening her sweater. "Well, at least she didn't come to the school and yell at Mr. Grandy about it."

Barb gasped. "Can you imagine?"

"Yes."

Charlotte had been stupefied by her mother's deranged outburst and it had taken her several minutes to understand the cognitive disconnect. Her mother had been so enraged that Charlotte couldn't explain the mistake to her, and had just gone up to her room with the remaining shreds of the book. She had then been flooded with dread, imagining her mother taking her Rage, with a capital *R*, to the high school, stomping in with hair and eyes wild, pocketbook swinging like a weapon, demanding to speak to the filth-monster who gave her daughter pornography.

Charlotte had had to wait until the next morning at breakfast, when her mother was calmly drinking her coffee, to explain that Sisyphus was a Greek king and not a venereal disease. Her mother had nodded and given Charlotte a paper bag and tape with which to bind the cover back onto the book. But she hadn't apologized. She never apologized.

"*The Myth of Syphilis*, ha ha ha. Hey, you're watching *I Love Lucy* tonight, aren't you?" Sue asked, shifting easily from the horrors of mistaken-identity pornographic literature to the popular topic of the week and completely forgetting about Charlotte's familial concerns. "She's having her baby!"

"Oh, absolutely," Barb answered. "Who *isn't* going to watch that?"

Charlotte wished she could be as excited as everyone else about Lucy and Ricky Ricardo adding a little baby to their family. She just couldn't escape the feeling that kept nagging at her about her own. There was something really wrong with her mother. She seemed to be teetering on the brink of something.

Chapter 19

In Vivian's life, she wanted to believe she was a Lucy, and everyone else was an Ethel. The thing was, all the bad stuff seemed to happen to Lucy. Lucy and Ricky'd had to go through all sorts of misunderstandings, and it would've been swell if that's all this was. This thing with Edward *and his other goddamned wife.* But Vivian was now certain there was no misunderstanding. As of tonight, Edward still had no idea she knew, and she still had no idea what she was going to do about it.

The Daltons' television set was tuned in to CBS, and Edward, Vivian, and Charlotte all seated themselves in the living room, in their usual spots, as if nothing had been very wrong for the past three weeks. Edward in his chair, Vivian on the end of the sofa nearest the TV, and Charlotte on the floor, leaning against the far end of the sofa, holding a bowl of popcorn in her lap. It was the same way they always watched *I Love Lucy*, as a family. Vivian looked over at Charlotte, in her pedal pushers and bobby socks, plucking kernels from the bowl of popcorn.

"Not too many old maids in this batch," Charlotte pointed out, throwing the few unpopped kernels into a small dish next to her on the floor.

Vivian murmured an acknowledgment. Old maids. She remembered shrieking, "Old maid!" at her sister Vera, after an argument over the McGinty claddagh ring turned ugly. Vera'd then gone and

slapped her across the face. Vera had always been the most aggressive of the McGinty sisters, and wouldn't hesitate to dole out
a slap or two if she was mad enough. Vivian could only bring
herself to slap back with words, and they were never great ones.
"You're stupid!" or "I know you are, but what am I?" with her fists
clenched so tightly her fingernails left little half-moon indenta-
tions in her palms. Poor little Violet would usually just crumple
into a sobbing heap on her bed, and Henry and Will would disappear into the backyard, uneasy with how the McGinty females
expressed themselves. Family was sometimes more trouble than
they were worth.

Vivian had ended up with the claddagh ring because her
Aunt Catharine left it to the first niece to marry. That was the
rule. And if everybody was just going to ignore the rules, Vivian
thought, what was the point of having them in the first place?
Aunt Catharine had, of course, played by her own rules. She'd
married three times, which was two more times than the Catho-
lic Church recommended. "Marriage," Aunt Catharine had said,
"is a wonderful thing, but people make mistakes." She'd made
two mistakes, but she knew God would understand that she was
just fixing them. No one should get too bent out of shape about it.

It was an open-and-shut case, as far as Vivian was concerned.
She was the first of the McGinty nieces to marry, and Vera
shouldn't have even argued about it. Vera had claimed Aunt
Catharine said the ring should go to the *oldest* niece, but no one
else remembered it that way. Vera, like Aunt Catharine, had her
own way of looking at rules. As she got older she scoffed that she
didn't want Aunt Catharine's ugly old ring anyhow, and started
calling Aunt Catharine "the slut" of the McGinty family.

Vivian twisted the gold ring around her right ring finger as
the band music swelled from the television speaker and the title
words swept across the screen. *I Love Lucy* drew the Daltons
into the merry, lighthearted, brightly lit world of the Ricardos
and the Mertzes like cartoon animals following the aroma of pie

cooling on a windowsill. For a half hour on Monday nights everything outside the Lucy world was forgotten, left suspended in the air around the television set. Vivian kept a suspicious eye on Edward, but soon felt herself sucked into the show, just like always. The happy families on television seemed to prove Vivian's mother right. *Everyone else has it better than us.* Vivian had always been caught between her father's good nature and her mother's gloom. She had to push hard against the gloom. It was heavy.

The Daltons all laughed at Ricky's anxious overbearing smothering. They all laughed when Ricky, Fred, and Ethel practiced dry runs of taking Lucy to the hospital. They all laughed when Lucy announced, "It's time," and the other three flew into slapstick chaos, with Ricky dumping out the contents of Lucy's overnight suitcase. And they all laughed when Ricky, Fred, and Ethel screamed at each other to get a cab for Lucy, and then all three of them rushed out the door to get the cab, leaving Lucy forgotten and by herself in the apartment yelling, "Wait for me!"

During the cigarette advertisement, Vivian thought back to the night Charlotte had been born, and how panicked Edward had been; how he'd been all doting and concerned and frantic, and how he'd argued with the nurses and attendants that he wanted to be in the room with his wife. "My wife needs me!"

When *Lucy* came back on the television, the doors to the hospital opened with the nurse saying "Another maternity case coming in," and then Ricky was pushed through the door in a wheelchair, followed by the pregnant Lucy, waddling in carrying her own overnight suitcase. Edward and Vivian laughed the hardest at this. Edward'd had his own fainting spell in the hospital where he, too, was "just a little dizzy" and had to sit himself down on the bank of chairs in the waiting room.

Vivian watched the screen as Lucy and Ricky kissed each other before Lucy was taken to the delivery room, knowing that the next time they'd be together, they'd have a brand-new baby in their family. Edward looked from the television screen to Vivian, lifted his hand to his lips, and blew her a kiss. His eyes were shining behind the glasses he wore. Vivian pressed her lips firmly together and looked back at the screen.

Ricky had to use a telephone in the hospital's waiting room. Since the telephone didn't have a dial he had to connect through an operator. Even though the operator wasn't there on the screen, Vivian imagined the girl on the other end of the line and knew she would've been wearing the bulky headset and holding the plug cords in one hand, and if she wanted to listen in on the conversation, she could have. Who knew what she would hear? *You know somebody named Edward Dalton? . . . He's married, right? . . . Well, he's got himself another wife.*

Lucy gave birth to a baby boy, and Vivian held herself together until they showed a close-up of a tiny baby on the black-and-white screen, with its tiny eyes scrunched closed and its tiny hands curled under its tiny chin. As the band theme swelled and the credits began to roll, Vivian felt the tears running down her cheeks, and she knew that if she had to speak, her voice would burst from her throat in choked sobs. Holding her breath, she pushed herself up from the sofa and stepped over Charlotte's outstretched legs, disappearing around the corner and up the stairs before Edward or Charlotte saw her face.

The toilet seat lid was cold under her backside and she pulled her knees up to have somewhere to rest her forehead, although her girdle was cutting into her flesh. The tiny baby. The love between husband and wife. She'd had all that, once. The tears flowed over the rims of her eyes and the choked sobs landed in her lap as snapshots from her life flashed across her mind. Happy! Smiling! Loving!

Vivian's body shook and she began to rock from side to side, sobbing as tears and drips from her nostrils fell into the valley of her lap. She cried and cried until it wore her out, and until each breath became a big effort. Until she'd figured she'd cried out everything she had, and now just felt empty. Nothing left.

Her feet slid from the toilet seat to the tiled floor with a thud, and she reached to pull at the roll of toilet paper to blow her nose. In the rational part of her mind, she knew she was mostly upset because of that sweet television baby. But it was just a television show. It wasn't real. Vivian gave a loud sniff, and final wipe under her nose with the toilet paper, then lifted her head, feeling the crackle of dried makeup that had run down her cheeks. She thought about how Lucy was now trapped in that marriage with Ricky. There'd be no easy escape from that. Now there was a baby.

The name *Sylvia Emerich* floated to the surface of her mind. She'd been trapped by a baby, Sylvia Emerich of Apple Creek. Forced to leave school because she'd been trapped by her baby. Men made a whole lot of noise about women "trapping" them into marriage, but women were the ones getting trapped. By men, by their own bodies. Boy, the women who weren't saddled with a kid were sure lucky, weren't they? That Flora Parker at the Building & Loan had been lucky. When there was no baby, you could just steal two hundred and fifty thousand dollars and run away, leave all your troubles (and your husband) behind. *And the trash ran away with the spoon.*

Vivian's lipstick had been wiped away over an hour ago with her dinner napkin, but the toilet paper she tossed into the trash bin was still smeared with mascara, Pan-Cake, and pink rouge. The face she tried to show the world, all messily smeared onto strips of soggy tissue.

She avoided looking at herself in the mirror as she stood over the sink, struggling to pry the lid off the bottle of sleeping pills. It had always been a stubborn bottle, and her hands were already shaking from being so tired and upset. The word "prying" ran over and over in her mind, as she twisted and pulled at the lid, like the word itself would help it come off. *Prying. Prying. Goddammit, come off!* Her hands began to cramp and she felt a new wave of tears building up behind her eyes just as the lid gave way.

The release of the lid snapped something in Vivian's brain, and she stared into the mouth of the bottle. *Prying.* Still holding the bottle in one hand, the lid in the other, she moved back to the closed toilet seat and sat down again, feeling like a foggy film had been peeled from her mind. She rested for a few moments, then gave another sniff. A determined sniff.

Vivian stood again and went to the sink, setting the lid of the sleeping pill bottle next to the soap dish. She looked at the bottle, then shook out two pills and popped them onto the back of her tongue. She twisted the Cold faucet on, and then swept a handful of tap water into her mouth. She wanted to be fast asleep by the time Edward came to bed.

As she lay there tucked under the covers and turned on her side, away from Edward's side of the bed, and waiting for the sleeping pills to do their job, she pointed and flexed her toes like she was kick-paddling through the bedsheets, with the word singsonging in her head. Pry . . . (point, flex) . . . ing (point, flex). Pry . . . (point, flex) . . . ing (point, flex). She'd put it off long enough. She scrunched her face up, squeezing her eyes shut as tight as they'd go so the tears wouldn't start again, and then blew out a tired gust of breath in defeat. She'd have to go see Mr. McAfee this week.

Chapter 20

Mr. Donald T. McAfee, private investigator, had been prying into Edward Dalton's past at Vivian's request. Two days before Christmas she'd set up a meeting with Mr. McAfee in the Literary Reference section of the Wayne County Public Library. Someplace where Vivian had never been before and didn't expect to see anyone she knew. They'd talked for twenty minutes, and then Vivian had suggested a special code to use the next time they talked on the telephone.

"You know," she'd said to him in a proper library whisper, "because the switchboard operators sometimes listen in on the calls."

Don McAfee was the same private investigator Wayne Building & Loan had hired to find Gilbert Ogden and Flora Parker, after their *abscondance*. Was that the right noun? Absconded, abscondance? It sounded right, but she'd have to check Charlotte's dictionary.

As far as Vivian knew, Don McAfee still hadn't found Gilbert and Flora yet, and she'd thought it'd probably be impolite to ask him about it. With all the newspaper stories of the Wayne Building & Loan robbery, though, she'd have thought he'd have more than enough clues to find those two.

Don McAfee and Vivian had agreed that she would wait to check in with him about the Edward investigation until after the holidays. When she'd telephoned him on January third Vivian had asked him just one question: "Do I need to come to your office?"

If Don McAfee had answered, "No," Vivian would've known that the rumor about her husband had been a bunch of nasty nonsense, and she'd have had to set the record straight with one Betty Miller. But when she'd asked Mr. McAfee if she needed to come to his office, Mr. McAfee had answered, "Yes."

Vivian had thanked him, replaced the receiver in its cradle, and stormed up the stairs to the bedroom to scream into a pillow. The Daltons' pillows had had to be cleaned more frequently over the past few weeks, especially if Vivian hadn't taken the time to wipe off her lipstick first. The pillow-screaming was the only outlet for her rage at life, which had increased tenfold since December fifteenth. Her nerves were raw and frayed at the ends, like some of the old jack cords at Bell that had worn away from the plugs from too much use and improper care.

The fact that Donald McAfee's investigation had been a success meant that Vivian's marriage, and most of her adult life, had been a sham. This was the thought that had been running on repeat through her mind for the two weeks after that call. One week of Vivian simply trying to understand what Mr. McAfee had told her, and another week of her valiantly trying to push the truth out of her mind. Maybe if she avoided meeting McAfee in person as she'd told him she would do (to see the proof, and to pay him), she could pretend it wasn't real.

Vivian's world had closed in on her and she was pretty sure nothing existed outside her brand-new little private hell. Her casual interest in anything outside her limited orbit of the house on South Walnut Street and the brick confines of Ohio Bell suddenly disappeared as the truth about her life sank in, colder than the January temperatures outside. She hadn't cared that the library had just received some historic journal collection from one of the town's founding fathers, she hadn't cared that the hardware store was planning to move its location one block farther north, and she hadn't cared that on January twelfth the first dial telephone was installed in Wooster, in Dr. Paul's medical office. Wooster and its technological progress would eventually make Vivian's job obsolete. If she'd cared at all, she'd have looked up "obsolete" in Charlotte's dictionary.

The *Lucy* episode, and Vivian's bathroom breakdown, had finally tipped her over the edge. A sliver of new moon shone brightly in the night sky, lighting the usually dark country road that led out toward the Heidelberg Chocolate Factory where McAfee's office was. It hadn't occurred to her to question why his office was in the chocolate factory, but if she'd asked, Mr. McAfee would've explained that he'd once done some work for Gunther Heidelberg, who'd paid him with the use of the upstairs office in the factory. He'd have also told her that he liked to work around the smell of chocolate.

Vivian sang out loud in awkward jagged bursts as she steered the Buick over the snow-packed road. It wasn't the joyous kind of singing she liked to do in church, it was something more troubled and halting.

". . . the cow jumped over the moon . . ."

How did that one go? Was that another one about a farm? Of course the cow lived on a farm.

". . . the little dog laughed . . ."

Goddamned dog. Was this even a song?

"And the dish ran away with the spoon."

I know people, Vivian thought, laughing at herself, and imagined all the things she could've done differently, if she'd really known people. She could've married one of the other boys who had taken her out riding in their cars, or on hayrides out in the country, or for an ice-cream cone at the soda fountain. Someone who wouldn't have made a damned fool out of her. John Reed! If she'd married John she'd be four-flushing her fancy self in some nice brick house on the north side right now, instead of slinking around Wooster with her head ducked low, from house to work to private eye's office.

Jesus Christ almighty, why in the hell did it have to be Edward?

If he hadn't bothered to tell her about his other goddamned wife, what else was lurking out there? Children? Did he have a whole other family living somewhere? A family that didn't nag him about his nose hair, and who'd let him have a goddamned dog? Vivian never told Edward about Rambles. She'd been seven and Rambles had been just over a year old, really still a puppy, when he'd scrambled off the front porch after a squirrel, out into the road, and into the path of Oscar Buckley's oncoming new Tin Lizzie, going much too fast for their quiet neighborhood. The pain of that loss was too sharp and too deep and she wouldn't go through it again. And she wouldn't have Edward and Charlotte go through it, either. She'd burst into tears every time she saw Mr. Buckley and that godforsaken car, and had crossed her arms with a "Humph!" when it finally went to the scrap heap. It'd been too hard after that to be around dogs; pet them or hold them, stroke their soft ears or look into their sweet faces, so she'd just avoided them altogether. *I'm allergic.*

Donald McAfee's office looked exactly like she'd imagined a private investigator's office would look, especially if he didn't have a maid. Almost empty as far as furniture went, but the piles of papers and folders made it seem like an overcrowded newsroom. Vivian went to sit on the only chair opposite the wooden desk and leaned her backside into a stack of papers and books that slid off the sides and front of the chair in a paper avalanche.

"Oh, mercy!" She sprang back to a standing position and then dropped to the floor, retrieving the stray pages. How did this man manage to find anything?

"It's all right," McAfee said in the deep voice that didn't match the way he looked. "I'll clean it up later." He "cleaned up" by just scooping all the papers and files together and patting them into a sloppy light-colored leaf pile. It worked for him, and he knew where everything was, more or less. "Peppermint?"

The office was not as much of a surprise as Don McAfee had been. Vivian supposed she had expected to see Humphrey Bogart lurking in the library stacks. She hadn't been able to hide her reaction to the slender, prematurely gray, almost delicate gentleman who'd held out a soft hand to her and given a confident, firm shake. You'd better believe she'd inspected his fingernails, which were cut evenly across the tops of his fingers, not gnawed down to the quick (like a Nervous Purvis), and she'd also made note of the fact that he did not wear glasses. Edward wore glasses. Why hadn't she thought of that before? Shifty, beady eyes, hiding behind their glasses. LIAR, LIAR, LIAR!

She settled herself back into the now-empty chair with a tight smile, and held her pocketbook in her lap. "No, thank you," was an automatic response to the peppermint candy. But her mouth felt like the bottom of the kitchen garbage bin, and she reconsidered after running her tongue against the roof of her mouth. "You know?" she said, before Don McAfee had a chance to sit down. "I will have one, thank you."

"Well, Mrs. Dalton." Mr. McAfee leaned across the piles on his desk and handed her a plastic-wrapped candy, then leaned back and placed a hand on the pile of documents directly in front of him. "I'm pleased you were able to find some time to meet."

Vivian pulled her lips over her dentures in a nervous frown, wondering if he was scolding her for waiting this long.

"Per our code on the telephone, I did find what you had asked me to find."

He picked up something that looked like a large negative of a photograph from the top of the pile and handed it to her. Vivian stared at what turned out to be a photostat copy of a marriage certificate from the year 1923. Fifteen years before she'd married Edward. Eyes frantically darting around the details, they landed on the name of the groom: John Edward Dalton.

"Oh, now, see here," she said quickly, shifting the candy to her cheek. She pointed to the name of the groom, as she uncrossed her ankles and leaned forward in the chair with excitement. "This is someone else. This isn't Edward."

For a few seconds the lump wedged in the middle of her chest loosened as she held her index finger firmly on "John." She could've cried with relief. That wasn't her husband's name. But Mr. Don McAfee leaned back in his chair with his fingers tented against his chin and shook his head slowly at her.

She pulled the sheet back in front of her face and ran her index finger along the other details. The groom's date of birth, the same as Edward's, and the place of birth, the same as Edward's. It couldn't be a coincidence. She swallowed the peppermint.

"John Edward Dalton," she read aloud, her breath an uncomfortable burst of mint.

Edward's given name was Edward, and his middle name was George, after his father George. There was no John in his name. THERE WAS NO JOHN IN HIS NAME! Edward *George* Dalton. *Georgie Porgie, pudding and pie, kissed the girls and made them cry.* Vivian had no idea where the name John had come from, but it seemed to her a sure sign he was trying to hide something, even if he hadn't bothered to change his birth information. An icy shiver ran under her skin and her mouth felt parched, but still minty, as she scanned the rest of the license. The name of the bride was Mildred Fischer.

"Mildred," she said aloud, and pulled a face as if she had just swallowed a glass of ipecac instead of the peppermint. "She sounds fat."

McAfee threw up his hands and raised his eyebrows as if to say, *She just might be.* Vivian smiled at him and looked back down at the photostat, biting the inside of her lip to keep from crying. She needed to feel like someone was on her side right now. Edward had been married to Mildred when he took Vivian out riding in his Model A. Edward had been married to Mildred when he'd proposed to Vivian. Edward had been married to Mildred on their wedding day.

"I found where she's living now," McAfee said in a gentler tone, speaking slowly, as if she might be frightened away like a bunny rabbit.

"You did what?" Vivian gasped, dropping the photostat, her pocketbook and gloves on the floor next to a pile of file folders. She wondered how he ever kept all those records straight.

"I found Mildred," he offered simply, in his deep baritone, as he rocked back in his office chair, his delicate hands clasped behind his head. "No extra charge."

"Well, garsh," Vivian said, feeling awfully sick and not too sure she wanted to know where Mildred was. She tried to breathe normally as she lifted the photostat from the floor and placed it on the corner of the messy desk. She couldn't be sick in front of Mr. McAfee.

Mildred Fischer. Mildred Fischer Dalton Taggart, as it were. Fat Mildred, now the ex–Mrs. Taggart, and ex–Mrs. Dalton, was still living in Syracuse, New York.

"Stayed near the scene of the crime, so to speak," Mr. McAfee joked.

"Eh." Vivian attempted a courtesy laugh, as she leaned down to pick up her pocketbook and gloves. She didn't want to seem rude.

The office seemed to be getting smaller and smaller and Don McAfee and his messy desk appeared to be swaying as Vivian withdrew the stack of bills from her pocketbook and aimed them in the direction of the desk. She slipped on a pile of papers on her way to the door, but caught herself in time, steadying herself on the broken coatrack next to the file cabinet.

"Mrs. Dalton, call if you need anything," the baritone voice boomed after her as she hurried away from the office that had shrunk down to a mouse hole behind her. Holding one hand on the wall, she teetered through the south end of the factory to get to the parking lot, the smell of chocolate filling her nostrils. It would never be the same for her after this, that smell. Chocolate. She would always associate it with this. This personal disaster that was ruining her life.

She made it to the Buick, opened the door, and slid onto the icy leather of the front seat, pulling the door shut. Breathing in and out and staring straight ahead over the steering wheel, she sat there. Watching her breath crystallize in the air, and remembering how she'd once sat in Edward's Model A doing the exact same thing on their very first date. The windows of the Buick had iced over while she was inside the office, and she knew she'd need to get out and scrape them off if she expected to be able to see while driving home. But first, she wanted to see what it felt like to get close to freezing to death. Alone.

Chapter 21

Charlotte waited until she was alone in the house to sneak up to her mother's weird office attic room. Her curiosity had previously been tempered by the fear of what she might find in there. She was reluctant to visit the room in much the same way she'd be reluctant to reach her arm into a dank, rotting log in the middle of the woods out at Christmas Run Park, but late last night, well after her mother had come home, she'd heard an incessant *rat-tat-tat-tat*-ing of the typewriter and wondered what it was that was so urgent her mother had to be typing it at three o'clock in the morning.

She stepped softly over the rug that ran along the upstairs hallway, and tiptoed up the short four-step staircase to the attic level, and then tiptoed some more over to the tiny terrifying attic room. The door opened with a loud creak. It wasn't a rotting log, but the room was cramped and musty, and for some reason smelled like cigarette smoke. Charlotte quickly crossed over to the desk, leaned over the typewriter, and pushed up the window sash. The air that slowly eased in through the window was frigid but clear.

She lowered herself into the sturdy wooden chair and inhaled the chilly air into her nostrils as her arm rested on a stack of pages next to the typewriter. She wasn't sure that she wanted to look at the stack just yet, so she let her eyelids close as she listened to the clattering of a trash can being dragged out into the alley by one of their neighbors. *Just rip it off, like a Band-Aid*, she told herself, and then turned her attention to the pile.

Dear Sirs,
  Can you please confirm if Edward Dalton was a student at the College of Wooster between the years . . .

Dear Sirs,
  I would like to know if you could tell me if Edward Dalton enlisted in the Army on . . .

They were all like that. Page after page of earnest pleas for information. Letter after letter typed to various civic and governmental agencies, inquiring about everything from her father's educational enrollment to his military service to his work history. The letters looked like first drafts, with many words run through with *x*'s. Charlotte peeled back page after page of the letters with her father's name somewhere in the body, and her mother's name in signature at the bottom. She shook her head and wondered if her mother had gone crazy.

In a separate, much smaller pile, behind the large pile, she found several pages of her mother's poetry. They were simple little poems, about flowers and butterflies and that kind of thing. These, Charlotte had already known about. Her mother had even submitted them for publication in *The Daily Record*'s Spindrift column. Some had been accepted and printed. Like the one on top of the pile:

Blue Monday

I wish I were a weather vane
Then I could vanish this quandry
Of brilliant sunshine versus rain
And know when to do my laundry!

Charlotte coughed out a guffaw, then dropped the clipping and slapped both palms to her forehead. She slid her palms down over her eyes and then down her cheeks, pulling the skin into a horror face the way she used to when she tried to make her little cousins laugh. *Oh, God.* So embarrassing. But there was a part of Charlotte that was a little proud. *Mother had even thought to use the word "laundry" instead of "the warsh."* She smiled to herself.

She picked up the clipping again, holding it with fingers and thumbs in front of her face as she propped her elbows on the little table. The editors at the Spindrift committee weren't exactly working overtime. "Quandary" was misspelled. She wondered if her mother had looked up the word in her dictionary. "Quandary" didn't seem like a word her mother would have used. For someone who claimed to hate books, her mother spent a lot of time on something some might consider literary. That was sort of a quandary.

If her mother had submitted a poem and *The Daily Record* published it, she'd go swanning around the house humming to herself and smiling at things that normally didn't warrant smiling. Like the sepia photograph of Grampy and Grammy Kurtz in front of the fence at their farm; an even more somber version of American Gothic.

On the other hand, if her mother had submitted a poem and it wasn't accepted, Charlotte would find her sitting at the kitchen table squirting Reddi Wip onto graham crackers and eating them one after the other. Those were a couple of pretty good indicators of her mother's unpredictable moods. If she was just a little bothered, she'd be eating the graham crackers. If she was very bothered, she'd be in her apron, banging around the kitchen baking something. But there was a third level to her mother's anger.

That night, after dinner, Charlotte had been on the way to the bathroom to brush her teeth when she'd heard a loud thump

from her parents' bedroom and then a faint whine. She peeked
through the keyhole, absolutely against her better judgment, and
saw her mother with a pillow pressed up against her face. She
was screaming into the pillow. Charlotte had slowly backed away
from the door and continued on her way to the bathroom. Then,
the next day, she had come home from school to find a pan of
seven-layer bars cooling on the counter, and two empty graham
cracker boxes in the kitchen trash can.

For a double recipe of "7 layer Cookies":

Have on hand:

1 large pkg, Nabisco Graham Cracker Crumbs
2 large baking pans (9x13)
~~1 Large pkg. Chocolate bits~~
1 " pkg. Butterscotch bits
At lease ½ pound butter.
1 Large pkg shredded Coconut
3 Cans Eagle Brand _Condensed_ Milk
About 2 cups chopped Walnuts.

1. Very slowly, melt the butter and stir in the
graham cracker crumbs, thoroughly mixing.
2. Evenly divide the crumbs into each pan.
3. Pat down all over the pans
4. ~~Scatter the chocolate bits lightly all over each
pan (A hand full at a time)~~
5. Then, scatter some of the butterscotch bits, all
over.
6. Then, scatter the coconut, lightly covering.
7. Follow this with the rest of ~~the chocolate bits~~
and the rest of the butterscotch bits.
8. Then, the rest of the coconut.

9. Open the three cans of Eagle Brand milk and pour over the coconut, being careful not to get too much along the edges. (One can per pan and divide the third can evenly over it

10. Then, scatter the chopped nuts all over each pan.

11. Have the oven preheated at 325 degrees and bake the two pans 50 to 55 minuts.

12. When the top of each pan shows a light brown and they are sort of bubbly, remove.

13. Cool <u>slightly</u>, and with a sharp knife, cut the cookies. Be sure to loosen along the edges.

14. Wrap in saran wrap and foil—put in the frigerator—or the freezer.

If Charlotte had had any idea about Mrs. Betty Miller's gossip-filled afternoon tea party, and what was coming, she might have started banging around the kitchen to whip up her own batch of cookies. Or perhaps a wedding cake would've been more appropriate.

Chapter 22

Ah, to be a blushing bride. A girl's wedding day was one of the most special days of her life, wasn't it? No one talked too much about the second wedding day, though, especially if you had to marry the same man all over again because he'd been a bigamist the first go-round. The blush of humiliation was a different shade altogether, and one that Vivian would say was unflattering to her skin tone.

There would be no cleaning up this can of worms, now that it'd been opened. Vivian had had to tell Charlotte first, before she sent the details for the story to Harry Sweeney at *The Daily Record*. She hadn't wanted to surprise her daughter any more than necessary.

The timing wasn't the best, though. If she'd had a full day to herself, to relax and prepare, it would've been better. But life was life, she'd had to work at the switchboard, and she'd been too tired to dress it up any better. *What was the point?* she thought. *It's like putting a blond wig on Edward G. Robinson.*

"Your father and I have to get divorced and then remarried because he had a wife he forgot to tell me about."

She'd waited for Charlotte's reaction, preparing herself for hysterics and tears, probably a little blame, since everything god-awful seemed to be Vivian's fault. But poor Charlotte must've just been in shock. She went as white as a sheet, and then the white turned a little green and Vivian helped her into the upstairs bathroom. Mother sat with daughter on the cold tiled floor. She stroked Charlotte's hair as she hung over the toilet, vomiting partially digested seven-layer bars into the bowl. Well, six-layer bars, since Vivian had taken out the chocolate bits.

"Me, too, honey," she whispered softly over Charlotte's bent head. "Me, too."

Vivian wanted off the emotional roller coaster. It had passed the point of Too Much. In addition to the whole mess with Edward, she'd heard Pearl say that one of those Siamese twins, the ones they separated in Chicago in December, had died. Only lived thirty-four days after being separated from his sibling. She'd broken down and wept right there in front of the switchboard. Forehead to forearm, jerking with sobs. Dorothy patting her shoulder. It just went to show that everything in the world was terrible.

Wooster Daily Record
Saturday, January 31, 1953

Daltons Wed Again to Make Sure Knot Is Legally Tied, by Harry Sweeney

The Edward Daltons of Wooster went to the altar a second time today just to make sure that the knot which was tied 16 years ago was done so legally.

Twenty-nine years ago Edward Dalton was a 17-year-old delegate to a Christian Endeavor convention. On a dare he and one of the other delegates were married. When the two returned to their native city of Syracuse, N.Y., and told their respective parents, there was quite a fuss. The marriage was annulled, forthwith, or at least everyone thought it had been annulled.

Dalton came to Wooster and attended Wooster College. He

served in the army from here. He made Wooster his home, settled down, and married a local girl. They have raised a fine daughter, who currently attends Wooster High School.

The first Mrs. Dalton also quickly got over the Christian Endeavor experience, and she, too, wed another person. They had a youngster. Everything would have gone O.K. if her husband hadn't sought to divorce her. In looking into the records he discovered to the amazement of everyone that the first marriage had never been legally annulled.

This discovery of course involved the Wooster Daltons. Mr. Dalton instituted court action immediately to have the first marriage legally set aside. This was done today by order of Judge Darius Martin who heard the case.

The five-day provision was waived by Probate Judge Wolford Hartley and the Dalton knot was tied again today in the sanctuary of the Forest Chapel Methodist Church by their pastor, the Rev. Arlen B. Alsop.

Fortunately Eddie had discussed the whole affair with his family, so, aside from a little embarrassing kidding no harm has been done.

However, as tradition goes, the Daltons will maintain their original anniversary which is June 5, 1937, and will truly rejoice in the knowledge that their friends understand this unfortunate situation.

It was official, and now everyone in Wooster would know about this unfortunate situation. This one would sit right at the top of everyone's lists of scandals so far in 1953. Although Vivian could take a little comfort in the fact that the story wasn't as much of an upset as the Gilbert Ogden bank robbery story had been, and the townspeople weren't affected by it the way they'd been with the robbery.

Publicly, the people of Wooster had emphatically criticized and condemned "that sneaky" Gilbert Ogden for what he'd done, but privately there were some who wondered if they could've gotten away with something like that. Two hundred and fifty thousand dollars. There had been a lot of sucking air through teeth, and exaggerated eyebrow-waggling, and "Whooo-wee, that's a lot of money!" declarations. Their fantasies varied a little, but most imagined their debts wiped clean, their troubles disappearing in the blink of an eye, and life rising up to meet them at every turn, with all that money. New homes, new cars, maybe even a boat, although they'd have to take it up to Cleveland or Sandusky to get it out on the water. Hell, they could just pay somebody to build them a brand-new lake right there in Wooster! With that kind of money, the world could be your oyster, and you could afford to buy all the oysters you wanted at Buehler's. That sneaky Gilbert Ogden had wanted the oyster, saw his opportunity, and seized it (along with Bill Parker's wife), and showed everyone in Wooster that maybe being sneaky wasn't the worst thing you could be. Nearly every one of the telephone operators at Bell had overheard at least one lamentation about Gilbert Ogden's "luck," and they'd all nodded along in secret agreement.

Nobody in Wooster was talking about Vivian Dalton's luck.

"Unfortunate situation," the article had called it. That'd been the understatement of the year, which Vivian had insisted upon with *The Daily Record*. Most unfortunate that Eddie had not discussed the "whole affair" with his family. Yessir. Most unfortunate that Vivian had instead heard about it while eavesdropping on Betty Miller's telephone conversation six weeks ago. Most unfortunate, that nasty little tick of a rumor which had dug its pincers into Vivian and then burrowed its head in deeper as she clawed and scraped at it, trying to pry it loose.

Wooster was *her* town, and he'd humiliated her in *her* town. Everyone, from Vivian's parents to her aunts and uncles to her kindergarten teacher to her doctor, her dentist, the checkout clerks at Buehler's to the college girls who worked at Beulah

Bechtel's to her coworkers at Bell, and everyone else she'd ever come into contact with in that town, now knew that her husband was a bigamist, their marriage hadn't been legitimate, and she'd been a fool.

That was the word she'd felt hanging over her head on her second wedding day. "Fool." Not "bride" or "wife" like on the first one. *Vivian Dalton, fool, pleased to meet you.* Vivian's second wedding day was busier than the first had been. In addition to getting married (again) in the morning, she knew she had to do the cleaning and the washing she usually did on Saturdays, later on. She was sure there'd never been a less romantic wedding. Not only did she not wear a beautiful white dress with a floor-length lace veil, she didn't even try to get a flower corsage to match her eyes this time. But you could bet your ass she wore her best dress and put her face on before setting foot outside the house that morning.

Vivian refused to look at Edward during the "ceremony," if you could call it that. She, instead, directed all her polite attention to Reverend Alsop, who kept pulling at his collar, shifting his eyes nervously back and forth between Vivian and Edward, and repeatedly clearing his throat. Charlotte, their illegitimate daughter, was not there. She'd asked to stay at the house, and before she left Vivian had pulled her close, Charlotte's head tucked under her chin.

After the newspapers had been delivered that morning, with the story about the Daltons, the switchboard at Bell had gone crazy, and the ladies who were working didn't get a moment's peace. The switchboard itself looked like a fireworks display with all the lights, and cords and arms were flying left and right as the operators plugged and unplugged, flipped up and flipped down. They hardly had time to listen in on any of the calls, but when they did they all heard, "Dalton!"

Dalton! Dalton! Vivian Dalton! Edward Dalton! Did you hear about the Daltons? There were people in Wooster who'd never heard of either Vivian or Edward Dalton before that *Daily Record* story, but after Saturday they sure had.

Vivian McGinty's older sister Vera had once said that she was "perpetually craving attention," and Vivian had eventually looked up "perpetually."

Perpetual:
```
1a: continuing forever: everlasting perpetual
motion b (1): valid for all time, a perpetual
right (2): holding something (such as an office)
for life or for an unlimited time
2: occurring continually: indefinitely long-
continued perpetual problems
perpetually adverb
```

Perpetual was how she saw the horror of this godforsaken day. It would never end. The telephone would keep ringing and ringing and she'd have to keep explaining and explaining. Vivian would've grudgingly admitted that she did like attention, compliments on her Beulah Bechtel hat, that kind of thing. Not this kind of thing. She did not want any of this. She did not want to have to get remarried to the man she'd thought was her husband for almost sixteen years. She did not want the entire town of Wooster, her hometown, where she'd been born and raised, to know about her shameful, embarrassing dirty laundry. And she did not want to have to explain everything to her family on the telephone that day. She had to make several attempts at a couple of the calls, because the switchboards were so backed up.

"Sorry, Viv, can you try again later? By the way, how're you doing? You doing okay?"

Vivian's brothers and her older sister had moved out of Wooster by then, to Fredericksburg and Akron, but the news would reach them soon enough. She remembered when she was going to be married (the first time), and how excited she'd been to tell everyone. Vera'd said nobody'd be crazy enough to marry her. The ring Edward had given her had belonged to his mother, whose fingers were unfortunately thick. Edward said thick, Vivian would've said fat. The delicate platinum band with elegant scrollwork surrounding a half-carat diamond slipped right off Vivian's ring finger, so until she could have it properly fitted by Orelin M. White of White Jewelers on East Liberty Street, she wore it with a piece of cloth tied around the back.

She'd pressed her thumb up against the knot in the cloth to hold it steady as she shot her hand out under Vera's nose, and letting out an accidental high-pitched giggle. The sun had been shining brightly through the window over the sink in the McGintys' kitchen, where Vera was filling a glass with water. Vera had jerked her head back, and then slapped Vivian's hand away in annoyance, so Vivian took a step back, cleared her throat, and held her left hand over her right shoulder, fluttering her fingers. Vera'd set her water glass on the counter, turned around, looked at the fluttering hand, and Vivian saw the briefest of scowls before Vera forced the corners to stretch out into a smile. The smile hadn't reached her eyes, though. Vivian had noticed that.

"Well," Vera'd said, her voice much higher and thinner than usual. "Good for you. Congratulations."

None of the responses from any of the other McGintys had been quite as satisfying as Vera's. Pawpy had crowed, "One down, two to go, eh, Vera? Violet?" And Vivian's mother might as well've thrown a barrelful of dirty wash water on Vivian when she suggested that Vera be her maid of honor.

This "announcement" of Vivian's second wedding was going to have to be different, and her only consolation was that everyone'd probably already seen the newspaper and wouldn't be gasping quite so much when she told them over the phone.

She dragged the heavy telephone base to the sofa and set it next to her as she sank into the cushion, which had a lipstick mark on the other side and she'd get to that later. She groaned and looked at her hands. The skin had started to wrinkle, and there were two spots she was calling freckles, but a doctor would've said were liver spots. She hadn't even worn the diamond engagement ring for a long time. It just got in the way when she was baking. She kept it safe in the velvet-lined silver jewelry box on her dresser. The rings on her fingers were the Irish claddagh on the right hand and her plain wedding band on her left.

She cradled the receiver between her shoulder and cheek, twisting the claddagh ring as she waited for an operator.

"Number, please," Pearl Fry's nasal tone came over the line.

Vivian thought the nasal tone made Pearl sound like she was complaining all the time, and that she'd sound less so if she'd sit up straight in her chair at work, but now wasn't the time to worry about that. Forgetting the chaos in the switchboard room, Vivian asked Pearl for some privacy when she connected the call. Not that she would've known if Pearl continued to listen in anyway. Listening and slouching and whining through her nostrils. Some people had no respect for family affairs. Vivian really wanted a cigarette.

"Hello, Mom?" Vivian said when her mother answered the phone.

"Vera?"

"No, Mom, it's Vivian." She rolled her eyes. How could her mother still get the two of them confused?

"Oh, oh," she stammered. "Vivy."

Vivian didn't have a chance to say anything else before the telephone was handed to her father.

"Hiya, Vivy," he said, cheerful as ever.

"Hi, Pawpy." Vivian took a deep breath.

"Aw, now, Vivy, love, you don't have to make a big to-do about it. We saw the paper."

"I . . ." Vivian felt her voice catch, and she bit her lip. She suddenly felt small. Small and overwhelmed.

"Now, nothing wrong with this, I tell you! A wedding, and I didn't have to pay for it!"

"Oh, Pawpy." Vivian laughed through the sob that came out. Spittle sprayed the telephone mouthpiece and Vivian pulled up a corner of her apron to wipe it away.

"There's nothing so bad that it couldn't be worse."

"Uh-hunh."

"You doing some baking today?"

"Yes, sir."

"Attagirl. Whatever it is, bring some by tomorrow, okay?"

And then, like he always did, he hung up the phone. Patrick McGinty didn't feel the need to waste time or words on the telephone, and his family had learned not to take the hang-ups personally. Just like that, the first call was over and Vivian felt like crying with relief. Part of her wanted to run over to her parents' house and curl up next to her dad on the couch like she used to when she was little. She'd felt like that a lot, lately.

Myrtle McGinty always complained that her children never visited, especially Vivian, since she lived just a few blocks away. Vivian winced as she thought of this. That sullen, gloomy attitude of her mother's was contagious. If you spent too much time with her, you'd soon find yourself filled with worry and dread and a general sense that everything was awful, until you were just as depressed as she was. Not quite what Vivian needed at the moment. She was glad her mother had handed off the phone.

She felt a little lighter after talking to Pawpy, so after giving herself five minutes just to breathe and muster some bravery, she made the next call to Violet. *And then I'm done for the day.* That'd be enough. Laura Eagan answered at the switchboard this time and Vivian asked for privacy, like she'd done with Pearl, although Laura was quick to pooh-pooh the thought, in her cutesy baby voice.

"Oh, Vivian, I never listen in on other people's conversations. We're not supposed to do that, you know."

168

Oh, for chrissakes. Vivian rolled her eyes up into her head. She could just picture Laura sitting there, with her eyes opened to their widest, like Betty Boop, and her spine straight as a lamppost. Laura sat up a little too straight, if you asked Vivian. It wasn't like there were any men hanging around the switchboard room. Laura was lying about the not listening, but she was also right. They weren't supposed to do that, you know. What would've happened if Vivian had never listened in on Betty Miller's phone call? Would they still be here, in this mess? Or would she still be oblivious, and more or less happy?

```
Oblivious:
1: lacking remembrance, memory, or mindful
attention
2: lacking active conscious knowledge or
awareness—usually used with of or to
```

Oblivious was one thing, but she also wouldn't have been legally married.

"Hello, Vi?"

"Well, hiiii, how are you?" Violet sounded tentative; careful and cautious, like she was afraid of breaking something just by speaking.

"Have you heard?" Vivian asked, wanting to know just how much she'd have to explain.

"Yes, Vivy, it's just awful, I'm so sorry."

"Well, there's nothing else to be done now. We're married again."

Several seconds of silence passed.

"And you're sure?" Violet finally said, speaking slowly. "You want to stay with him, even after all this?"

Violet had found herself a good man, and had no patience for the ones who weren't.

"You know, Vivy," she went on, "I liked Edward. I liked him all the way up until today. Now he'll have to do a lot of work to get back into my good graces."

Vivian almost smiled at that. Violet imagined herself as something of a lion, but Charlotte called her Aunt Kitty Cat.

"You're sure you want to stay with him?" Violet repeated her question.

Vivian took a deep breath and blew a few stuttered bursts of air that almost became whistles. She was holding back tears.

"I thought about it," (another deep breath) "but, Charlotte's still in school, and we've lived in this house for so long. And we've been together so long. I don't know, I just thought this would be easier."

But then she wondered about the word "easier." What was easier? She was just terrified at the idea of being alone. *This cheese will not be standing alone, Edward! This cheese is going to take a sheep! Or the sheep will take a wife!* Her mind was a tangled mass of thoughts and nothing was making sense. *Cheese, sheep, easier, easier, eeeeeee.*

"Is he there, at home, right now?"

"No. I told him to take Charlotte out to buy her some saddle shoes and take her for a malted."

She'd felt awful about the way she'd told Charlotte. Just dumped it on her like a load of greasy gravy covering up a turkey. And right after she'd eaten the seven (six)—layer bars, the poor thing. That'd been bad. If she were a good mother she'd have had a present for her or something. What kind of present did you give your child when you told them everything they knew about their family was a lie? No matter what the present might've been, it would've just reminded Charlotte of the reason she'd gotten it. The whole thing gave Vivian such a headache.

"He'll find a way to work in a stop at the hardware store, too, I'm sure."

It galled Vivian how easygoing Edward had been about all this. While she'd been tied up in knots, he'd just gone about his daily business, work, errands, Freemason meetings, as if this had all been no more of an issue than if he'd forgotten to take out the trash. *Mildred Fischer was the trash*, Vivian thought, *and the trash had been taken out this morning.* Before their marriage ceremony, Edward had signed a document confirming his divorce from Mildred, so that was done. *Oh, whoopsies, I forgot I had another wife.* That was his story.

"Do you want me to come over?" Violet asked.

"No, thanks, honey. I'm a little tired. I think I might go lie down," she said as she rose from the spot on the sofa she'd been sitting in for the past fifteen minutes. "Could you do me a favor, and call Henry and Will and tell them, and make sure you tell them I'm happy about everything, okay?"

"Vivy, does this remind you of Pawpy?"

Vivian didn't answer right away, but her shoulders slumped.

"The letters, I mean."

"I know what you meant." Vivian heaved what must have been her hundredth sigh of the day, and looked back at the sofa that now had a Vivian-shaped indentation. She took a few steps to the wall, then leaned heavily against it and slowly slid down, curling her legs against herself when she reached the floor.

Vivian didn't know if her father had written all three letters at the same time, but he must've mailed them at the same time. Those three love letters the "wickedly charming Irish *rogue*" Patrick McGinty had written to three different women, while he was married to her mother. At least one of the letters had been for her mother. That'd been a small consolation.

Vivian guessed he'd written the love letters at the same time, but then must've been careless and accidentally put each letter into the wrong envelope. It couldn't have gone any worse if Laurel and Hardy had been postmasters. Each of the three women got a letter that was supposed to go to one of the other ones. "Dear Myrtie" went to Adelia Harvey, and "Dear Adelia" went to Grace Cady, meaning that "Dear Grace" went to Paddy's wife, Mrs. Myrtle McGinty, and no matter how she read it, there just wasn't any way that letter had been meant for her. Her name wasn't Grace. And when Myrtle McGinty read the entire letter and saw the signature was her Paddy's signature, things went very wrong.

Don't get caught, he'd told Vivian about her eavesdropping. *Keep those secrets to yourself.* Oh, Pawpy. The betrayal felt personal, like he'd betrayed the whole family, not just their mother.

Just don't get caught.

Who were those other women? Apparently, as far as Pawpy was concerned, they were all just part of the great freedom he had working on the railroad. Some of what "this great country had to offer," was how he'd put it.

Vivian and her brothers and sisters had always assumed that their Pawpy stopped working for the railroad because he didn't have enough seniority to keep his job, because that's what their parents had told them. After the love letter fiasco Vivian suspected her mother might've demanded he quit that job and find something else to do. Something that would keep him close to home, where she could keep an eye on him.

Keep an eye on him. Like he was a baby with a hand too close to a hot stove. Why did these men need to be watched to behave the way they should behave? Grown men, for chrissakes. She'd have been better able to handle it if it'd been a regular old affair, like the one Farley Dean was having with his trampy blond secretary at the accounting firm. Vivian wouldn't have been happy about that, but it would've seemed at least kind of familiar. How would she have "kept an eye on" Edward before she'd even met him? It just wasn't one of the questions she had thought to ask him during their courtship. What do you think of jazz? Can you make a good bathtub gin? Are you already married?

"It's not . . ." She tried a sentence to answer Violet's question about Pawpy and Mama, but her thoughts were starting to swim. "It's not the same thing."

Pawpy, the railroad, Edward and Mildred, *It's "the farmer takes a wife" not "the sheep . . ."*

"No, no!" Violet blurted out, her words landing like stones tossed into the choppy waters of Vivian's thoughts. "No, it's not at all. I just wondered if it, you know, made you feel like it did back then."

"Yes."

"I'm so sorry."

"It hurts."

"I'm so very sorry, Vivy."

"I'll be fine."

"You sure?"

"I'm sure. Thanks, Vi."

"Okay, then, go get some rest. But call me later if you need to."

"Mmm-hmmm."

Vivian pushed herself up from the floor with a groan and reached over to the side table to place the receiver back in its cradle. She had counted nine steps up the stairs when the phone rang. Violet and her damned sympathy and attention to detail. She always liked to double-check things. Vivian would've let it ring but the noise was grating on her nerves. After the sixth ring she'd made it back down the stairs to the phone.

"Vi, I'm really fine."

"Vivian?" her sister Vera's voice came over the line.

Goddammit all.

But she should've expected it. Vera wouldn't miss an opportunity like this.

"Hello, Vera."

Vera didn't say anything else right away and Vivian wondered if one of her friends at Bell had disconnected the call for her. That would've been good of them. Merciful.

"I've been meaning to call," Vera's voice came back over the line.

Vivian felt renewed irritation for the Bell operators.

"Have you?" Vivian tried not to sound icy, but it was a lot of effort.

"Look, Viv, I just wanted to tell you I was sorry about what happened." Her voice was flat, and to Vivian's ears didn't sound all that sorry. Vera had never really been sorry about anything in her life. Vivian couldn't remember ever hearing her sister apologize, but she sure remembered a whole lot of "I told you so"s.

"Well, there's nothing to be sorry about. It was just a simple misunderstanding." Vivian's eyes widened with her attempt at bright and cheerful. If she'd had her Fire & Ice lipstick handy she'd have given her lips a quick swipe. "I mean, Edward told me all about it. It's all in the *Daily Record* article. I'll have a copy sent to you."

"Vivian." Vera, not fooled by the phony tone, sounded like her usual harsh self again. "I'm trying to be nice."

"Ha!" Vivian barked into the receiver, knowing good and goddamned well Vera was back to her irritated tone, and wasn't trying to be nice. "Well, I should be the one thanking you, then, shouldn't I? I know how difficult it is for you to be nice."

"I take it back," Vera spat, and her tone graduated from irritated to shouting. "Everything always goes your way, and the one time it doesn't, it's 'Oh, poor Vivian, poor, poor, Vivian,' and you still act like a spoiled brat!"

Vivian felt tired. This hadn't been her day. *Your wedding day!* She tried to think of a good response, but before she could, Vera struck again.

"You deserve this, you ungrateful bitch!"

And, with that, Vivian heard a sharp click, disconnecting the call.

She stood there, stunned. The word "bitch" rang in her ears and she held the phone in the air, staring at it. Then she slammed it down onto the base in a delayed response, screaming to the empty room, "YOU'RE THE BITCH!"

No one else was in the house, so Vivian didn't bother with a pillow, but screamed out loud as she stomped up the stairs. She went straight to her hiding place in the bedroom closet and fished out the packet of cigarettes. She took the cigarettes to the tiny attic room, where she pushed open the sash and nudged the table with the typewriter to the side so she could scoot the chair close to the window. Smoking really was a filthy habit, and she didn't want the smell in the room.

As she inhaled and blew the smoke in streams out the window she replayed what she could remember of the conversation. "Bitch." "Everything goes your way." Everything didn't go her way. NOTHING WENT HER WAY!

By the third cigarette her anger had simmered a little. She considered the fact that, even though Vera hadn't said anything nice, the know-it-all also hadn't said, "I told you so." *Goddamned Vera*, she thought. *She makes my ass tired.*

What could Vivian say about her sister Vera? What did anyone say about Vera? She had a strong personality, that was one thing. And a confidence as big as her backside, that was another. She was the oldest, the brashest, and the bossiest of the McGinty sisters. A know-it-all of the first degree, you didn't dare try to argue with her about anything. According to her, what she knew was law. When they were little and would go marching around the backyard, Vera was always the one wearing a pillowcase as a cape and pumping a stick up and down, leading the procession. No one was spared when Vera was in one of her moods. *Henry'll have to pay a girl to marry him. Vivian could dress up as a jack-o'-lantern on Halloween with those teeth of hers. Will could get himself beaten up by a girl. And Violet*, well, Vera never really picked on Violet at all. She was twelve when Violet was born, and Vera usually just treated her like a little doll.

Vivian remembered how her mother always said she'd never have to worry about Vera. Except for when she took up with that boarder the Brinkerhoffs were putting up in their house after the stock market crashed. Vivian heard her mother say she wished Vera had some better options for a beau. "But she's got my stout figure and sloping shoulders, and with that smart mouth she'll just have to settle for whoever settles for her." And Vivian had smirked and silently agreed.

Chapter 23

Betty Miller settled herself into the first pew at Forest Chapel Methodist and rubbed her gloved hands together, waiting for the Daltons to show up. She would have liked to draw attention to the Dalton scandal at proper social gatherings, where she could outdress, outclass, and generally outdo Vivian in every single way, but they did not run in the same circles, so it had to be at church. She was going to make Vivian into a glorious pariah, because her comeuppance was long overdue.

When Reverend Alsop read from James 5:19-20, Betty made loud murmurs of agreement and looked, pointedly, in the direction of the Daltons.

If anyone among you wanders from the truth and is brought back by another, you should know that whoever brings back a sinner from wandering will save the sinner's soul from death and will cover a multitude of sins.

"Wanders from the truth," Betty repeated in a low voice, but not so low most of the people around her didn't hear.

When Reverend Alsop read from Ephesians 5:15-20, Betty nodded her head and looked, pointedly, in the direction of the Daltons' pew.

Be careful how you live.

"Amen," Betty said, while still looking at the Daltons.

If Vivian noticed Betty's decidedly un-Christian behavior, she didn't let on. It drifted up and over her like Reverend Alsop's sermon. Something had shifted inside Vivian. Almost overnight. Was it the wedding yesterday? The conversation with Vera? She couldn't say. She just knew something felt different today, and she wasn't noticing the things she usually noticed. Like Betty Miller.

From her place in the first pew, Betty Miller was doing so much turning and murmuring that a few of the congregation's members were wondering if she might be possessed. She'd murmur and amen, and seek Vivian out with her angry stare, shooting visual daggers in her direction.

But Vivian paid no attention to Betty, the murmurs, the amens, or even the sermon, and, instead, was suddenly far more curious about minutiae she'd never bothered with before.

Minutia:
plural minutiae play \me-'nü-shē-,ē, -,ī, mī-, -'nyü-\
: a minute or minor detail—usually used in
plural <He was bewildered by the contract's
minutiae>

For example, the plaque outside the church, telling everyone when it was founded (1887), or the hymnbook she held during services, turning it over to see the gold stamp that would tell her where it was printed (Plattsburgh, N.Y.). Names, dates, places.

"I don't have any exact dates, just now," Betty Miller was saying from the podium.

Vivian was just barely aware the service had ended, and now Betty was jabbering to the congregation about something.

"Rest a-*ssured*, *my* father, *your* mayor, is working hard to make *sure* the *good* people who had their money *stolen* *will* be re-im-*bursed*. But, do *please* remember. We've *just* celebrated

Christ-mas, and as you *all* know, money is a *little* tight after the *hol*-i-days."

Almost as tight as Betty Miller's smile.

Vivian only saw the tight smile. The words were just an over-enunciated background hum to her. For some of the other members of the congregation, the ones who had never been able to afford sitting in the first five pews, the over-enunciated words were more grating than usual. If J. Ellis Reed was really the bighearted philanthropist his daughter was trying to make him out to be, he'd have reimbursed all the Wayne Building & Loan customers by now, not just the wealthier ones, or the ones who'd complained loudly enough to be heard. Roy Patterson was still making payments on the house he'd inherited from his dad fifteen years ago, Daisy Stucker'd been kicked right off the Stucker farm, and Jacob Starlin, who'd been laid off from the rubber factory some years back, feared he'd never own his property outright. He could hardly even keep his own wheelbarrow in his backyard.

Wooster and all its goings-on, once terribly important to Vivian, had lost their glossy appeal. She was suddenly consumed with a burning desire for information directly related only to her.

Every telephone call she would put through at Bell would now be listened to with extra squinting at the board, hoping to hear that unfamiliar voice again, to figure out who had called Betty Miller with that story. And every waking moment would be spent planning and plotting, and poring over the correspondence she had sent and received about Edward and his past. Even as they sat side by side in church that day, Vivian was only vaguely aware of her husband in body, but the facts and history of his life were marching across her mind as she mouthed words, just not the words to the hymns everyone else was singing. She was making plans.

Chapter 24

Betty Miller hadn't planned to address the congregation today, but she'd heard a few pointed grumbles directed at her that she was certain were related to her father's bank and the tardy reimbursements. She noticed Vivian Dalton didn't seem to be paying attention at all, but the Daltons had already gotten their money back, hadn't they?

Betty had been surprised and, she'd daresay, impressed yesterday, when the *Daily Record* article was published, telling the rest of Wooster about the Dalton scandal. She had then congratulated herself on having beaten the newspaper to the punch. At least with the people who mattered. She'd felt a great rush of euphoria as she'd made the announcement at her afternoon tea party, with all the ladies' powdered and rouged faces turned toward her in eager anticipation.

Vivian's timing in placing the story in the *Record* had been off by about two weeks, but Betty would grudgingly give her credit for having had the presence of mind to stem the flow of the hemorrhaging gossip by controlling the story. Well, good for her. Controlling the story was ninety percent of the battle, except, sadly for Vivian, the battle had ended. She was left with the carnage now.

Betty had kept a watchful eye on her own husband after hearing about Edward Dalton's secret first wife. What a strange story it had been, and to happen to a relatively normal family right there in Wooster. After her tea party, the rest of the women eyed their own husbands with the same low-level suspicion. How well did you ever really know your spouse?

Take Clara Weaver's husband, David, who spent long hours "at the office," and it couldn't have been all work he was doing, because he wasn't that successful an insurance agent. But it did take a certain kind of personality to get people to buy coverage they'd never need, and that was really David's problem. Or then there was Miriam Thompson's husband, Rex, who didn't have David's personality issues, but had other problems. He was the state representative for District 1 in the Ohio House. That position did require travel to Columbus, Betty supposed, but the drive was only ninety minutes, and Betty really didn't think it was necessary for him to keep an apartment there. And then there was Marilyn Dean's husband, Farley, who, as we knew, had given his secretary an outrageous Christmas bonus that year, and it had nothing to do with her bookkeeping skills. If you asked Betty, their behavior had all started to look incredibly suspicious.

Betty watched Charles undress for bed in the reflection of her gold-framed vanity mirror. He pulled on the new red and green pin-striped pajama bottoms "Santa" had brought him for Christmas, taking too long to tie the drawstring. He then slid his once-muscular arms, one by one, into the pajama shirt and proceeded to fasten the buttons, unaware that Betty was watching him. He missed the first button, so by the time he reached the last buttonhole there were no more buttons to fasten. He poked a finger through the lonely buttonhole and wiggled it, then shrugged, kicked out of his leather slippers, and climbed into his side of the bed.

Betty inhaled sharply through flared nostrils, rolled her eyes, and let a careful stream of breath out through her lips, keeping them just slack enough that she didn't whistle like a teakettle.

She then looked back at her reflection, twisted the lid off the jar, and dipped her fingers into the cold cream, rubbing it in careful circles over her face. She could not imagine Charles ever doing anything truly scandalous. The sheer laziness displayed with the button-fastening extended to other things as well.

She supposed Charles had always been that way, but a girl's vision was blurred at the beginning of love affairs, wasn't it? She wouldn't say she regretted marrying Charles; after all, he came from one of Wooster's very best families. Vivian Dalton obviously hadn't considered breeding when she made her choice. If she'd had any sense she'd have chosen Betty's brother John, although Betty promised herself she wasn't going to think about that anymore because her analyst had advised against thinking of anything that made her temple veins throb, and now they were throbbing again because, *How dare that common slut turn down Johnston Reed!*

Charitable Thoughts, she reminded herself as she pinched the skin beneath her wrist. That was the phrase Dr. Charlton had suggested. *Charitable Thoughts, and pinch beneath the angel charm on your wristwatch.* Betty shut her eyes and forced another sharp inhalation through her nostrils, and then another, and one more, until her blood pressure returned to normal and her veins ceased to throb.

She reminded herself that she and Charles had four beautiful children. (Not that the Daltons' daughter Charlotte wasn't a lovely girl, she really had very good manners, if Betty were being completely honest, but she did have a tendency to slouch, but Charitable Thoughts!)

Betty had often thought she might want to write her memoirs when she reached her later years. She had a lot of advice to offer young girls and women everywhere. Thoughts about posture and breeding and manners, as well as her own life story. Although, if she were to write her memoirs, she wasn't sure she would be completely honest about everything, unless her later years became her golden years, and she could finish the final chapter on her deathbed.

If things had gone differently in her youth, she might have married someone else altogether. But she had married Charles. All part of God's plan! Perhaps, if she hadn't gotten into trouble, she might have, *might have*, chosen someone else to spend her life with.

And, just every so often, she let her mind wander into an imaginary, unwritten chapter in her not-yet-written memoirs. A chapter where she'd lay her soul bare, and admit on the imaginary printed page that Charles's family money and social standing had taken precedence over a stronger urge deep inside her, all those years ago.

She hadn't thought about him in years (another lie). She couldn't even bring herself to think his name, she could only think of him as *that urge*, because of the way the memory made her feel. (That was true.) Uncontrolled. She was uncomfortable with the involuntary response of her body when she imagined his face hovering over hers, his strong arms pinning hers down as they both laughed, and she could almost smell him as she remembered. The mixture of the pleasant with the masculine and the acrid.

Her eyes closed and the chapter continued writing itself in her mind as she took another deep breath through her nostrils, half expecting to smell *that smell*. That smell was the real reason she had to have Dolly take the car to the filling station. Because she couldn't be around *that smell*. But when she inhaled in front of her vanity mirror, in the bedroom she shared with her well-bred, snoring husband, all she could smell was the cold cream.

That foul, grossly inebriated Santa Claus, endangering the innocence and wonder of Wooster's children, and polluting the very idea and spirit of Christmas. Jesus Christ was not born in a straw-filled manger in Bethlehem so that some filthy, drunken hobo could wreak havoc in the toy department of Freedlander's and desecrate the holiness of Our Lord and Savior's special day.

That was what she had said to all her friends. That was what had gotten him fired. Wooster was *her* town and he had some nerve showing his face and bringing *that smell* with him. To taunt her, to tease her, to *remind* her.

But that was all in the very, very distant past, and now she was Mrs. Charles Miller and she had a rock-solid toehold in the very firmament of Wooster, Ohio. And if Charles ever forgot that, if he ever took their marriage, their children, or their perfect life together for granted . . . if he ever decided to take a little wander, to test the waters in someone else's swimming pool, like Farley Dean or any of the other ones . . . She looked again at the now-sleeping mound and was almost one hundred percent certain he wouldn't.

But, if he did . . . she narrowed her eyes at her own reflection in the mirror, staring back at her like a sinister Japanese geisha girl from one of those god-awful movies they used to show at the, oh, what was the name of that theater? It wasn't important. If Charles Miller ever did anything to embarrass the family, she would have her father on it faster than you could say "Daddy's girl."

It didn't occur to Betty to wonder, *How well did you ever really know your father?*

Chapter 25

Charlotte Dalton had learned a little more than she cared to about her own father, and the Monday after the newspaper story was published, she refused to get out of bed, and who could blame her? Vivian had opened the door to her daughter's room and had seen a lump under the floral-sprigged bedspread, which was pulled snugly over the lump's head.

"Charlotte?" Vivian looked around the room at the disarray. Clothes thrown on the floor, over the chair, records out of their sleeves, books everywhere.

"Urmph."

"You're not going to school today? It's Groundhog Day." She made a halfhearted attempt at little animal squeaky noises she thought might've sounded like a groundhog, but there was no answer from the lump.

"Charlotte," Vivian singsonged. "If you don't come out, we'll have six more weeks of winter."

No response.

"Fine, then." Vivian's tone dropped back to normal, because it wasn't her fault their family was in this mess, and she didn't have time to go out of her way to entertain Charlotte. "I'll telephone them and let them know you're sick."

Another grunt from under the covers.

"Since you're staying home, I want you to clean up your room."

Vivian's rage had been personal and private, but now that the story was out in the open for all to see, the rage had melted and cooled a little into a hardened shell of shame and humiliation. She couldn't let all of Wooster see her as the angry wife (newly-wed!) because it would send the message that she hadn't really known about the first marriage before everyone else did. She'd made sure Harry Sweeney made it damned clear in his article that she knew everything. *I know people.*

Vivian, much as she wanted to, could not stay curled up under the covers of her bed like Charlotte. She was not a child anymore. She cooked up a pot of oatmeal, slid one bowl in front of Edward and the other in front of herself. They ate their oatmeal in silence, the newlywed Daltons: Edward with his nose in the paper, Vivian with her nose still very far out of joint.

As she stood on the bathroom tiles, holding her dentures in her palm and brushing over them with a toothbrush, she gave herself a little pep talk. *We're going to figure this out, all right.* After inserting her teeth and patting her mouth dry with a hand towel, she swiped the Fire & Ice lipstick all around her lips, and blew herself a forceful kiss in the mirror. She then descended the thirteen steps to the hall closet, which Edward had left open in his hurry to leave the house before her, and pulled her wool coat from the hanger. She fastened the buttons at the front door, tilted the brim on her Prussian-blue Beulah Bechtel hat, and held her head high as she walked to work. Heaven help the first bitch to give her a pity stare, because Vivian Dalton was not in the mood today.

Charlotte had ignored her growling stomach until she heard the front door close twice. The first time was her father heading to work, the second was her mother. Since her father had already left the house, the second door-closing had just been a snug pump. For the latter half of December, and all of January, if her mother left for work first, the door would be slammed so fiercely it rang through the house, peeling paint off the frame and sending a shudder through the windows, rattling them in their sashes, and now Charlotte finally understood why.

Two slices of buttered toast and a large glass of orange juice calmed the growling of her stomach, and gave her a little energy to face her reality. She glanced over at the cookie jar, which was full to the brim with the Nestlé Toll House Congo Squares Mother had baked the day before. "Baking calms me down!" For some reason she'd made them with butterscotch chips instead of chocolate, which made Charlotte wonder if the government was suddenly rationing chocolate. She hadn't seen or smelled any in the house in weeks.

Charlotte now considered the sheer volume of baked goods that had been produced in the Daltons' small kitchen over the past month and a half. Her mother had run through her full arsenal at least twice. Nestlé Toll House Congo Squares, sour cream cookies, seven-layer bars, peanut butter cookies with the forked crisscrosses, the Christmas fruitcakes. She'd also made divinity fudge before Christmas, and Charlotte idly wondered if that counted.

All in all, there had been a lot of "calming" going on in the kitchen that Charlotte would've said was more delicious than it was effective. Her mother was nowhere near calm.

Left hand sliding up the banister and right hand brushing bits of Congo Square crumbs from her lips, Charlotte slumped back upstairs to the bathroom. Her reflection in the mirror stared dully back at her as she guided the toothbrush over her teeth in careful arcs. *This is what a bastard looks like. Baaaastaaaard, baaaastaaaard.* She poked the bristles between her teeth in an effort to dislodge the walnut pieces. *That's really what you are, but you should stop feeling sorry for yourself, bastard.* She said the word "bastard" repeatedly in her head as she rinsed the paste from her teeth, and the more she thought about it, the less meaning it had.

She wandered into her parents' room and stared at the bed, with its white chenille bedspread pulled perfectly taut over the surface, like the smile her mother had been showing everyone since December. That frightening, tight, angry smile in Revlon Fire & Ice.

Charlotte picked up a tube of lipstick from the dresser and circled it around her lips. It was a bright pink that her mother never wore anymore. *Pink Champagne* was what the faded label said. She went and opened the closet and lightly skipped her fingers over the dresses and shirts on hangers, releasing the smell of her mother's perfume, which hung with the clothing. Lily of the valley. She dropped to her knees and reached for the boxes behind the three pairs of carefully lined-up shoes. The boxes were full of photographs of their family. Charlotte in the backyard, dressed in her Easter bonnet and flouncy dress, smiling. Charlotte and Mother next to the towering sunflowers in the garden. Mother and Dad on the dock at Little Sodus Bay in their bathing suits, smiling. Mother and Dad standing next to his old Model A Ford, smiling. Smiling, smiling, smiling. Appearances had always been most important to Vivian Dalton. Charlotte had been surprised her mother let her stay home today. She only did that when Charlotte was actually sick. She didn't want people wondering what was wrong with her daughter if she was absent from school too often or for too many days in a row. Appearances were everything to her. How people perceived her family. *Her family.*

Charlotte popped off the lid of a hatbox that sat on the floor of the closet, and there, instead of a hat, sat a half-used pack of Lucky Strike cigarettes and a little brown notebook. She crossed her legs, slid one of the cigarettes from the pack, and held it between her lips. It did not taste good, but she liked the way it felt. She tucked another cigarette behind her ear, then reached for the little brown notebook and opened to the first page. It was blank. She flipped to the second page, which was also blank. As was the next page, and the next page. She leaned forward and flipped faster until she reached a marked page. The first fifty pages of the little notebook had been left blank, and then when her mother started writing, on page fifty-one, it appeared to be notes on the family background. Hard facts. Birth, marriage, and death dates for parents, grandparents, aunts, uncles. Some were people Charlotte had never heard of. Charlotte skimmed through the information and turned the pages until she found this:

29 Inquiries
Churches
Syracuse.
James Street Methodist
3027 James Street, Syracuse, N.Y.
*Plymouth Congregational Church
232 East Onondaga Street, Syracuse
Records for September 14, 1922, show membership for George
and Letty Dalton 224 W. Yates St., Syracuse.

George and Letty Dalton. Charlotte's grandparents, whom her mother hated.

No membership what so ever, for an Edward
G. Dalton (OR John Edward)

No Mrs. Mildred Fischer Dalton, either!

Her mother had written twenty-nine letters to churches in the Syracuse area. The cigarette dropped from Charlotte's lips and she blew a low whistle and pulled her legs back under her as she rocked forward on her knees, her head brushing the bottoms of her dad's shirts. Her eyes were starting to hurt from all the squinting at the notebook, but she couldn't stop.

The notes weren't only research and family history, although there was a section labeled "Geneology," which Charlotte noted was misspelled. Beyond the Dalton family vital statistics, and beyond the addresses of churches and transcribed legal notifications and details about life insurance, there were a handful of quotes, such as:

> *Love is the emblem of eternity;*
> *it confounds all notion of time;*
> *effaces all memory of a beginning,*
> *all fear of an end.*
> MADAME DE STAËL

Then there were pages and pages where her mother had written titles of popular songs from earlier times.

> *1924*
> *"Yes Sir, That's My Baby"*
> *"It's Three O'Clock in the Morning"*
> *"No One but You"*
> *"Margie"*

There were more. And there was a page for 1925, and one for 1926, all the way through 1934 (although for that year there was only one song, "Stars Fell on Alabama"). Scribbled in the corners of some of those pages were bizarre random facts.

> *"Slang: 'So's your old man,'" "Portable radios introduced," "also 'Car heaters!'"*

Charlotte barked out an involuntary laugh at "Car heaters!" because it just sounded so absurd. Why the exclamation point? And, speaking of points, what was the point of all this? Was her mother reliving her own youth? The good old days, before she met Dad? Was she bemoaning the loss of her love affair with

Dad? Was she trying to reconstruct the love affair between him and his first wife? If there had even been one?

Charlotte felt a wave of nausea wash over her, as if she had just eaten a whole pan of Nestlé Tollhouse Congo Squares in one sitting. She briefly gagged at the memory of the seven-layer bars in the toilet bowl after her mother had told her the news. She placed the notebook on the carpeted floor of the closet. She felt ill. She worried that her mother was ill. She looked tired all the time, like she hadn't slept in a year, and now she was smoking and keeping a secret crazy little brown notebook.

Why can't my family be normal? Like "Ozzie & Harriet"? Or "My Little Margie"?

The little brown notebook was like a window into her mother's mind, and the more Charlotte read it, the more she wanted to pull the curtains closed on that window. Pull them closed and sew them up with a zipper that she could lock. She could see the change in her mother's temperament from page to page. The handwriting betrayed her frame of mind. When her mother wrote in cursive script, it was really quite pretty. She had beautiful, flowing penmanship, even if not everything was spelled correctly. But Charlotte could see, in the transition from cursive to print, the anger pouring out into the book. The more inflammatory passages were highlighted by aggressive pen marks that almost ripped the page. Exclamation points and underlined words filled the lines in front of her as she read through details that seemed to be nothing at first, but obviously weren't "nothing" to her mother.

Letter dated January 27, 1953, from Leahy, Mills, Vickery & Ahern states that the writer (and signed as such by Mr. Ahern) has no record, nor the knowledge of any application for an annulment proceeding, or Divorce proceeding which is said to have been contemplated by Edward George Dalton, or John Edward Dalton. Neither did he have any record nor

*knowledge of same by a Mildred Rose Fischer Dalton or by
the father of the groom, Mr. George W. Dalton. Adding that
he had handled all legal matters for both men since 1922.*

Her mother had borrowed her dictionary recently. Maybe for
"contemplated." Contemplating was something Charlotte had
been doing a lot of in the past few days. Contemplating her
family's scandal, contemplating never returning to high school,
contemplating the likelihood of graduating from high school
if she never went back. Where does someone in a small town
go to escape public scrutiny and scorn? She wondered where
Gilbert Ogden and Flora Parker had gone, if they were still in
the business of robbing banks, and if they had need of a young,
hardworking accomplice. Charlotte was wondering what would
drive someone to rob a bank as she placed the pack of Lucky
Strikes and the little brown notebook back into the hatbox, and
noticed the envelope of money taped to the underside of the
hatbox's lid.

Chapter 26

U.S. dollars to Canadian dollars. Gilbert Ogden kept a close watch on the fluctuation of the exchange rate, and would try to time his bank trips to maximize their funds. Never the same bank twice. His and Flora's top priority, as bank robbers on the lam, was to avoid suspicion. Blending in with, as well as keeping their distance from, the rest of their Toronto neighborhood was another priority.

They had spent significant amounts of time sitting in the window seat on the main level of the house, just behind the heavy crimson damask curtain, observing the comings and goings of the neighbors, and making notes of regularities in schedules, and deciding on the safest, low-activity times to leave the house.

"Does anyone live in that big house?" someone visiting their neighbors might ask. "Well," the neighbors would answer, "we haven't seen them yet, but there's usually smoke coming out of the chimney."

Flora had bought some French language books from the bookstore a few doors down from the third bank Gilbert visited to exchange money. She liked to curl up in the overstuffed chair by the fireplace and read.

"Just like Bonnie and Clyde used to do," she'd say to Gilbert with a curt nod followed by a laugh.

Flora Parker and Gilbert Ogden had to be the dullest outlaws in history. Playing Scrabble and chess, reading Chekhov and Austen, and practicing their *bonjour*s and *au revoir*s, just in case.

Flora had read good things about Quebec. If it got too hairy for them in Toronto, if suspicions were raised about the pleasant, quiet, seemingly invisible people who had moved into the neighborhood just a couple of months ago, they could go farther north, *Although not Montreal*, Flora thought. *Too big*. Heading north would really probably be their only option. They couldn't go back now.

Flora called "checkmate" after two hours of intense play, and Gilbert sighed and leaned back in his chair, cleaning the lenses of his glasses with a handkerchief while shaking his head.

"You're obviously cheating," he said. "But I haven't figured out how."

He hadn't beaten her yet.

"That's me," Flora admitted. "Big cheater. I'm just trying to make you a better loser. You're such a baby about losing."

Gilbert tucked the handkerchief back into his breast pocket and considered this for a moment before giving her a quizzical look.

"Why didn't you and Bill ever have any children?"

Flora's expression changed from cheeky grin, the triumphant, possibly cheating winner of the chess game. All the muscles in her face that had been holding up the cheeky grin went slack, the dimples disappearing completely. She picked up the queen and knocked over one pawn, then watched it roll back and forth on the polished surface of the board. A full minute passed before she spoke.

"We tried."

Gilbert said nothing, but quickly pushed himself up from his chair and went to her. He stood behind her and gently wrapped his arms around her shoulders, bending his forehead down until it touched her crown.

"I'm so sorry," he whispered.

Flora let just a few tears roll down her cheeks before wiping them away with the back of her hand. She was never one to wallow. Things had finally gone their way, and she wouldn't let the past ruin it. Together they had achieved the impossible, and managed to disappear from Wooster without a trace. Gilbert and Flora were now independent, financially secure, and grateful that neither one would have to struggle and scrape for money, or suffer petty humiliations at the hands of ignorant, undeserving fools.

But an even greater goal had been achieved through the clandestine, carefully orchestrated embezzlement of the Wayne Building & Loan. It was one the newspapers hadn't guessed at, and likely never would. It was something that was always in the back of Gilbert's and Flora's minds, a small nugget of truth sitting quiet and undisturbed, as it was at the tender moment the two were sharing in front of the chessboard. It was at that very moment that Flora's husband, Bill Parker, the Bill Parker of the rage and the shotgun and the scorched tire marks, appeared in the doorway.

Chapter 27

Bill Parker had met Flora Jacobs in New York City not too long after the Depression, in the sawdust-strewn backstage basement room where Madame Ososki held her acting classes on Monday and Wednesday mornings. Bill had fallen for Flora instantly, like he had with a number of women. But he told himself this one was different. He'd told himself that with all of them. Flora, with her smooth skin, quiet elegance, and the pronounced dimples in her cheeks that appeared when she smiled, and also when she put on what Bill called her "disapproving face." Although she mainly used that one during scenes. At least he was pretty sure it was just for scenes. Yes, Flora was different. Flora really was the one for Bill. He was at least eighty percent sure this time. Seventy-five at the very least. You couldn't blame him, though. It was hard to be sure with actresses.

Flora hadn't paid any attention to Bill Parker except when they had to rehearse scenes together, and she'd give the politest of smiles and then disappear into her character. There were around thirty people in the class, and even though there were maybe two other girls Bill thought he could be crazy about (or three, okay, maybe three, but Rita didn't always show up), he was always angling to be chosen for a scene with Flora.

In the years following the Depression, many in the New York

City theater community had headed out west, looking for opportunity and dough in Hollywood, but some eager hopefuls still went to New York to try to make it big on the stage. Some of the Broadway theaters had dropped admission prices all the way down to a quarter to try to keep drawing crowds, and repertory productions were sprouting up all over the Theater District to try to keep actors and directors working. Bill and Flora faced each other, or at least watched each other, two mornings a week in class, and over time (twenty-four classes to be exact, Bill counted) they became friends.

Flora was, like him, from a small town, and had arrived in the city around the same time. "Are you also from Nebraska?" Bill had asked her. "Nebraska" was where Madame Ososki insisted every small-town student of hers was from. Her very first small-town student had been from Nebraska, possibly from Broken Bow, or maybe Wahoo or Ogallala, but Madame Ososki was far too busy and creative to trouble herself with the minute details, so he was simply "from Nebraska." In the same way that students from Los Angeles or San Francisco were simply "from California." But Nebraska held a special place in Madame Ososki's heart because of that student, and she also loved to hear herself say, "Nebraska!" with the romantic rolling of the *r*, and the clean break of the *ska!* So, at any given time, Madame Ososki's acting class was made up of students from New York, Chicago, California, or Nebraska, and no one dared argue with her about it.

Both Bill and Flora had had some hits and misses finding success on the stage in the year and a half they'd been there. Bill went to see Flora when she played the Cheshire cat in a small, out-of-the-way production of *Alice in Wonderland*, and she'd be in the audience watching Bill in the few dwindling vaudeville productions he snagged. He was a natural, with his easy, lanky physique and malleable face, and had been praised by some for his physical comedy. Not Madame Ososki. She loathed vaudeville. "Words, Mr. Parker!" she'd cry, raising a forearm in the air. "It's the words that make a performance!" Bill disagreed with her, but stayed in the class anyway because Flora was there.

She let him treat her to meals at the Actor's Dinner Club, because they were free. The club offered free meals to those who couldn't afford to pay, and most of the time Bill couldn't. It wasn't high society, but the food was hot, and since it was free Flora didn't feel obligated to him. They'd also share lunches together and walks through Central Park, and Bill eventually admitted to Flora he wasn't too sure he'd done the right thing in moving to New York.

"I feel a lot more myself in a smaller town," he said.

"I do, too," Flora'd said, and that was when he knew she was definitely the one for him, and he forgot all about those other three or four girls. He hadn't been serious about them anyhow. He never took them to the Actor's Dinner Club. And when Flora'd told him stories about her childhood upstate, and admitted that she, too, sometimes wondered if it had been a mistake to come to the big city, he'd felt something serious. Like her slender fingers wrapping themselves gently around his beating heart.

Flora had finally let herself enjoy Bill's attention after four months of his obvious flattery, and only after he'd stopped flattering the other five girls from their acting class. Flora didn't miss a trick, and she'd frown until her dimples pierced her cheeks when he was winking or waggling his eyebrows at girls around the room. Mistrusting men, especially white men, had been something her mother had instilled in her from a very young age. She'd learned the lessons all black girls learned from their mothers, but her appearance made sure no one would ever know the truth about her unless she wanted them to. "Your eyes and hair," her mother would say, shaking her head in disbelief every time she lifted the fine, straight strands that would barely hold a curl. "They'll spare you."

Flora's being "spared" caused an uncomfortable overlap of relief and guilt that stacked like flapjacks on top of each other as she observed how the world treated her versus the way it treated someone like Lila Carter, her friend from grade school, or Ernestine Brown, the woman who mopped the hallway floors of Flora's New York apartment building. Flora would release the confusion of emotions in her acting exercises and in the characters she played onstage.

It was the vile words of a vicious-minded white shopkeeper hurled at a young black man begging for work that had smacked and stung worse than any blows might have. Hearing them had sent Flora racing down an alley to vomit behind a trash can and collapse in a frustrated, sobbing heap. The world was a cruel place. The next morning Madame Ososki's eyes had shone with tears, her breath held and hands clasped beneath her chin, as she watched Flora's performance.

"*Oy! Kak krasivo!*" Although the class didn't understand the words, they knew this was Madame's highest praise, and although she wasn't looking directly at him, Flora knew Bill Parker's mouth was hanging open in awed admiration. Flora's secret identity, as she sometimes thought of it, made her acutely aware of her environment.

Flora paid attention to everything and everyone, and one thing that stood out in her mind was that Bill Parker had been patient and open and more honest than anyone else she'd met in New York.

She was the one who'd suggested the move. She was the one who'd said, "Couldn't we be together and pursue our love of acting on the stage somewhere smaller? Somewhere less overwhelming, less intimidating? Somewhere easy and friendly?"

"You mean, like Nebraska?" he'd asked.

And she'd laughed, then said, "How about Wooster, Ohio?"

Chapter 28

Vivian's new fur-lined ankle boots crunched over the graying-brown snowpack as she walked to work. All the foot traffic, automobile exhaust, and soot covered every inch of what was once beautiful new-fallen snow. Charlotte sure had the right idea staying home "sick" today. If there was anything bleaker than Wooster in February, Vivian wanted to know what it was. Oh, wait one moment. There was something bleaker. Her marriage. If she'd known the meaning of the word "metaphor" she might've compared Wooster's late winter landscape to her marriage. The once-romantic, charming, and sparkling had sunk and crusted into something bleak, stale, and dirty.

```
Metaphor:
1: a figure of speech in which a word or phrase
literally denoting one kind of object or idea is
used in place of another to suggest a likeness
or analogy between them
```

The new boots were Edward's version of a metaphor. He hoped they could start fresh, following their renewed vows, and was going out of his way to prove to Vivian that she was important to him and that all that "other stuff" was in the past. The boots were the most expensive that Amster's carried, and they'd gone on sale, as it was the end of the winter season. Edward had bought them for Vivian on Saturday. The afternoon of their wedding day. Their second one. She was only sorry he hadn't had to pay full price.

Vivian hugged the sidewalk on the building side in order to pass Clyde Walsh walking arm in arm with Ginny Frazier, who must have finally agreed to go to the A&W with him, and now they were out morning-walking. Well, weren't they just a couple of lovebirds. Vivian sure hoped Clyde wasn't already secretly married. It wasn't an everyday occurrence, but she'd be the first to tell you, it did happen.

If she'd learned anything after the scandal began to leak, it was how quickly the scolding eye of judgment could turn on you. She'd had the awe and respect of the other girls at Bell when they'd figured out how good she was at figuring other people. How she *knew* them. But now?

The rumor'd started to trickle through the phone lines at Bell in the two weeks following Betty Miller's tea party. No one was cruel or outright scornful, but a chilly aloof blanket had dropped over the switchboard room. The smiles had been replaced by uneasy grimaces and awkward coughs, and now that the newspaper article had confirmed it, Vivian was sure work was only going to get more uncomfortable. She wondered if the other girls thought her situation was contagious. Like, if they got too close to her it'd happen to them as well. *Don't get too close, she's got the bigamy!*

She also wondered how long this would go on. Dorothy, Ruth, Laura, Pearl, and the others, they were all acting like Vivian had caught a venereal disease, for chrissakes. *Like syphilis.* The operators at Bell loved a good scandal, they just didn't want it so close to them. Vivian thought if they could find a cure for something like syphilis, some clever scientist needed to work on a vaccine for the bigamy.

"Well, wouldn't that be a fine how-do-you-do?" Vivian over-heard Ruth Craven saying to Dorothy as she entered the room. She might've been talking about Vivian, but she might not.

"I don't know why she's staying with him," Vivian later over-heard Dorothy whispering to Rose Troyer, one of the new girls. Dorothy was most definitely talking about her.

"Her poor daughter!" Vivian overheard Laura cooing to Ruth, in her gooey baby voice, as they came back from their cigarette break.

You know who wasn't acting like Vivian was about to wipe her headset all over their skin with her full-blown case of the marital plague? Maria Tomasetti. Now, how do you like that?

"Vivian, how are you doing?" Maria asked during a late after-noon lull at the switchboard.

"Oh, fine, thanks." Vivian kept her tone breezy and forced a Fire & Ice smile.

"Really? Because, if you need to talk about anything, I'm here."

Vivian kept her eyes on the switchboard, hoping for a blinking light.

"Well, thank you."

"Men are stupid, Vivian."

Vivian felt a tiny spasm of release in her chest cavity, and her forced smile relaxed into a genuine one. She sighed a little before a light blinked in front of her. She nodded gratefully to Maria, and noted to herself that Maria's English was really improving. Vivian plugged the rear key cord into the board.

"Number, please."

On her way home from work Vivian thought about the calls she'd listened to. The only one she'd recognized had been the mayor calling Don McAfee, Vivian's private investigator. That's how she thought of him now, as her own private investigator. She'd had to bite her tongue to keep from saying, "Hello, there!" over the line she wasn't supposed to be listening to. The call hadn't been terribly interesting, just the mayor telling Don to "keep working on our project," like he'd been doing. Vivian assumed the "project" was looking for Gilbert Ogden and Flora Parker. She wondered if they were even still alive, and if they were, what they'd been up to since they'd *absconded*, and how much of that money they had left. Then her thoughts flashed briefly to the hatbox in her closet.

She passed Freedlander's, like she always did, and looked in the window of the toy department, as she sometimes did. They'd changed the display from the miniature kitchen set, with a stove, refrigerator, and doll wearing a red gingham apron and holding a tray of plastic cookies, to a realistic model train set, with an impressive black steam engine, passenger cars, and cargo cars, and a caboose with a tiny die-cast engineer holding a striped cap. She stopped and stared at the train set and the tiny engineer through the glass, and felt a sharp fork of pain in her stomach. Trains always made her think of Pawpy.

Was it worse, what her father had done to her mother? Those letters to those other women? Was that worse than what Edward had done to her? Because not telling Vivian about his first wife was the same as lying to her about it. YES IT WAS!

Humiliation began to feel like something she had inherited from her mother, like her weak teeth or sloping shoulders. One of those had been easy to fix, and the other one could be helped by shoulder pads. What was the fix for the humiliation? Now she understood why her mother stayed with Pawpy. It was funny how easy it'd been, back then, for Vivian to say, "Well, I'd sure leave any man who did that to me." Time had a way of changing your answers for you, didn't it? The idea of ripping the family apart was too raw. Now, there was an image for you. *Ripping apart.*

Her brother Will had once ripped the arm of one of Violet's cloth dolls clean off, and you could see the stuffing inside and the severed threads sticking out from around the shoulder socket. Maybe that was just the best way to look at Edward now. As a doll's arm. The doll just wouldn't look right without it. Maybe Vivian could just put that old doll arm in a little makeshift sling for a while until it healed itself.

As she turned away from the display window to continue on her way home, she thought about the Betty Miller phone call again. Who had called Betty that night with the information about Edward? Who'd been on the other end of that line that night? Who was responsible for throwing the gigantic wrench into the cranking gears of Vivian's life?

She hadn't recognized that voice, but she'd know it if she heard it again. Frankly, the voice hadn't sounded like someone who would have kept up with Betty and her set. The way the lady talked, it wasn't highfalutin and snooty like Betty and the rest of the four-flushers. The voice had sounded more like Ruth Craven, who'd had even less schooling than Vivian had, and talked like one of Jimmy Cagney's gun molls. Thinking about the unknown voice just added another layer to the clouding of Vivian's thoughts, which were starting to feel like a big vat of pea soup. Cloudy pea soup in her head, and a twisted, clenching pain in her stomach. The twisted clenching had just gotten a little tighter with that thought. *Who had made that goddamned call?*

Chapter 29

"Did *he* call *her*, or did *she* call *him*?" Jeannie Thorson was asking Margie Miller, several yards ahead of Charlotte as she walked home after school.

Charlotte's first day back at school after the mortifying newspaper article had been pretty normal, aside from a few raised eyebrows, hushed whispers, and sympathetic nods, which she'd had to weather while fretting about what her mother was doing with a secret envelope full of money.

Jeannie Thorson and Margie Miller were both freshmen, and both four-flushers. Charlotte didn't really know what "four-flusher" meant, any more than her parents did, she just knew they had money they could throw around. Charlotte guessed they'd first go for malteds at the Rexall. Since Charlotte lived south of downtown, she often found herself walking behind them, sometimes pretending she was going for a malted, too.

Jeannie's and Margie's voices were carried by the wind blowing from the south, and although she hadn't intended to listen, Charlotte could hear the conversation as clearly as if she had been having it with them. They'd been talking about Ned Buss and Patty McGrath, and Jeannie had wanted to know who called who first, but Margie had ended that topic with a shrug and a "Who cares?" before changing the subject to the new Eddie Fisher record she was going to buy.

For once, Charlotte already had the latest Eddie Fisher record. On Saturday afternoon (the wedding day) her dad had taken her to the record shop right after Amster's, where he'd bought her new saddle shoes and a nice new pair of winter ankle boots for her mom.

"How about these?" He'd held up the first pair he'd seen on the stand, looking as awkward and out-of-place in the women's shoe section as a dairy cow on roller skates.

Charlotte had scrunched up her nose and shaken her head at that pair, and the next one, but the third pair had been very pretty and fur-lined, and from across the store she'd given him a thumbs-up.

She'd stood next to him at the cash register, holding the box with her saddle shoes, as he took bills from his beaten-up wallet and handed them to the saleslady.

"I'm sorry about all this, honey," he said quietly as he placed a hand on her shoulder. "I really screwed things up for us."

Charlotte had shifted from left foot to right, uncomfortable with her dad's uncharacteristic sheepishness, and aware of the saleslady's sideways glance at them as she punched the keys in the register.

"It's fine, Dad," Charlotte mumbled, not wanting to talk about it in the middle of the shoe store, in front of the powdered, coiffed saleslady. Maybe not wanting to talk about it at all, really.

Charlotte's thoughts zoomed back to the present as Howie Becker roared past in his hot rod, honking the horn loudly either at Margie or Jeannie or just because Howie liked to honk his horn. Because of all the noise, she hadn't heard what Margie said to Jeannie just then.

"My face would be a Russian flag," she heard Jeannie respond as the roar of the motor faded down the street. "The rumor was bad enough, but then the article in the newspaper, ugh. I would die of embarrassment."

Charlotte slowed her pace, suddenly wishing she had stayed at school to work on her history paper in the library. She knew they weren't talking about Ned or Patty anymore, and a flush crept over her face.

"I know," Margie agreed. "If something like that happened to my family, I'd shit a brick."

Charlotte gasped as *shit a brick* hovered invisibly in the air above Jeannie's and Margie's heads. She glanced at the back of Margie's beautiful fur-trimmed coat, half expecting to see a brick drop to the ground. The gasp had alerted the girls that someone was behind them, and to cover for the fact that she had been eavesdropping Charlotte quickly upended the stack of books she was carrying, spilling them out into the stiff snowbank.

"Oh, my God, is that her?" she heard Jeannie say, the words muffled behind a mitten.

"Shhh," Margie hissed at Jeannie. "Just hurry up, let's go."

Charlotte stood up and brushed the snow from the covers and corners of her books. Her embarrassment at being the subject of the gossip had been quickly replaced with shock. *Margie!* Charlotte just couldn't believe something like that had come out of Margie's mouth. *Shit a brick.* Gosh. Charlotte wondered if Margie's mother knew she talked that way. She'd bet Mrs. Betty Miller might shit a brick herself if she'd heard that. Charlotte tried to imagine Margie telling her mother she'd "shit a brick" over something. But everyone knew the things you told your friends sure were different from the things you told your family.

Chapter 30

Vivian told Edward she had to go up to Akron to be with her sister Vera, who was sick.

"Vera?" Edward looked at Vivian like she'd just announced she was going to spend a weekend in hell with Satan.

"Yes," Vivian simply said. "Vera."

Vivian knew Edward wouldn't telephone Vera's house to check on that, because he disliked her even more than Vivian did.

"Well, what's she got?" he pressed.

Vivian didn't answer and just threw him a withering look. She'd seen enough Bette Davis movies to know that sometimes a withering look was all you needed, especially if Gary Merrill had gone and done something really wrong. And she knew the only reason those looks were working was that Edward must've been feeling at least a little guilty. But guilty didn't mean stupid, and now Edward wanted to know what Vera had. Vivian had spent all her time planning the details of this trip and she'd forgotten to invent a believable sickness for Vera; something that her normally workhorse-strong sister might have gotten. *Syphilis*, Vivian thought, and then stifled a snort.

"Well, I suppose I can finish up work early Thursday," Edward said.

"No need." Vivian's tone was breezy. "I'm going by myself."

"You're what?" Edward finally laid the newspaper down and gave her his full attention.

"I am going by myself," she repeated, with almost Betty Miller—esque enunciation.

Vivian didn't wait for any more questions from Edward, and she knew there'd be some. She'd never taken the car out of town by herself. She'd started taking the family car without asking when she went to see Donald McAfee out at the chocolate factory, and Edward hadn't questioned her about it. After that, she'd done it a few more times. Almost as a dare. *I dare you to question me about taking the car, you sonofabitch. Just try me.* But, for whatever reason, he just let her take the car.

She went straight up to their room and began to pack before she lost her nerve. She untaped the envelope of money from the lid of the hatbox that no longer housed the hat. The black straw hat had been passed down to Charlotte ten years earlier for her dress-up box, and the hatbox had become a catchall hiding place for anything she didn't want Edward to find. Her cigarettes, her little brown notebook, and the money she'd saved for this plan of hers.

She guessed she'd need maybe seventy-five dollars for gas, food, and at least two nights at a hotel. She'd started putting part of her Bell money into the taped envelope before Christmas, not knowing what was going to happen to her and Charlotte if the rumors proved true. Well, the rumors were true. Edward had admitted it and apologized. He claimed he'd never known the marriage had been legitimate in the first place. "We were young and just joking around," he'd said. Vivian wondered if she just had the wrong sense of humor. At any rate, Edward was finally in a conciliatory frame of mind that Vivian planned to take full advantage of.

Conciliate:
conciliated; conciliating
transitive verb
1 : to gain (as goodwill) by pleasing acts

2: to make compatible : reconcile <It is hard to
conciliate the views of labor and management on
this point>
3: appease

The Buick pulled into the Sunoco station at a slow crawl, and Vivian pressed the toe of her new fur-lined ankle boot firmly onto the brake pedal to stop behind the powder-blue Lincoln Continental. She had expected to be the only car at the filling station at that hour on a Thursday morning. Saturdays were usually the busy days at the Sunoco. When the Lincoln pulled away, Vivian eased the Buick up next to the gas pump and rolled down her window.

"Fill it please, Albert."

"Sure thing, Mrs. Dalton."

Vivian rolled the window back up and rubbed her gloves together, shivering more out of excitement and nervousness than physical chill. It was something she'd done hundreds of times, filling the car with gas, but today was different. She'd wrapped a couple of ham-salad sandwiches in waxed paper for herself and packed a thermos of coffee, feeling like she should try to drive straight through and just get there before she had the chance to change her mind. She jumped at the knuckle rap on her window. It was just Albert. She rolled the window back down.

"Going somewhere special today?" he asked as she pulled five dollars from her pocketbook.

"Up to Akron," Vivian lied, again, with a smile.

"Well, drive careful! A lot of snow on the roads up there!"

There had been a massive snowstorm in northern Ohio two weeks earlier, and the temperatures had remained below freezing so nothing had melted.

"Thank you, Albert. Have a good day."

Albert Hixson was a little shit who tried to pretend he was a good boy. She knew the type. All polite smiles and brown-nosing to grown-ups, and when no one was watching he'd swipe a pack of cigarettes, stick up a middle finger behind your back, and run his smart-aleck mouth off to his friends. It wouldn't surprise Vivian one bit if Albert ended up married to two, or even three different women at the same time.

She stuck both middle fingers up as she held the steering wheel with her other fingers. No one was around, but it felt good. Gutsy. Strong. East Bowman Street stretched out ahead of her as she left Wooster, and would soon turn into Akron Road. Edward always drove when they went up to Akron, or in the summers when they'd head up to Fair Haven, so Vivian had tucked the Ohio and New York maps under the driver's seat before leaving the garage.

The road looked different from the driver's side of the car. *More control.* She'd been a good navigator on their road trips, checking the route on the map, and calling out the exits well before they'd need to veer off. Edward, on the other hand, was a terrible navigator.

Once, and only once, she'd asked to drive part of the way back from Fair Haven. And, twice, Edward said, "Take that exit, back there," after she'd passed the exit. After the second time, she'd pulled over into the gravel shoulder and slammed the gear into park. She got out of the car, slammed the door, and stomped around to the passenger side and whipped open Edward's door so fast that he fell out onto the gravel.

It'd almost evened things up for Vivian, who hadn't even bothered to suppress her smile, winking at Charlotte, whose eyes and mouth were a shocked trio of O's against the back window. But Edward dusted himself off, readjusted his glasses, and walked around to the driver's side without a word. She considered afterward that that might have been Edward's plan all along, to give her late instructions just to get himself back in the driver's seat. But, no matter.

She was the good navigator, and felt sure that she could make the seven-hour trip just fine on her own. Her little anxieties about dealing with people along the way, without the backup of her husband, were just that. Little. After all, she knew people. She'd be willing to bet that Albert Hixson had pocketed the money she just gave him back at the Sunoco, instead of putting it in the till. She knew people, that was for certain.

And how, exactly, had she *not* known the people (person) in her own life? she wondered, as the light gray of the winter sky almost blended into the endless stretch of snow-covered fields along Akron Road. The woman who prided herself on her keen understanding of people and their personalities. Ha. That was rich, now, wasn't it? She wondered if she'd have been any smarter about it if she'd had the chance to finish school. It always weighed on her, the education she'd missed.

The seven hours were long ones, and with no one in the car to talk to, Vivian fiddled with the radio until the static broke and a song came through, or in the long stretches between radio signals she'd talk to herself, noting things she passed on the drive: cars, farmhouses, wildlife. It seemed the only wildlife out at this time of year were crows, cawing and flapping up out of the tops of the naked trees of the woods that lined the snowy highway.

Four and twenty blackbirds, baked in a pie, Vivian thought.

Now, there was something she hadn't tried baking. Blackbird pie. She thought about baking for a few more miles, and then began singing softly. When she realized there was no one in the car to tell her to keep it down, she sang loudly and lustily, laughing at herself when she couldn't hit the high notes, "*my arms wound 'round you tight*," and her voice would squeal or knock mightily against the wrong notes. If a car was passing the Buick in the other lane she'd rush to clamp her lips shut and try to sing without moving them, like Edgar Bergen with Charlie McCarthy, but then as soon as the car was out in front of her she'd go back to full volume, holding the notes until her ears were ringing. "*And staaars fell on Alabama laaaast niiiight.*"

"*Night and daaaaay, you are the one . . .*"

"I'll get by, as long as I have you."

She sang lots of songs. Lots and lots of songs. And when she was worn out from singing, or if some of the words hit too close to home, she'd cry. Cry for the marriage she'd thought she had, and the life that had gone too wrong.

"I can't give you anything but love, baby . . ."

She only had to pull over once, when she'd been crying so much that her nose was running and she couldn't reach her purse, which had slid over against the passenger side of the front seat, to get to her handkerchief. She'd put the car in park, but left the motor running. The outside temperatures were below freezing and she needed the car's heater on, and also didn't want to risk not being able to start the car again if the motor got too cold too quickly. She finished blowing her nose and then unscrewed the thermos and took several large gulps of coffee before unwrapping one of the ham-salad sandwiches.

Lunch restored some of her energy. She took a packet of Sen-Sen out of her pocketbook, tore open the top, and shook out a handful of the tiny licorice pieces. As she chewed, the licorice wafted into her nostrils and stung her eyes. Wasn't it funny how smells could turn your mood right around? She rolled the top of the packet over to keep the rest of the pieces from spilling out, and returned it to her purse, then slid back into the driver's seat to get back out on the road.

It was two full hours before another bout of self-pity struck. As the tears began to flow, she reached for the rearview mirror to see if she really looked all that bad while crying. It was probably a skill to work on—looking attractive while crying. She'd have to practice. Then she fumbled with the latch on her pocketbook with her right hand, searching for the Sen-Sen while steering the white wheel of the Buick with her left.

Vivian had never checked into a hotel all by herself. She and Edward had only stayed in a hotel a few times in all the years they'd been married (*ha!*). Edward had always made the arrangements, and checked them in and paid the bill, while she'd stood next to the suitcases and checked her powder in her compact mirror. She felt the eyes of everyone in the lobby on her and nervously pulled up her coat collar. The way the desk clerk was eyeing her made her wish Edward were there.

"I need a room, please," she said, trying to keep her voice from shaking.

"For how many nights?"

"Oh, uh, two, please."

"Just you?" the clerk asked in a suggestive tone.

It was like that little shit Albert Hixson had aged ten years and was now working the desk at this damned hotel. Vivian wished she could think of something snappy to say. This wisenheimer needed to be put in his place, but all she could do was nod and avoid eye contact with him. As he slid the key across the desk to her he leaned in.

"Well, I'm right here if you need anything."

"I don't need anything from you," she managed this time, and snapped up the key, turned on her heel, and walked to the stairs carrying her small suitcase. When she got to the room she dropped the suitcase on the floor, closed the door and locked it, and then looked around at the furniture to figure out which piece she could push up against the door so she'd be able to sleep.

That was another thing. She'd been sleeping next to Edward for nearly sixteen years, and having a great big bed without him in it was unsettling. The sheets were scratchy. The mattress sagged. Every noise made her jump. The man in the room next to hers hadn't stopped coughing in the last hour and a half.

After lying awake in the dark for three hours, she lost her patience and kicked angrily at the covers. She sat bolt upright in the bed, grabbed the extra lumpy pillow, and smashed her face into it and screamed, "GODDAMN YOU, EDWARD!," allowing each muffled word to vibrate through the fabric and filling for several seconds. The force with which she screamed stiffened every muscle in her upper body, and when she finally let the pillow fall into her lap she felt pretty tired. She set the pillow back next to her head, collapsed onto her back, and fell right to sleep. The sleep was fitful. She dreamed her teeth were being pulled out all over again and she was scrambling to pick them up and jam them back into her gums.

The next morning Vivian stood on the porch of a late-Victorian clapboard house and pulled a Lucky Strike from the package. She'd quit the moment she knew she was pregnant with Charlotte, and hadn't planned to start up again, but everything had changed. Edward hated when she smoked. But who was he to have an opinion now? Who was he at all? Who was this man she had married, who'd married someone else before her and kept it a secret for sixteen years?

"We were just kidding around. It wasn't serious." These were Edward's words about his first marriage that were ringing in her ears as she stood on that porch on South Salina Street in East Syracuse in the biting morning cold, balancing the clipboard on her left forearm. She still held the cigarette between the first two fingers in her right hand, and with her thumb she pressed the doorbell.

Chapter 31

Mildred Fischer Dalton Taggart took her time in answering the door, as a small dog barked in the background. *Of course there's a dog.* Vivian felt her heart hop a little, and could see a short figure lurching down a long hallway behind the gauze curtain in the door's small eye-level window. She smoked the Lucky all the way down to the filter by the time the lurching figure reached the door. She quickly stubbed out the butt on the underside of the clipboard, dropped it into a pile of snow that hadn't been cleared from the porch, and pasted on what she hoped was a winning and official-looking smile as the door opened.

"Hello," she began in her sunniest tone of voice.

"Whaddya want?"

Edward's first wife was not fat, as Vivian had predicted, but was short and a little lumpy in the floral housedress that was cinched awkwardly at her bulging middle. Her hair was dyed a harsh mud-brown, which aged her. Already Vivian was feeling better, and she stood a little straighter in her fur-collared coat and new fur-lined ankle boots.

"I'm Shirley Smith, with the United States Census Bureau," she said, the way she'd practiced over and over in front of the bathroom mirror in her hotel room that morning. She'd never tried anything like this before and was more nervous than if she'd been walking onto a Broadway stage to sing "Oklahoma!"

"Census Bureau," Mildred repeated, looking from Vivian's eyes to the clipboard. "They already came here."

"Yes," Vivian agreed. "Mercy, aren't we a nuisance! But there was a small fire that destroyed the 1950 records for this neighborhood." She smiled apologetically. "We're having to do them over. Just a few quick questions, if you don't mind. Would you like a cigarette?"

"Make it quick." Mildred pushed open the screen door to step onto the porch, and the small dog made his escape.

Mildred held out her hand for the cigarette as Vivian gasped and whirled around to see where the dog went. *Out into the street*, the paranoid voice in her head shrieked. When she whipped back around she knew from the look on Mildred's face she sure wasn't going to be invited into the house, and the interview was going to be done right there on the porch, in the cold, as quickly and as hostile as you please. Vivian was torn between feeling giddy that Mildred believed her story and anxious about the goddamned dog, who, unlike poor Rambles, had stayed safely on the porch, and was now burrowing into the dirty piles of snow. She did notice that Mildred's voice was not the same voice she'd heard calling Betty Miller that night. So, that was one question answered.

She scrutinized Mildred's complexion as she held the lighter up to the cigarette, her hand wobbling just a touch. *Sallow and patchy*, she thought. She also couldn't believe anyone would answer the door without her lipstick on. Mildred took a drag and then leaned back and away from the lighter and narrowed her eyes as she inspected Vivian. Then it was the dog doing the inspecting. Circling her like a small furry porch wolf, its wet nose snuffling its way all around her ankles. *NO*, Vivian shouted inside her head, just in case the dog could read her thoughts. It could not. It stretched its dirty paws right up onto her skirt and continued its snuffling. If she didn't know any better, she'd swear the dog was smiling. She almost smiled back. *There was a Mildred had a dog and Bingo was his name-o.*

"Well, I appreciate you taking the time," Vivian said, fumbling to put the lighter back in her pocketbook and then find the dang pencil she was supposed to use for her interview while trying to gently push the dog off of her leg. *B-I-N-G-O.* "Now, let's see . . ."

"Brucie! Quit messing around and get back in the house!" Mildred's voice snapped as she held the screen door open for Brucie.

Vivian inhaled deeply through her nostrils and thought that little dog deserved a better name. What kind of a stupid name was Brucie for a dog? *B-R-U-C-I-E.* It didn't work with the tune. Stupid name or not, Brucie obeyed Mildred and plopped back onto all fours and tap-tap-tapped his way back inside the house on those dirty paws that'd probably left marks on Vivian's best skirt. Vivian grabbed the pencil and yanked it from the mess in her purse and then flipped the top page, which she had left intentionally blank, over the back of the clipboard.

"You were living in this same house in 1950?"

"Yeah."

"Fine, fine. And your full name?"

"Mildred Rose Fischer."

Vivian scribbled with the pencil, waiting for Mildred to say one or both of her married names, but she didn't.

"Mmm-hmm, could you spell 'Fischer' for me?"

"F-I-S-C-H-E-R."

"Thank you. And, miss, missus? Fischer, are you currently married?"

"No."

"Have you been married previously?"

"Yes."

"Mmm-hmm." Vivian didn't think she'd be able to get away

with asking "To whom?" or anything else specific about Mildred's previous marriages, so good old Shirley Smith would have to leave it at that.

"Who else lives at this address with you?"

"Just me."

Vivian kept her head down as she wrote on the page. The *Daily Record* article had mentioned that Mildred and her second husband "had a youngster," because that was what Edward had told Vivian. She wondered where that youngster was now. He or she would've been younger than Charlotte. Cooped up inside, Brucie had gone back to barking from what was probably the living room, and Vivian thought if Mildred were a friendly sort she might've made a joke about Brucie living there with her. She wasn't, and she didn't.

"And in 1950? Was there anyone else living here then?"

"No." Mildred drew on the cigarette, then blew the smoke over Vivian's head. "My son was here a few times, but the landlord knew all about it."

"Ah." Vivian tensed at the mention of the son. "That's fine. We don't share these results with the landlords. That is not our business. So, children. How many children do you have?"

"Just my son. YOU SONS OF BITCHES!" Mildred's attention had gone from Vivian and the clipboard to something just to the left of the porch and she marched through the piled-up snow to lean over the rail. "GET OFF OF THERE!"

Vivian followed Mildred's shouting to the birdhouse with a feeder that stood in the side yard. A couple of squirrels had been chitter-chattering and snacking on the bird feed, but scattered with Mildred's bellowing.

"Durn rodents," Mildred muttered as she clomped her way back to stand in front of the screen door, stomping her feet and brushing the snow from her ankles. Vivian's attention stayed on the birdhouse.

It sat on top of a wooden post and was shaped like a little

bungalow. Her heart gave a pained squeeze as she recognized Edward's handiwork. She'd seen enough of the things he made on his workbench to know he'd been the one who'd made that birdhouse. The little curved eaves of the house. The shape. He'd even added a chimney, which he loved to do. The dollhouse he'd made for Charlotte had a real chimney. And their birdhouse in the backyard did, too. "Makes it look like a real house. The birds'll love it!" *Oh, goddammit, Edward.*

"We done here?" Mildred had finished her cigarette and begun rubbing her arms with her hands.

Vivian looked back at her, then back down at the clipboard.

"How old is he?"

"How old is who?"

"You said you had a son?"

"Yeah. He doesn't live with me. What difference does it make how old he is?" Mildred crossed her arms over her chest and jutted out her chin, her eyes narrowed.

Vivian remembered she was supposed to be Shirley from the Census Bureau and forced herself to continue, being careful not to press her luck.

"Yes, you're right. That is only important if the child lived in the house with you. I'm so used to asking out of habit, sorry. And what is your age?"

"Forty-nine."

Well, that explained her appearance. But she was three years older than Edward. That was a surprise.

"Well, Mrs. Ta—" Vivian stopped herself as she realized she had started to say Mildred's married name, and then made a show of checking her clipboard, "I'm sorry, Mrs. *Fischer.* Thank you, Mrs. *Fischer,* for your time. The Census Bureau understands this is sure a bother."

She flipped the cover page back down over what she had written, and opened her pocketbook to deposit the pencil. The contents of her purse were in such a state of jumble and disarray that when she lifted the purse flap, a few things flew right out and landed at their feet.

"Oh, for garsh sakes," Vivian exclaimed, as she reached for the cigarette lighter and packet of Sen-Sen. At the same time, Mildred Fischer Dalton Taggart bent down and picked up Vivian's driver's license.

Vivian disliked admitting to personal weaknesses. She'd prefer you just didn't notice them. One of the things she might not have bragged about was being quick on her feet. She wasn't clumsy, but she also probably wouldn't catch anything you threw at her.

"Oh, thank you!" she cried, as both women rose from their bent positions, and Vivian tried to snatch the driver's license from Mildred's fingers. But Mildred held firm with those nicotine-stained fingers, pulled the license closer toward her face, and squinted at it.

"Shirley, you said your name was?" Mildred's tone had gone from generally unfriendly to downright nasty as she looked from the license to Vivian's face and back again.

Vivian's heart was pounding as she shoved the lighter and Sen-Sen back into her handbag.

"That's . . ." She let the word hang in the air and as Mildred's eyes met hers she made a mad grab for the license, swiping and scratching Mildred's hand with her Fire & Ice fingernails. But Mildred, counter to her slow lurching to answer the door, had the quick reflexes Vivian did not, and snapped the scratched hand, still holding the license, to her chest. Vivian stared into those angry, muddy-brown eyes, which did happen to match the hair dye, for a split second more before turning on her heel and scrambling down the porch steps, clutching the clipboard and her pocketbook to her torso.

"DALTON?" Mildred screamed at her from her front door. "YOU TELL EDDIE HIS SON WANTS TO SEE HIM!"

Vivian heard it, but kept shuffling down the street, her nylons rubbing together under the constrictive girdle and skirt. She rounded the corner to where she'd parked the car, out of sight of Mildred's house. She dropped everything she was clutching right there onto the snow-packed street, and then picked up the pocket-book, fumbling around for the car key as her heart pounded in her ears. She grasped the key tightly and poked around the lock until it finally slid into the slot. The lock sprang up, she flung the door open wide, scooped up the clipboard from the ground, and threw her purse onto the front seat before scrambling into the car.

The car peeled out of the parking spot, and she was willing to bet if there hadn't been snow on the ground she would've left skid marks like Bill Parker did as she tore down the street. At the sight of the black-and-white police car driving toward her she pulled her foot away from the accelerator and let the Buick coast as he passed. *Careful!* She could hear Edward's voice in her head from the afternoon way back when he'd taught her to drive.

"Oh, shut up, Edward," she wheezed aloud in the car. *Makes my ass tired even when he's not here.*

She passed four more stop signs before she felt like she could breathe normally. When she spotted a farm supply store she pulled the car into one of the vacant parking slots and turned off the motor and sat there with her chest rapidly rising and falling. The rearview mirror showed her exactly how frantic she'd become in the last five minutes and she gasped at the wild hairdo sticking out every which way from under her hat.

His son wants to see him.

Edward had said Mildred had a "youngster" with her second husband. Was that another lie? Something just for the papers? A wife, a son, and maybe even the damned dog. Brucie. How long did dogs live, anyway, if they didn't run after a squirrel out into the street and get hit by a car? Vivian closed her eyes and huffed through her nostrils in frustration. In her mind, all she could see was Mildred standing there in her doorway, shouting. Shouting and holding Vivian's driver's license in her hand. *Oh, Jesus Christ.*

It was a Friday. She didn't have time to worry about the driver's license. She also didn't have time to waste, going to sit in some restaurant with a nice hot cup of coffee and trying to collect her thoughts and work through what she had just seen and heard. *A-tisket, a-tasket*, she hummed, trying to calm herself with the nursery rhyme that had popped into her head as she ran from Mildred's house . . . *Easter basket . . . I can't believe I dropped it, I dropped it, I dropped it.* She pulled the car out of the farm supply parking lot and headed to the county courthouse.

Son wants to see him swam around her brain with the image of her driver's license. *Jesus Christ almighty.* Her hands shook as she steered into a parking space in front of the beige brick building. It had to be today. The office would be closed Saturday and Sunday, and she didn't have enough money to extend her stay at the hotel. Never enough time, never enough money. What Vivian did have enough of was questions. And more now than when she'd started out from the hotel that morning. She took the little brown notebook from her pocketbook with still-shaking hands, and flipped through the pages until she found what she was looking for:

> *Clerk's Office, Court House, Syracuse, New York—Ada M. Carr; Reg. Vital Statistics*

Ada M. Carr. The gatekeeper of information at the Syracuse Clerk's Office.

Chapter 32

Ada M. Carr sounded like a tidy woman. Someone sharp and efficient. She probably wore her hair in a tight bun and said things like "disclosures" and "proceedings." Vivian made her way from the car to the front door of the building, taking careful steps up the narrow, icy walkway, and wondered if she should have a cigarette first.

Stop wasting time.

She crossed the threshold into the somewhat heated entryway and had to walk a little ways down an echoing hallway before coming to an internal door marked "City Clerk." Her nerves hit again, the way they had as she'd climbed the steps to Mildred's porch with her well-rehearsed Census Bureau story. She hadn't prepared a story for this. With a deep breath, she pulled open the door and stepped into the office. The office appeared empty until she looked beyond the counter and spied a young man sitting at a desk near the back. He didn't look up. She cleared her throat and leaned against the counter to keep her balance as she shifted from left foot to right.

"Just a minute," the man called without looking up.

A minute passed. And then another. Vivian had removed her gloves and was tapping her Fire & Ice fingernails on the polished wood.

"I'm here to see Mrs. Ada Carr," she called out.

"Do you have an appointment?"

Shirley Smith from the United States Census Bureau probably would've had an appointment. Vivian wondered if she'd be turned away without one. She hadn't thought of that. Of course Ada M. Carr was a busy woman, and would have to schedule appointments. A woman who wore her hair in a tight, tidy bun would also run a tight, tidy schedule, wouldn't she? Vivian wondered if she should lie. Was there an appointment book he could check to see if she was lying? She was tiring from all her earlier lies that day and took a chance.

"No, I don't."

The young man heaved a sigh, then pushed himself away from the desk and strode over to the counter, still in his shirtsleeves, his suit jacket hanging on the back of the chair.

"Mrs. Carr is out sick," he said brusquely, offering no apology.

Well, she'd probably made herself sick from all that stress of keeping schedules and whatnot, was what Vivian was thinking when the door behind her swung open and a large man entered. She turned to see he was holding his hat in his hand and seemed to be in a hurry.

"Please . . ." Vivian gestured for the man to go ahead of her, while she tried to think of what to do.

The young man behind the counter raised his eyebrows at Vivian and then shrugged, turning his attention to the large man holding the hat.

"How can I help you?"

The large man nodded at Vivian and stepped up, laying his hat on the counter.

"I need to register this deed for my property," the large man said, pulling a crumpled envelope from his coat.

"Yes, sir," the man behind the counter said. "Do you have an appointment?"

"Um . . ." The large man cleared his throat. "No."

The younger man sighed again, and a smirk sneaked up around Vivian's lips.

"Well, did you bring your identification?"

The large man began rummaging around his inside coat pockets and finally withdrew a black leather wallet.

Identification. Vivian's smirk pulled into a frown as she looked down at the floor. She then very slowly turned on her heel and walked out the door to the office with her gloves in her hand, down the hallway, and out into the cold daylight. The fresh air would help her think, and the cigarette was something she should've had before she went in there. Her hands shook as she held the lighter up to the end of the cigarette balancing from the corner of her lips and she cursed under her breath. *Goddammit.*

She looked around for somewhere to sit. Why wasn't there a stupid bench at this stupid place? She looked all around her at the stupid civic building, which was supposed to be there for the stupid citizens of the stupid place, wasn't it? She leaned up against the beige bricks and tried to untangle the mess in her head. Mildred. Son. License. Jesus Christ almighty. Brucie. A black-and-white police car rolled by the building and her heartbeat sped up as she watched it pass. It took her seven minutes to smoke the Lucky Strike, and seven minutes to figure out a way around the identification problem.

She stomped the Lucky out under the toe of her nice new ankle boots, which did make her smile when she looked at them, and then walked back to her car, unlocked the door, and climbed into the driver's seat. Vivian thought about the young man behind the counter, and her own job at Bell. She remembered those early days at the switchboard when she'd connect or disconnect callers based on her moods and whims, the day she'd stood and wiped out a dozen calls with one sweep of her arm.

She angled the rearview mirror down to see her face and then carefully applied her lipstick. After puckering her lips, and then blotting them with her handkerchief, she picked up the clipboard and flipped past the first blank page, and then the second page, where she had written the answers to her phony census survey. The third page was the letter she had received from the city clerk's office. It stated the following:

We have Birth records on file from 1873 to the present. However, these records must be on file for seventy-five (75) years if you are not a relation.

Marriage records are on file from 1907 to the present. In order for marriage records to be searched, both husband and wife must be deceased and proof of death must be submitted along with the request.

It hadn't been seventy-five years since the birth of Mildred Fischer Dalton Taggart's son, and Vivian no longer had her driver's license to use for identification, but there were exceptions to every rule. Vivian needed to get back in that office and see how exceptional the exception needed to be.

Vivian guessed that the extremely unexceptional twerp in the shirtsleeves behind the counter was in his late twenties. Obviously, his mother hadn't raised him properly, or whoever had trained him here at the clerk's office had done what Edward would call a "piss-poor job" and hadn't taught him how to treat people. She supposed she shouldn't have expected much from a local government that couldn't even be bothered to put a bench outside their building. (If she hadn't just had her cigarette she might've said "a goddamned bench outside their goddamned building." Thank goodness she was feeling a little more relaxed.) Even Mayor Reed made it a point to add extra benches around Wooster's Public Square, so people had somewhere to sit, for chrissakes.

She approached the counter once again. The large man with the hat (who had not had an appointment) had gone, and there was no one else in the office that she could see.

"Back again?" the man asked wearily from his desk.

"I am." Vivian smiled, as she mentally turned her charm dial from one to ten. The eyelashes were fluttering, the finger was tracing coy little circles around on the countertop, and then she sneezed and one of her clip-on earrings dropped from her earlobe, bounced and clanked onto the counter and onto the floor. She'd been aiming for smooth and sly, like Rita Hayworth in *The Lady from Shanghai*, but the operation was probably looking more like Lucy and Ethel in anything.

"Ohh, no, Loooooocy," she muttered to herself in her Ricky Ricardo voice as she groaned and bent down to pick up the earring.

The file room was enormous, lit with horrible fluorescent light that cast a blinding white-greenish hue over everything. It smelled like paint, metal, and lemon floor cleaner. There was almost an echo as Vivian followed the young man, whose name she now knew was Nicholas, through the doorway and into the center of the room as he pointed out which filing cabinets held which records.

"I'll leave you to it," he chirped with a grin and a wink.

Nicholas, as it turned out, was a truly devoted *I Love Lucy* fan.

Vivian winked back and then waited until he closed the door behind him before setting her pocketbook down on the long table farthest from the door.

The vital records were grouped by date in the filing cabinets, and then alphabetized by last name. Vivian pulled out one group at a time, and then spent fifteen to twenty minutes seated at the table, flipping through the files. Some of the records were on full 8.5" x 11" pages, some were on half sheets, and still others were transcribed onto index cards. It was a messy mass of information.

For the most part the records were in proper alphabetical order, as Mrs. Ada Carr probably demanded, but as Vivian sat at that long table shuffling through folder after folder she suspected Mrs. Carr may have been out sick for quite some time, and that the careless Nicholas had taken to doing his own special brand of filing. (In fact, she'd watched him hastily stuff the hat-holding man's deed registration into a wooden tray marked "Marriage License Applications" before guiding her back to the records room.) Vivian had thought she was looking in the E–Fs, but as she shuffled through *Ingraham, Jefferson, James, Ikehorn*, she realized the records had been misfiled. She kept flipping the records in case an E–F might show up, because the tab on the outside did say "E–F," and then she did see that one of those misfiled records had a name she recognized, and it wasn't Mildred Fischer.

"Jesus Christ," Vivian whispered aloud.

She held her index finger to the page under the names on the record, and thought if it'd been one of her movie magazines it would've said "Illicit!" and "Scandalous!" For the next five minutes she couldn't look anywhere else other than at that misfiled record.

"How's everything going, *Looocy*?" Nicholas popped his head around the door, rattling her out of her astounded stupor.

"Oh!" Vivian jumped in her chair, startled.

"Can I make any copies for you?"

"Copies?"

"Of the record you were looking for."

Nicholas walked over to the table and took the record from her hand that had frozen in place like one of Freedlander's glove mannequins.

As he walked back toward the door she remembered herself.

"I'm still looking for one more. I think these I-through-Js may be in here by mistake?"

Nicholas raised his eyebrows and walked back to where she was sitting. She pointed at the names and then the folder tab. Nicholas scratched his head, "Hunh, what do you know." He then picked up the I–J folder and opened it to *Eberhardt*. "Well, there you go! The E-through-Fs!" He handed her the folder, unconcerned with the mix-up. "I'll come back in a little."

After a little, Nicholas did return, and by then Vivian had found what she came for.

"Nicholas, if you could copy these two records for me, that would be lovely. Would you mind?"

"Oh, Looocy." Nicholas shook his finger at her and gave her another wink.

And it was just that easy. Vivian had gotten exactly what she needed, and more. That poor Mrs. Ada M. Carr was going to have her hands full when she got back to the office, though. Who knows what other mistakes and messes Nicholas made?

Vivian sat in her hotel room in the armchair next to the window, eating her Italian take-out ravioli with the fork she'd had to borrow from the hotel's kitchen. She supposed the restaurant just assumed she'd be taking her food home to eat in her own kitchen because the bag held only the food and a paper napkin, and what kind of respectable lady stayed by herself in a hotel? She wondered if the cooks in the restaurant were authentic Italians, and if they were, were they using the good sauce recipe?

She put the ravioli and fork down on the little side table and got up to push the window open, brushing garlic bread crumbs from her skirt, which did have faint paw prints on it, thank you very much, Brucie. She'd also gotten a run in her stockings. They'd caught on the corner of the Buick's door as she was making her escape from Mildred.

Vivian settled back into the chair with an eye roll, a heavy sigh, and a cigarette, which she smoked out the open window as the water filled in the bathtub. It'd been the kind of day that required a cigarette and a proper relaxing soak in the claw-foot tub, where she tried not to think about the birdhouse or her driver's license, and just focus on the hot water soothing her muscles. *Edward*—she sighed to herself—*you make my ass tired.*

With her dentures soaking in a glass next to the sink, she slathered on her face cream, inhaling the familiar scent that almost made her feel like she was at home, but then she heard footsteps in the hallway outside her door that made her tense up until she heard, "Laundry!" yelled at the door of one of the other rooms. *Oh, shut up.* Vivian stomped over to the door, kicking out the bottom of her nightgown, and shook her fist at the voice in the hallway. She couldn't get more than a few minutes of quiet in this place. Couples laughing in the hallway, or the man in the room next to her coughing all through the night. What kind of person spent more than a few days here and needed to have his laundry done? Criminals. Gangsters. Husbands who'd been kicked out of their homes for lying to their wives.

Vivian's eyes rolled up and around and right over to the foot of the armchair where she'd eaten her ravioli and smoked her Lucky Strike. When she'd first gotten back to the room she'd plopped her pocketbook and clipboard there on the floor. The photostat of the second birth record Nicholas had copied for her at the clerk's office was sticking out of the clipboard. It was the one she'd been looking for, and shouldn't really have surprised her.

The year of the birth was 1922. Male, six pounds seven ounces. Mother: Mildred Fischer. Father: Edward Dalton. Vivian had already done the math while sitting at the long table in the empty file room. At the time that baby boy was conceived Edward would have been fifteen years old.

Chapter 33

Vivian had more than a couple of things to mull over as she maneuvered the Buick out onto State Street in Syracuse and headed toward the highway that would take her back to Wooster. On the one hand, there was the fury. She hadn't decided if her fury about Edward having a son was stronger than the fury she'd felt about Edward having had a first wife. Probably not. Once you'd learned that your husband had lied to you about one big deal, it wasn't too surprising to find that he'd lied about another. It sure didn't make it any better, though.

And then there was the shock of that other *misfiled* record Vivian'd found that had just about knocked her right out of that uncomfortable chair. *Jeeeeeeesus Christ!* She couldn't believe it. It had dropped her chin right on the floor. And once she'd picked her chin up again, after Nicholas interrupted her, she'd felt something close to what she'd felt when she'd gotten Aunt Catharine's Irish claddagh ring. Vivian felt satisfaction. No, she felt *smug*. Smug was better. Vera, always laughing at her, always pointing out her mistakes, making sure everyone knew she'd poured salt into the frosting batter instead of sugar. *Irish* rogue, *stupid, not Irish* robe. And tattling about her eavesdropping. Just like her sullen, grumpy mother, Vivian only remembered the bad things, so, yes, when she'd gotten Aunt Catharine's ring she'd felt smug. And she felt smug now.

Vivian pursed her lips into a tight grin over her perfect set of false teeth as she pressed the gas pedal down to merge onto the highway. My, oh, my, the things you could find at the city clerk's office in Syracuse. And she didn't even have her high school diploma! She wondered if she shouldn't just hang out her own shingle: "Vivian Dalton, Private Investigator," *pleased to meet you*. There were a lot of people, and a lot of *important* people, who would pay big money for the information she now had tucked into the bottom of her suitcase. When you were a big, important person, especially someone like the mayor of Wooster, everyone cared what you did and how you did it, that was for certain.

Vivian not only couldn't believe what she'd uncovered, she couldn't believe she was the only one who knew about it. *Li'l ole Vivian Dalton*. She felt the sense of control again. It almost made up for the confirmation of the mess Edward had made of her life.

Vivian had been missing something for the past couple of months, but didn't know what that something was. Like an invisible fiber floating on the surface of her eye that she couldn't grasp and pull away. It was there; she could feel it. Mucking up her life like those damned threads mucked up her mascara when she'd try to pull them out.

Well, she'd met the first Mrs. Dalton, and now that "something" had a face. A face she didn't bother to put makeup on when she answered her door, but a face just the same. And the birdhouse! The birdhouse had been another sharp jab in Vivian's side, and it left an ache somewhere between her ribs and her heart as she stared through the windshield at the barren, snowy highway. *Maybe he made it for their fifth wedding anniversary*, she thought. *Wood*.

The car radio had gone to static a while back, as she got farther away from Erie, Pennsylvania, where she'd stopped for a cup of coffee and the use of a clean bathroom. Vivian had been so preoccupied with her thoughts that she hadn't noticed the hissing from the speakers until she was crossing the border into Ohio. She was just reaching for the dial to turn the radio off when she heard a low whine, like a summer mosquito had somehow gotten trapped inside the Buick. It got louder.

Eeeeeeeeeeeee.

She looked in the rearview mirror and saw flashing lights on top of the approaching patrol car. Goddammit. Oh, good goddamned gravy on Christ crackers! Had she been speeding? She'd lost her focus after driving for so many hours, she may have been pressing a little too hard on the accelerator pedal, and now was going to pay for it. Boy, was she going to pay for it. Speeding tickets could run upward of thirty dollars, and Vivian had already spent nearly all of her cash.

She eased onto the brake and steered the car over onto the snowy shoulder until it came to a complete stop. As she put the gear in park she remembered her driver's license.

"Oh, goddammit, goddammit!"

She'd seen plenty of car chases in movies, and her glance jumped from the gear shift, to the road that stretched out in front of her, to the rearview mirror, where the officer had closed his car door and was crunching over the snow toward the Buick. Her nerves jerked and her hand hovered over the gear shift. She checked the rearview again. *Don't do it.* The figure in the patrol uniform was imposing, the black boots, the visored cap, and the dark sunglasses. *Don't.* She didn't always listen to that knee-jerk voice in her head; the one that piped up first when she needed an answer. But this time it was insistent. Logic (and recent events) told her she just wasn't built for a quick getaway. She suspected the Buick wasn't, either. It might even need a push to get out of the snow she'd just rolled into. She blew out a defeated breath and thought she might break down in tears right there. She waited until the officer rapped on the window with his knuckles before she rolled down the window.

"Well, looky here!" the officer cried, his breath crystallizing in the cold air outside the car.

Vivian squinted up through the tears that'd started, into the familiar face that matched the familiar voice.

"Uncle Hugh!" she exclaimed in a delighted gasp as the tears blurred her vision.

"What in the world are you doin' all the way out here?" he asked. "Are you crying?"

She laughed through the tears, not quite believing her good luck. It was about time she had some of that!

"Vivy," Uncle Hugh said more seriously, "what *are* you doing out here?"

And Vivian's relief at her incredible good luck turned back into tension with that question. She remembered where they were, and her smile faded a little, as she blotted her tears with the fingertips of her gloves. She was supposed to be in Akron, visiting her "sick" sister. She hadn't expected to have to come up with an excuse other than that one, and that'd just been for Edward and Charlotte. What could she tell her Uncle Hugh? *Poor Vera has syphilis.* But, even if she could've said that about her sister, she was much farther north than Akron, not to mention driving in the wrong direction.

"Ohhh," she stalled. "Edward..."—*think, dummy, think*—"...'s mother. Edward's mother. She asked me to go up to Fair Haven. To see about one of their houses."

That was good. Edward did have a mother, and she did have a couple of houses.

Vivian knew the McGintys were a little sore when it came to matters of property. They'd had to work hard for what they had, and saw Edward as something of a spoiled only-child whose parents owned more houses than they needed. She hoped Uncle Hugh wouldn't want to know any details beyond that.

"Oh, right," he said. "You and Edward plannin' on movin' up to ..."

"Uncle Hugh." Vivian's teeth had begun to chatter as the wintry air blew into the car through the open window, and the cold air must've jump-started her brain. "I lost my driver's license back in Fair Haven, and I'm a little worried about getting pulled over again. Could you follow me back to Wooster?"

If she were pulled over again it would be a problem. She had only one uncle on the Ohio State Patrol.

"Course I can, honey. Just lemme call dispatch first. And take it easy on that gas pedal!"

He ambled back to his squad car and Vivian rolled up her window, letting out a tiny squeal. *Luck of the Irish, today, Vivian.*

She waited until she saw Uncle Hugh's arm wave outside his window, and then pushed gently on the accelerator. The Buick's whitewall tires spun a little, but then gained traction as the car bumped its way from the shoulder back out onto the highway.

With her uncle following her in his patrol car for the rest of the drive back to Wooster, Vivian finally relaxed, and her mind began to run through the story she would tell Edward when she got home. Then she thought about what she was going to do with the information she had at the bottom of her suitcase about J. Ellis Reed. And then she thought about how she would now need to get a new driver's license. *Oh, for chrissakes.* She could picture her license, the small white card with "OPERATOR'S LICENSE" printed in bold uppercase letters at the bottom, and her name and home address typed in a block at the top. The license had her address. And now, so did Mildred.

Chapter 34

"Dad, do you have Aunt Vera's address? Should we send her a get-well card?" Charlotte had asked. Her father had said no, and they should just wait to see what her mother said about the visit.

After three days in Akron with Aunt Vera, whom her mother rarely spoke to, and whom she didn't seem to like all that much, her mother came back even angrier than she had been when she found out about Dad's first marriage. Aunt Vera must have done something to make her even madder.

"How is Aunt Vera doing, Mom?"

"Not good, Charlotte!" her mother yelled, as she opened and slammed cupboard doors in the kitchen. "Not good!"

Charlotte was really curious about whatever was ailing Aunt Vera. Was it terminal? Was it contagious? Was it polio, like her cousin James had a few years ago? She didn't think grown-ups got polio anymore, it seemed to just be children. But what could be so serious that her mother would go up to Akron for three whole days? Was that what the envelope of money was for? What with her mother's acid tone and violent abuse of the kitchen cabinets, she didn't think now was the time to ask.

She went upstairs to her room and looked at the Coca-Cola wall calendar hanging over her desk. Valentine's Day was Saturday. Charlotte traced a heart with her finger around the "14" square. She wondered what this Valentine's Day would look like.

Fingers crossed it would look like Max Zimmerman, but it might still be too early for that. It was a new thing, Max's apparent interest, and she didn't know if he really liked her or just felt sorry for her because of her family's "unfortunate situation." Most of her classmates—Sue, Barb, the other girls in the GAA—had really rallied around her after the scandal, knowing she was an accidental victim. Charlotte didn't like to think of herself as a victim, she just knew she didn't have the kind of antagonistic personality that would have encouraged anyone to say the word "bastard" out loud. She thought that if this had happened to Sue, there might have been a bit more whispering and probably some nasty comments. People tended to like it when bad things happened to Sue.

Some kids, like Margie Miller and her friends, gossiped about the bigamy story, but didn't aim any malice at Charlotte herself. Not that Charlotte would have cared very much. Margie was only a freshman. After the "shit a brick" comment Charlotte had overheard, she figured Margie probably did and said a lot of things just to get attention. *Because I know people*, Charlotte thought to herself, imitating her mother. She would say that her mother probably "knew" people maybe sixty percent of the time that she thought she did. Maybe sixty-five. There was a lot she missed.

Charlotte certainly didn't expect any displays of romance between her own parents in regard to Valentine's Day, although her dad had been going over and above to try to please her mother. When her mother had walked in the door with her suitcase, Charlotte's dad looked up from his newspaper and in a voice she rarely heard him use had said, "Pussycat, pussycat, where have you been?" Charlotte had thought, *I've been to London to visit the queen*, because that was how the rhyme went, but her mother had barked, "Akron, Edward, you know I was in Akron!"

In the Dalton household Valentine's Day used to mean sour cream cookies. It was the same recipe her mother used for her Christmas cookies, just with different cookie cutters. Heart-shaped and frosted in thick buttercream icing with a single cinnamon Red Hot placed in the center. When Charlotte was in grade school her mother would make an enormous batch of these, and then line a dress box from Beulah Bechtel's in wax paper and place the cookies in careful rows, separating the layers with more wax paper, for Charlotte to take to her class. Once Charlotte got older, she stopped taking cookies to school, much to the dismay of her classmates.

This year Charlotte wasn't sure what to expect. Everything felt electrically charged.

With her ears still ringing from her mother's shouting and banging around the kitchen, Charlotte went to the bathroom. When she came out she saw that her parents' bedroom door was ajar, and she could see her mother's purse sitting open on the bed. Charlotte glanced down the stairs and then tiptoed into the room, and as she drew closer to the bed she saw the little brown notebook peeking out of the top. Had her mother made any new entries? Were there any new discoveries? She quickly flipped through the pages, past the ones she had already seen to a new entry.

I felt I did trust in Christ, Christ alone, for salvation; and an assurance was given me that he had taken away My sins, even Mine, and saved me from the law of sin and death.

This was scribbled in fervent hand. It was not what Charlotte had been expecting, and she looked from the page to the bedroom doorway. She could hear her mother still banging around in the kitchen downstairs. What had prompted this? Aunt Vera's illness? Was it something she had heard in church? Charlotte was usually the one actually listening to the sermons, but this seemed a little more intense than anything that might be engendered by Reverend Alsop's mild words of worship. Was her mother doing something sinful that she needed saving from? Charlotte pulled a face at the thought. When Charlotte thought about sinning, she thought about Max Zimmerman, not her mother. She had decided that her parents had "sinned" only one time, in order for her to be conceived. Thank God, and, yuck.

She spent the next hour and a half lying on her back on the floor of her bedroom, listening to Eddie Fisher and constructing imagined conversations and scenarios with Max Zimmerman at the Valentine's Day dance.

When she went downstairs for dinner she noticed that the sour cream cookies were cooling on the countertop. Charlotte wondered if the "calming" had worked this time.

Sour Cream Cookies:

1 Cup Shortening (I use part butter)
2, Cups gran. Sugar
2 eggs, Large. (or more)
5 Cups Flour
1/2 Teas. Salt
2 Teas. Baking Powder
1 Cup Commercial Sour Cream
1 Teas. Vanilla.

Beat Shortening, Sugar and Eggs together ubtil smooth. ~~Mix~~ Sift Flour, Salt and Baking Powder together and bland into creamed mixture alternately with Sour Cream and add Vanilla. Mixing with you hands is much more thorough, at this point—then separate into one bunch at a time and roll to one eigth inch thickness. Cut out and bake at 350 degrees about 15 minutes. I always double the recipe which makes an awfully lot of cookies. But, I have mixed it up and frozen part of the dough for later baking.

Chapter 35

Dr. Charlton's calming technique only worked when Betty remembered to use it. And just how was she supposed to do that when she had so many events to organize? The good citizens of Wooster hadn't quite grasped their roles in this scandal and, once again, Betty Miller was having to pick up the slack. The Valentine's Day celebration was the second event she'd had to orchestrate in the interest of putting Vivian Dalton in her place. Like everything else she did, Betty deemed it absolutely imperative. Of course Vivian wouldn't be able to go to the event, it was being held at the country club. It was just a romantic peripheral reminder to Vivian (because of course she would hear word of the country club event, celebrating couples and romance) that her marriage was a sham. Betty had always had to go above and beyond a societal leader's usual call of duty to keep things in line and as they should be, but that was what made her Betty Miller.

For instance, last spring she'd had to take several weeks out of her extremely busy schedule in order to teach Dolly how to drive the Coupe, so that Dolly could take the car to the filling station when it needed gasoline. And really, if you thought about it, she had done Dolly a great service by teaching her to drive. There were people who might disapprove of Negroes being allowed to drive at all, but Betty thought that was preposterous. Being in service meant being able to do a wide range of errands, and occasionally that necessitated driving the car.

She didn't know what she'd do without their dear Dolly. She cleaned their house, mended their clothing, cooked their food. Why, Dolly even offered helpful suggestions for Betty's events every once in a while. Which reminded her, she would need to remind Dolly to pick up the flowers for the Valentine's Day gala.

"Betty, you seem a little preoccupied with this," Clara Weaver ventured uneasily. She had participated in the gossip about Edward Dalton's astounding bigamy as much as the other women, but the personal assault Betty appeared determined to wage on Vivian was excessive. Vivian wasn't even part of their social circle, and Betty spent just as much time harping on that; how she was "just so common and low-class." It was a touch hypocritical for someone with more than a few fairly unsavory cousins herself. Clara remained still, but was shaking her head on the inside. You never knew who Betty's next target might be.

Clara thought she saw the briefest shadow pass over Betty's face. A rare flash of doubt on the face of the always-certain, self-assured Betty Miller. Perhaps she realized she *was* going too far, and she just needed a friend to help lead her out of the bizarre vindictive trance. To Clara's surprise, Betty appeared to be reaching out for her hand when a traffic horn blared outside the shop, startling both women. Betty scowled in the direction of the noise, then turned back to Clara with renewed irritation. "You didn't see her at church on *Christ*-mas Eve, although I already de-*scribed* her be-*havior* to you," Betty countered. "And, I *spoke* with *David* at the *post* office. He *men*-tioned that he ran *in*-to her at the *open* house at the *high* school, and she was *aw*-fully *friend*-ly to him." Betty made sure to arch her eyebrows on the word "awfully." "Don't you *understand* what a *scorned woman* is capable of?"

Clara didn't know about scorned women, but she knew what

Betty was capable of. She could tell what Betty was trying to do, but she was going about it all wrong. Not only did Clara doubt her husband, David, had been at the post office with Betty (Clara was the one in charge of mailing letters and buying stamps), she doubted Betty would have even noticed him at the open house, with all the glad-handing she knew Betty did with the teachers and Principal Scott.

Betty needs to brush up on her manipulation tactics, Clara thought archly. If her father wasn't the mayor of Wooster, she wouldn't get away with her behavior nearly as much.

The level of suspicion regarding the husbands of Wooster had remained high for the country club set following the news of Edward Dalton. The seeds had been planted in the minds of the wives, just like they were planted in the soil every spring at the Trowel and Trellis Garden Club. Some were certain they'd rather not know, but others couldn't help themselves, and between the fear of unfaithful husbands and the fear of being publicly humiliated by a tawdry scandal splashed across the front page of *The Daily Record*, the women found themselves sneaking around corners and listening at closed doors. This new wave of upscale spousal paranoia meant sleepless nights for the wives, a dramatic increase in "checking in" telephone calls for the husbands, and more of his least favorite type of work for Wooster's top private investigator.

Chapter 36

If he were a kitchen utensil, he'd be a carving knife. If he were a hand tool, he'd be a mortising chisel. Or maybe the straight edge Elmer used for the cleanest, closest shave at Bowman Street Barber Shop. No matter what sort of inanimate object you used for comparison, Don was one of the sharpest PIs in Ohio, if not the entire mid-Atlantic region of the United States.

There were people in Wayne County who might have argued that if Don McAfee was such a great private investigator, then why hadn't he been able to locate Gilbert Ogden and Flora Parker? A couple of mild-mannered bank workers, and he couldn't find them? Don had heard more than his share on what people considered to be his great failure as an investigator. "Never found those embezzlers, did ya, eh, Don?"

Don took the occasional abuse about his professional "failures" in stride, tipping his hat to the few who dared confront him to his face, usually just people who were still sore about their money being stolen from the Wayne Building & Loan. Some of those same people wondered why the Building & Loan hadn't had insurance, but given what Don McAfee knew about David Weaver's insurance company, he wasn't at all surprised.

Anyone who had hired Don knew how good he was. They considered the Ogden Parker case to be one of the great unsolvables. Like Amelia Earhart or the Black Dahlia killer. And if

Don McAfee hadn't found Gilbert and Flora, then they probably couldn't be found. Don had located ex-cons, runaways; he'd exposed philandering husbands and wives; he'd even found the rightful heir to a railroad magnate's fortune, after combing through adoption records up in Cleveland. The discoveries were almost reward enough, and he would offer a sliding scale for his fees, depending on the client. Vivian Dalton had been a rough case, though, and she was on his mind tonight in particular. He always thought about all his maritally distressed clients when Valentine's Day rolled around.

He remembered Vivian's expression when he had shown her the marriage record from 1923, and explained that he had not been able to find any evidence that the Edward/Mildred marriage had been annulled, nor evidence of a divorce. He had also told her that Mildred was still living. It had been a lot for a person to hear all at once.

The husband-and-wife cases made up the bulk of his workload, but they were also the toughest for him. It was the criminal cases that kept him chomping at the bit, salivating for justice. And, just so you know, he could have found Gilbert Ogden and Flora Parker if he'd really wanted to. In fact, when business was slow, he did a little bit of snooping, just to satisfy his own curiosity, to see if his instincts were correct. And they were. Give old Don a couple of days, a week at the most, and he could've had them both back in Wooster, in handcuffs, standing in front of the judge down at City Hall. But he was infinitely loyal to his clients, and did exactly as they asked. The thing was, he was being paid *not* to find them.

Don sucked thoughtfully on a peppermint candy, looked at the date on the flip calendar on his cluttered desk. Friday the thirteenth, the day before Valentine's Day. He shook his head.

Chapter 37

The day before Valentine's Day was the day Gilbert decided to leave, so it was not in the least bit romantic for Flora Parker. Frantic was more like it. She rushed at the suitcase and started grabbing the folded shirts and pants and throwing them on the bed.

"You can't do this!" she begged.

Gilbert returned from the bathroom holding his shaving kit and stood in the doorway. He shook his head at the scene before him.

"Flora, please stop."

But she had upended the entire suitcase onto the pile of clothes and slammed both palms down onto the hard shell.

"You can't do this," she repeated, this time in a small voice, which threatened to crack.

Gilbert crossed the room to the bed and stood next to Flora, righting the suitcase and placing his shaving kit in the bottom. He rubbed his forehead.

"I have to go. She's sick. She doesn't have anyone else."

Flora turned around and then slid down until her backside hit the floor and she was leaning against the bed, her hands covering her face.

"If you're caught, you'll get the electric chair."

"I'm not going to get caught. I told you, I will be careful."

"Gil, that was a lot of money to steal. People don't forget about that much money."

Footsteps echoed on the stairs.

"Bill." Flora moved her hands away to reveal a tear-stained face. "Tell him not to go."

Bill hated to see his wife like this. Desperate and high-strung. It was completely out of character for her, but she had always been that way about her brother.

Since their mother's mind had begun to go, and she'd started to lash out at Flora for having married a white man, Gilbert had assumed all the communication with her. Gilbert was the only real family either Flora or their mother had left.

"Honey, if it was my mother," Bill said, stroking the top of her head, "I'd do the same. I can't stop him."

Well, she should have considered who she was asking for support, Flora thought with a mixture of exasperation and affection. Bill Parker had always been a mama's boy. It wasn't the worst quality in a husband, having an appreciation for his mother, but it wasn't her favorite thing about him. He had his strengths, though.

Bill's capacity for drama surpassed her own. If Madame Ososki could have seen them, she would have been surprised that the two naïve rubes from "Nebraska" had learned something from her. That they had paid attention in class, and worked hard to instill her lessons into the deepest depths of their very beings. And then she would have been proud, although she would have insisted that Bill "use your words!" to convey his rage. She would have been wrong. He had done beautifully without them.

Could there have been a better training ground for them than New York City theater? Although they'd both moved to Wooster half certain they'd never act again, the small town eventually became their stage, where both finally had the opportunity to give performances of a lifetime. Flora as a mild-mannered, double-crossing bank secretary. And Bill as a scorned and outraged cuckold of a husband.

Flora would have disagreed with Vivian Dalton's assertion

that everyone knew everyone else's business in a small town. She and Bill had kept to themselves, for the most part, and no one had any idea what they had been up to. Sure, the neighbors could get curious about where they were going, or what they were doing for the holidays, or she might have caught some nosy housewife inspecting her shopping cart at Buehler's, passing judgment on her groceries, but overall the Parkers had been able to live a nice, quiet, and private life there in Wooster, Ohio.

As they had done in New York, they rehearsed together in the evenings, after coming home from work. Bill had obsessed over his performance, spending hours asking himself, *What is my motivation?* and trying to come up with the perfect props to guarantee believability. Should he take the hat? Or would he have been too insane with anger and jealousy to remember the hat? Same question with the coat, although it was June. Maybe he should take a coat, just to prove how out of his mind he was. His winter coat would have hinted at serious derangement. A winter coat, in June? Why, that Bill Parker must be positively out of his mind, and who could blame him? Wife robbing a bank and running off with another man.

He had hemmed and hawed over the ideal time of day to stage his dramatic exit from their cozy little house. He didn't want to do it in the middle of the night, when no one would be watching; likewise, the middle of the day, when his neighbors would have been at work or running errands. Except, Flora had reminded him, she and Gilbert would be leaving on a Friday, and if everything went perfectly, no one would realize what they'd done until the following Monday. They'd had to concoct a story as to why Flora wouldn't have come home from work that Friday. Bill had told their neighbors that Flora had told him she was going out of town to visit her mother. "Glad to be staying here, if you know what I mean," he had said, chuckling, to Sam Goosson next door. Sam had guffawed and clapped Bill on the back. "I know what you mean!" *Mothers-in-law and whatnot.*

Bill had decided to commence his performance right around the time Sam Goosson came home from work that Monday. Some assistance he and Flora hadn't counted on, which worked in their favor, was that Boyd Hunsicker telephoned the Parker house from the bank that Monday to ask where in the hell Flora was, and also to ask him what he knew about the robbery, but Bill had been at work all day.

"I'm sorry, Mr. Hunsicker, but there's no answer," Vivian Dalton had said into her mouthpiece at the switchboard. "Would you like to try again later?"

The Parkers' telephone had been ringing when he got home, and Bill had watched the street in front of the house for Sam's car before he answered it. It was June, and hot, so the windows were open. He made sure Sam heard the phone ringing, and then the curtain went up on Bill's performance.

The shotgun had been a touch of genius. And he had recalled Jacob Starlin's volcanic rage, when Bill had borrowed his wheelbarrow out of his backyard without asking permission first. It was a piece of junk, that wheelbarrow. Rusted all around, with a hole clean through in the corner. Bill had felt so bad about Jacob's rage that instead of returning the rusty, battered wheelbarrow, Bill bought him a new one from Oliver's Farm Supply. But Bill never forgot Jacob's hot-red face, and the veins bulging in his neck as he screamed bloody murder in the backyard just opposite the Parkers'. Jacob had taken to the streets of Wooster, shouting at anyone who could hear him, about the "thievin', stealin' delinquents, got nothin' better to do than steal my personal property." Bill channeled that rage for his performance.

Since Jacob lived behind Bill Parker, he hadn't seen Bill's dramatic exit after the news broke about the bank robbery, but he had heard about it later. The neighbors on either side of the Parkers had said it was a wonder he hadn't driven the Studebaker right through the back of the garage, Bill was so steamed when he got into the car. "Carryin' his hat in one hand, his shotgun in the other," they all said.

They had also wondered later, when Bill hadn't returned after what seemed like an awful long time to be gone looking for your cheating wife. The burnt tire marks were a constant reminder of the wild episode, but Bill Parker never returned to his house. Some suspected he'd been so crazy with rage he must have driven himself right off a cliff to his death. Others thought he was probably okay, but just too darned ashamed to return to town.

"Maybe he found himself another girl," Roy Patterson said. "One who wouldn't screw around on him and run out of town with a skinny, four-eyed weasel and two hundred and fifty thousand dollars."

But not one person in all of Wooster thought that Bill had been in on the robbery, and had created a big to-do, just for show, before driving straight up to Canada to be with his wife and her sibling accomplice and all that money. Not even Vivian Dalton. Vivian hadn't thought that Flora Parker would've ever left her husband in the first place, so she would have at least been half right.

And after Vivian's trip up to Syracuse, she had the full story.

Chapter 38

Vivian had the full story, all right, but what she didn't have was her driver's license. And knowing who did have her driver's license caused a heavy pit of dread to settle in Vivian's stomach. There it was, sitting right next to the pile of festering anger that had Edward's name on it. If she made it through to summer without having an exploding ulcer, it would be a miracle.

If she hadn't had the dentist extract every one of her teeth, for purely cosmetic reasons, she was sure they'd be falling out by now. That had always been Vivian's solution: if something was giving her trouble, have it yanked out. Her teeth, her uterus, gray hairs on her head, chin stubble, and lately the cords at Bell's switchboard whenever Betty Miller was trying to place a call. But Vivian couldn't just have Edward yanked out of her life.

The idea of leaving him. Whooo, mercy, that was a doozy. Where would she even begin? Rent a room over the Laundromat and prostitute herself, like Daisy Stucker whose husband, Joe, had died in a horrible farming accident, leaving her with thousands of dollars in debt that she hadn't known about? Vivian wouldn't have to go that far, she did have her job at Bell. But if she kicked Edward out she'd be alone. Did she want everyone in town pitying her for having to live alone? Because that's what you were doing if there was no man in the house. Even if you had six kids to take care of. You were living alone. She couldn't decide which would be worse: having people talk about her because she was alone, or having them talk about her because she'd turned to prostitution so she could eat.

When it came right down to it, Vivian didn't think she could manage solely on her salary. The money from Bell gave the Daltons just enough extra to be able to buy new clothes when the old ones wore out, and to afford a nicer cut of meat at the butcher's on Saturdays. But it wasn't enough for a person to live on. That was the reason Bell hired women in the first place. They worked cheap. If Vivian let herself think about it for too long, she'd work herself up into a lather about how unfair it was, and how women ended up trapped in their marriages with mouths to feed, and how there was no chance of them ever getting out of that, and the next thing you know she'd be waving a sign or wearing a pair of trousers. So she didn't think about it too long. Just long enough to know that leaving Edward wasn't an option for her at this point in life. *The cheese stands alone.* That was all fine and good for the cheese, but it wasn't going to work for her.

To his credit, Edward had been bending over backward to please her. He'd even splurged for Valentine's Day. He'd paid a visit to Bowman Street Barber Shop and had Elmer take a little off the top and a lot off the sides and back, and while he was at it, he trimmed up the nose and ear hair as well. (He knew that Vivian hated that he'd been getting lazy about his grooming habits.) And there were a dozen red roses from Barrett's sitting in the Daltons' crystal (first) wedding vase in the middle of the dining room table on Friday. Where had he even found that thing? Vivian hadn't seen or thought about it in years. He must have gone into the basement and rooted through boxes, unwrapping all the newspaper-wrapped knickknacks in order to find it.

He even went to Beulah Bechtel's and bought her a new dress, which was the be-all-and-end-all, and it was sitting in a box on the dining room table next to the roses. Edward had once said to her that her half of the closet was like another planet to him, and he was afraid to touch anything, or it might leave him smelling like lilies of the valley or something. Wouldn't the guys at the Mason Lodge just love that? But he must've gone through her closet and looked at the labels of the dresses she hadn't made herself, in order to find her size. She could only imagine what he would've looked like, bumbling around Beulah Bechtel's, surrounded by hats and furs and gowns. If she hadn't been so furious about the secret son, she might've been able to appreciate all the effort he had gone to.

There were things you did for people out of love, and things you did out of guilt. Everything Edward was doing was out of guilt. When he was courting her, and even the first few years they were married, he'd show up at the door with clusters of lilacs or bouquets of wildflowers he had picked himself from the side of the road, because he'd been thinking about her. Roses were the "sorry blooms," the apology bouquets he'd buy her, later on in the marriage, whenever he messed up. He thought that since they were expensive, she'd like them and all would be forgiven. But every time she looked at them she was reminded of whatever stupid thing he'd done to make her angry.

If she'd been feeling the least bit romantic she might've considered going to Buehler's before work to pick up ingredients for a special dinner for them on Saturday. Pork chops, like he liked, maybe. With the mint sauce. Or was that for lamb? Or she might've asked Dorothy for her chocolate mousse recipe that she got from that fancy French cookbook her brother bought her when he was stationed overseas.

But Vivian wasn't feeling romantic, and Edward should consider himself lucky to be getting meat loaf and lima beans and another very tense dinner for Valentine's Day, while Vivian decided whether or not she was going to ask him about Mildred's birdhouse and his goddamned son.

Chapter 39

In an attempt to tune out her parents and escape the tension that filled the Daltons' house, Charlotte had been keeping her bedroom door shut. In her room, the only stress came from homework and wardrobe decisions. Charlotte was going to wear her red cardigan sweater today, in honor of Valentine's Day. Except Valentine's Day was tomorrow, and today was Friday the thirteenth.

Charlotte wasn't superstitious, unless a black cat crossed her path or she accidentally walked under a ladder, and she also couldn't remember what she was supposed to do to ward off the evil spirits of Friday the thirteenth. Something was wrong with today. She could just feel it.

"Darn it!" She stomped her bare foot on the rug, pulling at her hair in exasperation at the sweat that had broken out under her arms, dampening the shirt she'd just buttoned up.

She blew a gust of breath out into the stupid balmy warmth of her bedroom, which had the best-working radiator in the entire house. She usually had to open her window in order to sleep, which made her dad furious. "I'm not paying to heat the neighborhood," he'd mutter, along with a string of curses, if he was passing by her room and happened to see the window open. It didn't help at all, either, when she was trying to remain cool while getting dressed.

She went to the window and shoved up the sash, peeled paint chips dropping onto the rug. The bushes that separated the Daltons' house from the Giffords' house rustled, dropping a spray of dry snow on the Daltons' side. Charlotte did a double-take and squinted at the bushes. Was someone there? Her skin prickled and she stepped back from the window, her sweat chilling on her skin. She shook her head, trying to rid herself of the weird shiver. It was probably just the Giffords' cat (which was *not* black).

Charlotte tried to focus on getting dressed and not on the weird feeling that someone was watching her. If she pulled the roll shade down, her room would be too dark. No one was out there anyway. She shook her head again and reached into the closet for her boring old black pencil skirt. She remembered Max Zimmerman saying he liked when girls looked casual. "Like they don't really care."

Well, she thought, *nothing says "I don't really care" like this skirt*. She had flattened herself against the wall farthest from the window to pull on the skirt, and then reached out to snag the red cardigan from the back of her chair. Her paranoia flashed briefly with what she imagined Sue would say about her sweater as she fastened the buttons. "Ugh, red, on Valentine's Day, Char?" or "Oh, Charlotte, red? Really?" The thought annoyed her enough to distract her from thinking about the rustling bushes. She didn't care what Sue had to say on this occasion, because Max Zimmerman wouldn't be putting anything in Sue's locker. Not that he would be putting anything in Charlotte's, either; she had to remind herself not to get her hopes up.

Charlotte turned sideways as she eyed herself in the mirror, jutting out her chest and wondering if she should add just a little padding, maybe. Her mother refused to buy her a pointy bra, so she did what she could to draw attention to her breasts. She faced forward again, and then turned to the other side, smoothing the sweater over her stomach. She felt another prickle of suspicion crawl over her scalp, and shot a look at the window, wondering how much someone standing outside on the ground could see into her room.

"CHARLOTTE!" The shout came up the stairs.

"Coming!" she shouted back, quickly pulling on her white socks and penny loafers, then stepping over to the window to push it back down into place.

Charlotte had to keep the red sweater covered up with her winter coat for the walk to school. It was still freezing outside. And today she had too much to carry, so she had to bring her book bag, which always made her feel juvenile. The hat would mess up her hair, of course, but she, Sue, and Barb always left a few spare minutes before the bell rang so they could go to the bathroom on the main floor, next to the principal's office, and redo their hair. Charlotte brought a can of Spray Net, Sue brought the comb and brush, and Barb brought bobby pins and ribbons. By the time they were seated in first period, their hair was as perfectly coiffed and sprayed and pinned as if they had just come from Durstine's Beauty Shop.

The first few periods at school dragged, and Charlotte had a hard time focusing on the lessons. She couldn't shake the feeling that someone had followed her as she walked to school. She didn't see anyone, even the few times she stopped and turned around. But the feeling was there. It made her walk a lot faster than she normally would have, and in the boring black pencil skirt that wasn't exactly easy. As soon as she pushed through the front doors of the school, she stepped to the side and turned to look out through the window at the street, but she didn't see anything unusual. Just other students and a few passing cars.

The whole day felt off. *Darn Friday the thirteenth!* Sue hadn't said anything about her red sweater, Barb had forgotten the bobby pins, so they all had to use a lot more of the Spray Net, and Charlotte hadn't seen Max Zimmerman at all. She wondered if he had even come to school today. After lunch Charlotte went to her locker, and when she opened it she found a pink envelope that had been slipped through the locker vent.

She pulled her hat down over her ears to keep out the wind. The temperature had risen to the mid-forties throughout the day, but the wind was still fierce. She had stayed behind for a half hour to do some research in the library on her history paper, and also to avoid having to walk behind any four-flushers who might've still been gossiping about the Daltons' unfortunate situation.

All alone out in the late afternoon cold, she set a brisk pace, intent on getting home so that she could go to her room and reread Max's valentine. It said he hoped to see her at the dance. As basic and noncommittal as that was, she still wanted to read it again. Having a crush made you a little stupid. She knew that.

Charlotte was going to the Valentine's Day dance with her group of friends. It wasn't like Homecoming or Prom, where you had to be asked to go. She didn't need to be asked because she knew Max would be there, and he was "hoping to see" her there. Her penny loafers slapped over the damp sidewalk and she tried to keep her mind on the valentine, but, just like that morning, she had the distinct feeling she was being watched. If her hair wasn't all smushed down by her woolen hat it would've been standing on end. Every half block or so, she'd stop and turn her head to listen. The whistle of the wind was all she could hear. When the streets of Wooster were empty, they were really empty, and it was late in the day and getting dark.

She turned down the alley between Mulberry and Ohio Streets that she used as a shortcut, but as soon as she'd made the turn into the deserted alley she realized she was out of view of neighbors or drivers or anyone else who might help her if she needed it. She kept her stride even and tried to control her breathing as she pulled her book bag across her chest like a shield.

Her loafers were still slapping the pavement, but now she could hear another set of footsteps behind her. How far behind, she couldn't tell, and she was now too scared to turn around. Her anxiety prickled across the back of her neck and her breath had shortened to terrified spurts. The footsteps behind her quickened, and she could tell they were getting closer. She kept moving forward, but reached her right hand into her book bag and wedged her finger into the crevice between the Spray Net canister and its lid, pushing until the lid popped off. She then closed her fingers around the canister as the footsteps came up right behind her. *Don't wait, don't wait, just do it. Do it now!*

In a flurry of jerky movements Charlotte pulled her arm from the book bag and whipped around.

"Get awaaaaaaay!" she shouted as she pressed down hard on the nozzle of the Spray Net.

The aerosol went full-force into the face of the person behind her, and she heard an agonized cry and a loud "FUCK!" before she dropped the can and took off at a scramble down the alley and around the corner, moving as fast as her black pencil skirt would allow. She didn't stop running until she had shuffled up the porch steps, fumbling with the doorknob and then flinging open the door and slamming it shut behind her.

Her heart was beating its way out of her chest and her eyes zeroed in on the telephone sitting on the side table next to the couch. Would that be too rash? Hysterical? Calling for help? She hadn't exactly been attacked, had she? Charlotte stalked into the kitchen and peered out the window at the backyard, her arms wrapped around her chest as her eyes darted from the hedges to the back shed and beyond into the neighbors' yards. Going back into the living room, her heart still pounding, she looked out the front window. She didn't know what to do next, but the nagging pressure on her bladder steered her toward the bathroom.

She shot another look at the front door and then the telephone. Should she call someone? The police? Her mother? She imagined what they would ask her. *What did he look like? Could you tell us what he was wearing?* And she had no idea. But it had been a "he." That was the only thing she was sure of. She went to the hallway bathroom and locked herself in, feeling some comfort in the narrow, enclosed space. *Could it have been Max Zimmerman? Could she have just Spray Netted Max Zimmerman?*

She sat fretting on the toilet long enough for the seat to make a red ring around the back of her thighs, and she would have stayed there longer except her legs had started to fall asleep. She was drying her hands on the pink embroidered hand towel when she heard a knock on the front door. She froze and looked at the lock on the bathroom door. The knock came again and Charlotte unhooked the lock and cracked the door just a couple of inches.

"Vivian?" the muffled voice sounded through the front door sidelights. "Anybody home?"

It was Mrs. Gifford, their neighbor. Charlotte released her breath, left the temporary safety of the bathroom, and stumbled back through the living room, rushing to the front door, desperate to see a familiar face.

"Hi!" She flung the door open.

"Oh, Charlotte," Mrs. Gifford said. "Hi, honey. Is your mom home?"

"Not right now," Charlotte answered, no longer breathless, but still speaking more quickly than usual. "She'll be at work until eleven tonight."

"Okay, could you just give her these for me? I found them out in the alley, behind the Messners' garage, when I got home." She handed Charlotte the can of Spray Net she had dropped, and a small white card. "They must have fallen out of her purse. She must have been in an awful hurry if she didn't hear that can hit the ground!"

Charlotte looked down at the small card Mrs. Gifford had handed her and saw that it was her mother's driver's license.

"Thanks," she said, still staring, puzzled, at the license.

"Tell your mom to give me a call!"

"I will."

Charlotte closed and locked the door as Mrs. Gifford made her way down the porch steps. Her mother's driver's license. Could it have fallen out of her book bag when she grabbed the Spray Net? What was her mother's driver's license doing in her book bag? She went to the kitchen and placed the license next to the empty cookie jar.

Charlotte couldn't focus on her homework, or even on *My Cousin Rachel*. She had read and reread the same sentence at least ten times, so she gave up and decided to go to bed early. She and her dad had had a quiet dinner of leftover ham-noodle casserole, and then they'd played checkers for a while. She didn't know if she should tell him what had happened. The more she thought about it, the more she thought maybe even she didn't really know.

As she put on her pajamas, she glanced uneasily at the window. She had pulled down the roll shade as soon as she entered the room. It hadn't even been dark at the time, but she wasn't taking any chances. Now the room felt too warm. She normally would have raised the shade halfway and pushed the window open, just a few inches, to let in the cool outside air. But not tonight. Someone was still out there, and it wasn't Max Zimmerman.

Chapter 40

Vivian walked in the front door of the darkened house. She shut off the porch light as she stepped out of her ankle boots, which were no longer brand-new, and were another reminder of Edward's lies. As if she needed more of those. She hung her coat in the hall closet before heading for the kitchen, flipping the light on as she went to the counter. She was starving. She'd worked for Maria Tomasetti today, because Maria had taken her shifts last Thursday and Friday when Vivian had gone to "Akron."

The cookie jar stood empty on the counter, with light beige crumbs and pieces of white frosting lining the bottom. Oh, for chrissakes. She'd baked the damned cookies Saturday night, and now they were gone and it wasn't even Valentine's Day yet. She looked at the clock above the refrigerator. Twenty after eleven. She heaved a sigh and then spotted something on the counter that hadn't been there earlier. She leaned closer and saw that it was her old driver's license.

Vivian inhaled sharply as she picked it up, and her heart began to pound and she felt her bowels loosen and shift. Mildred Fischer. Oh, Jesus Christ, Mildred Fischer was in Wooster. Had she been to the house? How did the driver's license get there? She caught her reflection in the window over the kitchen sink. She'd kept meaning to put full curtains on that window. She couldn't see anything but the blackness of night, and she was suddenly aware that anyone outside could see her if they were looking in. She walked quickly back to the light switch and flipped it off, plunging the kitchen into darkness. She let her eyes adjust, and then squinted at the window. All the shadows along the perimeter of the backyard looked like people crouching, lying in wait. Vivian felt like screaming, but the house was quiet and she didn't want to break the silence.

She climbed the stairs quickly and looked at the door to Charlotte's room. The light was still on, a slim sliver between the door and the hallway rug.

"Charlotte?" she whispered through the crack in the door.

Charlotte shrieked.

Vivian pushed the door open wide to see Charlotte in her bed, with the covers pulled up beneath her chin, looking like she had just seen a ghost. Or a bat. One time they had a small family of bats in the attic, and Edward had to get after them with a broom.

"Honey, what is it?"

"Oh, Mother," Charlotte breathed.

"What? What is it, and why is my driver's license on the counter?" She was concerned about Charlotte's frightened reaction, of course, but not as much as she was about Mildred Fischer.

"Your license?" Charlotte asked, confused.

She must have been sleeping.

"My driver's license is sitting on the kitchen counter."

"Oh. Mrs. Gifford brought it over today. I think it fell out of my book bag."

"Mrs. Gifford," Vivian repeated, her voice flat. "Erma Gifford? Your book bag? Why would she . . ."

"Mother, someone followed me home from school today. I'm afraid he's still out there."

"Someone was following you?" Vivian reached out and placed her palm to Charlotte's forehead, like she always did when anything was wrong with her. "You said he? He who?"

Charlotte sat up, comforted by her mother's presence, sitting on the bed next to her like she used to do when Charlotte was little. But she kept the covers clenched in her fists.

"I don't know. I just know it was a man. I sprayed him with Spray Net, and I dropped the can and ran."

"Charlotte!"

Charlotte winced.

"When Mrs. Gifford came over she brought the license and the Spray Net. I had dropped it in the alley behind the Messners' garage."

"Oh, my goodness, honey." Vivian knit her eyebrows together and grabbed the points with her thumb and middle finger, as if she were experiencing pain. This was all her fault. The accidentally dropped driver's license had brought this mess to her doorstep, and to her family. *But, I dropped it, I dropped it, I dropped it . . . A little boy picked it up, and put it in his pocket.* She took a deep breath.

"Well, maybe it was someone who found my license and was just trying to return it."

The sentence came out in a calm, smooth, unbroken line, and Vivian hoped it might make Charlotte feel a little better. She almost believed it herself.

Charlotte frowned as if this wasn't something she had considered.

"You didn't put it in my book bag?"

Vivian ignored this. Why would her driver's license have been in Charlotte's book bag?

"You probably scared the poor person off, or maybe they had to rush to the hospital because of the Spray Net."

"Well," Charlotte began. "Maybe. That would make sense, wouldn't it? If you just dropped it somewhere." She released her grip on the covers.

Vivian reached out to pat Charlotte's now-relaxed hands.

"Don't give it any more thought, honey. Get some sleep."

Charlotte sank back against her pillow as a rush of relief

washed over her. Her eyelids drooped and she felt herself being pulled into a deep sleep triggered by exhaustion.

Vivian got up from the bed, leaned over, and kissed Charlotte's forehead, the way she used to do when Charlotte was little.

"Good night," she whispered.

As she closed the door to Charlotte's room behind her, she thought she heard a bump from outside. She crept along the wall to the window at the end of the hallway that looked out onto the Giffords' house. As her gaze traveled down, she saw a figure in the bushes up against the house.

I just know it was a man.

This was not a coincidence. There was no way that driver's license could have traveled itself all the way back here from Syracuse. This was someone who had been in Mildred Fischer's house.

She hoped Charlotte had fallen asleep already, but didn't have time to worry about that. She flung open the door to their bedroom, crossed to Edward's sleeping form, and shook him. Hard.

"Get up!" she hissed. "Get up, get up, get up! Someone's trying to get into the house!"

As soundly as he slept, his response time to being awakened was always immediate. Maybe it was from the few years he worked at the prison. Vivian didn't know. But now, Edward shot up in bed, grabbed his robe, and started down the stairs, with Vivian following close behind. Before Vivian reached the bottom step, there was a shattering crash of glass. She flew around the corner to see a brick lying in the hallway surrounded by the pieces of broken window.

It took four steps for her to reach the telephone in the living room as Edward went for the baseball bat in the hall closet.

"Dorothy!" she shouted into the receiver. "Dorothy, put me through to the police!"

Chapter 41

The newspaper story was all Wooster could talk about. It was all most of Ohio, not to mention the surrounding states, could talk about. It had first been published in Buffalo, New York, and then the Pennsylvania and Ohio papers had picked it up and printed their own versions of it.

Gilbert J. Ogden had been shot and killed as he was trying to cross the border into New York State from Ontario, Canada. That front-page story had revisited the details of the June embezzlement and robbery of the Wayne Building & Loan in Wooster, Ohio, and then borrowed details from the *Buffalo Courier-Express* to describe the recent scene at the border. One of the policemen involved had agreed to speak to Harry Sweeney at *The Daily Record*, and told a tale of police and FBI lying in wait for the fugitive. They had received a tip from a Buffalo switchboard operator by the name of Hazel Horschatz that Gilbert would be traveling to New York. Hazel had contacted local police after connecting and "accidentally overhearing" a call between a man in Toronto and a woman in Lackawanna, "a little nothing town just south of Buffalo."

"The lady, she sounded like an old lady," Hazel had said. "And she said, 'Gilbert!' and then the caller, Gilbert, told her to 'Shushh' and said, oh, what was it he said, it sounded like that guy in *Double Indemnity.* Something like, 'secrecy is of the most importance.' The old lady didn't sound too 'with it,' if you know what I mean," Hazel had said. "The man calling, Gilbert, had to repeat himself, and he just sounded nervous. Nervous and guilty of somethin'."

Hazel Horschatz, "that's H-O-R-S-C-H-A-T-Z if you're gonna put it in the paper," fancied herself quite the amateur sleuth. She'd been listening in on people's conversations ever since she started that job at the phone company three years ago. Three years was a long time to have a job, you know. She read detective novels, except not all the way through, and watched "film noar" movies, mostly all the way through, and boasted to her coworkers about her skill with "figuring things." Sure, sometimes she was wrong, like when Annie Fuller called her ma to tell her about the fella she was going with, and Hazel said Annie's ma would put a stop to that, "mark my words," but Annie ended up marrying the guy, with her ma's blessing.

It wasn't just detective novels and movies, neither, she also read the papers and followed crime stories, until they went dullsville. Back in June she'd latched onto the Wayne Building & Loan story down there in Ohio, due to her fascination with the names of the characters—that's how she referred to the people involved in the news stories, as "characters." Anyway, she thought "Gilbert Ogden" was maybe one of the best names she'd seen so far. She pictured him as a big, fat guy with crazy red hair, and a face just as red from drinking too much of the hooch. "He probably got his start in crime bootlegging," she'd said to the other girls at the switchboard, with a squeezing wink of her left eye (she couldn't wink the right one) and a tap of her index finger to her temple.

Hazel hadn't bothered to read the whole article, which included descriptions of the "characters," and a warning to be on the lookout for anyone fitting those descriptions. If she'd read the whole article, she would have realized how wrong her imaginary sketches were.

She'd told so many of the other girls about her theories about

Gilbert Ogden and Flora Parker that when Gilbert was shot and killed, the girls all scrambled to read about it in the papers the next day. A few of them read the article from start to finish and felt like they should point out to Hazel how wrong she'd been in her profiling. She didn't much appreciate being proven wrong, and had sniffed and reminded everyone that if it hadn't been for her, that bum never woulda been caught in the first place. Hazel had at least been spellbound enough by the name Gilbert and the fact that he was on the lam. That much had stuck with her. When he started stumblin' over that call with the old lady, she just knew it was him. She just knew it!

The Flora Parker woman wasn't caught yet but Hazel was sure she'd be easy to find, with her platinum-blond bouffant hairdo and all the heavy makeup she wore. Again, her coworkers pointed to the description of Flora Parker in the newspaper article to prove her wrong. Hazel had glanced at the page, shrugged, and cracked her gum. In her opinion, anyone named "Flora Parker" should have a platinum-blond hairdo. Well, what did she care, anyway? Richie was going to be proposing any day now and once she was married she could leave that lousy job. Who wanted a job where you couldn't get your ears pierced if you wanted to, that's what she wanted to know. Yeah, that was right, she'd leave that lousy job and those lousy dames who thought they knew so much. If they knew so much, how come they wasn't the ones tippin' off the coppers? Eh? Tell her that. It's Horschatz, H-O-R . . . oh, never mind. Richie'd be proposing soon enough, and she'd just be changing it to Rindfleisch, anyway. Make it Hazel Rindfleisch. That's R-I-N-D-F . . .

The newspapers around Wooster were beaten and battered, folded, unfolded, slapped, shaken, read, and reread over the Gilbert Ogden story, and the townspeople were responding in a variety of ways. Blue-haired Alma Kellerman, who had lived next door to Gilbert Ogden when he'd lived in Wooster, and had enjoyed having him as a neighbor, had gasped in astonishment when she learned he was a bank robber.

"Oh! That nice young man!"

And then this time, when she read he was shot, she was so sorry about it.

"Oh, that nice young man."

He really had been just lovely, helping her plant her hydrangeas and making sure the milkman left her milk up close to the door, instead of leaving it on the bottom step of the porch, where she'd have to limp down to get it.

"Oh, that nice young man!"

And she had been even sorrier when she'd read the part about Gilbert's mother's heart attack upon hearing the news that her son had been shot.

"Oh, dear. That poor woman."

Gerald Houder's wife had told him about the newspaper story, but he hadn't heard her, and had to wait until she was finished with the paper to read it for himself. He'd clenched his pipe between his teeth and shaken his head from side to side, before shouting, "IT'S NOT GOING TO GET YOU ANYWHERE, STEALING FROM HONEST FOLKS LIKE HE DID, THAT'S FOR SURE! SHAME ABOUT HIS MOTHER, THOUGH!"

Once she had recovered from her initial outrage at her Valentine's Day party at the country club having been relegated to page four of the paper, Betty Miller's response to the Gilbert Ogden cover story was stomping around victoriously, nearly growling in vindictive glee, and crowing, "I told you so!" and "He got what he deserved!" She showed not a shred of sympathy, even for Gilbert Ogden's mother. "His mother was probably just as much of a criminal as he was!" Apples didn't fall far from their trees. Everyone knew that.

She had taken it so personally when those criminals stole from her daddy's bank, and embarrassed him in front of the entire town and all the bank employees, when he had done nothing more than be a wonderful employer for them. How ungrateful people could be. The gall and the nerve it took. She would never understand it, never.

She had read the story over her coffee while sitting at the breakfast table, after sending Charles off to work. With the paper still in hand, she marched triumphantly to the telephone and proceeded to call everyone she knew to make certain they all read the story. It wasn't enough that she knew justice had been served, and it wasn't enough that it was the front-page story in *The Daily Record*, not to mention a few of the papers in the surrounding area. She needed everyone to know it, and couldn't just count on them reading it in the paper.

"Crime simply does not pay!" and "Rats will always get what's coming to them, in the end!" Her voice had reached levels of shrill her friends hadn't heard from her before, and they wondered if she had been drinking, so early in the morning. Marilyn Dean even considered calling Dr. Charlton to ask for a prescription for Dexamyl. She wouldn't mind running over to the Rexall for her, really. It wouldn't be any trouble.

That had been the first front-page story about Gilbert J. Ogden, but it wasn't the last. The details of his death were reported with the location, date, and time of day that he had died, and that the cause of death had been "gunshot wound." Gilbert Ogden's death certificate, which was seen only by the attending physician, the coroner, and the Buffalo city clerk who filed it away, would not have been released to the press nor available for public viewing. The death record contained more information than the newspaper story and would have created quite a commotion had it been made public. But it wasn't. And then the commotion happened anyway.

That first Gilbert Ogden story had triggered a wave of calls to the *Daily Record* office, and caused a ripple of shocked murmuring throughout the town of Wooster. But it was the second story that swelled the ripple into a tidal wave and upended the town completely. The envelope addressed to Harry Sweeney, sent anonymously without a return address, had held the smoking gun, so to speak. It wasn't the death record of Gilbert J. Ogden, but a photostat copy of his birth record, with the official stamp of the city of Syracuse. It showed fraternal twins Gilbert Ogden Jacobs and Flora Isabelle Jacobs, their mother, Isabelle Jacobs (mulatto), and their father, Johnston Ellis Reed (white).

Harry Sweeney had met with Lester Kaplan, his editor-in-chief, about the story before publishing. It was a stop-the-presses shocker because J. Ellis Reed was Wooster's mayor. Now, if the editor-in-chief had been the same man who published all the glowing stories about J. Ellis Reed's generosity with the Wayne Building & Loan scandal back in June, there wouldn't have been a problem. The story wouldn't have been a story at all. The birth record would have been mysteriously disposed of, and the matter would have been swept under the rug. Wooster was a town of you-scratch-my-back-I'll-scratch-yours local government and business dealings. But Lester Kaplan was new as editor-in-chief at the *Daily Record*, and he had not had his back scratched.

If Lester Kaplan had been one of Mayor Reed's ardent supporters, or even a friendly acquaintance, the story might have been quashed in a similar way. If Lester Kaplan's application for the Wooster Country Club hadn't been soundly rejected by J. Ellis Reed, Kaplan might've handled the story differently. But rather than scratching Kaplan's back, Reed had reached out his hands and given Kaplan a rough, aggressive push. Kaplan chose to print the second Gilbert Ogden newspaper story as he saw fit.

Betty Miller's response to the second Gilbert Ogden newspaper story was just a touch different from her response to the first. It was good that she had been sitting down when she read it, because when she reached the part with the birth certificate photostat, she fainted.

Chapter 42

J. Ellis Reed enjoyed being mayor. The position suited him. He had been born to be important, and the people of Wooster could see that. In the beginning he had followed all the rules, and made everyone happy. And then he'd thought it might be okay to skim a little off the top of the city coffers. His personal fortune had taken quite a hit with the embezzlement, and it hadn't been as easy as he'd thought it would be to replenish the stores. He had promised himself he'd keep it occasional and small, his dips into the funds. A happy, content community didn't question the local government. Especially after he'd had all those benches installed in front of the public buildings so people had a place to sit.

So the timing could not have been more inconvenient for the two unwelcome shocks that had started and ended his week. The first shock (Monday) was that Gilbert Ogden, the bank embezzler, whom J. Ellis had been paying a private investigator not to find, had not only been found, but had received a "spray of lead justice," "shot down in the street like the dog he was." The newspaper description had been overly theatrical and had made J. Ellis feel ill.

The second shock (Friday) was the one that threatened to kill J. Ellis himself, right there in his shiny leather chair behind his desk at City Hall. The shock of seeing his name alongside Gilbert Ogden's on the front page of *The Daily Record*, not only tying him to a criminal, but exposing his long-held lie. His firstborn son. The son he had abandoned, because he didn't fit with what J. Ellis thought his life should look like.

Gilbert Ogden's last name was actually Jacobs. His first driver's license had been issued in Syracuse by the state of New York, as had been his second. It was the second license that had been typed up by a distracted office clerk at the Department of Motor Vehicles, who erroneously listed him as "Gilbert Ogden," mistaking Gilbert's middle name for his surname. Gilbert, usually obsessively detailed and precise, had been tapping his shoe and gnawing at his fingernails impatiently waiting for the distracted clerk to hurry up and give him the license so that he could make it to the bathroom before disaster struck. Gilbert's groaning intestines (anxiety and undercooked chicken) forced him to snatch the card (without first reviewing it), tuck it in a pocket, and race to the nearest bathroom. Later, as he'd frowned at the driver's license, displeased at the prospect of having to return to the motor vehicle office to rectify the error, he'd had a peculiar thought. Perhaps the error might actually work in his favor. Pave the way for something else. Anonymous entry into the world of J. Ellis Reed in Wooster, Ohio.

J. Ellis Reed hadn't recognized the surname Ogden. He hadn't recognized Gilbert, either. A grown, bespectacled man he had never before met, who seemed extremely bright, with an aptitude for numbers. Perfect for the Wayne Building & Loan. It wasn't until after the robbery that he'd begun to put the pieces of that puzzle together.

J. Ellis stared at the front page of *The Daily Record*. He could no longer play the role of the magnanimous, trustworthy mayor after this goddamned story. The floodlights had suddenly turned on and were blinding him. He stared at the headline, the words blurring as he grew dizzy and felt a hot churning in his bowels. "MAYOR REED, FATHER OF WAYNE BUILDING & LOAN EMBEZZLERS." A great heat rose inside him and he gripped the arms of his leather swivel chair. The telephone on his desk began ringing, as did the one outside his office.

"Sir?" Darla Adams, his faithful secretary, poked her head into the office.

"Not now!" he shouted, slamming a hand on the ink blotter.

The door closed quickly.

Don McAfee had confirmed that Isabelle had never married and her name was still Jacobs, although she had moved from Syracuse to Lackawanna, just outside of Buffalo. She had worked at the public library there. She had always loved to read.

There was a part of J. Ellis that felt genuine pride in Gilbert and Flora. Clever, respectable, and clearly possessing a better work ethic than even his top executives. And he marveled at the sheer ingenuity with which the embezzlement had been executed. He couldn't believe they had pulled something like that off. In his most obtuse moments, he even took credit for how they had turned out as people, as though he'd had something to do with their upbringing.

Betty and Johnston had their trust funds. At the end of the day, he considered the money Gilbert and Flora stole as money that was probably rightfully theirs, in light of all the years he should have been sending funds to their mother but hadn't. His fear of the paper trail leading back to him and to his wealthy, well-respected family was too strong. Allowing them to get away made J. Ellis Reed feel like his debt had been repaid, and that he'd finally done the right thing. He was almost sorry he couldn't tell anyone of his unmitigated, covert benevolence, if only to have Betty revisit the idea of a J. Ellis Reed statue, or at least to have his grandchildren make him another sash.

He groaned and growled in frustration over the newspaper, beating his fists on the ink blotter and wiping the sweat from his face, sick over his imminent demise, or Gilbert's death, or both.

Chapter 43

In every person's life there comes a moment; an opportunity for redemption, a chance at genuine personal growth, to become a better human being. Sometimes this moment is preceded by a jolt of clarity or some startling occurrence or disaster; it often involves an unflinching, hard look at oneself and one's actions, an enormous, and likely painful, gulp of pride, and a Herculean effort at apology.

It would have been nice if Betty Miller had recognized that moment, if she had been a big enough person to apologize to Vivian Dalton. She had intentionally leaked a very personal, deeply humiliating bit of information, and then attempted to publicly embarrass and shame Vivian about it at every opportunity. But, in order to apologize, Betty would have had to acknowledge, not to mention believe, that she had done something wrong, something that begged forgiveness. That what she'd done wasn't a lesson that had needed to be taught, a score that had necessitated evening. But Betty Miller was almost blithely oblivious to her own behavior. How could she have been expected to find fault with herself, when she was so busy finding fault with everyone else? It was quite time-consuming, you understand. Everyone had to atone for *something*. Everyone except her and her father.

Despite several of her so-called friends drawing comparisons, she saw zero similarities between Edward Dalton's secret first marriage scandal and her own father's *alleged* illegitimate children scandal. She became pointedly resolute in proving that the photostat of the birth record had somehow been faked. It was impossible and inconceivable that her father, *her father*, would have done something so shameful.

Once the people of Wooster wrapped their heads around the fact that Gilbert and Flora had been of mixed race, they then began whispering that Gilbert and Flora had in fact looked a little like J. Ellis Reed. Something in the forehead, and maybe the jawline.

"*Non*-sense!" and "Pre-*post*-er-ous!" Betty had exclaimed.

Bystanders would have said she was shrieking, but Betty Miller did not shriek, she spoke very distinctly. The man who had impregnated the Negro woman (Betty made no distinction between mulatto and Negro), then abandoned her to raise two children alone (a shame, really, that was true), must surely have been someone else. She refused to believe it, even after her father admitted his wrongdoing.

He stated it very plainly Saturday afternoon (after everyone and their mothers had read both *Daily Record* articles about Gilbert Ogden), in the parlor of the Reeds' house. Betty was there, in the smart new skirt and jacket set she'd bought at Beulah Bechtel's, because she'd needed a little pick-me-up. In spite of the cost, the skirt and jacket hadn't quite done it, so after shopping she tried, repeatedly and unsuccessfully, to telephone Dr. Charlton at home to request a prescription for Dexamyl. The Bell telephone lines seemed to be backed up again, which was proving to be quite the regular problem.

Her younger brother, Johnston, was at the house (and in need of a haircut), as was their mother. She sat pale and silent, but as lovely as ever, in the Prussian-blue dress set against the coral damask of the wing chair. Her father would not make eye contact with any of them, but he spoke clearly. He admitted everything, from the love affair with Isabelle Jacobs to the unplanned pregnancy to when he fled town. He even cried a little bit, but squeezed his eyes shut tight to fight back the tears. And still, Betty wouldn't believe it. Her face became a grinning mask, like one of the Howdy Doody characters on the back panel of the Kellogg's Rice Krispies box in her pantry. Her body was so rigid she was getting muscle spasms in her neck and back, and her hands had been clenched into fists for what seemed like days, the little Charitable Thoughts angel charm hanging impotent and forgotten from her wristwatch. She had braced herself for that family meeting, and the truth her father was trying to impart just bounced right off her invisible shield, deflected.

Betty didn't try to understand why her father would have had a romantic relationship with a Negro, because to her it simply never happened. She might have tried to comfort her mother, like John was doing, but there was nothing to comfort her about. Everything was just fine. Mother was probably just tired. Betty was able to give her father a tight hug, because he was a wonderful man who had been treated very badly by the newspapers. Make no mistake, *The Daily Record* would be getting an earful from her. There were myriad ways she would make that paper suffer. She was privy to dozens and dozens of secrets and scandals of the people in Wooster, and she'd use that leverage to her advantage. Perhaps she would start her own newspaper. The kind of publication that would put out proper, wholesome content that would benefit the people of Wooster.

As she kissed her mother's pale cheek and hugged her brother goodbye, she had already begun planning the luncheon. She slid her pocketbook over her wrist and pulled on the short beige leather gloves. It would be a bigger challenge to boycott the town's most widely circulated newspaper, but she wasn't worried. What would be the best food to serve at the luncheon? She'd ask Dolly.

But as she exited the house and walked toward the Cadillac parked outside, Betty had to concentrate on keeping her breathing even and her shoulders squared. The Coupe was the latest model, more fashionable than Marilyn Dean's, but did that even matter now? Had it ever mattered? Her steps slowed on the driveway as she thought back to New Year's Eve, when she'd been basking in the warm, hazy glow of her third champagne cocktail while all four of her children played Parcheesi under the lights of their grandparents' Christmas tree. She remembered feeling happy then. Feeling happy and thinking that the only things that should matter are God, love, and family. *Family.*

She tucked herself onto the padded bench of the Coupe and pulled the heavy car door closed with a slam. Gripping the top of the steering wheel in her gloved hands, Betty let her shoulders slump and begin to shake as anguished sobs escaped her throat.

Chapter 44

"Gilbert Ogden!" "Ogden!" "Oh, my goodness, the Gilbert Ogden story!" "Did you read about Gilbert Ogden?" was what squawked out of every headset at the switchboard that week. The Eddie Fischer story had been buried by the Gilbert Ogden story. On any other day, it would have been big news, front page even, that someone had attacked that nice Charlotte Dalton (poor dear!), and then tried to break into the Daltons' house by throwing a brick through the window. But with Gilbert Ogden being shot on the front page, Eddie Fischer had been pushed back to page two.

He'd been apprehended by the police not far from the Daltons' house that night. Vivian had gone with Edward to the police station, grateful that Erma Gifford could stay at the house with Charlotte. It had been sad more than anything else. Here was this man, he wasn't a kid anymore, Jesus, he was in his late twenties, and he was angry and confused and frustrated. Vivian knew what that felt like, and she knew just what he was missing. A connection to his father. Vivian could see that much in his eyes. His eyes that looked just like Edward's, but a little more red and bloodshot from the Spray Net.

He wouldn't say much to them, or to the police. But he asked to speak to Edward in private. The police said no, but they sent one officer into a room with the two of them, giving them a little more privacy. Vivian'd watched the clock on the wall of the station, wringing her handkerchief in her hands, thinking about how everything connected to Edward's big lie just kept getting worse and worse. *Happy goddamned Valentine's Day.*

Vivian hoped Eddie Fischer wouldn't mention anything about her driver's license to Edward. She'd lose the upper hand if Edward knew she'd gone to Syracuse, and she couldn't have that. The upper hand was all she was hanging on to at this point. Holding on to the ends of slippery fingers.

She'd heard Eddie tell the police he wasn't going to hurt Charlotte, just wanted to talk to her. "She's my sister, right?" But he didn't have an excuse for throwing the brick through the window. Vivian saw that brick and she saw the rage. She knew what that looked like. He would go back to Syracuse, maybe to jail. Vivian wasn't sure if he had broken any laws by coming to Ohio, but she'd be glad when he left and went back to his life in New York. *You've seen your father now, so that's finished.* Vivian's insides clenched as a thought tiptoed into her mind. *What if it wasn't finished, though? What if this person was to be part of their lives now?*

Edward and Vivian had left the police station in silence, and rode home in silence. They had entered the house in silence, and Vivian had helped Edward tape newspaper over the broken window in silence. Vivian would've been aware of the silence if her mind hadn't been running a steady stream of chatter on its own. *Did his son tell him I was in Syracuse? Is he angry with me? Is he angry with his son? What gives him the right to be angry? I'm the one who should be angry!*

Charlotte skipped the Valentine's Day dance and kept herself shut up in her room with an acute case of temporary agoraphobia. She'd played her Eddie Fisher record all night, and then all day Sunday, and would have played it all that next week, except the smaller story, on the second page of *The Daily Record*, after the story about Gilbert Ogden, told her that Edward "Eddie"

Fischer was the name of the man who'd been arrested for destruction of property at the Dalton residence, and for assaulting Charlotte Dalton. Charlotte knew that she'd never again hear the name Eddie Fisher (no matter how it was spelled) without thinking of that attack.

It was all over school the following week. Eddie Fischer attacked Charlotte, and threw a brick through the window in their house. Some of the more gullible students believed it had been the crooner Eddie Fisher, and they wondered how Charlotte had even met him. She must have been some kind of girl to make Eddie Fisher crazy enough to throw a brick through her window. Sue, in particular, found that to be the absolute limits of hysterical. Not better than *The Myth of Syphilis*, but a close second. She went out of her way to encourage those rumors.

"Char," she had said over chipped beef in the cafeteria, "if Eddie Fisher was throwing a brick through your window, you'd invite him in, at least, wouldn't you?"

Charlotte had pulled a wan smile, wishing Sue didn't have to make a joke out of everything. Sue had no idea how terrifying it had been, and it would be a while before Charlotte could see the humor in the Eddie Fisher rumors. Barb was more sympathetic.

"You must have been so scared!"

Charlotte *had* been so scared, and the fear had usurped the rest of the weekend. The fear kept her from going to the Valentine's Day dance, and Charlotte also blamed the fear for sending Max Zimmerman right into the arms of Peggy Cline, who hadn't experienced any kind of fear that night. Max couldn't meet Charlotte's eye at school, and Sue's solution was, "He can take a handful of drop-dead pills, that's what I say," which sounded just fine to Charlotte.

After she read the details of the police report, Charlotte had broken the Eddie Fisher 45 over her knee, as well as her other Eddie Fisher records, and tossed them all in the wastebasket under the desk in her room.

Louis Jordan's "Saturday Night Fish Fry" had filled the silence in her bedroom instead. Upbeat and peppy, it was exactly that kind of shocking "Negro music" Mrs. Barnes had been complaining about when her son Raymond brought that fast New York City girl home to meet her. Charlotte knew her mother held those same narrow-minded thoughts, and was probably cursing at the ceiling as the music blared above her in the kitchen.

Charlotte would have been surprised to see her mother pick up the record and read the title with a little wistfulness, when she went into Charlotte's room to pick up stray items of clothing for that week's wash. The Fish Fry. The good old McGinty Fish Fry. What she wouldn't give to go back to those days, when her life in Wooster had been so much simpler.

Life in Wooster had become complicated for all the Daltons, and Charlotte couldn't wait for the day she'd finally get to leave. When she made the cheerleading squad at Wooster High School that spring, wearing the brand-new saddle shoes her dad had bought her, she felt like she could probably wait it out a little longer. She would add cheerleading to her growing list of accomplishments (she was a joiner, all right) and ignore anyone who told her it wasn't important. Max Zimmerman's new girlfriend Peggy Cline had tried out as well. She hadn't made it.

One more thing that made Charlotte feel a little better about Wooster was the exposé about Mayor Reed. She had read it until her eyeballs just about burst from their sockets, and she had finished the story with her mouth hanging wide open. She was willing to bet Mayor Reed's granddaughter Margie Miller was probably shitting a brick right about then.

Chapter 45

Vivian didn't know who had sent the photostat of Gilbert and Flora's birth certificates to *The Daily Record*. Her copy was still tucked safely away in the bottom of the hatbox. She'd just about fainted when she saw the front page of the paper that day. She'd hustled upstairs to the bedroom closet and thrown off the lid of the hatbox. But there it was. Still sitting next to the cigarettes, which she still needed every once in a while, and never you mind.

On the long drive back from Syracuse she'd considered it. Well, she'd done more than just consider it. In her mind she pictured it'd be like that time she'd stood at the switchboard and scooped her arm under all those connected cords and in one fell swoop unplugged them all. She'd used her personal power to disrupt Wooster, and it had felt good, at first. The story about J. Ellis Reed would definitely disrupt Wooster, she'd thought as she drove that endless, barren stretch of highway between New York and Ohio, letting her mind wander in all sorts of directions. Vivian's imagined version of the disrupting involved a dramatic scene where Betty Miller would be forced to read the details of the birth record aloud on television, during a commercial break for *I Love Lucy*.

Exposing J. Ellis Reed would've hurt that nasty Betty Miller the same way Betty's rumor-spreading had hurt Vivian. And she might've done it, at some point, if someone else hadn't beaten her to it. But . . . she also might've kept it a secret. It was all too muddled now to really be sure, but Vivian decided to give herself a little pat on the back for resisting temptation and keeping the document hidden in the hatbox. She decided to look at it as a spiritual boost, continuing to push her in the direction of Good. Everyone needed a little boost now and then.

The spiritual boost was almost as rewarding to Vivian as the reassurance she'd gotten from that birth record. She'd always sensed Gilbert and Flora weren't suited as a couple. *I know people, goddam*—She stopped herself in mid-thought, suddenly conscious that "goddammit" was not exactly in keeping with her spiritual boost. If she planned to continue on her route to Good she'd better watch her thoughts. Anyway, that sneaky Gilbert Ogden'd been shot, but there'd been no word of Flora Parker. Vivian wouldn't be one bit surprised if she was off somewhere with her husband, Bill, enjoying the rest of that Wayne Building & Loan money. Because those two had looked like a couple of lovebirds to Vivian, and *Vivian knew people*.

The typewriter in the little attic room at the Dalton house had seen a whole lot more poetry, and not quite as many desperate letters to civic officials, as a result of the spiritual boost and the route to Good. She found that the poetry brought her a more peaceful sensation in her stomach, but the knots hadn't disappeared completely. It was as if they'd been soaked in liquid and shrunk in size, but were now also just a little bit tighter and just a mite more difficult to untie.

Vivian's leather pumps slapped over the damp pavement as she passed Freedlander's on her way to work. Last week's snow had melted and it was looking like that groundhog might have been wrong after all. *Let's hope so*, she thought. *I've had enough of winter. I'm ready for spring.* She hummed "Row, Row, Row Your

Boat" as the runoff from the melted snow ran in a mini-river along the curb next to her.

Vivian didn't have a new spring hat, but she did have a new invisible, self-appointed halo. She left that in place, but hung her beige cotton gabardine coat on its hook, over her pocketbook, then entered the switchboard room and made a declaration to her fellow operators.

"I will no longer be eavesdropping on the telephone conversations."

She made this declaration in a whisper, out of earshot of their supervisor Leona, because the switchboard operators at Bell were not supposed to listen in on the conversations. It was definitely there, somewhere, in the rule book. And now, suddenly, Vivian agreed with it.

Her announcement had been met with dubious furrowed brows, both black-penciled and brown, and the switchboard operators at Bell decided to give Vivian some space in the minutes, hours, and days following that odd announcement. It was one thing to decide not to eavesdrop herself (Maria Tomasetti had just shaken her head and laughed), and quite another to pass judgment on all the others. But they'd all read the newspapers about Edward's secret, dangerous, delinquent son attacking poor Charlotte. Vivian deserved some compassion and some space to breathe, and they just ignored her when she judged them; when she pursed her lips and shook her head if she spied Dorothy, Ruth, Pearl, or Laura flip the mute switch and lean in to listen.

The rest of Wooster had been catching their collective breath as well, as the hysteria of late February gradually subsided. The month of March had ushered in at least one significant change. J. Ellis Reed resigned his position as mayor, out of embarrassment over the scandal, and had taken an early retirement in order to spend more time with his wife, who was standing by his side, pale, poised, and wearing a forced smile, in the face of it all.

Harold Richardson, the council president, had to be sworn in as interim mayor, but when the term was up there would be another election. The grapevine was already buzzing that there was a lady—A LADY—who was considering throwing her hat in the ring. Dorothy Hoffman had overheard something about it at the switchboard.

"Didjya catch her name?"

Vivian frowned her disapproval at Pearl for asking the gossipy question, then scowled when one of her lights lit up and she had to answer the call instead of hearing the name of the lady running for mayor. *A lady mayor?*

Vivian quickly connected the call, then flipped the mute switch.

"When her kids were in high school she studied right along with them . . ." Ruth offered, from what she'd heard.

"She got her diploma . . ." Laura's baby voice chimed in. "And then went to Cornell! That's Ivy League!"

Cornell was a serious college. Even more serious than the College of Wooster. Vivian began to wonder if she might vote for a lady mayor, if the lady'd gone to Cornell.

"And, now, what do you know," Pearl marveled. "She's thinking of running for mayor of Wooster."

Vivian's smug self-righteousness about no longer eavesdropping lasted for a whole week. Then she rationalized that she could be more compassionate to her fellow Woosterites if she knew what was going on in their lives.

Chapter 46

Edward Dalton had never been a man of too many words, but his son's surprise visit over Valentine's Day weekend had sent him into a long spell of troubled silence. It'd been four weeks since the near-attack on Charlotte and the attempted break-in, and Edward had spent every waking moment in the shed out back, in the basement, at work, or at the lodge. Vivian wondered if he was speaking to anyone outside the house, or if his vocal cords had just shriveled right up from lack of use. When Charlotte asked him questions, he'd answer with a shake of his head, or by placing a hand on her shoulder or a kiss on the top of her head.

Vivian had enjoyed having the upper hand for that brief time she'd had it, what with Edward being a lying bigamist and her being the unsuspecting wife (mistress!). But the little drop-in from Eddie Junior had messed things up. Now Vivian wasn't sure where to direct her lingering anger, which had lost a lot of steam with Edward's sudden silence.

Vivian had asked if he wanted to come with them to Grandma Kurtz's ninetieth birthday party, and he hadn't responded. She kept talking to him, in spite of his muteness, because she knew the silence had to break sometime and he'd say something eventually. Wouldn't he? Of course he would. Wouldn't he? She didn't know. It dawned on her that she didn't know Edward like she'd thought she did. She felt like she'd been smacked diagonally by life, like in Looney Tunes where the smack froze the cartoon character into a sideways, flattened-out position. Vivian felt like she was now limping around all off-kilter, and maybe veering a little bit off the Road to Good.

Grandma Kurtz's house was packed with relatives, from the crotchety ninety-year-old matriarch herself all the way down to the youngest, messiest great-grandchild, one of Cousin George's kids. Vivian brought Charlotte, who wanted to see her great-grandmother and spend some time with her own cousins. Vivian didn't really want to spend time with anyone, after being the humiliated center of attention of the family last month. But she wouldn't let her bruised ego keep her from making an appearance. *Fine, thank you!* It was a momentous occasion, after all. Ninety years, sakes alive. And you just never knew; maybe the old bag had some money she'd leave them in her will. Grandma McGinty had been her favorite grandma. Grandma Kurtz had just been a pain in the neck. But, happy birthday, old lady!

The living room and adjacent parlor were packed to the gills with Kurtzes and the people they'd married, and Vivian had somehow ended up standing next to Vera while their Uncle David was making a speech. She hadn't spoken to Vera since she'd called her a spoiled brat and an ungrateful bitch, and Vivian didn't suppose she should expect an apology anytime soon. No, instead, right while Uncle David was talking about Grandma Kurtz's long, incredible life (Vivian wanted to know what was so "incredible" about living on a farm and having too many kids), Vera had the nerve to grab Vivian's right hand. Vivian felt Vera's fingers fumbling around the claddagh ring, before she grasped it and yanked down, making a clumsy attempt at being playful, but really trying to pull it right off Vivian's finger.

"Come on, Vivy," she said in a low voice. "You weren't really the first one to get married, now, were you?"

The few relatives who were standing nearby let out a collective gasp. It was a low blow, even for Vera.

"Vera!" Cousin Ruby hissed at her, while Uncle David, who could only hear the sound of his own voice, continued to talk. Vivian moved behind Ruby, away from Vera, her face reddened to the color of boiled beets.

After he finished his speech, David led everyone in a rousing chorus of "For She's a Jolly Good Fellow," and while they all applauded the birthday girl, David received a wrinkled, smiling "Thank you, dear" from Grandma Kurtz. She must have been mellowing in her very old age, Vivian thought as she turned and took to the stairs.

Who the hell did Vera think she was, anyway? *Calls me a bitch when I've just been through the worst time of my life?* Vivian stomped past the second floor and continued up the staircase. Her skin felt prickly and the sting of tears threatened. Her self-esteem was hanging on by maybe just a ring and a ring finger. She could not believe what her sister had just done.

While friends and relatives milled around on the first floor, gabbing and eating cake, Vivian found herself alone and holding back tears while waiting to use the special bathroom Grandma Kurtz had had installed on the third floor of the house. "Because when I'm rememberin' in mah picture books . . ."—"picture books" was what Grandma Kurtz called the photo albums her children and grandchildren gave her—"when I'm rememberin' in mah picture books I don't want to have to hightail it all the way down the stairs if I hear nature callin'."

Almost no one else bothered with the third-floor bathroom because they had no interest in Grandma Kurtz's picture books, and also because of all the stairs, but Vivian had made the extra effort to get away from everyone else at the party so she could be alone. But, wouldn't it just figure, there was someone else in the special bathroom, and she had to wait.

Finally, the door to the bathroom swung open and Vera's husband, Wally, and a fresh spritz of a woodsy cologne, greeted her. Vivian forced a smile (*Fine, thank you!*). She was never without her manners at events and gatherings, regardless of who was there. Wally stood in the doorway, all protruding stomach, armpit stains, and wide eyes, surprised at seeing someone else on the third floor. He then slapped a hand to his cheek and tilted his head.

"Well, if it isn't the second wife of Edward Dalton!"

And that was all she'd needed.

She shoved her way past Wally into the bathroom, slammed and locked the door, and reached for the beige bath towel that hung folded on the rod. She didn't even wait to hear if Wally had started down the stairs before she held the folded towel to her face and let out a muffled scream. She then sat down hard on the wooden toilet seat cover (which she'd had to put down, of course, since Wally was a typical animal who left the seat up) and screamed into the towel again.

When she opened her eyes the edges of her vision blurred and she grabbed the seat under her to steady herself. The small room looked to be tilting from one side to the other. She squeezed her eyes shut again and tried to slow her breathing. There was a faint ringing in her ears and she could hear the faraway voices of the party two floors below. When she opened her eyes a second time the blurriness had cleared. She looked over at the towel and smiled at the lipstick mark Grandma Kurtz would yell about later, long after all her guests had gone. She felt a hiccup of giggle in her throat. Then Charlotte was calling up the stairs after her, and she stood quickly, smoothing her dress and the stray hairs around her face. In the mirror she rubbed Fire & Ice from her dentures and from the edges of her lips.

When she reappeared downstairs in the parlor with Charlotte, Ruby came at her with a small plate of cake and a fork. "Vivy, did you hear about the lady who might be running for mayor of Wooster? Are you feeling okay? You look pale. Charlotte, honey, there's more cake in the kitchen."

This was how Ruby offered comfort, and Vivian appreciated it. She accepted the cake and fork and shot a quick look around the rooms. She could see her mother near the kitchen and her father next to the picture window, talking to Henry and his awful wife, Norma. Awful in the way that she was just so prim-and-pretty perfect, and had been lucky enough to snag Henry for a husband.

"Vivy?"

"Hmm?" She looked at Ruby. "Lady running for Wooster mayor?"

"Yes!" Ruby clapped her hands together. "She went to Apple Creek High School, so you wouldn't have known her. She had to drop out, but sakes alive if she didn't get right back into it after her kids went there."

Vivian had poked the fork gently into the cake and pried off a corner of the piece.

"Can you imagine it? Mayor Sylvia!"

"Sylvia?" Vivian repeated, letting the name settle properly on her tongue. "Sylvia *Emerich*?"

"Why, yes!" Ruby was thrilled that Vivian knew who she was talking about. "It's not Emerich anymore, though, it's Yoder. You know, she married that sweet farmer." Her voice lowered to a whisper. "He, uh, got her into trouble, you know. That's why she had to leave school."

The farmer takes a wife. The farmer takes a wife. Eeeeeeeee!

When Vivian got home after the party she removed her pumps at the front door, hung her coat and hat in the closet, and stomped straight up to the little attic room, leaving Charlotte to bring in the plate they'd brought the banana bread on, and to lock the car and close the garage. Vivian closed the door to the room, and then sat and cried over the typewriter for a half hour, before she eventually dried her eyes and then began to hammer away at the keys.

Outside My Window

Spring is only a glimpse away
With holiday seasons in the past
In simple thanks to God we pray
Our labors in usefulness to cast

Give us strength to lift the soil
Plant seeds with loving care
Achieve happiness through our toil
And feel your guidance always there

This quiet, between-the-seasons stage
Is like a hand upon my shoulder
Releasing power to turn the page
And face our new spring bolder.

First thing Monday morning Vivian dropped off the envelope with "Outside My Window" in person to the Spindrift committee office out on RD 4, just past the chocolate factory where Don McAfee had his office. Rather than sending her a mailed response, the committee telephoned her on Wednesday to tell her it had been accepted, and as it had such a timely, springtime theme, they would be printing it in the following Saturday Spindrift column.

Vivian spent all day Thursday and all day Friday smiling and sailing about everywhere she went. Work, Buehler's, out to the shed to tell her mute husband his dinner was getting cold. You could not wipe the smile from her face. This was more than her usual happiness at having her poetry published in *The Daily Record*. She'd seen the acceptance from the newspaper as a sign.

The freedom she felt, and the new knowledge that Apple Creek's Sylvia Emerich had turned her life around, gave her a little hope that maybe she wasn't as stuck in her life as she'd thought.

Chapter 47

"What on earth would I do with this?" Vivian exclaimed, holding her Mother's Day gift (what she would later be able to describe as) *aloft*.

Charlotte had given her mother a brand-new copy of *Webster's New World Dictionary*.

"Oh, Mother." Charlotte rolled her eyes with a little smile, then went up to her room, leaving her parents sitting together on the sofa in the living room.

Vivian placed the dictionary on the coffee table and scooted back against the lipstick-free sofa cushions.

"Edward," she said. "I know you don't want to talk about it."

He frowned and looked at his fingernails, which were still stained and beaten up from the flower window boxes he'd made her.

"Will you just tell me one thing?"

When he didn't get up from the sofa she continued.

"Did you take that prison guard job so you could keep an eye on him?"

Edward pursed his lips and looked at the floor.

Vivian watched him stare at the carpet for about a minute before giving a slow nod of his head.

"You remember . . ." he began, and Vivian stayed as still as she could so he wouldn't stop. It was time he said *something*.

"You remember how you used to talk about those girls who

got themselves into trouble before they got married?" He raked his palm back and forth over his forehead a few times, then rubbed the rough, weathered skin on his cheeks and chin. Vivian sat and waited.

"I still remember that one, Sylvia Emerich. You never stopped talking about her."

Sylvia Emerich. Vivian nodded and wondered why it was that everyone was suddenly talking about Sylvia Emerich all the time. But she knew what he meant. She remembered. She'd carped and harped about Sylvia for the first couple years of her marriage. "That tramp," and "ruined her life," and "what kind of idiot does something so irresponsible?" and so on and so on. She was a little surprised that Edward had been listening to her. Most of her grumbling back then'd been because she was stuck all by herself in that crummy little bungalow, lonely and bored and grumpy.

She stared at the *W* on the *Webster's* cover for a few minutes while Edward just sat there next to her, elbows on knees, holding his forehead in his hands. Nothing more was said, except the talking inside of Vivian's head. Finally, the talking started to make sense to her. Wasn't that just a hoot? She'd never thought that her own husband might've done something "so irresponsible" himself.

Vivian hadn't really thought about it up until now, but if Edward had stayed with Mildred this whole time, instead of leaving her and coming to Wooster, they'd be going on their thirtieth anniversary this year. *Oh, poor Mildred*, Vivian thought as she continued to stare at the dictionary cover. *Thirtieth is pearls.* Vivian's head shook slowly from side to side. *Tsk-tsk. That was a shame.*

She finally reached out her manicured hand for Edward's paint-stained one. He'd never been a big talker, and what he'd just said to her was plenty. She knew him enough to know that. Edward closed his fingers around hers and they sat that way, quietly beside each other on the sofa in the living room.

"Eddie broke his parole leaving Syracuse to come here."

"Mm-hmm," Vivian murmured.

"They sent him back to prison."

"Mm-hmm."

"I'd like to visit him there in the summer."

Vivian said nothing, but nodded and squeezed his hand. Then they sat staring ahead through the living room picture window for what seemed like hours.

"Did you hear?" Vivian finally broke the silence and turned to face her husband. "Sylvia Emerich might be running for mayor of Wooster next year?"

Chapter 48

Charlotte would have said she had had quite enough shocks and surprises to last her through the rest of the year, thanks a bunch. However, one Sunday afternoon, a couple of weeks after Mother's Day, she had come home from Barb's house to find her mother tucked in a corner of the couch, with her new dictionary open on the coffee table and her nose buried in Charlotte's repaired copy of *The Myth of Sisyphus*. Sisyphus, the Greek king who stole the secrets of the gods and was punished for it; condemned to roll an enormous stone up a hill for all eternity.

At this point Charlotte would have chosen that stone-rolling rather than the impossible task of trying to understand her family. Her mother, who normally would have been wearing her apron and banging cabinets in the kitchen (which she had not done in months), was in a housedress and a pair of Charlotte's dad's socks, curled into the far corner of the couch, reading. *A book.*

"Sisyphus was an absurd hero," Mr. Grandy had said, standing at the chalkboard in Charlotte's English class.

What was absurd was Charlotte's mother, Vivian "I-don't-trust-people-who-read-books" Dalton, reading classic literature in the Dalton family living room with nary a movie magazine in sight. Charlotte stood gaping like a fish at the aquarium glass, her mouth dropping open and pulling closed.

"I have decided," her mother announced that night at dinner, "that I would like to get my high school diploma."

The word "diploma" hung in the air over the casserole dish of cheese and burned chicken; a fancy, swirling invisible banner that suddenly sounded very foreign to Charlotte. *Did she say "diploma"?* Charlotte stared, and her dad stared, and her mother picked up her fork and was using it to prod at a few peas rolling around her plate.

"What?" her dad asked.

"I *said*—" her mother began again, really leaning into the word "said," drawing it out into several syllables. *Sa-a-a-a-ai-d*.

"You're not going to be in classes at the school, are you?" Charlotte blurted out, interrupting. She could picture it now, starting her junior year with Mrs. Kelvin saying: "Why, Vivian Dalton, did you make that dress yourself? And I just love that rooster brooch! Come sit here, next to Charlotte."

"No, Charlotte," her mother said airily. "I've spoken with Principal Scott, and he's going to have some of the teachers coordinate a home curriculum for me."

Coordinate. Curriculum. Charlotte stared at her mother, eyes wide. She then felt a sickly, sticky veil of horror descend over her at the idea of her mother meeting with the principal. Then she frowned at the absurdity. *Absurd.*

"Why do you want to do that?" Charlotte's dad asked.

"Yes," Charlotte chimed in, in what she hoped was a more pleasant tone. "Yes, why?"

"Because, I want to. That's all."

Her dad shrugged, and went back to eating his cheesy chicken, with a slight smile playing around the corners of his lips. Charlotte's eyebrows furrowed again and she watched her mother scoop the peas onto the edge of her fork and guide them into her mouth.

Charlotte's desire to leave Wooster returned with the strength of a late spring tornado. But not until she finished high school. Until she could get out, maybe this wouldn't be the worst thing. The dictionary on Mother's Day had been kind of a joke, but was it really a bad thing that her mother wanted to learn? With any luck she would use that dictionary to expand her vocabulary and her mind, so she could stop using the racial epithets that she didn't really understand and that made Charlotte cringe with shame, and maybe she'd finally learn what "four-flushers" really meant.

Chapter 49

June crept up on Vivian almost without notice. All of a sudden it was time to flip the page on the wall calendar in the kitchen. Edward had installed the screens in all the windows, which were now open, just above the freshly planted geraniums in Vivian's new flower boxes, to let the occasional warm breeze circulate throughout the house.

Springtime had come late in Ohio that year, but it'd finally brought back the kind of weather where Vivian wanted all the windows and doors open so she could smell the flowers, feel the warm breezes, and hear the crickets chirping at night. A lovely scent wafted in from the honeysuckle bush just outside the kitchen window, and Vivian found herself lingering over the dishes just to enjoy it.

"You think whatever was wrong with her in February had anything to do with it?" Edward asked from the table.

"Mmm." Vivian shrugged but kept her eyes on the backyard.

Vera hadn't really been sick in February, as far as she knew, but if it made more sense to Edward that she had been, and that Vivian had been a good sister and gone to see her in Akron, all the better.

"She seem sick at the party?"

"No." Vivian suppressed a grimace remembering Grandma

Kurtz's birthday party, and Vera's rude and awful behavior. "Healthy as ever."

Vivian had been stunned speechless when her sister Violet telephoned to tell her about Vera's stroke.

"She's in the hospital right now, but should be able to go home with Wally in a few days," Violet had said over the line, before taking a long drag on her cigarette.

Violet, too, had quit smoking to have James and Emily, like Vivian had with Charlotte, but had started up again when James got polio. He was fine now, but Violet hadn't completely recovered. Her smoking was here and there when things were good. After learning of their eldest sister's stroke, she was back to a pack a day.

"Unh," was all that had come out of Vivian's mouth.

"The doctor says she can't talk, but she understands everything. And she can't move the whole left side of her body. Wally's hiring a nurse to help her when he's at work."

Vivian had pulled the telephone cord to its limit and was almost to the top of the stairs. She wanted to lie down on her bed, but instead slumped into a sitting position on the tenth stair.

"Viv? Did you hear me? Are you there?"

She steered the Buick over to the curb in front of Violet's house and honked the horn. Violet still couldn't drive, and said she had no intention of learning. Why would she? Robert drove her everywhere. Vivian had rolled her eyes. It was almost as if Violet enjoyed being a little bit helpless now and then. That wouldn't have annoyed Vivian so much if the helplessness came along with a considerate punctuality. Violet was always late.

Vivian turned the rearview mirror toward her and patted the skin under her eyes. The makeup didn't quite cover the shadows, evidence of the sleepless nights she'd endured since hearing about her sister's stroke. Vera was only forty-four. And Vivian had been struggling with flashes of *Good!* that squashed the charitable pity she should've been feeling one hundred percent of the time. She'd held on to much of that anger toward Vera, and also thought that Vera's stroke was probably her just desserts for being such a horrible sister all these years.

Five minutes passed before Violet came out of the house, and through the open windows of the Buick Vivian heard her calling back into the house to Robert that she'd be back in time to cook dinner. She climbed in the front seat, and the McGinty sisters started on their drive up to Akron.

"Vivy, gosh, you're thin!" Violet exclaimed. She hadn't seen Vivian since Grandma Kurtz's birthday party. "You look like Katharine Hepburn."

Vivian made a face. Katharine Hepburn was one of those women who wore trousers.

"I haven't been baking as much. Except for these."

She patted the tin of peanut butter crisscross cookies beside her. Vera had always liked peanut butter cookies.

Vivian might have dropped a few pounds, but it was nothing compared to Vera. Vivian inhaled sharply when they stepped into Vera's bedroom. She'd never seen her older sister so weak, so diminished. Her skin lay atop her bones like wax paper across a rickety ladder. In fact, she looked like a skeletal version of their mother. Violet took Vivian's hand and pulled her up next to the bed, where Vera was propped up against a lace-edged pillow, with their mother's crazy quilt pulled up around her torso. Two straight-backed chairs had been set next to the window, to the left of Vera's bed.

Vera's eyes lit up when they drew closer. They were watery, but alert, and there was a brightness in them that Vivian'd never seen before. That scared her even more than her sister's sickly appearance. There'd never been a time she could remember when her older sister looked pleased to see her. Vivian was properly unnerved and had to put her hand on the back of one of the chairs to steady herself.

"Hi!" Violet greeted Vera in a cheery but soft voice, as if speaking too loudly would give Vera another stroke.

The right side of Vera's mouth pulled up in a ghastly way. On the nightstand next to the bed was a glass of water and a notepad and pencil. The stroke had paralyzed Vera's vocal cords and the left side of her body, so she couldn't speak. But she could write what she wanted to say on the notepad.

"She's smiling, Viv," Violet said, explaining the lopsided facial expression that was sure to give Vivian nightmares.

Vivian stood next to the chair, still holding it with one hand, the other holding her pocketbook. The nurse had taken the cookie tin to the kitchen when they'd arrived. Seeing Vera in her current condition threw Vivian's emotions into a choppy washtub of confusion. From the bed Vera lifted her right hand and waved for them to sit in the two chairs.

"Come on, Vivy," Violet coaxed, patting the empty chair like she was talking to one of her cats.

Vera's hand moved to rest on the notepad, and then she tapped the cover with her middle finger.

"You want to write something?" Violet asked, getting up from her chair and reaching for the notepad.

She held it open and handed Vera the pencil. Vera guided the pencil in awkward motions over the page. Her muscles on the right side, although recovering, still weren't operating as they had before the stroke. When she put the pencil back on the nightstand, Violet turned the notepad toward herself and read what Vera had written.

"Oh, in the back here?" she asked as she paged forward in the notepad, past blank pages, until she was almost to the last one. She held the open notepad out to Vivian, who had crossed her ankles and placed her pocketbook in her lap.

"Hmm?" Vivian said, but accepted the notepad, laying it on top of her purse.

She looked up at Violet.

"She wants you to read that," Violet offered with a shrug, and then turned to Vera. "Are you hungry? Can I get you something to eat?"

Vera offered the grotesque half smile again as her gaze went to the notepad.

"Oh, yes." Vivian handed it back to Violet, who opened it to the front again, where there was blank space to write.

"Some toast," Violet read, after Vera had picked up the pencil and labored over another bit of writing on the page. "All right, you just sit tight, and I'll be right back." She handed the notepad back to Vivian, who leafed through to locate the message in the back again.

As Violet's pumps clacked across the floor and out of the room, Vivian started to read. As she read, she realized that her sister had written her an apology. An apology for exposing the secret about Edward's first wife.

Chapter 50

It'd been just after Halloween, and Vera McGinty Irwin had been sitting on Zella Johnson's front porch in the late afternoon sunshine up in Akron. Zella went around with Forest Sadler, one of Wally's drinking and gambling buddies. The one who'd been fired from Freedlander's department store for being a drunk Santa Claus. Vera and Zella had been laughing about Wooster.

"They're country club people, the Wooster relations, you know how they are."

"I do, I do," Vera said, remembering the year and a half she spent taking care of the Dean and Thompson kids. It'd been the height of the Great Depression but Edith Dean and Beverly Thompson came home from shopping in town, bragging about how Beulah Bechtel's was selling every dress for just $14.95. They'd bought two each! Vera would've had to work forty hours just to make enough to buy one of those dresses.

"We're not the cousins the Reeds and Millers like to parade around, if you get me." Zella said "we" like she was talking about more people, but she might've just meant herself. "How 'bout a drink?"

"Sure," Vera said.

The screen door slammed as Zella disappeared into the house. It was too warm for November, and Vera removed the cardigan sweater she'd been wearing and let the late afternoon sun warm her bare arms. The whole day had been a lazy one, and Vera wasn't about to ruin that with the washing or housework. She stretched her legs out on the steps in front of her and leaned back onto the heels of her hands. A leftover Halloween jack-o'-lantern sat just inches from her fingers, grinning out at the street. It looked a little like Vivy used to before she got her pretty new dentures. Vera smirked to herself, but the smirk quickly faded. She took a deep breath and blew it out through puffed cheeks. She didn't quite know how to feel about Vivian, her husband, their marriage, and this new fly in the ointment of it all. The fly Vivy didn't even know about. Vera's thumb ran back and forth across a nail head sticking out of one of the porch planks. Sticking out there like her nagging thoughts about her younger sister.

Vivy'd always gotten just what she wanted, and she'd always gotten it first. Vera was the oldest, but Vivian was the one who got herself a proper job first, got married first, and had a baby first. Vera might've been mistaking Vivian's pride about all that for smugness, but it was hard to tell. "A fine line" like their Pawpy liked to say. Vera'd wanted kids but it hadn't happened for her and Wally. They'd settled for a different kind of life. The kind her mother'd warned her about when she'd done all her complaining about the "criminal element seeping into Wooster" way back when. Back when the Brinkerhoffs next door started renting rooms to a couple of down-and-out men during the Depression. Well, her mother'd been right. Wally Irwin had what Vera would call a "colorful" past, and he had the colorful friends that went along with it.

Wally was the one person who could stand up to her, and she liked it. Or, she liked it until she wanted to have her way, and then things could get rough. There had been a few black eyes, hers and his, because Vera gave as good as she got. She'd suffered a broken rib or two, but those healed up if she was careful about how she slept, and made sure not to hold the wash basket on that side. It didn't happen when Wally's friends were around, though, so Vera learned to like the gambling-casino/boarding-house atmosphere of their house in Akron, because it meant a more or less peaceful household and unbruised knuckles for both husband and wife. Vera played poker with them, she drank with them, and she fed them. And she listened to all their stories.

The screen door creaked open again and Zella stepped out holding two tall glasses of what looked like iced tea. Vera took one of the glasses.

"It's lemonade with whiskey," Zella explained. "But the way I make it, it looks like iced tea, so the neighbors won't get nosy."

Vera held out her glass and clinked the edge of Zella's drink.

"Here's to that."

As they drank their "iced teas" Zella told her all about her cousins Betty and John, and how their mother was her mother's sister, but they didn't really talk anymore, because you know how sisters get. Vera had glanced at the jack-o'-lantern. Once Zella got past mocking all the Wooster Country Club stuff, sticking her nose high in the air and putting on a prissy tone of voice, and complaining how different her cousins were now, Vera could hear wistfulness behind the resentment.

"You know," Vera ventured, "my sister went around with John, way back in the day."

"John Reed? My Cousin John? No foolin'?"

Vera nodded. "Before she got married."

"What's your sister's name?"

"Vivian. Vivian McGinty at the time."

"Hunh." Zella took a drag on a freshly lit cigarette. "She pretty?"

Vera's our sturdy one, Vivy's our pretty one, and Violet's our baby. All her life. And it never got any easier to hear.

"I suppose." She managed to grunt out the words.

She didn't even like to admit it to herself, but maybe, just once, Vera would've liked to hear that she was pretty.

"I wonder if she was the one he was so crazy about. There was one of those girls he was just head over heels for, just plumb nuts about, and when she threw him over, he was pretty sore about it." Zella squinted at a squirrel jumping across the road. "Yep. He was sore, but Betty took it even harder. She was fit to be tied."

Vera hadn't paid too much attention to Vivian's beaux, but she remembered John Reed because he was one of the north siders. A four-flusher. Once, Vera'd tried to tell Wally that "four-flusher" meant a richie, when he'd been saying it had to do with card playing, but he hadn't been in the mood to argue and Vera hadn't been in the mood for another bruised arm.

People always said Vivian was pretty, but Vera'd thought Vivian was just pretty *stupid* not to marry John Reed. She could've had as many Beulah Bechtel dresses as she wanted; clothes were so damned important to her.

Vera felt herself getting all worked up again over Vivian being the goddamned belle of the ball. Everything went Vivian's way, and she didn't even notice it. She was always feeling sorry for herself. Maybe it was about time somebody gave her something to *really* feel sorry about.

Vera'd heard it from the mouth of Marvin Taggart, one of Wally's buddies "from the old days." The old days, right after that lousy Wally'd left the Brinkerhoffs' boardinghouse, leaving a smitten Vera high and dry and stuck in Spinster City for eight years. He'd taken the Brinkerhoffs' other boarder, Ralph Eberly, with him and Vera'd shouted after them that she hoped Ralph would keep him warm at night.

The men had hitched on the railroad around Galion, and the New York Central line took them to Cleveland, then Buffalo, then Syracuse, then Albany, and back to Wooster. While most everyone else was heading west after the Depression, Wally and Ralph thought they'd be smart and head in the opposite direction, picking up jobs where they could. One of the jobs had been construction, in Syracuse, New York, in '33. Some big shot relocating his baseball franchise to Syracuse had to have the stadium finished in three months. The rushed deadline meant the pay was good; Wally loved to tell Vera all about when "the pay was good." *Because those were the days,* he'd say. Wally, Ralph Eberly, Forest Sadler, Marvin Taggart. They'd all been there, and though they'd gone their separate ways afterward, they reconnected now and again in Akron to drink and play poker at Wally and Vera's place. Marvin had gone his separate way straight to the prison at Auburn after he'd been caught stealing a car near Syracuse.

"Betty's a big 'society gal' now," Zella said, swirling the ice cubes around and around in her drink. "You know, 'la-di-da.' But when we were kids, we sure had fun. Betty had a little too much fun herself, you know." Zella held her cigarette while pointing her index finger in Vera's direction. Her eyelids had lowered to half-mast, and her drink was even lower than that.

"Ye-ap. Betty had too much fun, and got herself in a family way. Had to marry Charlie Miller right away. That was too bad for Forest."

"Forest?" Vera asked. "Your Forest?" Forest Sadler'd been the one who laughed the hardest when Marvin Taggart told them all he had to divorce his wife, Mildred, because turns out she was already married.

"Yeah." Zella was starting to sway gently back and forth as she sat on the top step of the porch. She stared off into the distance and her words began to get a little slurry.

"Betty wenn with Foress before Charlie. But Foress should've known it wouldnn go nowhere, not with Betty and her parents, and what with Foress working at the Sohio station, smellin' like gasoline all the time. It was funny, he took that job 'cause the Sohio was on the north side, and he wanned to see how many of those rish bishes he could meet. I guess he never spected to really fall for one. Those two had a spark, all right."

Vera had more than half of her drink left, and swirled it

around in the glass. She shook her head and tried to follow Zella's ramblings. Maybe if she drank a little faster.

"I might juss be his consolation prize. Same gene pool, differen breeding, you know?"

"Unh-hunh," Vera agreed, but was thinking about how she'd nearly fallen over when she'd heard who Marvin Taggart's wife, Mildred, was already married to.

Zella had settled into her liquor and lemonade.

"Oh, Forest ain' too much to look at now, I know. An' he drinks too mush. He didn' start on the bottle until Betty an' Charlie got hitched."

"He took it hard, did he?"

"An' how. Now, Vera," Zella said, turning her swaying head toward Vera and reaching out her fingers to tap on Vera's forearm. "I woulnnet spread it around, but I was never too sure Margie was Charlie's, you know? She mighbe Forest'ssss." As she extended the *s*'s in Forest's name she began to laugh.

Vera laughed along with her, but let her thoughts drift back to Marvin Taggart sitting at the table in her dining room, eyes bulging out of his head as he shouted about "Mildred that double-crossing, no-good dame." Marvin's face had been beet-red, fists clenched, showing them all just how steamed he was about his ex-wife who was already married to "some guy named Edward Dalton."

Zella's laughter had tapered off along with her drink, and when it finally stopped she became philosophical again.

"Yeah, they had 'it' back then. Betty used to love goin' to the Sohio station to see him there inniz lil uniform withiz cap oniz head. She said she loved the smell of the gasoline." Zella hiccupped. "Said idwas zexxy." She rolled her eyes and circled a finger around by her ear. "She's real differen' now. But we still talk on the phone from time to time. If I got a good story or sumthin'." She rolled her eyes again and sighed.

It was that last sentence of Zella's that rang in Vera's ears long after she'd said goodbye to her, handed her the empty glass, and made her way back to her own house. It rang in her ears, and stayed lodged in her mind for weeks after that conversation. *We still talk on the phone from time to time.* And when the weather turned and the snow began to fall, and Vera called Vivian to ask what Charlotte might like for Christmas, Vivian was in one of her moods. She mentioned "all Charlotte's high school joining," which Vera'd thought she'd have been proud of.

"Well, good for her!"

But that just made Vivian even madder.

"*You* don't know what you're talking about. *You* don't have kids."

Vivian may as well have smacked Vera right in the face.

So, on December fifteenth, Zella Johnson was practically salivating as she asked the telephone operator in Wooster to connect her to her cousin Betty Miller's number. She'd just heard the juiciest gossip from her neighbor up there in Akron.

Chapter 51

Vera hadn't written all that in the notepad, of course. She couldn't have even if she'd wanted to, which she hadn't. With her partial paralysis and overall weakened condition, it'd taken half a day and all of her strength just to get the important bits down on both sides of one page.

Vivy,

I can't say that I'd ever have admitted this if it hadn't been for this damned stroke. It's funny what it's done to my mind. I'm still all in here, and even though half of me's asleep it's like my brain's been shook up and shaken out. The things I did right, from the ones I didn't. And what I did to you just wasn't right. And I didn't even know it then, how bad it would hurt you, mess up your life.

I told somebody what I knew about Eddie and his first wife. I told somebody I knew wouldn't keep it to herself and I knew who she'd tell. I guess in my mind, the way it was at the time, I thought it would serve you right. Cut you down to size a little. I thought everything always went your way. It was jealousy. Just real small-minded jealousy. You being the pretty one, and Pawpy's favorite, and always getting what you wanted. I will tell you now, I feel a lot of shame about it all!

You'd think me being stuck here now in this bed I'd be even

sorer about things. Oh, poor me! But, it's strange. It's not like that. I'd like to be able to feel the left side of my body, and be able to get up out of this bed without help, but I think it's God's way of showing me how good I had it. And, maybe I messed that up, not appreciating it more, you know? Or maybe the stroke messed up my brain more than I understand. But, I sure did mess up with you, and you gotta believe I'm sorry about it. Really and truly sorry. I never thought it would turn out this bad. I know we've always had our troubles, you and me, but I do love you, Vivy. And if I take a turn for the worse, I need for you to know that I do, and if I could take it all back, what I did, I'd do it.

—Vera

Vera watched with her watery eyes as Vivian read the notepad, and the tears filled and began to spill over. It was a strain to move her right hand up to brush them away. She couldn't feel it, but the tears were rolling down the left side of her face, too. Violet came into the room carrying a tray with some toast and peanut butter crisscross cookies. When she saw Vera's face, she rushed to set the tray next to her on the bed, grabbing the cloth napkin to wipe her tears.

"Oh, no, what's happened?"

Vera knew if that nurse Wally'd hired didn't work out, her baby sister would happily step in. She'd always been that way.

Vera kept her eyes on Vivian, who looked like she was in a mild state of shock, and Vera didn't blame her one bit. Vivian, to offer some explanation to their youngest sister or maybe to try to understand it better, opened her mouth and started to read aloud from the notepad she'd just read to herself. As she read, Violet brought a hand to her mouth, wrapping the other arm around her middle. She stood there, with her back to Vera in the bed, shaking her head in dismay. Vera didn't blame Violet for that, either.

Vivian finished reading and then closed the notepad. She couldn't look at Vera, lying there helpless in the bed, the tears now unattended by Violet starting to mingle with snot dripping from her nose. Without a word Vivian stood, set the notepad back onto the nightstand, and walked out of the bedroom. Violet looked from Vivian's retreating figure to Vera in the bed. Vera and Violet heard the front door open and close, and Violet went to the window to see their middle sister (perpetually craving attention!) walking away from the house. She walked right by the Buick parked at the curb, and kept walking down the street until she disappeared from view.

Vera, in her still-alert mind, would never have been able to admit if she'd meant for the gossip about Edward to have the kind of disastrous effect it did. Trickling down through the telephone line from Akron to Wooster, and then exploding in a burst of flames, like a lit cigarette dropped on a stream of gasoline leading right to the pump.

A few neighboring porch lights had switched on by the time Vivian got back to the Irwin house. She hadn't looked at her wristwatch, but she'd have guessed she'd been gone two or three hours. Her pumps creaked on the floor of the entryway, and she looked into the parlor, where Wally was sitting, staring at the empty, darkened fireplace. He didn't look up. Vivian guessed the nurse must've gone home.

Wally would eventually sleep with the nurse, causing a big scandal in the neighborhood and in the family, but for now he was still in shock, and mourning the loss of his wife the way she used to be. Wondering if he was partly to blame for the stroke. Thinking he shouldn't have hit her the way he did.

Vivian climbed the stairs slowly, counting them the way she sometimes did in her own house. Fifteen. A much luckier number than thirteen, although less lucky if you happened to fall from the top. Fifteen. Like the day on the December calendar when

Vivian's world had crashed around her. Vivian would forever after connect the date of December fifteenth with the fifteen steps she had to climb up to her sister's room. Violet had turned on the lamp next to Vera's bed, and was sitting in the chair Vivian had left hours earlier, watching Vera sleep. No longer bothering to blot the drool dripping from the left side of her mouth.

She looked up when Vivian entered the room, and got up from the chair. Her hands went to her heart, and she mouthed, *I'm so sorry.* Vivian just gave a slight, defeated nod, and walked to the side of the bed, where she stood over Vera. Her eyes flicked briefly to the alarm clock sitting on the nightstand. A long time ago its weight would've felt good in her hand. But not now. Instead of reaching for the clock, she slipped Aunt Catharine's Irish claddagh ring off her right ring finger, lifted Vera's frail, weakened right hand, and slid the ring over the knobby knuckle of her third finger. She then turned to Violet and jerked her head toward the door. Violet left the lamp on, but closed the door to the room after them. Neither said a word to Wally as they walked past the living room and out the door into the mild summer night.

The two younger McGinty sisters sat silently in the front seat of the Daltons' Buick, and stared straight out the windshield following the path the headlights made on the drive back to Wooster. The car's engine and the constant vibration of the wheels on the highway kept the silence from seeming awkward. Vivian replayed the words from Vera's notepad over and over inside her head, just like she had when she'd gone out for her long walk. Violet thought about the notepad confessional, too, and Vivian's strained voice as she'd read from it. And then she thought about Vivian's actions, and would think about them long after that day.

That McGinty claddagh ring had always meant more to Vera than it should have, in Violet's opinion. She couldn't believe Vivian had given it to her after what Vera had done. But Vera was sick and not likely to get any better; that was for certain. Violet sneaked a look at Vivian while she steered the Buick from the highway onto the exit. Vera had always been the know-it-all of the family, but Violet would point out that her sister Vivian really knew people.

"Did you see the papers?" Vivian finally broke the silence as they drove into Wooster, the glowing streetlamps coming into view. "They're executing the Rosenbergs in a couple of weeks. The electric chair."

"Oh?" Violet responded. "I didn't see that. Robert said something about it, though. You're reading the papers now?"

"Mmm-hm," Vivian murmured. Her gloved fingers tapped on the top of the steering wheel as they drove south on Beall Avenue, past the entrance to the Wooster College campus, where she used to mutter curses under her breath at the carefree coeds laughing and swinging their books around. Just seeing them used to flatten her mood and sour her outlook on the day, making her feel like she wasn't good enough.

The new feeling inside her, bubbling up from her belly and spreading out into her extremities as she drove past, was one of excitement, nervous hope, and possibility.

"And, did I tell you?" She kept her eyes on the coeds but leaned toward her sister. "I'm going to get my high school diploma."

Chapter 52

Vivian felt good about her plans to get her high school diploma. She wasn't as sure how to feel about her anniversary this year. It was their sixteenth year together, if you counted the first fifteen years and seven months that weren't legitimate in the eyes of the law. If she'd considered a piece of paper with Reverend Alsop's signature to be more sacred than sixteen years of semi-faithful devotion, well then, that might have ruffled her feathers a little, but a lot had happened since that day. The sixteenth anniversary didn't have any specific traditional gift attached to it. Last year, fifteen, had been crystal, and she'd hoped for candlesticks, but Edward hadn't gotten her anything, because he forgot. But that had been before. There was no chance he'd forget this one.

Edward presented Vivian with a large box. He must've been keeping it out back in his shed, because she hadn't seen it in the basement or in any of the closets. It was heavy, and wrapped in beautiful silver ribbon, and he set it on the coffee table in front of her. It looked like he'd had it professionally wrapped at Freedlander's, which was something he always scoffed at. "I've got two good hands. I can put tape on paper and tie a bow." Not to mention, it cost money to have that done at the store. The corner of Vivian's mouth pulled a little and she shot him a queer look as he brushed a hand on the sofa cushion next to her and sat down.

She turned her attention back to the gift, and gently pulled at one end of the ribbon, watching as it slid out from the bow. She worked the knot apart with her fingernails, now painted in Revlon's Plum Beautiful, because she'd had enough of Fire & Ice, then slid the rest of the ribbon out from under the gift and set it beside the box to save. Edward's foot began tapping next to the table. The unwrapping was going a lot more slowly than usual, since Vivian wasn't too sure she wanted to see what was inside. She'd had plenty of disappointments that year and didn't think she could handle any more. She carefully plucked at the tape holding the wrapping paper together, trying her best not to tear it. The wrapping paper could, and should, be saved, too, and she folded it into a square and tucked it under the ribbon sitting next to the box.

When she pried open the top of the box and looked inside, her eyebrows drew together in confusion. She reached in and pulled out several brand-new notebooks, opening the cover flaps to see that that was just what they were. Blank notebooks. She set them on the table next to the wrapping paper and ribbon, and reached back into the box to pull out a ream of paper. Also blank. She peered into the box and then took out one book, then another book, then another. As she read each title, she realized these were books she would need for her freshman-year courses of high school.

She'd saved the card for last, but tears were already stinging and blurring her eyes as she slid a Plum Beautiful fingernail under the flap to open it. She was afraid she wouldn't be able to read it. She was embarrassed to be crying, and wished Edward wasn't watching her. He'd stopped tapping his foot and handed her his handkerchief, and she poked the fabric into the corners of her eyes to soak up the tears before they could spill out onto her cheeks and muss up her makeup. The card, unlike the wrapping, was not professionally done. It was just a piece of paper that Edward had folded into quarters and written on himself. A homemade card like the ones Charlotte used to make when she was in elementary school.

The outside read:

"Happy Anniversary to my Favorite Wife"

Vivian almost crushed the paper in her palm and threw it at him. She refused to look at him, even when she heard him snickering next to her. The nerve that man had. She pursed her lips and flared her nostrils, afraid that if she looked at him she'd start to laugh, and she wasn't sure he deserved that just yet. She gave a sniff and a quick shake of her head, and then opened to the inside of the card. The words, "To New Beginnings," were written in large letters and then the number "1," and in parentheses the word "Paper."

She looked down at the stack of notebooks, the paper, and the books. It was all paper, for garsh sakes. Paper, for the first anniversary. And then she turned and looked at Edward, whose forehead was wrinkled and his wild, graying eyebrows tented together. If Vivian hadn't known any better, she'd have said he looked nervous. Honest-to-goodness nervous, leaning forward, rubbing his palms on the knees of his trousers and watching her, his fingers all scratched up with paper cuts. There were no roses in the crystal vase. No "sorry blooms" for this anniversary. This was not a gift given out of guilt. It was love, and it looked like Vivian and Edward Dalton were going to be starting over.

"Vivy"—Edward gave her a gentle nudge—"why did the guy keep hitting himself on the head with a hammer?"

She took a deep breath and arched an eyebrow, but didn't look at him.

"Because it felt so good when he stopped."

She sighed and felt the tears starting up again as she placed her hand over his on one knee. "Edward, you make my ass tired."

Then she began to laugh.

Epilogue

Flora Parker had mailed Gilbert's copy of his birth certificate to Wooster's *Daily Record* the day after he'd been shot and killed. Harry Sweeney hadn't bothered to check the Canadian postmark on the anonymous envelope. If he had, he could've made the story that much more intriguing, but Harry could be careless like that. That was one of the reasons he hadn't been promoted to editor.

Flora and Gilbert had both kept copies of their birth certificates with them throughout their lives, as their mother had insisted upon it. She had been certain that having that information would be important and useful to them one day. Gilbert had harbored more anger toward their biological father, but Flora's anger toward him might have just been dormant. It came exploding to the surface when she heard about Gilbert being shot. The news reaching her over the police radio Bill had rigged up in the attic of the house. J. Ellis Reed deserved to face the consequences and be held accountable, something she was sure he had never before had to do in his long, privileged life.

People in Wooster would gossip that the entire criminal caper had been premeditated. They would concoct wild speculative stories about Flora and Gilbert and J. Ellis Reed. That Flora and Gilbert had been plotting their revenge on their birth father since before they even moved to town. Flora would expect nothing less of the good people of Wooster.

From what her mother had told her, Ellis had promised to marry her, and insisted that race didn't matter. But then he had gone running back to Wooster "like a yellow-bellied river rat," when push came to shove. That was also how her mother had described giving birth to twins, "Push coming to shove," and then she'd laughed, and said, "Flora, you were pushing your brother before you could even breathe for yourself."

Isabelle Jacobs had too much pride to go chasing after a man who ran from her, and too much sense to love a coward. The attending nurse in the Colored Wing at the hospital offered her counsel when it came time to fill in the details of the twins' birth certificates. Isabelle had told Nurse Tucker about Ellis.

"Would you like your son to have his name?" Nurse Tucker asked, her stiff blond curls springing wildly from beneath her starched cap. "I've seen this a lot in my time here, and women like to make sure the father knows that child belongs to him."

"No," Isabelle responded. "That man was a disappointment. A foolish mistake. The boy will be Gilbert, after my brother. And Ogden, for my stepfather."

"All right, then," Nurse Tucker said. "Let's make sure I'm getting the spelling correct." She held the form out in front of Isabelle.

"That looks good," Isabelle confirmed, pleased that Nurse Tucker hadn't assumed she couldn't read.

"And what about your daughter?"

"I've always liked the name Flora," Isabelle said with a dreamy look in her eyes. "You know, Flora is the Roman goddess of flowers and spring."

Nurse Tucker's mouth slowly came out with, "That's very pretty," after a prolonged pause, but her face said, *Well, look at you!*

Isabelle was used to people underestimating her.

"It's not their fault," she'd later explain to her children. "They're just ignorant. They need to learn."

Flora would have liked to have had a private memorial service for Gilbert and her mother, in the living room of the Toronto bay-and-gable Victorian she, Bill, and Gilbert had called home for a little while, but there wasn't time. As soon as she and Bill had heard about the shooting, they knew their neighbors would soon, too. They had to get out of there quickly. It took them a half hour to pack up their clothes and Bill threw some books and board games into a box on top of the suitcase that held their money. Flora took special care with the mink Gilbert had given her, holding her handkerchief to her eyes so the tears wouldn't drop onto the coat.

There was still the odd day in late spring where she'd pull the mink around her as she sat in front of the fire in their new cozy little house, roughly one-third the size of the bay-and-gable Victorian, and the perfect size for the two of them. Flora was helping Bill with his French, because if they wanted to be cast in the local theater productions, they'd need to be able to understand their lines. She was also trying to think of the best time to tell him she wanted to send the rest of the money back to the Wayne Building & Loan. She wanted to be rid of it. Rid of the memories it brought and rid of the way it still tied her to J. Ellis Reed.

Flora was happy where she was now, and when she was ready, she'd tell you the name of the town. For the time being, Flora would just say it was "somewhere small." Somewhere just like Wooster.

Author's Note

The recipes and poems in this book are my grandmother's (typos and all—don't blame the copyeditors), and the newspaper articles are verbatim from *The Daily Record*, just with name changes and an extra detail in one (the "youngster"). I've exercised some artistic license in other historical details of this book, and wanted to acknowledge them. The story is loosely based on my grandmother, but "loosely" is crucial to keep in mind. The portrayal of Vivian McGinty's parents is pretty close to the truth; however, the portrayal of her siblings is fictional, and their characters do not resemble my grandmother's own family (other than the fact that her youngest sister, my Great-Aunt Ginny, really did thwart the armed robbery at the William Annat Company department store). *The Myth of Sisyphus* was not translated from French into English until 1955, so Charlotte would not have read it in her 1952 English class. Wooster's A&W was not established until 1957, so Clyde Walsh would have had to take Ginny Frazier somewhere else for their first date. The A&W also, apparently, never served burgers, just hot dogs and chicken sandwiches, in their early years. The Heidelberg Chocolate Factory is not a real place, at least in Wooster. Quinby Elementary School, Forest Chapel Methodist Church, and Wayne Building & Loan were also created for the story. Alphanumeric telephone exchanges were really only used in the larger cities, but I liked the way "MAson-8812" sounded, better than "32" or something similar. Some of the telephone numbers for Wooster in the early 1930s were just two digits. The switchboard operators sat in non-wheeled chairs (based on photographs), which was far more practical, but I wanted the chairs to have wheels. Just because. I tried to keep everything else as authentic as possible but, not having lived during that time, I'm sure there will be discrepancies. My apologies in advance.

Acknowledgments

I have to thank Kate Jackiw and Donna Quathamer for their early reads of this book, when it was in its most infantile, messy manuscript stages, because that is not fun. "Here is a big mess. Please read it." Kendra Cleveland also did an early read of the first chapter and sent me probably-excellent comments which I never received because they were sent from her not-excellent and not-smart flip phone. The thought counted, though. Ann Schluter Kowaliczco, although too distracted by ankle surgery painkillers and Words With Friends to early-read this, has read so much of the other stuff I've written, and offered so much in the way of encouragement and support, and photography (see author photo). Jim Redmond has also read so much of the other stuff, and has been a staunch bedrock of encouragement, support, unwarranted praise, and invaluable constructive criticism.

My all-the-superlatives, Columbo-esque agent, Susan Ramer (and the always-thoughtful Cara Bellucci), whose notes, suggestions, and tireless attention and efforts made everything so much better. And my astute, thorough editor, Jennifer Brehl, who made me dig deeper into the character motivations (and ultimately made everything so much better). Nate Lanman, who was so wonderful and made sure everything ran smoothly, and the rest of the "behind the scenes" team at William Morrow for all their hard work. Two literary agents, who aren't mine,

Stefanie Lieberman and Janet Reid, who offered excellent advice and encouragement very early on (before this book) that kept me writing and learning along the way. (I still read Janet's blog daily.) I've used the word "encouragement" three times now because it's pretty important. *En-courage-ment*. Gives you *courage*, and whatnot.

Eternal thanks to my high school typing teacher, Mrs. Gentry. *"A, a, a, space! A, a, a, space! A, a, a, space! Return!"*

Brad Harmon, president of GateHouse Media's Central U.S. Division, for his lightning-fast response to my request for permission to use the clippings from *The Daily Record*. Elaine Fletty at the Wayne County Public Library, who had already been so helpful with my genealogy research, and who dug up some of my grandma's poetry for this book.

The Firmdale Hotels Instagram page, where I would go for meditative warm-fuzzy moments before, during, and after writing. (Their hotels are mainly in London, and are so incredibly lovely and relaxing and the photos provide a beautiful backdrop.) The Turner Classic Movies channel, which was frequently on the television in the background, putting me in a 1930s, '40s, or '50s frame of mind.

Thanks to my family (immediate and extended), in particular my mom and my Aunt Rosemary, who made quirky and funny contributions to the book via their memories, Cousin Sandy for the railroad letters story, and Cousin Leta (who still lives in Wooster) for her ironclad confidence that this would be published. And, finally, thanks to my dad, who ended up being extremely supportive, in spite of himself. He'll be encouraging once he sees this in print.

About the Author

Gretchen Berg was born on the East Coast, raised in the Midwest, and spent a number of years in the Pacific Northwest. She has taught English in South Korea and in northern Iraq and has traveled to all the other continents. A graduate of Iowa State University, she lives in Chicago, Illinois. *The Operator* is her first novel.